IF NOT YOU, THEN WHO?

Steven J. Peterson

Published by

MELROSE BOOKS

An Imprint of Melrose Press Limited
St Thomas Place, Ely
Cambridgeshire
CB7 4GG, UK
www.melrosebooks.com

FIRST EDITION

Copyright © Steven J. Peterson 2011

The Author asserts his moral right to
be identified as the author of this work

All characters in this book are fictitious and any resemblance to
actual persons, living or dead, is purely coincidental.

Cover designed by Jeremy Kay

ISBN 978 1 907732 38 6

All rights reserved. No part of this publication may be reproduced, stored in a retrieval system, or transmitted, in any form or by any means electronic, mechanical, photocopying, recording or otherwise, without the prior permission of the publishers.

This book is sold subject to the condition that it shall not, by way of trade or otherwise, be lent, re-sold, hired out or otherwise circulated without the publisher's prior consent in any form of binding or cover other than that in which it is published and without a similar condition including this condition being imposed on the subsequent purchaser.

Printed and bound in Great Britain by:
CLE Digital Solutions. St Ives, Cambridgeshire

CHAPTER 1

Sitting at his desk, gazing out of the large, plate glass window of his ground floor office, Phillip could just see the car park and the road beyond it, traffic rushing past, people hurrying, perhaps to offices or shops or maybe hurrying because that was what they always did. He could also see the sign, or rather the back of it, placed where anybody entering the building could see it, and he imagined the letters arranged on the front. 'Phillip Everett' it said in large letters and more discreetly, in smaller letters underneath, 'Private Detective', a phone number and his office address.

It had taken him eight months to get to this stage after that interview with his senior manager, Steven Walsh, when he had been more or less told that his future was not as a trader with this particular bank. In fact, at the moment, there was not much future for anyone working in the financial area, banking as a whole was in crisis. It appeared that they had followed their American counterparts in lending unbelievably large sums of money, to anybody and everybody, with only the flimsiest chance of being repaid in full. The men at the top had apparently ignored the warning signs and reassured the Government with pages of figures, all of which proved nothing. Credit had been advanced to all and sundry but with no guarantees that they would ever be able to repay it.

Walsh had told Phillip that he liked him, thought he did a good job, but others in the building blew their large bonuses on champagne at £80 a bottle, flashy foreign cars, rented expensive apartments or properties whereas he, Phillip, appear to spend within reason and even save money. If he took redundancy now, it would be on very generous terms and he would be able to look around for another post, before the flood of out-of-work bank employees came on the market.

"Of course, you don't have to listen to me, you could stay on till the bitter end – I have nothing to gain either way."

"What about you?" said Phillip, curiously.

Walsh replied, "I've got plans of my own. I'm a lot older than you, though I hate to admit it, and this is maybe the last high pressure job I'm going to hold down. I tell you this in confidence, you understand, but I've made some wise investments over the years, took out a pension scheme years ago when I could hardly afford it, so if this job dries up and they tell me 'my services are no longer required', I shall have a good laugh and retire with dignity, with or without my gold watch."

Phillip gave Walsh's advice some careful consideration, weighing up pros and cons, and a week later he applied for a redundancy package, giving a number of vague reasons as to why he wanted to leave. He was very pleased with the results of the termination of his contract, considering that later on many of his erstwhile co-workers were told to pack their possessions in a cardboard box and were simply shown the door.

He was financially in a strong position, having taken care to avoid investing in anything with an unjustified risk. At the moment he was living alone, with no excessive expenditure, so he bought a house on the main road, plenty of passing customers to see his modest sign, and after querying a change of use for the ground floor with his local council offices, he made the downstairs lounge into his office and left the upstairs as his living accommodation. There were four bedrooms, two with attached bathrooms, so he made the front room into a study/lounge/TV room with a comfortable sofa and used the downstairs kitchen/diner for any cooking he decided to undertake. The house had been built on an odd plot of land only the previous year so all the electrical fittings were completely up to date and he had installed the latest IT equipment, enlarged the front window to let in more light and placed his desk where he could look out over what had been the garden and was now the parking area.

When he had finished the alterations to the house, he spent three months on an intensive correspondence course – 'How to be a Private Detective' – covering all aspects of the law as it pertained to private detection. He knew how to organise the financial side of the business and money was spent on advertising in local papers, business journals and Yellow Pages but so far, not a single enquiry had been made. His advertisement in the local paper came out every Friday morning so here he was, sat at his imposing desk on a Thursday morning, looking out of the window at the passing traffic.

The phone rang and he jumped at the sudden sharp noise at his elbow, picked up the receiver and said, "Phillip Everett, Private Detective Agency."

There was a slight hesitation, as if someone was making up their mind whether to speak or not and a voice said, "Gordon McIntosh here. I wonder if you remember me?"

Phillip wracked his brains to pin down that elusive memory and the voice went on, "Last time we met was before my assignment in Edinburgh. I know you guys in London are not sure about geography north of Watford but Edinburgh is in Scotland!"

Phillip knew who it was now and said, "Scotland, I remember it, it's a small piece of land where men wear skirts and all the natives eat sheep stomachs filled with various sorts of unspeakable innards that we normally use to fill our landfill sites?"

"Not nowadays, we send the haggis down south and sell them to Londoners," said Gordon.

"Anyway, how are you, you old sinner, long time, no see?" said Gordon.

"I'm fine, just a bit bored."

"Why's that?"

"I'm sitting in my office, waiting for my first customer."

"You'll have to explain that remark," said Gordon. "What happened to banking? I'm back in London now, so you'll have to explain to me what it is you're doing. Let's meet up and we can reminisce about the old times; how about tomorrow. Do you remember the old Friday nights in the past when we went hell raising on the town? What about our old watering place?"

"You'll have to tell me which one you mean. There were so many and places have changed names in the meantime!"

"What about that wine bar, just off Regent Street, the one where you picked up the gorgeous girl who turned out to be a fella, remember? Meet you there about six o'clock, okay?"

"Trust you to bring that up," said Phillip. "See you tomorrow," and put the phone down.

Phillip remembered Gordon from the past. They had a lot in common and a similar sense of humour; he was feeling much more optimistic already. This was just what he needed, a night out with an old mate. He looked up at the sound of an engine and saw a black four-by-four turning into his parking space. Nice motor, he thought, looked like a brand new Jeep, just pulling up in front of his office. Who do I know who drives one of those, he thought, nobody I can think of, perhaps it's my first customer. I sincerely hope he doesn't think he can just park there while he goes to do some shopping elsewhere! But no, a moment later the doorbell rang and Phillip was in two minds whether to rush to the door and welcome the man into the office but on second thoughts, he decided that would not be appropriate, he would play it cool.

The doorbell sounded again and Phillip opened it and said, "Please come in, can I help you?"

"I hope so, are you the private detective Phillip Everett?"

"Yes, I am, would you like to take a seat and tell me what I can do for you?"

"Do you take paedophile cases?" said the man bluntly, looking to see how Phillip would take this inquiry.

"Why don't you explain what you mean by that and tell me what the circumstances are? I'll do my best to give whatever help I can," said Phillip.

"This is going to take up a bit of your time because I have to explain it from the beginning and there's no quick way round it."

"Please carry on," said Phillip and drew a notepad and pencil towards himself.

"For a start, my name's Edward Dunn and I and my wife and family now live in California, not far from Los Angeles, where I'm a civil engineer. My father and mother wouldn't come to live with us, although we begged them to do that; we could have built them a lovely bungalow on our property but no, they wouldn't budge. My mother died over a year ago so now my father's on his own. He retired on full pension from his job as headmaster of a private school some three years ago and he misses her so much. I'm the only child and I did my best to persuade him to come and stay with us but he wouldn't listen. You know how it is with older people, they can be very stubborn and they don't like big changes in their lives. Moving to a new country was just too much of an upheaval for him.

"Being very lonely he went for a walk in the local park, perhaps hoping to see a friend or acquaintance he could chat to, when he saw a young schoolgirl, sitting on a bench crying. At that time, he found out later, she was only thirteen but gradually, as they developed a platonic father/daughter relationship, she gained the confidence to tell him one or two facts about her home circumstances which were not very happy. She is the only child and her mother is unmarried but she always seems to have a boyfriend around, many of whom stayed in their house for varying lengths of time. The mother took every opportunity to tell her daughter she was fat and ugly and if it had not been for her, life would be so much better. Otherwise, she pays her very little attention so the girl binged on junk food and was grossly overweight; when she looked in the mirror she started to self-harm and was bullied at school so she started to play truant. When my father first saw her, she was sitting on a bench crying and he went to sit next to her to see what was the matter. The mother's name, by the way, is Doris Herne and the girl is called Betsy.

"As time went on, my father persuaded her to take better care of herself and she agreed to try and lose weight and pay more attention to her appearance. He bought her a new school uniform if she promised to stop playing truant and paid for her to go to a hairdresser to have a more attractive, modern hairstyle. As Betsy started to have more attention paid to her, she began to have confidence in herself and behave like a normal teenager. She no longer allowed her mother to walk all over her and arguments developed between them when she realised there had been a change in their relationship and she could no longer ignore Betsy. She completely lost her temper with her daughter one day and slapped her face several times so Betsy told her if she hit her again she would tell Mr Dunn, who would report her to the police for child cruelty."

Edward Dunn went on to describe Doris's reaction. Up till then, Doris had had no idea that the new uniform and hairstyle had not been paid for by Betsy alone, assuming either she had been stealing money or perhaps had managed to find a job delivering papers or something. She took so little notice of her daughter, it had not occurred to her up to now, that anybody else could be involved in her daughter's life. Doris asked her if she had managed to find herself a boyfriend and if so, who the hell was this Mister Dunn? She said she was going to put a stop to it because Betsy was only thirteen years old. Betsy shouted that she was nearly fourteen but Doris knew immediately what she was going to do.

Next morning, she went to the nearest police station and said to the police sergeant at the desk, "My name is Doris Herne and I've come to report the sexual abuse of my thirteen-year-old daughter Betsy by a dirty old man!"

The Desk Sergeant looked sceptical and said, "Can you clarify that remark madam? I'm not sure exactly what you mean."

Doris announced importantly, "What I mean is that my daughter has had an improper relationship with an older man!"

The Desk Sergeant sighed imperceptibly and said, "What's his name?"

"She won't tell me," said Doris.

"Well how do you know all this?"

"Because my daughter started to get new clothes and she's been going to the hairdresser and the gym; I'm a single mother, living on benefits and I haven't given her any money for this."

"Well that's hardly conclusive evidence, now is it?" said the Sergeant.

"Well how about this then, yesterday we had an argument and the little monkey shouted at me that if I didn't stop picking on her, she'd go and see Mr Dunn!"

"What's his other name?" said the Sergeant.

"That's all she'll tell me – why don't you talk to her. I'm reporting a case of child abuse and it's up to the police to investigate," shouted Doris.

"From what you tell me, it sounds as if someone is being kind to the poor kid and you can't call that 'child abuse'."

"Have you ever heard of an old man being kind, as you call it, to a thirteen-year-old, without wanting something in return?" said Doris, triumphantly.

The Sergeant felt he had no choice but to enter the complaint in his log book and told Doris he was writing down her complaint and he would get a policewoman to call on her and her daughter, to try and resolve the situation.

"This is how the whole thing started," said Edward Dunn, "and a police investigation followed. Betsy told how she met my dad and how he paid for various items such as the school uniform, some shoes, the hairdresser, the gym and how she grew to look on him as if he was the father she never knew and never had. My father was arrested and at the hearing in the Magistrates' Court, the police asked for a remand without bail, to stop him approaching the schoolgirl. They felt they had to protect the girl from someone who was possibly a paedophile and who might be grooming her for the future, who had undue influence on a young child. My father is now in prison, waiting for his case to come up in court and the police are still investigating the circumstances, dwelling on the fact that he was headmaster of a mixed sex public school. They will not find anything against him but one never knows what might happen in court. Nowadays, one has only to suggest that an older man is a paedophile and their reputation is ruined forever."

"Where do you want me to start?" asked Phillip.

"I'd like you to get him out on bail. He is having a terrible time in prison; even if you have not been convicted, the inmates still give you a bad time and being on remand, he is kept in an ordinary prison and not separated, as are convicted paedophiles, so you can imagine how he is being treated."

"I think it's only fair to tell you," said Phillip, "you might have been better with a solicitor who's experienced in these kind of cases."

"I shall hire a good lawyer when the time comes but he won't investigate in the way I would like you to do. He will present the case in court, hopefully working from evidence and statements you have acquired. I can't go to the police because they are gathering evidence for the prosecution so what I would like you to do is talk to my father, Betsy, the girl, and her mother. My father has been very foolish to have a friendship with this girl but he is not a paedophile. Both my parents always wished they had both a son and a daughter but it was not to be; finding this girl crying upset him and he tried to help her; the relationship of father/daughter just developed naturally and he would never have done anything to harm her. The real villain of the piece is her mother; she always saw the girl as a nuisance, never cared for her at all and is pursuing a vendetta against my father with all the venom in her."

"I'll certainly do my best to get your father released on bail and then we can take it from there. There is just one thing…" said Phillip, rather embarrassed, "my fees for something like this—"

"Of course, of course, what do you charge? let me have a note of it or if you prefer, I can write you a cheque for an advance straight away."

"I charge £30 an hour with expenses," said Phillip.

"That seems reasonable enough," said Edward Dunn and fished out his cheque book. "Here you are… a cheque for £5,000 on account and you will let me have a note of your investigations, won't you? If you have any problems, here's my mobile number, the hotel I'm staying at and a list of addresses you might find useful. This phone never leaves my side, damn things have become so useful, can't think whatever we did without 'em. By the way, no need for formalities, just call me Ted."

"Thank you Ted, this is my business card, you can call me Phil or Phillip, whichever you prefer."

They shook hands and Ted thanked him for taking up the case and with that, they parted company.

Phillip watched him drive away, returned to his desk and started to make notes. First, prepare to request release on bail – need a good solicitor to represent us in court, I just don't know enough about making an appeal myself. I can make a start by visiting Betsy and getting her side of the story, but I have to interview her with her mother's permission, otherwise she will start accusing me of something. I can't do any of this until I get that cheque paid into my account. He locked up and walked along the road to the local branch of his bank to deposit the money.

Chapter 2

On Friday night, Phillip and Gordon met in the wine bar where they had met many times in the past, and Gordon eyed him up and down saying, "Now that I see you in the flesh, you look great. Of course, having a long holiday does that to you! No pressure, just taking it easy."

"What do you know about pressure?" said Phillip. "You have a benevolent employer, a job for life. I bet you never broke sweat once in your career."

"I can assure you, that's not the way it is. When I got back after just twelve months away, most of the people in my Department had gone; I lost all the friends I had before I left."

"What do you mean, gone? Where did they go?" asked Phillip.

"Got the push, left after being told they had no future in their jobs, or left because their pay was relatively low and they could do better somewhere else."

"That amounts to promotion," said Phillip, lightly.

"I'd hardly call it promotion when you have to leave one bank to go to another."

"Anyway, enough of that… fill me in on what's been happening to you while I've been away from the smoke."

Phillip told him about his talk with Steven Walsh, the hints that there would be redundancies in the near future and his decision to play it canny, accept a redundancy package and set up in business as a 'Private Eye'. He told him about buying a house, turning the downstairs into an office and his aim to become a private investigator.

"I didn't know such people still existed any more," said Gordon.

"Why would you think that?" said Phillip. "There'll always be people who are not in a position to go to the police when they want evidence for a divorce, finding a missing person, tracing relatives or just assembling facts together. Anyway, I've just started my first case today."

Gordon looked at him. "And what would that be, catching a partner playing away?"

"No, it's more serious and challenging than that but let's not talk about it."

"Whatever happened to whatshername, Samantha, your live-in partner?" queried Gordon.

"When I left my job, she realised that all the perks I had went with the job, so she left as well!"

"Was it not supposed to be 'for better, for worse'?"

"It appears that the better got worse and the 'worse' too much to take," said Phillip, lightly.

"So who's she with now?"

"I haven't got a clue, haven't seen her since she left, months ago, but it will be someone with money, lots of it," said Phillip.

"So you haven't got a woman now?" asked Gordon.

"If I'm honest, I have to say that I've not really thought about it."

"You are kidding, aren't you," said Gordon, "a young, good-looking man like you not getting his leg over for so long, it's not natural. As I remember, you used to be a randy sod, always on the lookout for it before Samantha got her claws in you."

"Aw, come on," said Phillip, "I've been a bit busy buying a house, coping with the builders making alterations; then I took a correspondence course to fit me for the job, registering, applying for my licence, advertising etc, I've not exactly had time to be trawling around for female company, have I?"

"Yes," said Gordon, "it's a good job I'm here to save you from turning into a dithering wreck. All work and no play, makes Jack a dull boy, as you well know. You've not lost your libido have you?"

"We'll soon find that out," said Phillip.

The bar was crowded with the usual Friday night drinkers either partying or drowning their sorrows, they observed.

"I'm amazed," said Gordon, "according to the newspapers, half of the finance jobs have disappeared and many other positions which relied on finance companies have gone down the Swanee. I suppose a lot of the people who are in here tonight are working out their notice and came in here, hoping they will hear on the grapevine of some vacancy which nobody else knows about! Fat chance!"

After a protracted battle to get to the bar, Phillip brought back some drinks for them when two girls made a beeline for their table and said, "You two guys are hogging a whole table to yourselves, mind if we sit here as well?"

Phillip tried to turn on the charm and said gallantly, "Two such gorgeous girls are welcome to sit at this table, I'm Phillip and this is Gordon."

"Wow," said the first girl to her friend, "we'd better watch him, he's very smooth!" The friend replied, "Don't you worry, Jasmine, my mum told me about men like him!"

"What else did your mummy tell you?" laughed Phillip.

Jasmine said, looking down and fluttering her eyelashes as if she were shy, "My mummy told me that the smooth, good-looking ones are dangerous!"

Phillip said seriously, "My mummy told me I must be very careful with beautiful girls who have great figures, but I always ignored her!"

"Alright, you lot, when you've quite finished being funny, who wants another drink?" Gordon asked.

Turning to his friend, Phillip said, "This man works for the Bank of England and therefore is very rich. In fact, he owns half of it so you can ask for any drink you like."

"You can ask, but that doesn't necessarily mean you'll get it. Do you ladies know that we at the Bank of England are the lowest paid in the financial market?" said Gordon.

"He is going to make me cry in a moment," said the other girl, "and I forgot to bring my handkerchief. How about it if we rich secretaries brought you two poor bank employees half a lager to cry into?"

"Which century do you live in? Even in the wilds of Scotland, caber tossers use tissues to wipe their faces with after the strain of the Highland Games!! And anyway, what's your name? You, the cheeky one?" asked Gordon.

"It's Isobel and are you asking us to believe that a six-foot-four hairy Scotsman, after tossing his caber, or whatever, turns to another hairy Angus and says 'Pass me the tissues please'!"

"When you've all finished laughing," Gordon said, "does anybody want a drink or not because I'm going up to the bar now?"

"Same again," said Phillip, pointing to his bottle of beer.

"I'll have a glass of red house wine," said Isobel.

"And me too," said Jasmine.

As they pushed their way to the bar, Gordon asked Phillip, "What about it?"

"What do you mean," said Phillip, deliberately misunderstanding his friend, "the wine bar or the drinks?"

"Don't be stoopid!"

"Sorry, just winding you up," Phillip said. "As women go, they're okay, but it's difficult to tell when they're both wearing trouser suits with blouses buttoned up to their necks!"

"Oh well, if that's the case, when we get back to the table, I'll just ask them to stand up and take off all their clothes to see if they meet your exacting standards," said Gordon.

"That would help," agreed Phillip.

"I'm thinking more of their personality," said Gordon, loftily.

"Why didn't you say so?" said Phillip. "Personality-wise, I don't have a clue."

Returning to the table with their drinks, they could see two men talking to Isobel and Jasmine. Gordon put the drinks down on the table and said, "If you four know each other, we'll just be moving on some place else."

"They're not with us," said Jasmine, "and they're just going," she added to the men who were trying to chat them up.

"And there we were, getting on so well," said one of the men. "I thought you liked us."

"You might have thought that but we didn't," Isobel said, and they walked off in a huff.

"What made you think that we knew them?" said Isobel. "Apart from having never seen them before tonight, they had the worst chat-up line you could think of, real suggestive."

"I thought from your faces they were not doing very well." Phillip sat down. "It's been a long time since I've done any chatting up so I'm probably not very good at it either."

"You've done alright so far," said Isobel, "you could always practise with us, chatting up I mean!"

"Tell me, where did you get such beautiful Christian names?"

"There's a song called something like 'Jasmine in Bloom' which was one of my mother's favourites so she christened me Jasmine."

Phillip said, "The name Isobel reminds me of an island in one of Italy's lakes, near the town of Stresa, and there is a really romantic story told about it. Apparently a Count married a beautiful young woman and he was so much in love with his wife that he bought this small island and had landscape gardeners make it look like a ship with the most beautiful gardens and terraces, and he called the island Isobella, after his wife. You can go and visit the island if you ever go to the Italian Lakes."

The two women sighed. "That is romantic," said Isobel.

"You've got to watch this guy," said Gordon, "he is very good at telling stories, to get you in the right mood."

"Well I think he's very nice," said Jasmine. She turned to Phillip and asked curiously, "Why has it been such a long time since you were trying to chat up any girl?"

He shrugged and said, "I had a live-in partner until about eight months ago."

"Was it serious or was she just a lodger?"

"I thought it was... she did not."

"So what happened?" asked Jasmine.

"It's a bit of a long story and I don't want to spoil the evening by harping on about it. What about you two?"

"We both live in Welwyn Garden City and work for Banco Santander in Town. We are both single and currently, we don't have any close attachments."

"You could have had those two tonight," said Gordon.

"Do you mind! We're not looking for a quickie in the back of a car, or anywhere else, for that matter," said Isobel, indignantly.

"Anyway, what about you Gordon?"

"I am Scottish on my father's side and originally, we lived in Edinburgh, I got a post with the Bank of Scotland but the salary was low at that time so I moved to London and managed to get a job with the Bank of England and so far, I'm still working for them."

"Where do you work Phillip?"

"I'm my own boss, I did work in the City for a bank but I decided to take a redundancy package and started my own private detective agency."

There was a short silence until Isobel asked, in awed tones, "Are you really?"

"Yes, I am really!" he replied.

"I think it must be fascinating work!"

"I wouldn't really know as I only got my first case yesterday and I've not even started on it yet."

At this point the two girls said, "You'll have to excuse us for a moment, we are just going to powder our noses," and got up from the table.

As they headed for the toilets, it gave the men a chance to have a good look at them. Isobel was very slim and slightly taller than Jasmine. She looked very smart in her black trouser suit with the contrasting white blouse and medium heeled shoes, perhaps this was what they all had to wear at the bank. She had blonde hair, just brushing her shoulders and was very attractive. Jasmine was probably about five feet six tall but she appeared as tall as Isobel because she was wearing high heeled shoes. She wore a similar black trouser suit with a white blouse but somehow she looked to have more curves; with her light brown hair swept back from her pretty face, you could say she was definitely the more attractive of the two girls, with well-rounded breasts and a cute bum in her tight trousers. Gordon looked at Phillip and asked if he still had to ask them to take all their clothes off or had he seen enough to pass a reasonable judgement.

"They look very nice," said Phillip, defensively.

"Oh, so you approve, do you?"

Phillip took a swig of his beer and asked, "What makes you think they would want to date us two anyway, never mind anything else?"

"I saw the way Jasmine looked at you, hangs on every word you say, I can tell she fancies you," said Gordon with satisfaction.

"Time will tell," and at this point the two girls came back to the table.

As they sat down, Isobel said, looking at both of them, "And what were you two talking about while we were gone?"

"Why you of course," Gordon said.

"Oh, and have we passed the test?" asked Jasmine casually.

"When we were standing at the bar," Gordon began, "Phillip said, 'With you both wearing…' ouch… that was my foot, that hurt."

"Oh, sorry, I didn't realise your foot was just there," said Phillip. "You'll recover. Gordon was about to say how smart you both looked in your black trouser suits."

"Hmm, somehow I don't think that was it," said Isobel, "but thanks for the compliment, if that was what it was."

She looked at her watch and turned to Jasmine, "We'd better be going if we want to catch our train," she said.

"No need to hurry," said Gordon, "you could stay the night at my flat and then you don't have to rush off."

"Oh yes," said Isobel, "and why would we want to do that?"

"It's not what you think," he said. "That didn't really come out the way I meant it. What I meant to say is that my flat has two bedrooms as well as the lounge. One bedroom has twin beds and one has a double bed and there's a sofa that converts into a bed in the lounge. One bedroom even has an en suite shower room and you two could sleep in there, it's quite separate from the other bedroom. You could barricade yourselves in there and bolt the door if you want! I invested in this flat when property seemed like a good idea and I've got so many relatives who think nothing of paying good old Gordon a visit and getting free bed and board," he said in explanation. "Besides which I need the space for my hobbies!"

The girls looked at each other, a little doubtfully, but then Jasmine nodded her head so Isobel said slowly, "That sounds okay, we'll take advantage of your kind offer. What about you Phillip, where will you stay?"

"Oh, I'll bed down on the sofa, it's very comfortable, I know, I've stayed there before. Now, how about another round of drinks, is everyone having the same again?"

"Do you want me to give you a hand?" queried Gordon.

"Why," said Phillip amiably, "is your hand detachable? No, you stay here and fight off the opposition, I should be able to manage four drinks."

When Phillip headed off for the bar, Isobel turned to Gordon and said, "Now you can tell us what you were going to say when Phillip kicked you!"

"Now I come to think about it, it was probably not the best thing to say," he said.

"Come on, you've aroused our curiosity now so you've got to tell us what it was!"

Gordon hesitated, afraid he was going to put his foot in it when the present situation was heading in a very pleasant direction, so he tried to be as diplomatic as he could and said, "I asked Phillip if he didn't think you looked nice in your trouser suits and high necked blouses and he said it was difficult to tell."

"Was that it?" said Isobel.

"No," said Gordon, "I said I was going to ask you to strip off so he could pass judgement. It was just a joke, more like a sarcastic comment really."

"Well for an innocent remark like that," she said, "I certainly don't think you deserved a kick on the shins like that."

Phillip reappeared, carrying a tray with their drinks on it. "You'd make a good waiter," said Isobel.

"Don't mock, if my detective agency doesn't take off, that may well be my next job."

"What sort of exciting things do you two get up to at Banco Santander?" said Gordon.

"I'm secretary to the Area Manager and Jasmine is a PR," said Isobel. "That's about the most exciting it gets."

"What does a PR do?" asked Phillip.

"I smooth over difficult situations with major customers."

"Give us an example," he said.

"Say Company X sends us a letter saying they are not happy about the way the company is being served by our bank and they are now thinking of transferring their account to another bank, then I have to liaise with them, try to work things out to both parties' satisfaction and try to prevent their account being moved."

"Sounds very tricky," said Phillip.

"Do they make unusual demands of you, being a young and good-looking lady?" asked Gordon.

"You mean, do they ask me to sleep with them? Fellas are bound to try it on but I just ignore them and they soon realise there's nothing going to come of it."

"What if the top boss of an important company says I will only keep my account with Santander if you agree to sleep with me?" said Gordon.

"I say I will go straight back to my manager and quote exactly what you just said. I would then go back to my office and tell my manager, who by the way is a woman. She would jump on anyone who made a statement like that and she would tell him that if he took the account away from our bank, she will sue him for a number of sexual offences, demand a large sum in compensation and plaster it all over the newspapers!"

"Wow," said Phillip, "don't ever introduce me to your boss, she sounds like a real man eater."

"She won't tolerate any sexual nonsense from any man."

"She must be really hot stuff, I think I might take up the gauntlet," said Gordon.

"What will you do?" said Phillip, egging him on.

Gordon boasted, the beer starting to give him false courage. "Oh I've handled some difficult women in my time and managed to tame them."

"But they must have been Scottish highland women who are used to being clubbed over the head and dragged into your cave!"

"Scottish women aren't really like that, are they?" said Isobel.

"Don't listen to that Sassenach, his knowledge of women doesn't extend beyond the M25. He thinks the world ends there!" said Gordon.

"I can see that you two are good friends. I wouldn't like to see how you treat your enemies."

"Don't pay any attention to what Gordon says, he loves me really!" said Phillip. "It's just a bit of friendly banter."

"We don't get that kind of thing at Santander."

"Well the Spanish always were a miserable lot," said Phillip. "A bit of humour is vital in any place of work, it helps to get things done."

"So what was work like in your office Phillip?" asked Jasmine.

"A big room with three rows of desks and all sorts of IT gear, twenty-two-inch screens, with a person sitting at each desk trading all sorts of different commodities and shares on the money market. Sometimes, the atmosphere was so tense you could cut the air with a knife and sometimes, there was a lot of hilarity. It was like a mixed ward in an NHS hospital, mixed sexes, quite a few young women. One of them was known as 'Drop My Drawers Angie' who was very eager to oblige in any way she could!"

"And did she 'oblige' you?"

"No, I always pretended to have a low sex drive and I told her I could never do justice to a sexy lady like her, then I would point her in another direction to somebody else."

"Was that really fair, to point her towards some other poor sap?" said Isobel.

"All the other poor saps, as you call them, were perfectly capable of looking after themselves. Besides, two or three were quite happy to take her on and they used to say she was nice and cuddly and why miss out on the opportunity."

"You men, the way you talk about us, just as if we were some sort of toy you could pick up and play with while it gives you pleasure and then chuck us away when you lose interest!"

"In my experience," said Gordon, "that's not always true; usually it's the other way around, more guys are ditched by you ladies."

"That's because men just go and have affairs, rather than admit the relationship is over and it's time to move on."

"I think," said Phillip, "that both sides are guilty of doing either of these things, wives have affairs as well as husbands."

"But you don't have a wife or a partner in a long term relationship, do you?" said Jasmine.

"No, I did have but she walked out when the money ran out!" he said.

"What do you mean, the money ran out?" said Isobel.

"I took a redundancy package and all the advantages I had in my job came to an end, so she went as well," said Phillip.

There was a moment's silence and then Gordon said, "That's a very good example of what I was talking about!"

"Where is she now?" asked Jasmine, softly.

"I did hear that she latched on to one of our supervisors but I haven't seen her in nearly a year," he said.

"You don't look too broken hearted about it," Isobel said.

"It was a bit sad at first, but in the long run it turned out for the best. I was in the middle of a major life change and everything that went with it so it would have happened, sooner or later, and in this case, sooner was better."

"What's it like in your office, Gordon?" asked Isobel. "Is there anything like that going on where you are?"

"I assume you mean the sexual thing but this depends a lot on managers and the Bank of England has a long tradition of being like an old lady and they don't like changes. On the surface, the staff appear serious and get on with their jobs but if you scratch the surface, there are intrigues going on all the time. It's just that they're more discreet about it! What about Santander?" he asked.

"It's a very conservative bank and if there was a serious infringement of a sexual nature, it would probably mean the sack or possibly, movement to another location," Isobel said.

"So you don't have any boyfriends?" Gordon asked.

Isobel raised her eyebrows and said, "Is that a casual question or a serious one or do you fancy your chances?"

"While there's life there's hope. I might be interested, I'll let you know! Anyway, I can see Jasmine's eyelids are drooping, it must be past her bedtime; shall we get a taxi and go?"

They finished their drinks, after Phillip had rung for a taxi, and were soon on their way to Gordon's flat. It was in a very impressive block, newly constructed on the riverside, and the lift moved them silently to the fourth floor, after Gordon had keyed in his security number. He gave the girls a guided tour, pointing out all the advantages such as the marvellous view, which looked down river towards Greenwich, the spacious bedrooms, one with an en suite shower room and the other next to a luxurious bathroom, the open plan kitchen and the spacious lounge, looking out of floor to ceiling windows onto a small balcony. They were very impressed and when they saw the bedroom they were to share, they were glad they had accepted the invitation to stay overnight, provided they were not expected to sleep with either of the men.

Chapter 3

Phillip knew the layout of the flat because he had previously owned one very similar, two floors above, which he had sold to buy his house. Gordon had bought this flat fully furnished from a couple who had not been able to keep up the enormous payments on their huge mortgage and their flat had been repossessed so he had benefited from their good taste. He had met Phillip at the in-house gym and squash courts, and both being of a similar nature, they had soon become friends.

"This is a really beautiful place," said Jasmine, "makes our flat look a bit down market in comparison."

"Anybody want anything to eat or drink before bedtime?" asked Gordon. "Only thing is, I've just got whisky and some of that dark rum, but I've got tonic water or coke to go with it."

"I'll have a rum and coke with plenty of coke in it," said Isobel.

"And I'll have the same, please," said Jasmine.

"I think I'll have the same," said Phillip and moved over to help Gordon.

"Did you have a flat like this one?" asked Jasmine.

"Yes, almost exactly the same but two floors above. We met at the gym and became good friends, but in fact, this is the first time I've seen him for about a year because he's been in Scotland on a special assignment."

Jasmine giggled. "It sounds like he's a special agent in MI5, does he carry a gun?"

Isobel looked at her and at the large glass of rum and coke she was sipping and said to Phillip, "I'm not surprised your lady friend did not want you to give up your flat, where do you live now?"

"I bought a four-bedroom, detached house on the outskirts of Croydon so that I could combine work and home."

Isobel looked at him in amazement. "What on earth possessed you to go and live in Croydon?"

"I go where my destiny leads me," said Phillip, only very slightly drunk.

"Poor old Phillip," said Isobel, "relegated to the sofa!"

"I always sleep on the sofa when I stay here," said Phillip. "It's very comfortable, unless you would like to give up your bed for me to sleep on.

"What, and leave Jasmine on her own with you, what kind of a friend would I be if I did that!"

Jasmine announced, "Hey Isobel, I completely forgot, we don't have any toothbrushes or anything to sleep in and no make up for in the morning, what are we going to do?"

"It's hardly a tragedy," said Isobel. "You can have a shower in the morning and you must have a comb and lipstick in your bag…"

"No probs," said Gordon, "I've got a stock of new toothbrushes in the bathroom cupboard and as for what to wear in bed, Marilyn Monroe always said she only wore Chanel No. 5 perfume, but I've got a couple of large T-shirts I wear when I go to the gym which are long enough to hide all your naughty bits and keep you decent, how about that?"

"Thank you," said Jasmine, formally, "that sounds much better than having to sleep in bra and pants."

"Yes, I'm sure of it," said Phillip, solemnly, trying to make her laugh. "I gave up wearing bra and pants years ago, somehow they didn't suit me!"

Isobel told Jasmine to get ready for bed first and she would join her in a moment. Gordon offered her a nightcap of brandy but Phillip butted in with, "You know what they say about alcohol, 'Whisky makes you feel frisky, brandy makes you feel randy'."

"In that case, I don't think I'll bother," she said.

"See what happens when you open your big mouth," said Gordon indignantly.

"Sorry, but you wouldn't want either of these two ladies to succumb to your wiles by some sort of subterfuge would you, that's not cricket. Play the game!"

"I told you, there'll be none of that," said Isobel, calmly.

"There you are, a woman who knows her own mind so you'll have to put away your handcuffs and contraceptives and charm her with your winning personality instead."

With Jasmine getting ready for bed, Isobel was curious to know whether they were used to getting changed or undressed while they were with other boys or young men.

Phillip roared with laughter. "We've both been to university and I played rugby where you had a communal bath or shower rooms and you soon get used to being naked in a room full of other men. God forbid if you showed any kind of modesty, your mates would never stop ribbing you about it."

"Have you led a sheltered life, Isobel?" asked Phillip.

"I don't think so but I've lived with my family and ever since the age of five, I've had a room of my own so I can't say I'm used to sharing with anyone."

"Does that make you feel uneasy about dressing and undressing when other women are around?"

"Perhaps a little," she said.

"From what I can see, you have a lovely figure so I don't see why you shouldn't be proud to show it. The female body is a beautiful thing and artists have been drawing and painting naked bodies for centuries."

Isobel looked down at her lap and blushed. "But it's just not me," she said. Then she said firmly, "I think Jasmine will be in bed by now, so I'll say goodnight," and went towards the second bedroom.

"Were you trying to persuade her to sleep with you?" hissed Gordon, as soon as the door closed.

"No," Phillip whispered back, "she's a bit too thin for me, I'll leave her to a randy sod like you."

"I do rather fancy her," said Gordon, quietly.

"Well you'll have to make love to her in the dark, she's got some sort of hang-up about taking off her clothes when anybody else is there and it could take you a very long time to win her over."

"Yes, I think this will require a lot of hard work and above all, patience. Come on, let's get some sleep and I can plan my campaign in the morning!"

Phillip pulled out the sofa, found a pillow and a duvet and soon fell into a sound sleep. He woke, suddenly aware there was a warm body next to his and in the dim light reflected from the balcony, he wasn't sure if it was Isobel or Jasmine but when he turned over and his exploratory hand touched a naked buttock, he was suddenly sure it was Jasmine. She started to kiss him gently, pressing her full, voluptuous length against him, sliding her arms round his neck, but Phillip, although still half asleep, joined in their embrace with enthusiasm, not really caring who it was but determined to make the most of his opportunity. Had he really not made love to a woman for all those months – this was exciting but he tried to hold back just a little, not wanting her to feel it was just a "wham, bam, thank you ma'am" type of encounter but she was as eager as he was, wrapping her legs round him, and pushing her body against him. All too soon they had climaxed and it was finished but they relaxed against one another, each totally satisfied with the outcome. He nuzzled her neck, not saying anything, and still entwined, they fell asleep.

★ ★ ★

Light flooded the room from the uncurtained window and Phillip woke with a start, aware that he was on his own. Did I dream what happened, he asked himself, did I want it to happen so much, I went to sleep and imagined it? Then he became aware that his shorts were missing. He threw the duvet on the floor and searched the sofa for his underwear, finally discovering the missing item wedged between furniture leg and floor, whereupon he grabbed the rest of his clothes and scuttled into the bathroom. Much refreshed, he emerged half an hour later and found the two girls talking in the kitchen.

Phillip said, "Good morning, ladies, I hope you slept well?"

"Yes, thank you," they chorused. Phillip avoided looking directly at Jasmine and she gazed anywhere but at him. Gordon joined them, switching on the kettle and asking what they would like for breakfast.

"Any complaints?" he asked jovially. "No-one was assaulted or forced into white slavery or anything like that? I'm just checking, as your host, after all I am responsible for the wellbeing of my guests am I not? If anyone would like a cooked breakfast, we can order it from the place downstairs and it will be delivered shortly?"

"Not for me," Phillip said.

"Nor me," each of the girls replied.

"That being the case, let's go out for breakfast," said Gordon.

"Actually, we really have to be going," said Isobel, "or the family will be wondering what happened to us."

"You did ring home and tell them you were quite safe, didn't you?" asked Phillip.

"Oh yes, but they still worry if we don't get home the same day!"

"You're both over eighteen aren't you?" said Gordon, making a face.

"Course we are, silly."

"Thank heaven for that, I don't want to be arrested for abducting under-age girls."

"I'll have to go as well," said Phillip. "Got to start preparation for my first case or I'll never make any money. Can I walk you two ladies to your nearest station or the nearest Underground station?" asked Phillip.

"It will have to be the Underground," said Jasmine. "I'm not walking all the way to the station in these heels!"

"Right you are," said Phillip and turning to Gordon, "See you next Friday, or shall we make it Saturday night? What about you two ladies, will you be there?"

Isobel looked at Jasmine and said, "We're not sure, we might pop in straight from work on Friday but it just depends…"

Gordon looked somewhat forlorn at the thought of spending the rest of the weekend on his own but urged the girls to let him know what their plans would be and gave them his mobile number and they all said goodbye.

The nearest Underground station was only a short walk away, once they had taken the lift to street level and nothing was said. Isobel went to look at the timetable and Jasmine hung back, saying quietly to him, "Thanks for being so discreet."

"Thank you," said Phillip politely, and Jasmine blushed, smiled and turned away to join Isobel on the platform.

Chapter 4

He made his way home to Croydon, letting himself in and making a large pot of coffee and some toast in his kitchen, and started his work by ringing the prison to make an appointment to see his client's father, Mr Walter Dunn, at two o'clock on Monday afternoon.

At ten o'clock on Monday morning his phone rang and he answered. "Phillip Everett Detective Agency."

A well-educated voice answered, "Are you a detective?"

"Yes, madam, I am."

"Well, my name is Lady Pennington and my dog is missing, can you find it for me?"

"I am sorry madam, but I don't handle cases involving lost dogs."

"And may I ask why not?" said an offended voice.

"I'm afraid it would be too expensive for you; I charge £30 an hour, plus expenses and I can't guarantee finding the dog after even one day of searching."

"I have contacted the police and they have refused to take any action, so I wish to engage the services of a detective agency!"

"Why don't you advertise your loss in the local paper?" said Phillip soothingly. "I'm sure that will get some results and if your financial position allows, offer some reward, say £50, and this will be as quick a way as any of getting your pet back."

There was a short silence and then, "I shall get my secretary to place an advertisement in various papers but I warn you, if this is not successful, I shall be in touch with you and will expect you to place yourself at my service, regardless of cost!"

Phillip put the phone down with a sigh of relief. That might have been my first case, one lost dog. I wonder how many of them I'm going to get! But now I'd better be on my way to prison to interview Walter Dunn.

They kept him waiting twenty minutes while they checked his credentials and finally ushered the man into the interview room as if he had leprosy. Their faces said it all in big letters, "paedophile". Phillip hoped Walter Dunn did not feel as bad as he looked. He appeared wretched, hair grey and lifeless, eyes with dark shadows under them, glancing from side to side in fear as if being followed all the time. He looked in very bad shape and when Phillip introduced himself, he looked apprehensively round the room as if expecting a blow at any time. I've got to do something for this man, thought Phillip; if I don't, he won't last until the date is set for the trial.

He put out his hand and said, "Mr Dunn, my name is Phillip Everett and I have been asked by your son to investigate your case and get you out on bail."

Mr Dunn took the proffered hand and grasped it as if he would not let go. "Do you mean that?" he said eagerly. "Is it possible? You can't imagine what it's like in here with everybody being convinced I am a paedophile; they shout names at me and the warders treat me like dirt; I get pushed and shoved about and everything is done to make me feel guilty, when I know I've done nothing wrong. They just won't listen to me and I can't stand much more of it. Sorry to go on like this but you are the first friendly face I have seen in weeks and it's all been such a nightmare."

He was near to tears so Phillip asked him to sit down and he would make a few notes.

"The police have a very poor case and there is no evidence that anything inappropriate took place between you and this girl. They must be relying on the mother's charge that you acted sexually towards her daughter and when the full facts are known, a good solicitor will demolish her case.

"I need to hear exactly what took place between you and the girl, I must have the facts before I can build up a case to get you out on bail. Take your time, I am going to record what you say because this could help us during the appeal hearing."

Phillip switched on the little recording machine and asked Mr Dunn to start talking.

He began in a weak voice: "My wife died over a year ago, getting on for two, and we were very close. I know we all have to go sooner or later but I found it very difficult to get used to life without having her around. At first, my son said to go and live with them but I couldn't see that working out with him having this young family and I thought I would only be in the way. So I decided to stay in our bungalow where I'd been so happy with my wife. One or two friends said I should find a companion, to help me come to terms with losing my wife, so on the spur of the moment, I joined one of those dating agencies.

"They arranged a few meetings for me and some of the women were younger than my wife was and in their own way, they were quite nice but it's not like when I was courting, things have changed so much, I felt completely lost. I know the agency did their best, they arranged meetings with several different ladies but it never led to anything. It was probably my fault, I didn't put enough in to it or maybe I was too choosy and then my friends talked me into going on a singles holiday; I was too old for it. In the end, I became resigned to confining myself to a small number of friends.

"One day, I was feeling very lonely; I did a bit of shopping and then went for a walk through the park. It's quite nice there, lots of flower beds and ornamental trees and things. I started to feel a bit more cheerful when I saw this schoolgirl sitting on a bench, sobbing her heart out. Well I couldn't just walk past so I sat down on the other end of the bench and asked her why she was crying. She just ignored me so I had a good look at her and I could see she was a bit fat, obese they call it nowadays don't they, and she looked, oh it's hard to put it exactly, she looked a bit scruffy, her white blouse was grubby and her shoes were down at heel. Her hair was stringy and her coat had a stain or something on the sleeve, altogether not really a pretty sight.

"She went on crying and in the end I said to her if she didn't stop, people walking past would think it was my fault. She finally stopped crying and I gave her my handkerchief to dry her face and asked what had made her so unhappy and was there anything I could do to help her. She looked at me in amazement and said I was the first person who'd ever said that to her. Then it all came out, she was fat and ugly, her mother told her so and said she was just a nuisance. They called her names at school and laughed at her because she didn't have a father but her mother always had a boyfriend to go down the pub with and she was no good at school work; the teachers said she was stupid. If anything went wrong at home, it was always her fault and her mother blamed her for everything so she started pinching money from her purse and buying chips and takeaways and now she had burst the zip on her skirt, she was so fat, and she was going to run away but she didn't know where to go. That woman who calls herself a mother wants locking up for cruelty to children!!

"So I said to her that the only person who could really help was herself. I told her she was not ugly and if she stopped guzzling takeaway food and went to a gym, she would lose all her excess weight. She was not taking any trouble with her clothes and hair, and yes, she needed some new school clothes and shoes. She looked at me very scornfully and said that her mother would never pay for any of that and I was just a stupid old git to raise her hopes. I had to think quickly because I knew if I did nothing now, there was another young life ruined for ever so I told her we would not ask her mother for any money, I would come up with a programme for her to follow and if she followed it, I would pay for everything.

"The first thing she needed was to have her hair done – I remember my wife saying how it always made her feel so much better when she came out of the hairdressers, and how personal hygiene was so important if she wanted to improve her appearance. We would find a gym who would make out a programme of exercises specially for her and she must stick to them for at least one month before deciding if it was worth going on; then we will buy you the correct school uniform and decent shoes, but no playing truant and you must do any homework you are given and try to concentrate on your school work. How did that sound? The difference in the expression on her face was worth anything I might have to spend and it was as if I had a purpose in life again.

"We found a hairdresser, not one of the frightfully trendy ones, just a nice quiet one, and she looked very nice when she came out; her hair was much lighter, nearly blonde. She gave her name as Betsy Herne and arranged to make regular visits. I took her to a gym one of my friends had recommended and paid for six months; one of the female trainers worked out a schedule to aid weight loss without putting on too much muscle and suggested a possible eating plan. Being a new member, Betsy was entitled to a discount so I bought her some trainers, a track suit, some socks and shorts and asked her which sports bag she would like to keep all these things in. She chose one in pale blue and it was as if nobody had ever given her anything before, she was speechless.

"Outside, I told her that it was up to her and if she kept up the exercise and avoided all those fatty foods, she would soon be slimmer and fitter and feel much happier. She said she could only eat the food her mother gave her so I told her to offer to do the shopping and occasionally make a simple meal for her mother and that way she could make sure they were eating sensibly. I said I would get her one of those cheap pay-as-you-use-it mobile phones and she could keep in touch with me, if she needed some advice or help."

"So how did all this go wrong?" asked Phillip.

"To start with, everything went very well: her mother never paid much attention to her and it seemed as if she was so involved in her own life, she did not notice the changes taking place in her daughter. Betsy settled into a routine, calling at the gym most evenings, cutting back on the junk food and going to the hairdressers regularly. She kept in touch with me with the occasional text message and when she had lost some weight, I bought her the clothes I said would, both for school and for casual wear, and she became a really pretty teenager, not without the occasional spot! But that was also her downfall. Some of her mother's various boyfriends she met at the pub started to notice the difference between mother and daughter and one of them said jokingly that she would have trouble keeping the men away from her pretty daughter.

"One night, when Betsy had gone to the gym, Doris went into her room, went through all Betsy's things and realised that most were nearly brand new and she had not given her any money with which to buy them. That made Doris furious because she thought her daughter had a rich boyfriend who was buying all these nice things for her, things she could not afford to buy for herself, so she waited till Betsy came back from the gym, thinking how she could turn this situation to her advantage. She shouted at Betsy, threatened her and wanted to know who it was had bought the things and how often she had to sleep with him to get all these expensive clothes.

"Betsy had a little more confidence in herself and she stood up to her mother, telling her it was disgusting that a mother should speak to her daughter like that and just because she slept with different men, didn't mean to say that she, Betsy, was sleeping around. Doris was about to slap Betsy on her face when she played her trump card, as you might call it, and told her not to even think about attacking her, saying she was fitter than her and she might finish up worse off. The days of knocking her about were over, and she went into her room. Doris was so surprised at the change in Betsy but now, everything was falling into place and she started planning what she would do next.

"Doris worked out a plan where she would take her daughter down to the local police station and tell the desk sergeant that a man was buying her clothes and having sex with her and she was only thirteen. Doris didn't know who it was because Betsy refused to tell her, but he was spending a lot of money on her and she wanted the police to find him and charge him with the offence. At first the police were very sceptical about the story; they knew Doris quite well from trying to eject her from the pub at closing time, and were inclined to think she ought to be pleased that someone was being kind to the kid. But Doris had got the bit between her teeth, and threatened that if the police didn't take action, she would go to the papers, her local councillor, her MP, in fact she would make as much fuss and bother as she was capable of.

"Reluctantly, the police knew they had to investigate the story so they sent a policewoman round to the flat and while Betsy was at school, Doris showed her the clothes which I had bought her. Apparently Doris made a big dramatic scene, saying, 'I'm a single mum who has to scrimp and save for every penny I earn and I can't afford to buy my child anything like this. She also goes to a gym, a private one that must be expensive; I think that some man is buying these clothes and everything for services rendered, if you know what I mean.'

"The policewoman said, 'I take it you mean illegal intercourse with a minor below the age of consent, do you?'

"'Course I do,' Doris said, 'why else would he do it?'

"The policewoman listened to all Doris's outpourings and told her that this did not amount to evidence any more than that Betsy had accepted gifts from a generous benefactor, and whoever that person was, he had not committed anything more than an inappropriate relationship with her daughter.

"'Listen,' said Doris, 'no-one would spend money on my daughter without getting something in return.'

"'I'm afraid we cannot arrest anyone on such vague information when there is no evidence of sexual misconduct but I think I should talk to your daughter and see what she has to say about this.' "

Mr Dunn stopped talking for a moment and then carried on: "I don't quite know what happened after that, but the police came round to my house and interviewed me and said there would be a hearing in the Magistrates Court and they were going to ask for a remand in the case as more investigation was needed. I thought it was just a storm in a teacup, never even bothered to get myself a solicitor, thought everything would be straightened out at the hearing, but before I knew where I was, I had been remanded in prison, without bail. Doris was in court saying that I had complete control over her daughter and she was afraid I would influence her if I was allowed out on bail, and I now think she had a word with her current boyfriend to pass the nod to any of his cronies inside to make my life as uncomfortable as they could."

Phillip asked, "Did you not have a solicitor in court?"

"Yes, the court appointed one for me but once the case had been heard, my usual solicitor who deals with my legal affairs, he refused to take my case because he said it was a 'bit unsavoury' and not the sort of thing his firm usually dealt with and I would be better off being represented by someone 'who deals with this sort of case' as he put it. Apparently, I was already guilty of being a paedophile before I had ever been tried. I contacted my son and thankfully, he flew straight over here to stand by me; I can't tell you how grateful I am to him for taking over the reins and backing me up one hundred percent. In fact, I feel better already." And he gave Phillip a somewhat watery smile.

"I think this is a very poor case of justice not being done, but what was the name of your solicitor?"

"John Standish," said Walter, and Phillip made a note of the name on his memo pad.

"This will do for today. I have enough here to start collecting evidence to report to the lawyer you son has retained so that he can at least get you out on bail."

Walter looked worried. "Do you think it wise for me to be out on bail, little though I relish staying in here? I have heard of cases where paedophiles were beaten up and even killed," Walter said.

"I think these cases are quite rare and usually happen to men who have been convicted and then released after serving their sentences. You are not a paedophile and you have not had sex with Betsy, have you?"

"Of course not," said Walter indignantly.

"Well, there you are," Phillip said. "Don't even think about yourself like that, have confidence – understand? Right, now I'm going to leave you, but keep your chin up; you, me and your son are going to fight to get your name cleared, and while I'm here, I think I might have a word with the prison governor or a staff officer about your treatment in here and see if I can give them a subtle hint about improvements. You never know, you might be going to write an expose about prison treatment for prisoners on remand." And he winked.

Chapter 5

Back at his office he got straight on the Internet, looking for John Standish, solicitor, found his phone number and dialled it, asking the person who answered if he could speak to John Standish.

"Who shall I tell him is calling?" said the woman's voice.

"My name is Phillip Everett and I wish to consult Mr Standish about a case I'm involved in," said Phillip smoothly.

"Would you hold on a moment and I'll see if Mr Standish is free to speak to you."

A moment later a voice said, "John Standish here, how may I help you?"

"I hope you can Mr Standish. I believe you were representing Walter Dunn during his hearing at the Magistrates Court quite recently?"

A pause.

"Yes, I was."

"I have just been to interview Mr Dunn on remand in prison and he told me about the way you represented him, or rather, misrepresented him."

"Who are you?"

"I am a private investigator acting on behalf of Mr Dunn."

"And what right do you have to question the way I represented a client in court?"

"I know enough about the law to know that your performance was at best inadequate and at its worst, negligent. We are looking into your conduct of the case and might bring about an action to accuse you of negligence. Because of you, Mr Dunn was remanded in prison when in fact, the evidence against him was so inadequate, he should have been given bail. He is now suffering mental and physical abuse and his mishandling by the other prisoners and warders amounts to a threat on his life."

There was silence at the other end of the connection.

"Why are you doing this, Mr Everett?"

"I have just come back from the prison after speaking to Mr Dunn for two hours and I have left an elderly gentleman slowly being destroyed by our so-called justice. This is an innocent man who did nothing more than befriend a little girl, crying on a park bench; he took pity on her when he heard about the circumstances of her home life, which, I might add, nobody in authority disputes, and did his best to help her."

Silence again.

"Now see here, I'm not admitting any failure on my part to do my job but alright, I can see your point; what do you think should be done?"

"I want you to do what you should have done in the first place and prepare an appeal against the remand and get him released on bail. This should not be difficult for an experienced solicitor like yourself. For my part, I will help you to build a new case, quoting reliable evidence, the key points of which are, Mr Dunn and Betsy Herne have only ever met in public places such as the park, the gym, or various shops, they have never once been alone where any kind of impropriety could have taken place and there is only the biased word of Doris Herne spoken out of jealousy. She, I might add, slept with various men while her daughter stayed in her own small room and is hardly a fit mother to be in charge of a teenager. She dislikes her daughter and blames her for her own inadequacies. You get the case prepared and the date set for a hearing as soon as possible and between us we will have Mr Dunn out on bail very quickly."

"Very well Mr Everett, leave it with me and I will be in touch with you very soon."

Three days later the phone rang and John Standish told Phillip that a hearing was set for the 24th at ten o'clock, a week on Tuesday, and if Phillip would like to call at his office on the previous Friday, they could go over the salient points of the presentation of the case together.

"That sounds great," said Phillip. "Look forward to seeing you then."

He put the phone down and then barely five minutes later, it rang again so Phillip answered, thinking it was something Standish had forgotten, when the female voice said grandly, "This is Lady Pennington here. I have tried all your suggestions pertaining to tracing my missing dog, but none of them has met with any success. I have advertised, offering a substantial reward, in all the local papers, for the safe return of my darling Bruce and I have not had a single reply. My secretary contacted the editor of one of the papers for me and I offered to increase the reward money but he advised against this step; he said there were all sorts of evil persons about and it might encourage them to kidnap dogs and hold them to ransom, threatening them with cruel treatment if the owner did not 'cough up', I think was the phrase he used!"

Phillip interrupted politely and said, "He's a smart man, your editor, I totally agree with that. Wouldn't it just be a better idea to buy a young puppy, or even rescue a dog from the Animal Shelter, to replace your Bruce who might possibly not be with us anymore." He paused. He didn't want to tell her the brutal truth that the dog was probably dead by now; he tried to be diplomatic.

"Mr Everett, I take it you have never owned a pet dog. If you had you would know the pain and deprivation you feel when that animal disappears and you don't know what has happened to it. It's almost like losing a child and although you are obviously of the opinion that the animal is now dead, I cannot stop thinking that he may be trapped somewhere in distress, perhaps suffering cruelly. I am very attached to him and I must do everything in my power to find him or else I shall never have a peaceful night's sleep again!"

"I'm very sorry," he said, not wanting to admit that years ago he had kept a pet hamster and wept bitter tears when he found it dead one morning, "but I cannot think of anything else that would help."

"You can help me, Mr Everett, I want you to search for Bruce until you either find him, his body, or what ultimately happened to him. I will pay you as if you were looking for a person – £30 per hour and expenses, was it not? Please take my case. You are the only person who has been completely honest with me."

"Very well, Lady Pennington, perhaps you can give me some information so that I know where to start. Could I have your full name, address and telephone number, a photo of Bruce, details of his disappearance, the times of day he was exercised and most importantly, was he left alone at any time on the day he vanished. When I have these details and anything else you think would help me, I shall be able to formulate a plan of investigation. I'll also need a deposit of, say, a cheque for £300, no cash please. Is this alright with you?"

"Yes, certainly. You will have the information and cheque very soon. Good day to you Mr Everett."

★ ★ ★

On Friday evening, Phillip went to meet Gordon at the wine bar; no special plans had been made to meet the two girls. He arrived ten minutes early and ordered a bottle of beer. He didn't really like bottled beer, he preferred it on draught, but, it being a trendy wine bar, they only sold beer in bottles. He was just considering what he would do, if Gordon didn't turn up when he heard a feminine voice close to him, saying, "Now this is an example of a sad looking guy, Holly!"

Phillip turned his head, to see two girls sat on bar stools and it was the one next to him who had spoken.

"Do your mothers know you are out?" he said, glancing sideways.

The girl sitting next to him turned to her friend, "Cheeky, as well as being sad," she said pertly.

"Which school do you go to?" he said. "I might be able to put in a good word for you with your teacher!"

"That's age discrimination in reverse isn't it Jennifer?"

"Yes, we'll have to report him to Esther Rantzen, Holly."

"So it's Holly and Jennifer is it? Are you two young ladies waiting for your escorts or could I entertain you this evening?"

"It all depends what you can do" said Jennifer.

"Well, let me see, I can do a Roger Moore impression of acting."

"Okay, do that," Holly said.

Phillip lifted one eyebrow.

"What was that supposed to be?"

"That, my dear, was acting," said Phillip, beginning to enjoy himself teasing them.

"What other bits of acting can you do?" said Jennifer.

"I can do Clark Gable," and without pausing he said, "Frankly my dear, I don't give a damn."

"Who's Clark Gable?" they both asked.

"I give up," he said.

"No, no, don't give up, next time you might even make us laugh," said Holly.

"You two are the type of person who would probably laugh if I fell off my stool," he said.

"Ooh yes, now that would be funny," said Jennifer.

"Sorry, you'll have to wait 'til the end of the evening before I do that; when I've had enough to drink, I just slide down the side of the bar and they carry me out. Anyway, what brings you two here?"

"We only came in here for a drink first and now we're going to our favourite bar, just off Piccadilly Circus, they have music and a great DJ."

At that moment Gordon made his way over to them.

"Sorry I'm a bit late."

"Now that you've arrived you can help me babysit these two schoolgirls!"

"Are they over sixteen?" said Gordon.

"We haven't got around to asking that yet."

"Well you should always ask that first, it will keep you out of trouble," said Gordon, pretending to be serious.

"We're not stopping here, just having a warm-up drink and we're going to this fab bar where they play all the latest hits and the DJ's really funny. Come with us, we can have a laugh," said Jennifer.

"Yes," said Phillip, "the DJ plays his comb and paper."

"Yes, I've heard of people doing that but it lacks volume," said Gordon.

"Very funny," said Holly. "He only plays the latest hits."

"God forbid," said Phillip, rolling his eyes. "It would turn my drink sour!"

"Don't you like the latest hits?"

"I would not listen to them if I was alone and bored out of my mind."

"If you don't come with us, you won't find out what you're missing," said Holly.

"Are we on a promise there?" said Gordon.

Holly smiled cutely and said, "You never know what it could lead to."

"You don't know what you would be missing," said Phillip. "This fellow here is a true Scot and later on he changes into his kilt and if you asked him nicely, he would show you his sporran."

The two girls giggled and said, "We're off now, bye."

* * *

After they had gone, Gordon asked Phillip what sort of week he'd had and he replied that it hadn't been bad, got a few things moving.

"Did I tell you about Lady Pennington and her lost doggie, Bruce? I think he must be a Labrador from the way she described him. A few days ago she rang me and asked if I would help her find her lost dog so I gave her some advice and managed to palm her off by saying I charged too much to go looking for missing pets. Well, today she came back to me and persuaded me to take her case!"

"Good grief," said Gordon. "Is she going to pay you?"

"I said that I needed a deposit of £300 before I started and she agreed!"

"So now you've got two cases already, do you think you'll be able to make a living out of looking for lost dogs?" and he was laughing uproariously.

"Don't laugh," said Phillip. "I made good money at the bank and unlike many others I put my bonuses to good use. I didn't splash out on expensive wine or cars and £1000-a-time suits so I reckon even if I don't earn enough to cover my living expenses at first, I'm going to build up the business and eventually, everything should fall into place. In the meantime, I can subsidise the business with my savings and if ever my savings get too low, I'll have to get another job. What about you Gordon?"

He shrugged his shoulders. "Financially, I am getting by okay but I'm not in quite the same position as you. To change the subject, I don't think those two girls we met last week are going to turn up tonight, do you?"

"Well, to be fair, we didn't make a definite date with them did we?"

"No," said Gordon, "it's probably for the best; I think that Isobel is the old fashioned type who still believes in no sex before marriage. We didn't get very much out of last Friday's meeting, did we?"

Phillip just nodded; he wasn't going to tell Gordon about his exciting encounter under the duvet with Jasmine that night.

Their attention was grabbed by the appearance of a very beautiful woman, trailing some man behind her. She was fashionably dressed, to make the most of her curvaceous figure, and there was an air of confidence about her, as she looked round the bar, that showed. Gordon was staring at her with his mouth slightly open.

"Close your mouth Gordon," said Phillip dryly, "you're causing a draft."

"This is your 'Ex' isn't it?"

"Yes, that's Samantha," he said. "I wonder who that saphead is with her?"

"Whew, never mind him, the way she looks, I wouldn't mind being that saphead myself, you must have had some great sex with her," said Gordon, enthusiastically.

"Unfortunately, life is not all about sex, Gordon; after you've lived with someone for any length of time, sex can begin to lose its novelty!"

"Well, it would take me a very long time before I got bored with her in the bedroom and sex lost its novelty, I would probably die of old age before that happened!" Gordon said.

At this point Samantha, looking around, noticed Phillip and headed straight to him, completely ignoring her escort.

"Well, if it's not my ex-partner, Phillip, how are you?"

"I'm fine and there's obviously no need to ask how you are. I heard you were an item with the office manager?"

"Well you know how it is these days, James lost his job so I'm with…" – she waved a hand in the direction of the man she came in with.

"Dear me," said Phillip sarcastically, "at this rate you're going to run out of men!"

"I can always come back to you my darling," she cooed.

"No, my darling, you wouldn't like my circumstances now, just a small house and a second-hand car, no real job or the prospect of one, too far beneath your exacting standards, sweetheart! Now Gordon here, he has a job for life, a flat two floors below the one we used to live in, a snazzy sports car and what's more, he fancies you as well!"

"Yes, I have met Gordon before."

"Oh I know that, but you don't know him intimately, do you?"

At this point, Samantha turned, waved her hand and walked away.

Gordon returned to his drink and said, "What a woman, totally arrogant but exciting with it. Looks like you and me are getting drunk on our own tonight."

"Yes," said Phillip, "but I'm not sleeping with you!"

Gordon laughed and told Phillip that he was a highly desirable sleeping partner and he had had no complaints from any of his partners. They heard a voice behind them say, "There they are, in the usual place, propping up the bar again and they already look half drunk!"

"We were just saying how disappointed we were because you weren't here," said Phillip and gave Jasmine a quick hug.

Gordon smiled, mainly at Isobel, and said to Phillip, "You look after these two ladies and I'll get some drinks in and don't let any men near them till I come back. Kick a few of those drunkards out so that we can all sit at a table!"

An older couple indicated they were just leaving so Phillip ushered the girls over to it but there were only three chairs.

"I'm not sitting on anyone's knee," said Jasmine.

"There's a chap over there, seems to be sitting on his own, go ask him if we can have his chair," said Isobel.

"Are you being funny?" said Phillip. "Do I look as though I want my face re-arranged!"

"Use diplomacy," said Jasmine, "tell him he would be better off sitting on a bar stool where all the talent is and thank him for giving Isobel his chair because she has a bad back and she will give him an angelic smile and he will be so flattered, he will immediately jump up to please her. Believe me, I've seen it happen!"

Phillip approached the big man warily and explained that the young lady with blonde hair had hurt her back, moving her computer from one office to another and as he was sitting on his own, he might be better off at the bar, that is, if he wanted to get to know anybody. Isobel smiled radiantly at him, when prompted by Jasmine, and with a little wave in her direction, he allowed Phillip to take his chair.

"You two will get me murdered," he complained. "I don't think that story took him in for a moment and I have been forced to tell a lie!!"

"Oh dear, do you hear that Isobel? Your knight errant who went into battle for you, has had to be untruthful on your behalf; what shall we do for him, shall we make it up to him in some way?"

"Yes please," said Phillip.

Gordon returned with the drinks in time to hear this and said, "Whatever it is, can I have some as well as him?"

"You didn't do what he did and get us a fourth chair so that you could sit down."

"How did you manage that?" Gordon said.

"I just said that he looked very comfortable on that chair and now I wanted to be comfortable so off he want just like a big pussy cat, leaving me in possession of said item, for which my two grateful friends here are going to reward me. You don't come into it, you only went for the booze!

"Actually, I tell a lie. I said to him if you don't give me this chair, I will get that wild Scotsman at our table to come and beat seven bells out of you. He stood up, all six-foot-seven of him, his shoulders blocking my view of the room, and putting both fists, the size of large loaves of bread on my shoulders, he ground his teeth in a snarl and said, 'Tell your friend I will see him later,' and he gave me his chair!"

Gordon groaned. "Thanks a lot, that's all I need, several weeks in hospital while my bones mend."

"Don't take any notice of him," said Isobel, and turning to Phillip, "You know you didn't say that to him," indignantly.

"I withdraw my offer of compensation."

"I don't," said Jasmine, cheekily, and turning to Phillip, "I keep my promises!"

I hope you do, he thought, and in just the way I would like best. He looked at her properly for the first time and noticed her wide, brown eyes. Her hairstyle reminded him of a film star of the 1940s called Hedy Lamarr. She had obviously changed out of her trouser suit and high-necked white blouse she wore at work, into the clinging, v-necked, knee-length dress she wore now, showing her shapely legs and just a hint of cleavage.

Phillip could see the shape of her full breasts and the slightly tanned look of her skin. Would he be lucky enough to make love to her tonight? He heard a distant voice saying, "He's fallen asleep, look at him, dead to the world."

"I heard what you said," protested Phillip. "I couldn't think of a suitable reply."

"What, the sharpest wit in this room couldn't think of anything to say, that must be a first," said Gordon satirically.

"That could be put down to lack of alcohol," said Phillip. "I'll go and top up our supplies."

He gave his order to the bar person when a voice behind him said, "And two glasses of house white wine please."

Phillip turned to find Holly standing behind him, smiling at the expression of surprise on his face.

"If you wouldn't mind?"

"No of course not. What brings you back here, thought you left because you liked the other place better?"

"How much do I owe you for the wine?" said Holly.

"Oh that's on the house," said Phillip gallantly. "Never let it be said I made a lady pay for her own drink."

"So long as you don't think it entitles you to anything, thanks a lot." She picked up her two glasses just as Gordon came over to see what was holding him up.

"What's keeping you, did you decide to brew the beer yourself or are you chatting up this young lady?"

"Ignore him, he is just a crude Scotsman."

"I remember him from earlier on."

"Such a common face," said Phillip.

"Take the tray to our table, there's a good boy, I'll be with you in a minute."

He went with Holly to where Jennifer was standing. She passed her the glass of wine and said, "This kind stranger has bought us our drinks."

Jennifer said to her, "I think he deserves a reward for that!"

"And I would be pleased to accept it but my friend and I are otherwise engaged tonight; that's my table over there. I was just curious to know why you two decided to come back here?"

"Well I never wanted to leave here in the first place," said Jennifer, "it was Holly's idea. I would have been quite happy to stay here and chat to you."

Holly said disgustedly, "Listen to her. I think she's developed a crush on you already. We left here because the other bar is much bigger, they have music and you can even have a dance, but tonight there were no interesting men."

"I hope you two can find some interesting men in here tonight but I have to get back to my table now," Phillip said.

"Just a moment," said Holly, putting her hand on his arm. "Were you trying to chat us up for a future encounter?"

"I'm trying to widen my circle of friends. I've led a very sheltered life for the past few months and prior to that, I lived with a partner. Now I have more time for myself so I'm spreading my wings. Nice to have met you. Bye!"

Phillip returned to the table.

"Who were they?" queried Isobel.

"Just two girls I met earlier this evening when I thought Gordon wasn't going to turn up. Their names are Holly and Jennifer."

"As you can see," said Gordon, "he is a very popular guy!"

"You can stop that," said Phillip, aiming a playful punch at Gordon's arm. "They are only the second couple of girls I have spoken to for well over a year!"

"Are we staying the night at your place?" said Jasmine to Gordon.

"Of course, you are more than welcome, and Phillip as well. It means you don't have to rush to catch any late trains; besides it's not a good idea, getting off trains at nearly deserted stations and either having to walk home or catch a bus or something."

"Oh good, that would be great, shall we do that Isobel? I've brought my toothbrush and one or two other things with me, just in case."

"Well, if we've been invited, we might as well accept," said Isobel.

"You're quite right Gordon, I'm always a bit apprehensive about when I get off the train; there are usually no taxis about so we have to walk quite a long way and you hear such awful stories. Thanks."

They finished their drinks, went for a taxi, and on arrival at the flat, Gordon announced that he had stocked up with a few more different drinks and they only had to tell him what they wanted and he would provide them with it.

"What a kind man you are," purred Isobel, "but what I would really like is coffee; shall I go into the kitchen and make it? What about you Jasmine?"

"Yes, that's just what I need after all that red wine I drank tonight."

"Looks like it's just you and me, two alcoholics," Phillip said.

"I'll have a whisky and soda, please."

Gordon poured their drinks and Jasmine asked Phillip about the case he was investigating for the 'dog lady', as she called her.

"Her full title is Lady Pennington and she wants me to find out what happened to her dog."

Isobel came back with the coffee and said, rather puzzled, "She's lost her *dog* and wants you to find it?"

"Yes, she's a very nice lady and to her, that dog is almost like her child and the same as a best friend."

"But if she has plenty of money to pay you to find this dog, why doesn't she just buy another one of the same breed?" queried Jasmine.

"Exactly what I suggested to her but she said she couldn't just abandon her pet like that and it might be somewhere trapped or starving, so hearing how upset she was, I agreed to take on the case," Phillip said, "and she is willing to pay."

They sat chatting and laughing for a short time and then the girls said they were ready for bed and said goodnight.

"I don't know what you were saying to them while I was getting you a drink," said Gordon, "but it must have totally bored them; next time, try and keep your conversation more cheerful and don't talk about work."

"Hey, don't blame me, it's your bank work that puts people to sleep, sitting down all day, playing with your abacus. Oh sorry, abacus is what they call advanced technology in the Bank of England."

"We use far more sophisticated technology than you will see in most private banks," said Gordon, offended. "However, what do you think has happened to the girls?"

"What do you mean?" asked Phillip.

"They asked for coffee, didn't they? Now you don't ask for strong coffee before you go to bed if you want to get to sleep, do you?"

"Perhaps they have worked out some Machiavellian plan to seduce us when we go to bed," said Phillip.

"Let's hope so," said Gordon.

They finished their drinks. Phillip prepared the sofa, stripped off to his boxers and lay down, willing himself to keep awake. He was nearly asleep when the soft, lithe body slipped under the duvet with him, naked except for a pair of lacy briefs. Phillip needed no urging and, suddenly fully awake and alert, started to kiss her mouth, her neck, the tips of her breasts, while she returned every kiss with the same urgency, her breathing gradually coming faster; their passion mounted. He was thanking god for the wonderful sensation of satisfying a passionate woman. Their enjoyment was over all too quickly, for a few moments he held the lush body close and wondered how long it would before they could do it again, but she pulled herself reluctantly away and with a final, lingering kiss, went back to her single bed, next to Isobel's.

Phillip woke reluctantly, discovered his boxer shorts to be under the sofa again and went to use the bathroom. Refreshed by a shower and shave, he went into the kitchen to make himself a mug of coffee, although he didn't hold out much hope of finding very much to eat; Gordon usually ate out or sent in an order and had it delivered to his flat. His exertion during the night had made him very hungry and after much searching, he found some cornflakes, a carton of long life milk, searching the drawers he discovered a dessert spoon and was soon munching his way through a large bowl of his favourite breakfast cereal.

Jasmine came into the kitchen, fully dressed and smelling gorgeous; she came over to him and gave him a long, lingering kiss, savouring the taste of milk and cornflakes.

"Good morning, how long have you been up?" she enquired.

"Half an hour or so, and how are you feeling this morning?"

She smiled and said, "I feel great, are we doing anything today?"

"Whatever you like, I'm at your disposal," he said grandly. "Is Isobel awake yet?"

"She was still asleep when I was getting showered and dressed."

"If you're awake so bright and early, sounds as if I didn't do you justice last night," he said.

"Do you need to ask for reassurance?" she said and punched him lightly on the arm.

Phillip pretended to be hurt and said, "Is that the punishment for my lack of effort?"

"No, that's for asking for points out of ten," she said.

"We'd better not carry on with this line of conversation any further, or you'll be getting me too excited!"

Gordon came into the kitchen, asking where Isobel was.

"Isn't she up yet?" he said.

"Here I am," she said, as she entered the kitchen. "What are we going to do today?"

"Won't take no for an answer," Phillip said. "We're all going out to have breakfast and then we can decide what to do for the rest of the day!"

"Ooh, isn't he masterful this morning!" said Isobel.

"Yes, I'm feeling very domineering and if anyone disagrees, they will get a spanking. Not you Gordon, of course!"

"I'm a bit disappointed by that," he said. "I think I might like spanking but it would have to be done properly by Isobel."

They all burst out laughing and left the flat to find a place for breakfast.

Chapter 6

The following Tuesday, after checking that both amounts had been credited to his bank account, he rang Walter Dunn in prison to tell him that a date had been set for the hearing of his appeal and he had retained the same solicitor who had made such a poor showing at the Magistrates Court, the reason being that he had shamed him into feeling guilty about his treatment of the case and after being told he might be sued for negligence, he ought to make a much better job of the appeal. Mr Dunn sounded a little unsure but Phillip assured him that there would be a good outcome, and he then asked for Doris Herne's address and phone number as he wanted to interview Betsy, and her mother or some responsible adult would have to be present when he did. He made a note of the address and number and after telling Walter to keep his spirits up, with only a few days to go now before his appeal, he rang off.

Phillip thought Walter Dunn sounded a bit more upbeat and he rang Mrs Herne's number, wondering where she would be at this time of the morning. But she answered the phone almost straightaway with one word, "Hello."

"Good morning, Mrs Herne, this is Phillip Everett speaking."

"Who…?"

"I am investigating your daughter's case and I need to speak to her as soon as possible, to corroborate some of the details in her statement; could I come round this afternoon?"

"You from the police?" asked Doris, removing the cigarette from her mouth.

"No, actually I'm a private investigator and I've been employed by Mr Edward Dunn to speak to all the witnesses involved in the enquiry."

"In that case, there's no way you're going to speak to her, the little cow, she's caused me more than enough trouble already and I'm sick of her whining on."

"Mrs Herne, before you put down the phone, I would advise you that I'm perfectly entitled to speak to Miss Herne and I did not ring you to obtain your permission. I rang only as a matter of courtesy and I would have thought you would have wanted to be present at that interview. If not, some other responsible adult must be present."

"You're going to defend that pervert, ain't you?"

"Every accused person is entitled to the best possible defence and Mr Dunn was only acting out of the kindness of his heart to someone he saw as a child, perhaps the daughter he and his wife were never able to have. If you do not wish me to speak to Miss Herne when you are there then I shall have to request her attendance at the police station."

"Well you can believe he's not a paedophile if you want to but I still say he was grooming her to have sex with her, if he hadn't done it already."

"Mrs Herne, you should not judge others by your own somewhat dubious standards."

She slammed the phone down.

That would appear to be that, and he would now have to request a meeting with Betsy at some other time, to go over her statement. Evidently she had not pleased her mother by not agreeing to back up the complaint she had made against Mr Dunn; this was quite understandable, as she saw him only as her benefactor. Phillip put his notes to one side for the time being.

He started to read the information which had arrived this morning from Lady Pennington. The dog was allowed out into the garden between nine and ten o'clock. When he had run about for a time, he would lie down on the step outside the door and this was a sign he wanted to come in. He had a large basket in the hall where he slept at night. In the early evening he would be taken for a long walk, either by Lady Pennington or one of her staff, and would then spend the rest of the night inside the house.

On the evening of the dog's disappearance, Lady Pennington took him for his usual walk, took off his lead while she opened the door, and heard him bark. As she turned around, she saw Bruce run through the opening in the wall and out onto the road. She called to him but could not see the road because of the high garden wall and when he did not come at her call, she went to look but there was no sign of him. She called to the handyman to search up and down the road and she kept calling but there was no sign of the dog. She had stayed up all night, thinking he would soon be scratching at the door to be let in, but since then she had not seen or heard of him again. The photograph showed a large black Labrador and Phillip concentrated all his attention on the doggy face and said musingly, "Now Bruce, if you can tell me where you are, you will save us all a lot of trouble and your mistress a great deal of money!!" The dog in the photograph did not answer.

Now where the hell do you start looking for this sort of dog, he thought. What is the most likely scenario? He wrote down: *The most obvious one is dog runs into road, vehicle going too fast knocks him over and kills him, driver panics, puts dog into boot and drives off. Later on, he disposes of the body where nobody will find it. Two, a driver could have seen the dog and thought "I've always wanted a dog like that", picked him up, taken him home as a pet, perhaps somewhere at the other end of the country or intends to ask for a reward for returning him. On the other hand, they could deliberately have lured the dog out of the garden and stolen it for dog fighting. I know they usually use Staffordshire bull terriers but I have heard of cases where they used*

Labradors and he's a pretty big dog, but probably too good-natured to be made into a fighter.

It's no good, he thought, after all this time it's most unlikely I could find him but I'm being paid so I'd better do my best. He rang the Pennington number and was answered by a lady with a completely different voice, somewhat older, he thought.

"May I speak to Lady Pennington, please?" he said.

"Speaking," said a puzzled voice.

"Oh, I'm sorry, but the lady I spoke to previously sounded a little different to you," he said, diplomatically.

"It must have been my daughter Sarah, whom you spoke to before; are you the man she asked to find Bruce, have you found him already?"

"I'm Phillip Everett and yes, your daughter is employing me to find out what happened to her dog but so far, no luck. What I wanted to ask you is would it be in order if I came to your house, to see the surroundings where the dog went missing? I don't want to park outside without you knowing who I am and, then be arrested for stalking."

"Certainly, Mr Everett, that will be quite in order. Park your car close to the front door and I will tell my staff that I'm expecting you so there will be no difficulties put in your way."

An hour later, he arrived at the address he had been given and to start with, he parked on the grass verge, trying to judge how busy the road was and what sort of traffic was using it mainly.

There was a gap in the wall where the drive swept up to the front of what was quite a large manor house, roughly fifty metres away; add to that the width of the grass verge and pavement, it was around fifty-five metres in all. The traffic seemed to be well spaced and the vehicles were not travelling at excessive speeds; there would probably be peak times early in the morning and late afternoon/early evening but between these times, he could not see that the road would be extremely busy. If the dog's lead was taken off at the front door, he would have to run fifty-five metres across the garden before disappearing through the gap and be out of sight at the far side of the walls. If, at the same time it was barking, cars travelling on the same side of the road would have plenty of time to pull up. He reasoned that if it had reached the far side of the road, it could have been run over, but if it was on the house side, someone must have taken it. If it was deliberate, how would anyone know that the dog was released from its lead at the house door at any particular time of the day! Curiouser and curiouser!

Why would anyone park here, hoping the dog would be free to come running to say, a portion of food or perhaps to a female dog in season? Why would anyone choose this particular house? Admittedly, it was large and obviously well kept, indicating someone with plenty of money who might be prepared to pay a few hundred pounds to get their dog back, and it would mean a nice little earner with the minimum of work or risk. After all, if caught, they could always say they found the dog running loose or chasing cars on the road and they picked it up to save it from being run over, waited for the owner to come forward but meanwhile, they were just looking after it! It would make a very plausible story; let's just hope that is the case; at least that would be a chance, to get it back alive. There were far worse things he could think of but he didn't really want to dwell on that at the moment. A car screeched to a halt in front of him and an irate young woman came towards him, tapping on the driver's door.

As Phillip let the window down she said imperiously, "What are you doing parked on private property? this is not the place where you stop to look at your maps or something and I want you to move on immediately, or I shall call the police and have you removed forcibly." She was obviously in the middle of a huge temper tantrum!

Phillip knew the importance of first impressions so he was wearing an expensive suit, white shirt and a smart silk tie, and he opened the car door and stood up next to her. He knew he was in good shape as he made regular visits to the gym and he was hoping she would notice this and calm down a little. He was not really used to dealing with furious females who looked as if they would like to murder him!

"Please excuse me," he said meekly, "I'm not really parked here, I'm just examining where Lady Pennington's dog disappeared; I thought it might give me some ideas as to what could have happened."

She had the grace to blush a little. Phillip went on, rubbing salt into the wound, "Lady Pennington told me she would inform her staff that I was coming and that it was perfectly alright to look wherever I wished. I take it you work in some capacity for Lady Pennington, her secretary perhaps?"

She said very stiffly, not looking at him directly, "Sorry, name's Sarah Pennington actually, didn't know my mother had spoken to you. You must be Phillip Everett, we talked on the phone."

That was the only apology he was likely to get this side of Christmas so he smiled and said correctly, "How do you do? Please call me Phillip if you wish."

"Sarah; actually I'm the Hon. Sarah Pennington but most people call me by my first name. Follow me up to the house and I'll try and rustle up some coffee for you." Phillip got back in his car and followed her car up the sweep of the drive, coming to a halt in front of the Grade II listed manor house. Some place, he thought and followed her into the large hall.

"Come through into the morning room," she said. "Have a seat and I'll be back with you shortly. I'm not sure where my mother has got to but…" Her voice trailed off as she disappeared, possibly into the kitchen.

She reappeared some ten minutes later, apparently in a better temper, after having given him time to study the paintings on the walls and the myriad photographs in silver frames, dotted about the room on various shelves and tables.

"Now what can I do to help you with finding Bruce?"

"If you wouldn't mind going through exactly what happened at the time he went missing then I can get an accurate idea of the geography of the place and see if it fits in with any of the theories I have come up with."

She sat down and started to give her account: "I took him for a walk in the evening and we came back up the drive to the front door – it was about nine o'clock. I took his lead off and turned to open the door; I half stepped into the hall when I heard him barking. I turned round to see what he was barking at just in time to see his tail going out of the garden."

Phillip said, "Can you think carefully, which way did he go? To the right or the left?"

"He went to the left."

"You're quite sure?" asked Phillip.

"Yes, absolutely sure, is that important?"

"It just gives me an idea of the direction in which a car might be travelling, if he were to be knocked down."

"Have you had any ideas so far?"

"You mean about the dog?"

Sarah looked closely at him, the worried frown on her face suddenly relaxing. "Yes, about the dog for now," she emphasised, smiling.

"I'll tell you about one possibility I have thought of and that is, when dogs chase traffic, they usually run at the side of a moving vehicle; I have only seen an animal killed or injured when it ran across to the other side of the road and it was hit as it ran in front of nearside moving traffic."

Sarah looked a little puzzled.

"I can explain it better if we were to walk to the end of the drive."

As they walked towards the entrance of the drive, he was able to get a good look at her. She appeared to be about twenty, quite tall, maybe five feet eight inches, wearing jeans and pale blue sweater with long sleeves, and expensive looking black and white trainers. She wore her blonde hair in a ponytail and if she was wearing any make-up, he couldn't tell. A very pretty girl, thought Phillip, in a rather insipid way.

They stopped at the end of the drive and he explained his theory.

"Imagine a car was parked on the other side of the road with a barking dog inside it. Bruce hears this and runs towards the noise, straight across the road and gets hit by a car travelling in the opposite direction on this side of the road."

Her eyes filled with tears. "So you are saying Bruce was killed?"

"That's one possibility."

"But wouldn't that driver stop, come to the house and say I just hit your dog or something?"

"You would think so; there is even a law that states any accident involving a dog should be reported to the police but sadly, a lot of people today pay scant regard to the police," he said.

Sarah looked downcast and said stubbornly, "I still want to know exactly what happened to Bruce, I want you to go on investigating" – she looked straight into his eyes – "please!"

"If that's what you want, I'll go on investigating but you do understand the difficulties, don't you?"

"Come back to the house and have that coffee I offered you; it should be ready by now."

"It's very tempting but I need to be somewhere else shortly. I'll let you know how I progress."

He was aware of some perfume she was wearing which subtly attracted him and he had to remind himself the meeting was strictly business. But if he ever met her socially, he might make it his project to find out where she sprayed that delicious scent!

CHAPTER 7

Next morning, Phillip rang John Standish to tell him he was trying to arrange an interview with Betsy Herne but Doris, her mother, flatly refused to allow him to visit her house so he was unsure what should be his next step.

"Today is Wednesday and we are meeting to discuss the case on Friday, so why don't you wait until then?" said John.

"Okay, I'll do that," said Phillip, "and now for something completely different! Have you ever been involved in the case of a missing dog?"

John laughed. "Are you joking? Missing dogs…? Never! How did you manage to get yourself involved in something like that?"

"It's a Lady, no less, and although at first I turned her down, she came back and persisted and she sounded so distressed that I took the case on, seeing as she was willing to pay my fees."

"So where are you now, are you getting anywhere with your case?" said John, somewhat amused.

"I'm almost sure the dog was lured away, possibly by using a bitch in season, and when he got the scent, off he went. What I don't understand is why have they gone to all that trouble? It's been a number of days now and there has been no request for ransom or a reward for returning the dog which is a big, soft, black Labrador. If it had been a Staffordshire bull terrier I could have understood it; they might have wanted to use it for dog fighting, but I can't see that being the case."

"I once sat in court when three men were up before the magistrates for dog fighting and it was horrific. Apparently, they used a big non-fighting dog to fight with a bull mastiff, to build up the atmosphere. Of course, the mastiff tore the other dog to pieces and what with the smell of blood and guts, all the rest of the dogs get very excited and then they start the real fights going. These men are ruthless and they are fined nowhere near enough, even when they are caught red-handed. Occasionally they are sent to prison and banned from keeping dogs for a number of years but I don't know whether the police are able to keep a check on them."

"That's barbaric," said Phillip, "but that's my next move. I have to find out where these meetings are being held and then try to infiltrate the place to see if I can spot the dog. How do I find out a venue?"

John said, "As far as I know, the men in it who want to make the most money out of betting will put an advert in local papers in some sort of crude code and those in the know will recognise it and word will get round as to location."

"Give me some ideas as to what to look for," Phillip said.

"Well it could be something like 'The Old Friends' Reunion next Thursday, at Area 5, 7.30 to 9.30 pm, see you there'. You wouldn't be much wiser because you don't know which is Area 5; but to everyone in the know, it's obvious," said John. "I would think nowadays, they might be more inclined to use the Internet, in which case they could be more informative but if you do decide to go, be very careful, these men would just as likely put you in the ring with two of their fighting dogs and then bury your body somewhere on farmland, along with all the carcases of dogs that had been ripped to pieces."

"Thanks for the info and the warning, see you Friday!" said Phillip.

Putting down the phone, Phillip went straight onto the Internet to see what information could be gleaned about dog fighting. There was a great deal of factual information, mainly of a historic nature, which he skipped through rapidly, and then he found data which told of the resurgence of dog fighting, especially in the London area. It said that South London in particular was the place for meetings. Painstakingly, Phillip trawled through pages and pages, looking to see if there were any indications as to how he could find a future meeting and when he had almost given up, he saw a note at the side of the page saying Meetings. He clicked, only to find a telephone number, of which he made a note. He was not going to use his office phone or his mobile in case it could be traced back to him so he went out to find the nearest phone box which had not been vandalised.

He remembered seeing an isolated phone box when he had been coming back from Lady Pennington's and decided to use that one later in the afternoon. He decided to work out his plan of action by assuming that he could find a meeting and go to it and then what? I would have to be the luckiest person in the world if I saw someone bringing in Bruce, ready to push him into the arena and start the dog fights, chances would be thousands to one. Okay, I just visit one meeting, go there to see if I can find him and if not, I will close the case and send my bill to Sarah Pennington for the time I have spent looking for her dog. That's all I can do. The phone rang and it was Sarah, asking him if he could come to her home this afternoon, as she felt their first meeting had not gone too well.

"Just park in front of the house and I will be looking out for you." Puzzled, Phillip agreed to drive over this afternoon, and put the phone down.

What had got into her head, he thought, I thought we'd sorted everything out with no apparent difficulties; I was on my best behaviour as a private investigator, but she was an attractive girl and well worth another visit. I'll ring that phone number on my way there and see if I can find where the next dog fighting meeting is to be held. He drove in the direction of Sarah Pennington's home and stopped at the telephone box. He had his story all ready and when a person with a gruff voice answered. "Yea," he said, "I've seen your advert and I want to go to the next meeting."

"What's yer name?"

"Bert Green."

"What's yer address?"

Phillip made one up, quoting the road he was on: "3 Argyle Street."

"Phone number?"

Phillip gave him the phone box number.

"Next meeting's on Monday, Porton Farm, off Roxby Road, 7.30 to 9.00. You goin' to enter a dog? If you are, you'll have to pay fifty quid to the Boss when you get there so have it ready." And he put the phone down.

A man of few words, thought Phillip to himself, wishing he didn't feel quite so apprehensive. Taking out his Ordnance Survey map of the area he soon found Roxby Road but nowhere along its length could he find Porton Farm. I'll work that one out later, he thought, but after writing all the information down, he drove on to meet the delectable Sarah.

He saw Sarah coming out of the house as he unbuckled his safety belt and slid out of the car. They shook hands, rather awkwardly, and both began to speak at once. Phillip started to say how nice she looked in the dress she was wearing, then thought it was a little too personal for a 'hired hand'. He then realised Sarah was suggesting that they go for a walk and nodded his head in agreement, wondering what she had in mind. She began to question him about his life and background and as they walked along, carefully keeping a short distance apart, he had to give her a potted version of his earlier life, saying, "I hope I don't bore you!

"Born first, followed by sister Emily, to parents with a flourishing business. Emily now works in Paris in the fashion industry, so I don't see very much of her; as far as I know, she isn't married or with a partner. Uneventful childhood, went to grammar school, then London School of Economics, graduated in economics and law, started working in the City and stayed in banking until June last year. I was given the hint of future redundancies in the offing by a good friend so I got out while the going was good, took redundancy payment and set up in my own business. In the meantime, my live in partner, Samantha by name, found that when I left the bank, all the perks that came with my job had evaporated into thin air, so she left and is now living with someone who still has a banking job and the 'perks' to go with it. That brings us right up to date."

"You mean she left you because you left your job?" asked Sarah. "There must have been someone else."

"That's what she said, 'I'll find someone else who still has the things I'm used to having'," said Phillip.

"But that is so cold hearted and terrible," she said, "you must have been really cut up about it."

"It was not completely unexpected but yes, it did upset me for a while. Then I had to think about my future career and make the most of the money I received. Later on, bank employees were being sacked in droves, with nothing to fall back on and I was lucky I had been tipped the wink by that friend."

"What made you decide to become a private investigator?" she asked.

"I think it must be because I always had a curious mind, I'm good at analysing a situation and I have the persistence of the proverbial bulldog!" he laughed.

"I suppose you could have joined the police force."

"Well, the police force is too rigid for me, they have to operate within certain boundaries and I don't know if there is any room for using your imagination, particularly in the lower ranks. If you want to try something and it's not in the rule book, you have to get permission from various levels of management and the answer is often 'no'. At least, that's my understanding of it. That's enough about me, what about you?" he asked.

She was a little embarrassed but started with, "My great-grandfather built up a fortune during his lifetime, my grandfather went into the business and continued to make money by buying up run-down businesses and making them more efficient and profitable and then selling them on with a great deal of profit. My father still works in the business, I think they're called 'Enterprize Businesses', my older brother works with him and they seem to be very prosperous although not quite so lavish with their lifestyle as they were when my great grandfather bought this manor house, way back in the nineteenth century! I went to a private school for girls and then to London University where I came out with a BA in English Language and economics. I'm working for my father at the moment as a PR."

"How old are you?" queried Phillip, without stopping to think.

"You should never ask a lady her age," she said, pretending to be shocked.

"I just don't want to be told that you are far too young to be alone with me without a chaperone!" he replied.

"Actually, I'm twenty-one. It was my birthday three weeks ago."

"You look about eighteen," said Phillip, honestly.

"I'm not sure whether that's a compliment or not!"

"I wish I looked eighteen," he said.

"Why, how old are *you*?"

"Twenty-nine."

She nodded her head wisely and told him she preferred older men, they acted more maturely, because at university her fellow students acted like silly kids.

"Do you have a girlfriend at the moment…?" she asked hesitantly.

"Not really, for the past eight months I've lived like a monk, just the occasional visit to a pub for a few beers but a couple of weeks ago, a long-time friend came back from an assignment in Edinburgh and we've started going out again. We met two girls but I would not call them girlfriends, just acquaintances, really, someone to chat to and have a laugh with."

"A good-looking man like you will have no difficulty in finding a partner," said Sarah.

"After my last disastrous relationship, I'm in no hurry to plunge into another one."

Unaware, they had walked in a complete circle and found themselves at the front of the house again.

"Let's go into the walled garden at the back of the house; it's nice and sunny and there is a bench we can sit on, we've been walking for ages."

"Do you want me to tell you the latest about Bruce?" said Phillip.

"No, it would rather spoil the atmosphere I think, I just wanted to enjoy your company; when all the family work in the same business, and at home there's nothing new to discuss except some grotty television programme and I usually talk to my friends on the computer but it's nice to have a real, live man to talk to."

"Thank you," said Phillip cautiously. "Do you have a boyfriend?"

"My father's a bit over-protective with me; I always lived at home, even when I was at uni. and so far, I don't have very much of a social life except going to boring dinner dances with my parents where everyone's about seventy-five. The other students I was friendly with have gone back to their homes in Yorkshire or Cornwall or somewhere way out in the sticks, so I've not met anybody who would be suitable."

"And I'm definitely not suitable," Phillip said, "being twenty-nine and having one foot in the grave!"

She put her arms around his neck and gave him an inexpert kiss on his mouth. Without thinking, his arms went round her and he made a very good job of kissing her, pulling her body close so he could savour the soft curves; he could feel her mouth opening beneath his lips and he was just about to try thrusting his tongue against hers when he realised this was neither the time nor the place and he gently withdrew his arms.

"There you are," she said, very pleased with herself, "an old man you certainly are not."

Phillip didn't know what he should say to her so he said that someone from the house might be watching them but she pulled him over to the bench, saying eagerly, "Nobody could see us here," and putting her arms around him again, pulled his head down to hers and started to kiss him again. Phillip was so tempted by this open display of attraction that for a few moments he could have stretched her out on the bench and started to really make love to her. Her breathing was becoming erratic and her soft cheeks flushed rose pink as she abandoned all restraint and it would have been so easy for him to take advantage of her. It took all his willpower but he pulled his mouth away from her face and said to her, "Sarah, we can't do this."

The frustration in her expression, as she came to realise what he meant, made her say bitterly, "I thought it was always the girl who said 'No'."

Phillip took her hand and sat stroking it until she calmed down and then kissed the fingertips. "I think I have to go now," and he walked her to the front door where his car was parked. With scarcely a glance in his direction, she told him to let her know if he found out any more about Bruce, opened the door, walked into the hall and slammed it closed with all the strength she possessed. Phillip was mentally kicking himself and calling himself a variety of names: You promised to behave professionally with all your clients and the first attractive girl you come across, you behave like a sex-starved teenage boy. Not only have you lost a promising friendship but you've also lost the possibility of getting some more rich clients. Totally stupid behaviour on your part. Having told himself off, he drove home, made himself something to eat and started to think about his next move.

He wrote down – *Monday evening – dog fighting, Tuesday morning – Court attendance. This Friday – a planning meeting on strategy at John Standish's office.* Once he had written down his plans for the next few days, he read the newspapers and went to bed. In the morning he was at John Standish's office at the appointed time and they started to discuss the handling of Mr Dunn's appeal.

"How are you thinking of handling it, John?"

"We can only overturn a court decision by presenting new evidence," John said.

"That being the case, we have to think of everything in the way of new facts that we can produce and put it to the judge to convince him or her of Walter's innocence so that he can be let out on bail."

"Okay," said John, "give me an example of why you think he is innocent of the charges laid against him – try to convince me as if I were the judge and I can then assess his chances!"

Phillip marshalled the facts in his head, without glancing at his notes, and started by saying, "Walter Dunn's relationship with Betsy Herne was entirely innocent; they had at no time any opportunity to have sexual intercourse because they were never alone and he always met her in a public place such as shops, the gym, or out on the street. When he met her for the first time, it was in the park, in the open air, with people passing by constantly. Nothing sexual could have taken place between them and the mother's assertion that Betsy was being 'groomed' for sexual favours in the future is ludicrous! She appears to be a neurotic woman with a grudge against her own child. She thinks having Betsy ruined her life and her treatment of her daughter amounts at the least, to child abuse. She has herself had sexual affairs with several different men, exposing Betsy to moral corruption and when one of her men friends complimented Betsy on her appearance, the mother was jealous and decided to punish her by bringing a charge against her benefactor."

"That's very positive: so far, Doris has very cleverly claimed that Dunn was grooming Betsy so that he could use her in the future for whatever purpose he had in mind and therefore he was so in control over her daughter, if he was allowed to remain out on bail, his corruptive influence over her would be exerted to the detriment of her teenage years. I shall present this new image of Doris, jealous mother, neglectful of her daughter's welfare, worried that she was maturing into a pretty girl and would be her rival in the future. I shall emphasise the various reasons why she was insistent he should remain in prison without bail and I think you may possibly be correct in thinking her boyfriend might have urged his cronies already there, to bully and intimidate Mr Dunn. The only thing is I can't produce that in the appeal because we have no concrete evidence this has taken place. Pity, but there it is. I must say I am rather surprised that she didn't try a bit of blackmail on Mr Dunn. You know, 'I'll withdraw the charge if you give me XXX amount of money'."

"I thought that as well," said Phillip; "when I spoke to her on the phone she didn't seem the brightest spark on the bonfire, but I'll bet one of her boyfriends might have thought of making a fast buck out of the situation. If she had asked for money, we would have got her, wouldn't we?"

John shuffled the papers on his desk and enquired how Phillip was progressing with his search for the dog.

"I've managed to track down a phone number and when I rang, I was given an address in Roxby Road. The man at the other end wanted to know my name and address and phone number, which I made up, and he told me there is a meeting on Monday night so I'm going to have a go."

"You realise you will be in danger, don't you?" said John. "To protect their perverted pleasure, they would eliminate you on the spot and feed you to the pigs; anything that remained would be buried deep in some godforsaken hole, if they even suspected you were an informer!"

"I've no intention of dying," said Phillip, "and if I'm caught, I shall tell them that you know exactly where I am and what they are doing and if I don't get back in person to a pre-arranged meeting place, you will have Special Branch on to them before they can say boo!! I'll go now and let you get on with the appeal and I will see you on Tuesday, in court."

"Better make it nine o'clock in my office, then we can go over our presentation."

Chapter 8

Back in his office, the answering machine was blinking and when he pressed Play he was pleased to hear Sarah's voice saying "Please ring me", but when he tried there was no answer. He made himself a quick sandwich, decided he and Gordon should go out for something to eat this evening, instead of drinking beer all night, and when the phone rang an hour later he was pleased to hear Sarah's voice on the other end.

"Phillip, it's Sarah, I wanted to apologise for my behaviour the other day."

"No, it's I who must apologise to you! You were just being friendly and I behaved like a jerk, I don't know what came over me. I always try to behave professionally, but there I was, behaving like an idiot. My only excuse is that I lost my head a bit, you being such an attractive girl. I can promise you it won't happen again."

"Phillip, you're exaggerating, it was only a few kisses and I behaved like a silly schoolgirl. When you decided to stop me making an utter fool of myself, I felt I had let myself down, behaving like a frustrated teenager and I should have had the experience to handle the situation a whole lot better. I guess I'm not very experienced in relationships and I want to apologise to you by taking you out for dinner. Would you forgive me and let me do that?"

"I'd be delighted to go out for a meal with you, how about

tomorrow night?"

"Do I have to wait another full day before seeing you?" she pouted.

"You must have a boyfriend, nearer your age, to take you out tonight?" he queried.

"If you don't stop harping on about you being too old for me, I shall hit you with my handbag, that is when I see you!"

"Well I am eight years older than you—"

"No more silly nonsense about age differences; you've got under my skin, I like being with you and I'm over twenty-one, not a stupid adolescent with a crush on an older man and that's my final word!"

"Yes, ma'am, I got you."

"I suppose you'll be out chatting up your birds this evening."

"Gordon and I have a standing arrangement for a night out on a Friday, being best friends from way back and if one of us doesn't turn up, it leaves the other high and dry. So we do our best not to let the other one down, go for a meal first and then to the same wine bar, have a few beers, a few laughs and then I stay overnight at his flat, a nice place facing the river. I usually get back to my place about two o'clock."

"If I'm taking you out for dinner, perhaps I could call in in the afternoon and you could show me your house," said Sarah.

"Yes, that would be great, only don't come too early as I'll have to do my housework first," he said jokingly.

Sarah said puzzled, "Do you have to do your own cleaning and dusting? Shouldn't you have someone like a housekeeper to do that for you?"

Phillip swallowed a laugh and said seriously, "I don't earn enough in fees to be able to afford domestic service but I hope that one day, when I've built up my business, I can employ some staff!!"

"Oh, that's all right then, I shall see you tomorrow afternoon, bye bye," and she rang off.

Gordon met Phillip with the remark, "And how's my private dick, sorry, private eye, this evening?"

"I don't know, how is your private dick?" Phillip replied. "I personally am starving after a busy day of work, work, work, so lead me to the nearest eatery!"

"If you're in that much of a hurry, there's a McDonalds' place not far away, how does that suit you?"

"I know it's out of your class as a city banker type but I'm just a humble private investigator and I need to eat to keep my strength up," said Phillip.

"Don't give me that crap about being poor," Gordon said. "They don't usually see customers wearing the kind of expensive casuals you've got on. Hoping to make an impression are you?" he jeered.

"I know where we'll go, it's just near Piccadilly Circus and the food's really good. Off we go!"

Twenty minutes later Phillip was satisfying himself with large amounts of Beef Bourguignon, followed by a mountain of sponge pudding centred in a lake of custard, while Gordon contented himself with steak and kidney pudding. Appetites satisfied, they hopped on a bus for the short journey to the wine bar which proved to be the wrong decision.

A number of youths wearing hooded sweatshirts seemed to come out of nowhere and jumped onto the bus behind them. They were shouting, pushing, swearing at each other and then one lit a cigarette.

"Wot you looking at?" he said, speaking to Phillip.

Phillip looked the youth up and down and then said softly, "I wouldn't know, it appears as if the label has fallen off!!"

The other youths laughed raucously but the smoker said threateningly, "Do you want to get done over? Me and my mates can have you just like that," and he snapped his fingers.

Phillip drew himself up to his full height of six foot one and said, still very quietly, "Listen, you little dirt bag, one more word out of you and I shall throw you off the bus, preferably landing under an overtaking car. Take that cigarette out of your mouth and show some respect for the other passengers or else I will stuff it down your throat, and teach you some manners. Have you got that?"

The bus came to a juddering halt and one of the other lads shouted, "Quick let's get out of here, the bus driver's called the police!"

The lads scrambled to leave the bus and Phillip watched carefully as they pushed their way past, suspecting that some of them were armed with knives. The smoker tried to stub his cigarette out on Phillip's jacket, at the same time pulling out a wicked, serrated edged blade but Phillip had seen it coming and he punched the youth so hard that he fell back against the bus seat. Phillip caught his right arm and had the greatest satisfaction in twisting it up behind his back until he yelped with pain.

"Drop that knife or else I'll break your arm," said Phillip evenly.

The lad could hardly believe the complete reversal of circumstances – one minute he and his gang of thugs had been going to have some fun with the bus passengers – and the next, he was in agony, with his mates all running away and this big geezer was threatening to break his arm. He dropped his precious knife and the awful pressure was released on his arm.

"Now disappear before the police get here and remember, I know your face and if I ever see you again up the West End, I shall make a citizen's arrest and haul you down to the nearest police station!! You got that?" The lad ran as if his life depended on it.

Gordon looked at Phillip with new respect. "That was a very sticky moment." The understatement of the year. "What are you going to do with the knife?"

"I'll just drop it down the nearest drain."

"It doesn't look as though the police are here yet."

"Well what can you expect? Busiest night of the week, they must get so many calls, they won't know which one to answer next. Let's get going, we'll be a little late at this rate!"

The girls were in the wine bar already and wanted to know what had held them up. Gordon explained the circumstances while Phillip bought a round of drinks and when he got back to their table, Jasmine was telling Gordon what advice he should give him.

"Tell your brave but crazy friend never to do that again and be very careful for the next few weeks. These 'hoodies' are worse than animals and they will be looking for you two to get their revenge because you made them lose face in front of other people. They will be laughed at by their peers and that will spur them on. They hunt as a pack because singly, they are cowards," said Jasmine, sounding quite worried.

"Well, just to set your minds at rest, we don't live in their area, we won't be taking any more bus rides and once they retire to lick their wounds, they'll forget all about us," Gordon said reassuringly.

"Let's change the subject and you can tell us what you've been doing during the week," said Phillip.

"We've been looking forward to seeing you," said Isobel, flatteringly. "Isn't that what you want to hear?"

"Of course," said Gordon. "I shall now tell you a joke! A man visits a mental hospital and he asks the chief psychiatrist how he decides who can be released or who should remain. 'Oh, that's easy,' said the psychiatrist, 'I fill a bath with water and leave three implements there, a spoon, a cup and a bucket and tell each patient to empty the bath.' 'I see,' said the visitor, 'the one who is fit to be released is the one who uses the bucket.' 'No,' said the psychiatrist, 'he is the one who pulls out the plug!'"

Silence.

"I'll explain it later," he said, gloomily.

"Here's a better one than that," said Phillip. "Why do bees hum?"

"You must have got that joke from a Christmas cracker," said Gordon.

Isobel looked a little serious. "It's something to do with the speed at which they flap their wings isn't it?" she said.

"Isobel," said Jasmine, "if that was the answer, it wouldn't be a joke would it, silly."

"Anything that flies makes a noise," said Gordon, wisely.

"What are those things with lovely blue wings that fly over water?" Isobel said. "Those don't make any noise!"

"They do," said Gordon, "but you're just not near enough to hear them!"

"I don't think you can hear an ordinary house fly," said Jasmine, enjoying the expression on Phillip's face.

"Yes, you can," said Gordon, "it sort of buzzes like—"

"Before you three come to blows and my patience is exceeded, I'd better give you the punch line," said Phillip, "and it is – Bees hum because they don't know the words! Da da! Get it?"

After they had laughed at the silly joke, they finished another round of drinks and in high good humour, called a taxi to go to Gordon's flat. In the taxi, Gordon sat with his arm around Isobel, trying to gauge her readiness to accept a plea to share his bed that night but apart from smiling at him she did little to encourage his passion and once more, he went to his room alone and the two girls went to the other room, leaving Phillip to prepare his sofa and wait for Jasmine to join him. Whether Isobel was aware of Jasmine's leaving their room to join Phillip under his duvet, she never gave any hint of it in conversation. Jasmine was as excited as he was when they came together, but somehow, he felt a little guilty, thinking of tomorrow and his date with Sarah. Probably nothing would happen, they would just enjoy a good meal and chat like the friends they were becoming but he fell asleep, thinking about that bench in the walled garden and what could have happened.

He woke on Saturday morning, and wandered into the kitchen, to find Gordon with a very smug expression on his face which told Phillip what he was going to say, almost before he said it.

"Isobel and I got it together last night and she came into my room after you and Jasmine were wriggling about under your duvet. Why didn't you tell me about that? If things go to plan, you won't have to bother using that sofa again; if Isobel comes in with me, you and Jasmine can have the other room. You notice I don't say you can 'sleep' in the other room; from what Isobel's told me, Jasmine gave her all the details of what you get up to and it's a wonder that sofa's still got four legs on it! You sly devil, I might have known you were having it off with her while I was sleeping alone."

"Well you're not now are you, and you always fancied Isobel more than Jasmine so I thought I'd keep her occupied while you tried to seduce Isobel and it worked, didn't it?"

"And how! But I'm too much of a gentleman to discuss things like that with you; get ready and we can all go out for breakfast, I feel as if I could eat a horse."

When the girls came out of their room, looking a little self-conscious, it was Gordon who paid compliments to Isobel and he was obviously smitten. I wonder how long that will last, thought Phillip. Once he gets them into bed and they start to think he might be serious about a future together, he chickens out and decides he can't make a commitment. Ah well, we'll see. They enjoyed their meal together and then Phillip excused himself, saying he had an appointment with a client at his office which in a way was perfectly true, except it was with an attractive girl who was going to take him out to dinner and he had to make sure the rest of the house was at least tidy before she arrived.

He was now used to keeping his place presentable; what he had said about not being able to afford a cleaner was partly true, but he also avoided having anyone who could have access to his premises when he was out. As yet there was no-one he could trust. After an hour's work, he looked round and thought it would stand up to an inspection, when he saw Sarah parking her car, next to his advertising sign. Exactly on time.

He opened the front door and said, "Hi, welcome to my pad," and felt extremely silly. They made the usual small talk, how are you, nice to see you, etc., etc. and Phillip tried to take in what she was wearing. She had obviously dressed for their forthcoming dinner date and when she slipped her coat off, she was wearing a black dress and short jacket with a pearl necklace and earrings which, he thought, could be diamonds, and how she had driven her car in those high heeled shoes, he shuddered to think.

"Would you like a drink or shall I show you around?" said Phillip vaguely.

"Bit early for a drink," she said. "Show me where everything is."

He showed her his office, the kitchen, the stairs, the lounge, the bathroom, and Sarah said, "How many innocent females have you led up these stairs into your bedroom? Which is your bedroom by the way?"

"That one, and the answer to your question is none. Even Gordon has not seen this place yet." Sarah walked into his bedroom and Phillip followed, almost in a daze. He had a feeling he knew what was going to happen and this was confirmed when she turned round and, putting her arms around his neck, she kissed him.

Phillip said, "Are you sure you want to do this, because you look so sexy, if we start something, I won't be able to stop this time?"

"Don't be silly, I've been waiting to do this since you first kissed me, now help me take off my dress because I don't want to get it creased!"

She shrugged off the little jacket and he slowly unzipped the back of her dress; the material dropped to the floor, leaving her wearing only a lacy bra and pants. Somehow he was out of his clothes, pulling at buttons and zips; he pulled her towards him, fumbling behind her back for her bra hooks and pushing the straps over her lovely smooth shoulders and down her arms, eager to fondle and kiss her breasts, firm, generous breasts. They didn't even bother with the bed, they lay on the carpet, kissing, caressing until he realised he could wait no longer. She was insatiable and then, in what seemed like only a moment or two, it was over and they relaxed, still entwined.

They smiled at each other drowsily and quite without meaning to, they fell asleep just where they lay. Phillip woke with a start, wondering what he was doing asleep on the carpet and then he looked sideways. Sarah was curled up like a dormouse, fast asleep without a stitch on. A stray thought passed through his head, wondering whether, if he gently woke her, she would be ready to have sex again and they could forget about going out for an elaborate meal and just stay in the bedroom for the rest of the evening, but he found his shorts, lifted Sarah, still fast asleep and laid her on the bed, pulling up a sheet to cover her, when he became aware that her eyes had opened and she was looking straight up at him.

"Did that really happen or was it something I dreamed?" she said.

Phillip laughed and said, "You certainly weren't dreaming and yes, we did make love."

"I know *I* did, but what about you... did you — I only know the soppy terms they use in women's magazines — were you satisfied? You know, did you...?" Her voice trailed off.

"Yes, of course I did."

"I don't have much experience in this area but I thought both of you had to go all the way to reach the final climax!" she said coyly.

She got up off the bed and started to dance towards him until Phillip said, "Your dancing is very exciting but there are a whole lot of people out there enjoying it as well as me!" She looked down and realised she was still completely nude and automatically crossed her arms over her breasts to cover herself and began searching for her bra and pants.

Phillip sat there laughing at her until she realised that they were in an upstairs bedroom and nobody could possibly overlook them so she grabbed a pillow and began to thump him with it.

In between thumps, she gasped, "You bastard, I ought to punish you for that!"

"Sorry, this house is not licensed for corporal punishment, so you can forget that!"

"You've spoiled my celebration about the wonderful way you made me feel. I never realised it could be as good as that!"

"You can dance naked any time you want, if it makes you feel that good," he said teasingly.

She dropped the pillow and put her arms around his neck. "I'm beginning to think I'm falling in love with you." Phillip stayed silent, unable to think of anything to say without hurting her. "Please say something..." she pleaded.

He began to explain to her that at the moment they were feeling very happy but there was a lot more to love than just good sex.

"The true test comes when you are very unhappy with someone but still love them. Let's just continue to be happy and enjoy ourselves and don't look too far into the future."

"But don't you love me a little bit?" she said, putting her head on one side like an appealing little bird.

"Sarah, I think you're fabulous but I told you I'm just getting over one unhappy relationship and it wouldn't be fair to you to say things and make promises when..." He thought of his forthcoming meeting with the vicious men who organised dog fighting. "Well, let's wait and see," he said lamely.

She kissed him and then saw his bedside clock. "Look at the time, where's my dress, have I got time for a quick shower? It could be quicker if we showered together but no, it would ruin my hair and somehow I think that once we got in the shower together, it might be a long time before we turned off the water. Perhaps we could save that pleasure for another time!"

Showered and dressed, Sarah drove them to the restaurant she had chosen and the head waiter, scenting a large tip from the young, attractive couple, showed them to an excellent table and sent over the wine waiter to take their order. Sarah was quite expert at ordering the kind of wine she liked, after months of accompanying her parents to various functions, and was completely in her element. The menu was enormous and mainly unreadable, although Phillip had a slight knowledge of French; in the end he chose a pasta dish and settled down to sip his wine while they waited for their first course. Their conversation was interrupted by a voice saying to him, "Remember me? I'm the girl who left you in the wine bar, only to find the other place boring so my friend and I came back to find you already had another lady friend." The air would have frozen an ice cube as Sarah looked at him enquiringly.

"Yes, of course I remember you. May I introduce you to my fiancée, the Honourable Sarah Pennington?" He emphasised her full title because he was only too aware of the fact that Holly or (he had forgotten the other girl's name) was in a mood to cause trouble.

It was as if a balloon had deflated as Holly said, "Oh, pleased to meet you, congratulations I'm sure. Well we might see you again I dare say," and she and her friend walked over to the ladies toilets.

Sarah put her hand on Phillip's and said quietly, "Thanks for saying I was your fiancée, but who were those two?" She didn't dignify them with the title "ladies" or "girls", just "those two".

Phillip replied to her question, "They were a couple of girls Gordon and I talked to before," and he was on the point of saying Isobel and Jasmine turned up, when he realised that would not be very diplomatic, "before we left the wine bar to get something to eat," he finished. "Sarah, do you mind if I order a pint of lager? The wine was delicious with the meal but I usually drink lager and as you're driving tonight, I can indulge in a few more pints."

The evening ended very pleasantly with relaxed conversation and a glass of excellent cognac then Sarah drove them to Phillip's house.

He opened the front door and Sarah said, "Upstairs or down?"

"Wherever you lead, I will follow," he said.

Sarah walked up the stairs, humming quietly to herself and on the landing, she stopped and said, "I think I've had quite a lot to drink tonight, so I can't drive all the way home can I?"

"You're very welcome to stay here," he said soberly. "There are four bedrooms and you can sleep in any one you want, but you must ring your parents and tell them where you are and that you're staying the night. I can't have your father or any of your servants breaking in and attacking me with a meat cleaver, or some such object!"

She smiled and said, "It's my mother you have to worry about, but I'll ring her and tell her I'm staying with a friend and she can reach me any time on my mobile, so that should set her mind at rest." She did just that and reassured her mother that she would be home next day, although she wasn't quite sure what time it would be.

"Okay, which room would you like to sleep in?"

"The same one as you," she said saucily.

"That'll be the back bedroom then." He walked into the room and closed the curtains with a definite swish.

"Now we'd better take our clothes off," she said. "Do you have a coat hanger which I can hang my dress on?"

He supplied her with a plain wooden coat hanger and she carefully hung her dress on it. She put the dress in the wardrobe and then turned to him as she closed the door.

"Now let me see, I think I made it a little too easy for you this afternoon so now, if you want me to satisfy your overpowering lust, you're going to have to catch me first!"

He made a grab for her but she easily eluded him and they started chasing each other from room to room, scrambling over beds and banging doors until they were nearly helpless with laughter.

Phillip came to a halt and said, "Phew, I'm not as fit as I thought I was, I need a can of beer."

"No refreshments allowed," she said, relaxing her concentration for a moment, which was when he caught hold of her in a strong grip and said, triumphantly, "Gotcha, I win, I win."

"You cheated, now let me go!"

"You know that old saying, 'All's fair in love and war', so I won, fair and square madam, what are you going to do to satisfy me?"

She wriggled and struggled, her breath coming faster as he pulled her towards his bed, pushed her over and collapsed beside her, thoroughly aroused. The kissing started and there was no thought now on Sarah's part of getting away from him as their lovemaking reached its climax. Phillip lay beside her, thoroughly satiated, and fell asleep.

He woke some time during the night, aware of the bare skin close to him and the possessive arm thrown over his waist, kissed her gently and drifted off to sleep again. The next time he woke it was just after eight o'clock and he turned to find her eyes wide open, looking at him.

"What are you thinking about?" he said.

Her eyelids lowered. "I was hoping that you are feeling as happy as I am, lying next to you," she said, honestly. He leant over and gave her a gentle kiss.

"Who's first in the shower?"

"You have a shower? I want to take a long, luxurious bath!"

"This is a man's bathroom, don't expect to find any of those creams and lotions that I'm sure you've got in your bathroom at home," he said.

"Oh I expect I'll manage," she said, carelessly.

He showered, shaved, brushed his teeth, dressed and still she was in the bath! He went downstairs and spooned out some ground coffee into the percolator and soon the aroma of fresh coffee was wafting upstairs. She yelled down from the landing, "I can smell gorgeous, fresh coffee. I'll be down in a moment."

She appeared, wearing his bathrobe with the sleeves turned up several times and the belt tightly fastened so she wouldn't trip over the excess length and said gaily, "There's not much to wear here, and I didn't pack an overnight bag in case you turned me away, but it's better than my birthday suit, isn't it?"

"Are you wearing anything under that robe?"

"Of course not, I'm still a bit damp, why, do you want me to take it off and show you?"

Phillip groaned. "Come and get some coffee and have breakfast, don't start putting ideas into my head. I've only got cornflakes and some muesli, but I've put some partially baked rolls in the microwave, they're quite nice with plenty of butter spread on them and some marmalade." He poured out a mug of coffee for her and together they enjoyed breakfast.

"Am I the first female to enter your bachelor pad?"

"Yes, you are. My previous lady partner moved out of the flat we were living in, when I sold it to buy this place. It was in the centre of London, near the river, and I got a good price for it, so yes, you are the very first lady to enter this house. After breakfast I thought we could go for a drive and find a pub in the countryside somewhere, to have lunch and maybe a walk, although how you're going to manage it in those high heels you wore last night, I don't know!"

"Well, that's something you don't know, isn't it? I keep a pair of comfortable flats in the car to wear when I'm driving, I don't want to ruin the carpet on the floor round the pedals."

They had a leisurely lunch and afterwards, a stroll by the lakeside and all too soon for Sarah, she had to take him back to the house.

"I must get back to reassure my parents that I'm all in one piece; I don't usually stay away overnight, except when on holiday."

They kissed goodbye and she murmured to him, "Love you lots," and drove off, leaving Phillip to enter a silent house, feeling a little lonely.

He shrugged his shoulders, told himself not to be stupid and to get down to some preparation for the following night. He could find no more information about dog fighting on the Internet, which he had not already taken note of, so he turned to his map and, after a minute search, he found the farm but it appeared that it was in ruins, according to the information given. That kind of made sense; deserted buildings situated on a rarely used road, the only people who wanted to be there would travel in great secrecy and the gang would have lookouts posted out of sight, ready to warn them if say, the police were spotted approaching. In his mind, he worked out how he was going handle the situation and, feeling hungry, he switched off all the equipment, locked up and went for a sandwich and a couple of pints of lager.

On Monday morning, Sarah rang, telling him what a wonderful time she had with him and she hoped to see him again soon. Apparently her parents were not thrilled about her staying away all night but she had managed to pacify them. She told them that now she was twenty-one, she was perfectly entitled to have a private life of her own but reassured them by saying that she loved them very much and was not going to let them down. Finally, she told Phillip that they should spend every Saturday and Sunday together from now on, to get to know each other really well.

"Is that all right with you?" she said hesitantly. "I know I sound a bit bossy but…" she trailed off, waiting for him to end the unbearable silence.

"I take it you are booking me and my house for the foreseeable future and I'm to provide my services free?" he said, in a serious tone of voice.

Sarah panicked. "Oh, no I don't mean anything like that, or…" she began to falter, wondering what she could say to retrieve the situation and then she heard him laughing and realised he had been teasing her. "You rotten so and so," she spluttered, "making me think you'd taken offence like that. Wait 'til I see you face to face, I'll make you suffer for that!"

"I take it we have an agreement?" he said. "I'll meet you next Saturday and we can go to the cinema, if you'd like, or have a meal or something."

"It's the 'something' I like the sound of," she said cheekily. "Anyway, I'd better get some work done, speak to you later, love you, bye."

His mood lightened after Sarah's cheerful call and he went upstairs to pick out some old clothes to wear that night. He set out at seven o'clock to find the farm, hoping he looked the part of a farmer in his anorak, flat cap and Wellington boots and could blend in with the rest of the crowd when he got there. He found Roxby Road with no difficulty and followed it until he came to a signpost indicating the village of Roxby itself. He turned into a narrow lane and drove along until he came to an even more dilapidated sign indicating Porton Farm. He bumped slowly along what appeared to be a cart track, all the time aware that hidden eyes were following his progress and perhaps even noting his car registration number. As he neared the clump of buildings which was probably the farm, a dip in the countryside hid a field where a large number of vehicles were already parked.

Phillip parked his car as near as possible to the entrance of the car park; if by any chance he found the dog, he would have to make a quick exit. He looked round slowly to get an idea of his bearings and became aware of the hum of conversation of quite a large number of men and the occasional yelp from an excited dog. He followed the noise towards an open barn door and a glimpse inside told him this was the dog fighting area. The hairs on the back of his neck stood up as one of two well-muscled bouncer type guards grunted to him, "I'll have twenty quid off you if you're going in to see the show an' if you want your own dog entered, that'll be another £50."

"Right," said Phillip, and gave him a £20 note and went inside the barn.

He estimated there were between a hundred and fifty and two hundred men present: correction, there was even a sprinkling of women of all ages, scattered round the barn, concentrating on the area fenced off in the centre of the room, as the main dog fighting area. There was an overhead battery of lights, shining down on the straw filled arena which once put inside, the dogs would be forced to fight until one was the clear winner. There were a number of men who were obviously bookies, ready to take bets, and someone was selling cans of beer, judging by the number of drinkers.

There was a sudden hush as a man wearing a long white overall shouted, "Gents and ladies, we are about to start our evening's entertainment with a warm-up bout, just to get you all in the mood, between a German shepherd and a Staffordshire bull terrier and then the serious bouts start!"

The two dogs were put in the ring, their owners keeping them on their leads and urging them to attack. The bull terrier was growling and baring its teeth but the other dog seemed uncertain as to what was expected of it and then the audience started to shout, "Let 'em off the leash," and the dogs were set loose.

The German shepherd dog tried its best to defend itself but the bull terrier went straight for its throat in a frenzy, hanging on until blood was spurting out all over the straw. It let go of the throat, only to attack other parts of the dog until in the end it just lay on the straw, unable to get up. The handler leaped into the ring and put the bull terrier on its leash and hauled it away from the other dog which was now obviously dying. Two other men lifted the wounded dog out of the ring by its hind legs and dragged it away through a rear exit out of sight, and the next two yapping, growling dogs were put in the ring and the slaughter started again. Nobody was going to miss him, he hoped.

Phillip felt physically sick but had to force himself not to spew up. He had not been allowed to get too near the fencing because of the other keen watchers and he found it fairly easy to get to the entrance door without obviously pushing. The two bouncers were not on duty at either side of the door, probably gone to watch the entertainment, so Phillip found himself outside gulping in the fresh air and made his way to where he had parked his car. Nobody was around, as far as he could tell; they were all in the barn and it seemed like a good idea to look at some of the other cars; there might be other dogs left in their owners' vehicles and he could make a quick not of some car registration numbers. You never knew when an item of information like that would come in handy.

The first three vehicles were empty and the fourth turned out to contain a vicious looking Rottweiller, which, thankfully, was securely locked in! He realised he would have to be quick and after another six cars, he peered in a white van and saw a large black dog asleep. It might possibly be a black Labrador, he called "Bruce" trying to keep his voice down and the dog sat up, pricked his ears and began to wag his tail. "Is that you Bruce?" The dog stood up and started to vigorously wag the whole of his behind, and came up to the window, snuffling and trying to lick the window. That's got to be him thought Phillip. He wrote down the registration, went back to his car and picked up a tyre lever. He used it to force open the rear doors but was not prepared for a large, black excited dog who wanted to show his thanks for being rescued and whose only wish was to lick Phillip all over to show his happiness.

"Get down, you idiot," he hissed. "Shush, you big stupid animal, if you don't keep quiet and behave, we won't get out of here alive!"

He looked round and saw the two muscle bound entrance guards, heading towards the car park, appearing to search for something. He thought it might be him; they were gesturing to each other and split up, each one going in a different direction; he held his breath, waiting until they passed him, talking to each other and saying something he couldn't quite catch. Then he saw a woman coming out of the entrance to the barn and heading towards the men, waving as though she had arranged to meet them. The first one grabbed her and started to pull at her clothes and he heard her laugh, saying, "You're in a hurry aren't you? I thought there were going to be two of you, that's what we arranged didn't we? Oh there he is; come on don't be shy, we can do it one at a time if you like but that'll cost you and I want the money now before you start!" She held out her hand and each man put some notes in it which she counted rapidly and stuffed in her handbag.

"That dog fighting don't half excite you doesn't it, where's the van then, I don't fancy lying down in this grass!" They dragged her over to the far side of the car park to a large van, opened the doors and jumped in, pulling the doors shut behind them.

Phillip worked his way back to his own car and Bruce followed him, tail wagging incessantly. The dog jumped into the car without any difficulty and he started the engine, cringing at the loud noise it appeared to make, and slowly edged his way back to the lane, praying that no-one would see or hear him. Once back on the road, he drove as fast as he could, hoping that Bruce was Bruce and not some family pet left in the car while his owner went to watch the dog fighting. Thank God I never had to stay any longer thought Phillip. I would definitely have been sick if I had to see any more dogs ripped to pieces and the 'audience' egging them on, and loving every splash of blood and every wound inflicted; evidently from what that prostitute said, it excited them so much they were quite willing to pay her for sex after they had been watching the ghastly spectacle, or maybe they just went back to their wives and 'got it for free'!

He headed for Lady Pennington's and rang the bell. Lady Pennington herself answered the door, rather surprised to see him.

"Mr Everett, isn't it? Please come in. That looks just like Bruce; where did you manage to find him?"

"I seriously hope it is your Bruce, otherwise I might be charged with kidnapping a pedigree dog!" Bruce went up to Lady Pennington, wagging his tail, and she made a big fuss of him.

"There's only one way to prove whether or not he is our Bruce; he is microchipped and I shall go and get the little machine to check that." She disappeared and came back with a small device which she passed over Bruce's neck and sure enough, it clicked with the correct identification number. "Yes it's Bruce alright. Sarah will be delighted to have him back; she will be here shortly, she is taking a course at an evening class, but tell me… how did you manage to find him?"

Phillip debated with himself whether to tell Lady Pennington the details of his night's work but on thinking about the events, he rather thought that the less she knew, the better it would be.

"I'd rather not say at this point Lady Pennington; it's a rather sordid business connected to dog fighting and I'm just pleased I've managed to reunite him with his real owner. I won't be able to wait here until Sarah gets back, because I still have some research work to carry out, but I'll be in touch tomorrow some time."

"Thank you once again Mr Everett for finding Sarah's pet; somehow I think there's more to this investigation than you are telling me, but perhaps you know best by saying nothing." Accompanying him to the door, she told him to drive carefully and said goodnight.

He drank a couple of cans of lager from the fridge and tried to calm his nerves before he went to bed. The reaction had started to set in and all the possible dangers he had been in kept coming back to him as he realised that at best, he had avoided a severe beating if he had been caught by the two bruisers trying to smuggle Bruce out of the car park in his car. He had seen no sign of weapons but that didn't mean to say that no-one was armed with a knife or some knuckle dusters or possibly a gun, which could have been used to threaten anyone suspected of being a police informant. He sincerely hoped that nobody had made a note of his car number because it would be fairly easy to check. He went to bed, hardly expecting to sleep, and although he thought he had dreamt some lurid dreams, he woke up feeling quite refreshed.

At nine o'clock the next morning, he arrived at John Standish's office and they exchanged the usual greetings.

"Have you ever been to court as a witness or as the accused?" asked John.

"No, neither, but I have some experience of the law!"

John laughed and said, "What you mean is that you have read books and studied cases!"

"Well," he said defensively, "I've attended court as an observer, part of my studying to be a private investigator."

"You can forget all that," said John rudely. "This is for real. We've got a formidable solicitor facing us. He is young, clever and ambitious, and determined to win. He is still building his career and every case he wins is another feather in his cap!"

"John, this is just an appeal, not a trial for a grisly murder."

"How little you know. Anyway, first the basics: this hearing is in front of a judge so you address him as 'your honour', the other lawyers are addressed as 'my learned friend', and if you speak to the court, what's known as 'addressing the court', you say 'If it pleases the court'. Can you remember that?" asked John.

"Get on with your presentation," said Phillip. "I've seen enough court cases on television to know the procedure!"

"Okay, now I will have to present our case as if it was completely new evidence which was not available at the first hearing. I have to do that because I was appearing for Walter at the first hearing and the judge will want to know why this was not used then. The opposition will present their case, requesting that Walter Dunn be kept in custody and then I will offer the new evidence as a reason why he should be released on bail. At this point, we are not trying the case, we just want him released on bail. I will call on you fairly quickly and it will be up to you to do your best."

"What are the best points that I should emphasise?" queried Phillip. "And will you be calling Walter into the witness box?"

"I am not planning to call Walter, why?"

"I think it's important that the judge sees him, what an old, frail and rather pathetic man he is. It will be obvious to everybody that he is hardly a cunning, manipulative, devious man, grooming an innocent thirteen-year-old girl for future sexual favours, which the opposition is suggesting him to be."

"Of course, he'll be in court but whether his appearance will be enough to get him bail, we can't bank on that."

"Leave it to me," said Phillip.

"It's time to go to court and do our best for him," said John.

An usher told them which court they were appearing in and it proved to be a small room with the clerk to the court already seated and Walter Dunn was shown into the front row of chairs (rather like pews in a church, thought Phillip) and they all shook hands solemnly. John set his armfuls of impressive papers and files on the table in front of him and told Phillip he should sit at the side on a bench, until called to give evidence. Phillip watched the opposition, a young man, obviously the solicitor, indicating where a middle-aged woman and a young girl should sit, before he too spread his papers and files on the table in front of him. Of course, this must be Doris Herne and her daughter Betsy, and he studied them closely.

Doris looked closer to forty than thirty years of age, rather well-upholstered, with her hair dyed an improbable shade of yellow. She was wearing a black skirt, which ended just above her knees and was far too tight, together with a matching black jacket which might have benefited from a blouse or top of some sort except that without either of these, it showed her all too ample cleavage.

"Foolish woman," though Phillip to himself, "she's made herself look more like the tart she no doubt is."

Betsy was wearing her school uniform, white blouse, grey pleated skirt, dark green blazer and green and red tie, no doubt to emphasise to everyone in court that she was a young schoolchild, except she looked mature for a fourteen-year-old, quite pretty but still with traces of the excess weight she had tried desperately to lose.

The judge came into court and everyone stood; the clerk of the court said, "This court is now in session," and the judge said to the prosecuting solicitor that he could now proceed. The young solicitor outlined his case stating that Walter Dunn had, over a length of time, developed a corruptive influence over Betsy. He had used his money to buy a young and emotionally immature girl various gifts which her mother, existing on benefits, could not possibly afford. Through doing so, he had gained total control over a vulnerable girl so that she would do anything for him.

At this point John Standish said, "Your honour, I strongly protest," but before he could finish, the judge said, "Yes, yes," and to the young solicitor he said, "You will keep to the facts of the case and you may carry on."

He called Doris Herne to the stand and everyone in court watched her waggle into the witness box. Betsy looked down at her clenched hands.

Asking questions, the solicitor elicited, without much difficulty, how Betsy had changed, from being a well behaved, obedient child to a disruptive, arrogant person who no longer listened to her mother or did anything her mother asked her to do. At this point, John Standish reminded the judge that they were not trying the case, they were only appealing to have Walter Dunn out of prison on bail and this should be remembered by the prosecuting solicitor.

"Your honour, we object to bail on the grounds that if Walter Dunn is allowed out of prison on bail, he will commence his previous activities again, and try to regain his control over an immature child. He is an extremely cunning and devious person, a man who will go to any lengths to get his own way. Your honour, I cannot see any logical reason to reverse the original decision of the prisoner being remanded in custody without bail, if only to protect his victim from undue persuasion."

"Is that the prosecution's case?" asked the judge.

"Yes, your honour, but I reserve the right to question any witnesses for the defence when they present their case, but for the time being, the prosecution rests. Thank you Mrs Herne, you may now leave the witness box."

"Is that all?" hissed Doris, when she returned to her seat. "I had a lot more I could have said!"

The judge indicated to John that it was in order for him to state the case for the defence's appeal against remand without bail. John stood up and began to speak pleasantly in his well-modulated voice.

"Thank you, your honour. According to the prosecution, we have here a wily, devious and conniving man who would stop at nothing to have his way with the child called Betsy. I would like to show you this gentleman, sitting next to me in court, and would ask you to take a good look at this poor man, a gentleman in every sense of the word, who only recently lost his wife of over forty years to whom he was totally devoted.

"He finds himself alone, with nothing much to occupy his time except a little gardening, a little reading and the occasional conversation when meeting a friend out walking. He set out for a walk one afternoon and came upon a little girl, sitting on a park bench, sobbing her heart out and he immediately tried to help her. He managed to persuade her to tell him what the problem was, thinking it was perhaps a lost schoolbook or someone had been bullying her but it was more serious than that. She said her mother hated her, called her fat and stupid and was always laughing at her and so she had started stuffing herself with junk food and playing truant from school. Even worse, when she caught sight of herself in a mirror, she had such a low opinion of herself, she started to self-harm, cutting her arms and legs with an old razor blade she found. Her mother said that if she did not have her, by this time she would be married to some rich husband and having a happy life."

Doris jumped to her feet and started yelling at the judge, "These are lies, all lies. I've never said anything like that to her!"

"Will you control your client," said the judge. "If she does not sit down and remain silent, I shall bar her from the court for contempt!"

The prosecution solicitor glared at Doris and told her to sit down and be quiet and then apologised to the judge and promised her she would have her chance to speak later. Doris sat down, highly incensed on hearing the words quoted which she had spoken many times to Betsy.

"Please continue," said the judge.

"My client, Mr Walter Dunn, took pity on the girl, seeing her as the daughter he and his wife had yearned for but never had, and he decided to help her. Yes, he paid for a new school uniform but only on condition she did not play truant and concentrated on her school work; yes, he paid for her to have her hair cut regularly so that she looked more presentable, yes he bought a gym membership for her, but only on condition that she gave up eating the junk food, ate sensibly and exercised to lose some weight. Her mother never noticed the improvement in her daughter until one of her numerous boyfriends remarked on how nice Betsy was looking and it was this remark which started all the trouble, Mrs Herne reporting a case of supposed child abuse to the police out of sheer vindictiveness, and this farrago of nonsense led to Mr Walter Dunn being imprisoned."

"Were you not the solicitor who acted for Mr Dunn at the committal stages?" asked the judge.

"Yes, your honour, indeed I was but at that stage there was very little evidence for me to place before the court."

"And now you have this new evidence."

"Yes, your honour."

"Well, you had better present this new evidence!"

"I would like to call Mr Phillip Everett."

"Your honour, we were not informed about this new witness," said the prosecuting solicitor, loudly.

John turned to the judge and said patiently, "Your honour, I have sent all the applicable information to the Prosecution Department. If it has been lost or mislaid, I am sure I cannot be held responsible for that."

"Of course we have not lost relevant information but we do not in fact, appear to have received it!"

The judge asked if they wished to adjourn the hearing while they were given copies of Mr Everett's evidence but this placed the prosecuting solicitor in a difficult position. He had allowed only one day for this hearing in his diary, thinking it would be very straightforward and if there was an adjournment, he would be forced to schedule the case some time later in the month when he had a much more important (to him) case which would have more newspaper coverage and ensure he got his name prominently displayed, perhaps even on the front page. Phillip had been studying the table in front of Doris and her solicitor when he spotted an A4 brown envelope mixed in with the files and papers displayed and what was more, it had been opened. He turned to the judge and asked if he was allowed to speak and when given permission, he pointed to the envelope, saying "This envelope look very similar to the one I sent to Mrs Herne's solicitor some days ago, and as you can see, it has been opened."

The solicitor pulled the sheets of neatly typed paper out of the envelope, desperately searching his mind for an excuse and said smoothly, "I apologise most profusely your honour, this must have been passed to me just as I was leaving for court and I was unaware of its contents."

"I suggest we adjourn for lunch, while you study the papers and perhaps when we all return to court, we can proceed with the hearing, without any further delay."

After lunch, which Walter seemed to enjoy very much, he told Phillip how his son Edward had been forced to return to California due to a sudden crisis in his business, but he would be returning shortly; in the meantime he was keeping in touch with his father as often as he could and would be waiting hopefully for the results of the hearing.

After lunch, Phillip was asked to give evidence on behalf of Mr Dunn and John started by asking the judge if it would be in order for Phillip to describe his first meeting at the prison with Walter.

"No Mr Standish, it would not," said the judge. "This is a court of law, not a storytelling club, proceed with your first question!"

"What was your first thought when you met Mr Dunn?"

"I was confused," said Phillip.

"Confused, perhaps you can explain why?"

"I had been told I had to meet a paedophile and listen to his story and this person sitting in front of me looked to be a sad, broken old man. What he told me made me even more confused."

"And why was that?" said John.

"He was an elderly gentleman, a retired schoolmaster with not a blot on his character, who was suddenly charged with behaving like a paedophile. It seemed to me to be unprecedented behaviour as this pattern of behaviour is usually caused by some sort of physical or sexual abuse perhaps in childhood. Even before I had met Mr Dunn, at least three people told me not to take the case, as public opinion is running strongly against their activities and there are vigilante groups who take matters into their own hands and pass out summary justice even before a court case takes place. I was warned that people who represent this sort of person in court were also in danger of being punished in some way, to discourage them."

"So why would you, a young, inexperienced private investigator, choose to take on a case like this, when you knew nothing of Mr Dunn's background at the time?"

"Because I am totally convinced that he is innocent!"

At this point the prosecuting solicitor protested. "Your honour, is any of this relevant, the witness's opinion is of no relevance."

John said blandly, "Your honour, what I am trying to establish is the good character and appearance of my client in order that he may be freed on bail. This witness is merely stating what is perfectly obvious, which is that my client is a gentleman and would never have done anything of an underhand nature."

"Very well, you may continue but do not labour this point unduly."

"Thank you, your honour."

"To continue Mr Everett, what factual evidence have you established so far?"

"As I was not allowed to talk to Betsy, the young person on whose evidence this case rests, it has made it very difficult to ascertain the full facts, particularly in view of the mother's hostile and vindictive assertions which have no basis of truth. However, I have been unable to find a single occasion when Mr Dunn and Betsy have ever been alone together and they have never met anywhere other than the first time in the park, in full view of numerous passers-by, when Mr Dunn accompanied her to a hair stylist, a shop selling school uniforms, the vestibule of a reputable gymnasium and a sports goods shop for her to select a pair of trainer shoes and a track suit!"

The prosecuting solicitor was beginning to see his case quite literally disappear so he asked, rather sarcastically, "And does the witness have some kind of special insight whereby he can see where other people meet and in what circumstances?"

"Your honour," said Phillip, "there is no evidence of the two persons concerned meeting in private!"

"If the opposing solicitor does not quite understand the word 'evidence', then I will be more than willing to look up the word in the *Oxford English Dictionary*," said John, with tongue firmly in cheek.

The judge said, "I have heard quite enough. Do you have any proof that Mr Dunn and Betsy had meetings other than the ones stated?"

"No, your honour, but the defence cannot *show* that meetings did not take place!"

"Since there is no evidence that any meetings did take place between Betsy and Mr Dunn, other than the public ones already stated, I am therefore going to release Mr Dunn on bail but the onus on his good behaviour is entirely the responsibility of his Defence solicitor and he must promise not to go within one hundred metres of Miss Herne, or try to contact her in any way. Failure to do so will result in immediate re-arrest and imprisonment. Is this understood, Mr Standish?"

"Perfectly, your honour."

"Normal bail conditions will apply but for now you are free to leave this court," said the judge to Walter, who looked as if he was about to cry.

At this point, Doris started to shout, ranting and raving at the judge, "What about my rights as a mother?" she screamed. The expression on the judge's face was one of amazement that anyone should behave like this in his court and banging his gavel on the desk, when the prosecuting solicitor had managed to quieten Doris, he said, "I was not going to intervene but in view of this disgraceful behaviour, the court grants Mr Everett permission to interview Miss Herne, in the presence of a policewoman. The interview will take place at Mr Everett's convenience," and to the court ushers, "Now clear the court," and he swept out of the door.

Phillip walked up to Walter and patted his shoulder, smiling and congratulating him; he turned to John and they shook hands, very pleased with their day's work.

"I don't know about you, Walter, but I should think you will want to go home. Let's go back to John's office, I'll pick up my car and take you home but perhaps you might like to get one or two bits of shopping on the way because I don't suppose anyone will have bothered to stock up for you. You'll have to point me in the right direction, I don't have one of those sat-nav gadgets in my car." He shepherded the bewildered Walter out into the fresh air and they went back to John's office.

Walter asked John what would happen to him now.

"You carry on leading your normal life. Phillip here is going to keep on investigating the background to your case and I shall be in touch with you as soon as I know the date set for your hearing. Provided you go nowhere near Miss Betsy Herne or try to get in touch with her by any means, you have nothing to worry about."

Walter gave him the directions to get to his house in the suburbs and while Phillip was driving, he gave him a very amusing but well edited story of how he had come to find a lost dog for its lovely owner who was now his girlfriend. Walter's 'house' turned out to be a spacious bungalow and as he turned the key and ushered Phillip into the lounge, he could see it was spotless.

"How did you manage to keep everything so tidy while you were in prison?" asked Phillip.

"Oh, I have very good neighbours," said Walter, "and Hilda, I pay her to do a bit of cleaning. I wonder if she's got me a drop of milk and then we can have a nice cup of tea."

He went into the kitchen, opened the fridge door and said, "Bless her, she must have known I would be back, look here, she's stocked up with everything I could want for a few days. I must go round and pay her and tell her the good news. I'll put the kettle on and you show yourself round, I won't be long."

Phillip made some tea, although he was more of a coffee man himself, helped himself to some chocolate biscuits and when Walter came back in, with a beaming smile on his face, said, "Do you want me to drive you anywhere to pick up some shopping or anything?"

"No, thank you, but the sooner I get back to normal, fending for myself, the quicker I'll settle down. It's going to seem a bit funny, sleeping in a normal bed instead of a prison bunk. I can't thank you enough for what you've done for me and I hope my son's paying you for everything; if you're running short, just tell me; 'I'm not short of a bob or two' as my Yorkshire friends would say."

Phillip stayed a little longer, chatting while Walter busied himself looking at a pile of mail.

"There's one here from my son, usually he just sends me messages on that mobile phone machine. Always on at me to get a computer and he says he can send me emails and pictures of the family but it seems too complicated to me. Whatever happened to good old letter-writing, much simpler! Anyway, he says he'll be back for the court case when the date is fixed."

Phillip laughed and then said that he would have to be going but he would keep in touch and if there was anything worrying him, just give him a ring and he would do his best to sort things out. They put a lot of emotion into their handshake; after all they were grown men, it wouldn't do to show their feelings, and then Phillip left.

Chapter 9

He switched on the answering machine: the first call was from Sarah saying, "Please call me." The second call was also from Sarah, saying, "Please, please call me as soon as you can." The third call was a man's voice, giving the name Barry Spencer and asking to make an appointment to see him and giving a telephone number. Phillip rang Sarah's number first but it was her mother who answered. She said Sarah was at work and would he like her office number? Phillip wrote the number down, tapped out the numbers and was answered by a man's voice saying, "Pennington Investments."

"May I speak to Sarah Pennington please?"

"Who is it?"

"Phillip Everett, I received a message to ring her."

A few moments later Sarah was on the receiver saying, "I'm so pleased to hear from you, are you alright?"

"I'm fine."

"I rang last night, you were not answering so I left a message. I rang again this morning and left a message but I was beginning to worry that something might have happened to you."

"No, really, I'm fine," said Phillip. "After I took Bruce back and left him with your mother (I'd had quite a busy evening, I'll tell you about it some time), when I got back, I just had a can of lager, switched on the answer machine and went to bed. This morning, I went early to the solicitor's office to plan our campaign for Mr Dunn's release on bail, before we went to court, but I'm sorry I didn't ring you before, I've just this moment got back to my office and found your messages."

"I'm so glad to hear that you're okay," she said. "May I come and see you tonight? I can't wait till Saturday!"

"That sounds lovely, I shall be pleased to see you; what shall I do about food?"

"Leave it till I get there; see you tonight, love you!" said Sarah.

Phillip put the phone down and pondered about Sarah's feelings. I hope she's not getting too serious about our relationship, thought Phillip; she's a lovely girl but I'm not sure I want to get too involved with anyone at this point in my life. I must try and keep the relationship with her under control.

Sarah arrived at half past six, just as Phillip had finished showering and dressing. He ran downstairs lightly, opened the door for her and as soon as he had closed it, she took off her coat and put her arms around his neck kissing him as if she had not seen him for years, instead of days. "Let's do this in more comfort," and taking his hand, she pulled him back up the stairs, and into his bedroom. She stood back from a him a little, while she slowly peeled her outer clothes off, revealing her black net bra with matching panties. She purred like a contented cat who knows it's going to be stroked, and said, "I'm going to leave the rest of the undressing to you," and lay down on the bed, propped up by some pillows.

Phillip swiftly removed the clothes he had just donned and said, "What, no running around tonight? All the better, we can save our energy for making love." He started gently at first, kissing her, moving all over her body, nuzzling her neck, while he slipped off her bra, amazed at the firm, round breasts which responded to his caresses so readily. She wriggled out of her panties to possession of her most intimate area while all the time the sexual tension was building up to a climax. Now they were one person, wildly enjoying their total abandonment. Finally they both fell back and lay side by side.

Sarah woke first and poked Phillip in the ribs. "Hey, wake up and feed your hungry guest!"

He opened his eyes and said, "Are we going to eat naked?"

"I should hope not, what is there to have? I'll have a shower while you decide." He watched from the bed while she picked up her discarded clothing and sauntered into the bathroom, wiggling her behind at him, laughing and banging the door in his face when he tried to pinch her bum. He pulled his clothes on, went downstairs and searched his fridge for something they could eat but he hadn't shopped for some weeks and apart from a few eggs and a carton of cottage cheese, which had been on a '2 for 1' offer and now looked decidedly out of date, there was nothing to be had except a few cornflakes and some stale bread. Sarah came downstairs, glowing from her shower and the vigorous sex they had just shared.

"Not much here," said Phillip. "I really will have to get some supplies in, but in the meantime, may I suggest a takeaway and then you can advise me what I ought to get at the supermarket." He picked up the phone and ordered a Chinese meal for three, thinking that should satisfy their hunger with a mixture of dishes, of which they would enjoy at least one.

They settled down to await the delivery of their food and Sarah said, "I haven't really thanked you yet for bringing Bruce back to me."

"That is what you are paying me for," said Phillip. "How is he?"

"Absolutely fine, none the worse for his absence but go on, tell me how you managed to find him?"

"It was more good luck than anything really; when no-one called and asked for money and there were no replies to your advertisement offering a reward for his return, I thought it was possible he had been stolen for the purpose of dog fighting."

Sarah was puzzled. "What do you mean, dog fighting? He's not the sort of animal to be aggressive like a Rottweiler or a bull terrier, he's as soft as butter! I've had him since he was a puppy."

"I know that but apparently, these gangs who organise dog fights, like to pit a large, amiable type of dog, against a fairly fierce one, just to start the proceedings off and get some blood flowing which apparently gets the really nasty dogs very excited by the smell of blood."

Sarah was shocked. "You mean they are wounded, these pet dogs and what happens then? Although I think I already know the answer to that."

"I'm not going to say any more about that," said Phillip gently. "Suffice it to say that I discovered there was going to be a fight, so I went to the meeting and while the rest of the audience were watching the dogs fight, I went round the car park and found this big, black Labrador, cooped up in a van, and when I said the name 'Bruce' he looked up so I broke open the doors and he seemed very happy to see me. He followed me to my car with no trouble so I drove straight to your mother's, and she checked his microchip identification code and it proved it was Bruce, without any doubt. One mission successfully accomplished. Do I get a kiss for that?"

"I hope no-one saw you doing this or followed you or anything because from programmes I've seen on television, these gangs are criminals and they are often violent. Oh Phillip, do take care and no, you don't get a kiss because the delivery boy is knocking on the door now with our Chinese feast!"

They sat in the kitchen, hungrily sharing their favourite dishes, drinking from a bottle of wine Phillip suddenly remembered he had stashed under the sink, for some reason, and Sarah asked, between mouthfuls, "Do you always drink wine with your meals?"

"No, only when I have guests," he said. "I try not to drink too much alcohol."

"What is 'too much'?"

"It's when you feel yourself sliding under the table, then you've drunk too much alcohol."

"So long as you are still upright," she said, "you can go on drinking?"

"Men have another way to test whether they are drunk or not but you are too young and too much of a lady to be told!!"

She laughed. "I think I can guess what that is!" When they had eaten their fill, Phillip poured the last of the wine into Sarah's glass and told her to make herself comfortable on the couch in his office. "I'll clear up and be with you in a moment."

After packing the food, which had not been eaten, into the freezer section, he stacked the plates and glasses in the dishwasher and switched it to On. He took a can of strong lager out of the fridge and joined Sarah in his office, part of which he had furnished with comfortable armchairs and a couch. "So is this room your office or your lounge?" asked Sarah.

"Well I don't really need much room for an office, a small space for a desk, filing cabinets and other paraphernalia, but people will be coming here by appointment and they will feel more at ease in a comfortable chair, which helps to produce a more relaxed atmosphere."

"You mean, while you interrogate them, give them the third degree," she laughed.

"Oh I have a separate room with handcuffs and shackles on the walls, fancy whips and the rack, but that's a secret!" he said, solemnly.

"Oooer, do you think some of your customers would like that?"

"Well I try to please everybody but I'm not going to put you in there unless you seriously misbehave. You are far too pretty to endure anything but the most gentle lovemaking!"

"You say the nicest things to me but I expect you say the same things to all the girls you meet!" She stood in front of him, wearing only her underwear.

"Are you going to sleep like that or are you driving home in that outfit?" said Phillip, sardonically.

"I want to sleep in your bed tonight," she said. "Can I, please?"

"But this is a working day and tomorrow is another working day," he said.

"What difference does that make?" asked Sarah. "You're not going to ruin my evening by sending me home are you? You're not that sadistic!"

"Okay, you can stay if you wish but you must ring—"

"I know, I must ring my parents and let them know I'm staying the night with a gorgeous, handsome man."

"If you tell them that, I shall be hung from the nearest tree and then my body will be fed to the pigs."

Sarah came close to him and putting her arms around his neck she said, "I'm falling in love with you. When we make love, you make me feel so wonderful, I can't even begin to describe it, how you make me feel!"

"That, young lady, is not love, it's lust and sex!"

She looked at him scornfully. "Don't say that, I'm not a stupid teenager."

"When you do fall in love, you will know the difference," Phillip said.

"So you don't love me?" she asked."

Phillip decided to be very firm and he faced her and said, "I won't allow this to happen and I don't want to have the same discussion taking place every time we see each other. You are a gorgeous creature and a good lay," he said crudely, "and any young man would give all he had to be in my position but I can't allow myself to fall in love with you; when, with the best will in the world, you finally decide to leave, I would be a broken man. I've already had one setback but with you it would be far worse than with Samantha." It was as if he had told her he never wanted to see her again; Phillip groaned inwardly and thought she was about to cry, she looked so unhappy. He put his hand gently under her chin and lifted her face for his kiss. "I will be your friend and your lover as long as you want me," he murmured in her ear and she turned and smiled.

"For the time being, I'll settle for that, but I'll make you fall in love with me one day."

He changed the subject and asked her what she was going to wear in bed, offering her the top half of a pair of pyjamas his mother had bought for him one Christmas. He gave her a light slap on the bottom as they went upstairs and she accused him of being fond of spanking young girls. "Get your pretty rump into bed and let me get some sleep, I've got a busy day tomorrow." She curled up around him and he pressed the light switch, plunging the room into darkness. He felt her lovely soft body at his back and felt happy. Now then Phillip, he told himself, don't get used to this because it's not going to last, and that was the last thing he remembered before he fell asleep.

He was woken by Sarah, fully dressed and ready to set off for work. "Sorry to wake you up so early, dream boy, but I had to kiss you goodbye before I left." She gave him a lingering kiss and said, "I'll be in touch, bye," and she was gone. He felt the same empty feeling he had last time she left but told himself not to be so stupid. Might as well get up and go through the usual routine and after breakfast he'd settle down to some work. He rang John Standish and asked him to arrange for him to meet Betsy Herne with a policewoman present, and John promised to ring back. He listened again to his messages on the answering machine, deleting the two from Sarah, and concentrated on the third one. He rang the number given by Barry Spencer and a male voice answered, "Vasily Bukow's office, Barry Spencer speaking."

"Good morning, Mr Spencer, Phillip Everett speaking. I received a message to contact you. Can I help you in any way?"

"Mr Everett, I'd like a meeting with you to talk about the possibility of using your agency for some work we might be undertaking shortly." Phillip heard a note of hesitation in the man's voice, the words 'possibility', 'might be', 'shortly', this did not sound very promising and he was tempted to make his apologies and say he was too busy but the trouble was, he had no further work once the investigations in Mr Dunn's case were completed so he might as well take the chance and at least see what the proposition was. "I'm Mr Vassily Bukow's personal assistant and we would both like to meet you to talk over a proposition we have in mind. We would like to make it this afternoon as Mr Bukow's schedule is very busy at the moment, would that be convenient?"

Phillip pretended to consult his diary, no need for them to think he was nearly unemployed, and said, "If you wanted to come about two o'clock, that would be fine with me. Are you familiar with this area of Croydon, Mr Spencer?"

"There'll be no difficulty finding you Mr Everett, we are usually good at finding people and places, see you then." Just for a moment, the thought occurred to Phillip that he might have been under observation but he dismissed that as ridiculous.

After he put the phone down, Phillip went straight to the Internet to see what information he could discover about Mr Bukow. He found the Bukow Investment Co., but no details of the kind of investments they dealt with; he did however, discover that Mr Vasily Bukow was a Russian billionaire who moved to London from somewhere in Russia, bringing his billions with him. Reading between the lines, Phillip guessed that he was probably a shady, underhand wheeler-dealer whom the government in Russia would dearly love to see back in the Mother Country, where no doubt he could be subjected to some pressure to disclose how he had managed to take out his unspecified assets and perhaps he might be persuaded to return some of those said assets! He might be one of the big spenders and could indulge himself in employing a near penniless private investigator on some dodgy case. He was quite sure now that some kind of check had been made on him.

The two men arrived exactly on time; Phillip let them in, trying to get a look at the transport they had used, shook hands with each one and ushered them into his office cum lounge. He asked if he could get them a drink, which they both refused and he tried to make a quick appraisal of his two visitors. Mr Bukow was a fairly short man, without an ounce of fat on him, bulging with muscle and emitting an aura of power which said "Don't start anything because you might regret it"; not a person to forgive and not a person to make an enemy of. Spencer, on the other hand, was a tall, slim, handsome young man, probably an Oxford or Cambridge graduate, in a perfect job as PA to a business tycoon. The only surprise was that most of these PA jobs were given to young, pretty girls, especially if they had nice figures to match their pretty faces. Phillip hoped this had no significance.

Seating himself opposite his two guests, Phillip asked, "What can I do for you, gentlemen?"

"Do you trace missing people?" said Spencer.

"When you say 'missing', do you mean a young person running away?" queried Phillip.

"Not running away, lured away," said Spencer.

"I think you had better tell me the whole story, otherwise we are going to spend all afternoon asking each other questions!" said Phillip.

Spencer nodded his head and after a quick glance at his companion said, "Mr Bukow has a seventeen-year-old daughter; she has always been very well behaved. She is a lovely young lady and there were many young men trying to date her but she stayed out of the drug scene and binge drinking and any criminal behaviour and Mr Bukow is very proud of her and her sensible way of managing her life. Then one day, she went to one of her girlfriends' eighteenth birthday party, but when Mr Bukow's driver went to pick her up at midnight, she was no longer there. The driver and other guests there searched the whole house and grounds but found no trace of her so he rang Mr Bukow who told him to call the police. The police arrived shortly afterwards and questioned everyone there but the only real fact they discovered was that she had spent a lot of time with a very good-looking young man. They were seen dancing and sitting together by many of the other guests but no one knew exactly who he was or had seen them actually leave, although several persons said they had not been there towards the end of the evening."

"These cases are best left to the police," said Phillip, "they have massive resources, including Interpol."

"Mr Bukow has done just that but last week, a police inspector called to see him and told him that the case had been investigated for nine months and they had come up with nothing. They had to assume that the girl went willingly with the young man and the pair of them do not want to be found. Apparently, this is not unusual with girls of that age; the police do not suspect foul play so they have no choice but to scale the investigation down. They never close a case, as you know, but unless anything specific comes up, they have to put this on the back burner."

"Was there a demand for ransom or some other demand on Mr Bukow?"

"There was no ransom demand, and what other type of demand do you mean?" said Spencer.

Phillip said directly, "Mr Bukow is obviously a very rich man and wields a lot of influence in certain circles. He could have been approached and asked to do someone a 'favour', or perhaps some kind of political manoeuvre they wanted him to back?"

The two men spoke in Russian for a few moments and then Spencer turned to Phillip, saying, "Mr Bukow wants me to tell you that he knows nothing about anything like that and he is not interested in politics; he does not think he has any enemies or, at least, none he knows about!"

"I need to know the correct answers to my questions as I am totally dependent on Mr Bukow's replies, if I get the wrong answers, it will lead me to the wrong conclusions and I will never be able to discover what happened to the girl," Phillip said seriously.

"So will you accept the case?" said Spencer.

"Only if Mr Bukow meets my conditions of employment."

"What are they?" asked Spencer, sitting back on the couch with a satisfied expression.

"First, I charge £30 an hour, plus expenses. Second, I always ask for a deposit and in this case, the deposit will be large. This is the kind of investigation which will take time; if the police, with all their resources, could not find anything to go on, it's going to take me some time to check up on the background of people involved, such as guests at the party and others, before I can even get to the starting line of the investigation. The last one is, this is Britain and in this country I have to stay and operate within the law. I am not licensed to carry any weapon and as you can see, I do not have a broken nose or a cauliflower ear; I do not engage in any physical violence. What that means is I do not rough people up to get the answers I want to hear," finished Phillip.

Once more, Spencer and Mr Bukow rapidly conversed in Russian and then he said to Phillip, "If Mr Bukow wanted a muscle man, he could hire a dozen quite cheaply, but he wants someone with brains and for that reason, he wants to hire you. He will pay £30,000 into your bank account immediately, as a deposit; he will write you a cheque right away and he wants you to start work as soon as it has been credited to your account. Is that in order?"

"Yes, I agree," said Phillip and while Mr Bukow was writing out the cheque, he told Spencer to give him all the information he had, names and addresses of guests at the party, anything which might be considered relevant because what might appear to be an unimportant item, could well lead to the girl's being found. "I would also appreciate knowing what the police told you during their eight months of investigation, anything to get me off to a good start."

Spencer told him that all the information collected during the months since the party, everything known so far, would be sent to him by courier the following day. Mr Bukow gave the cheque to Phillip and they prepared to leave. They all shook hands and Phillip said, "I work hard and get good results, I hope you will be satisfied when I have finished."

Barry Spencer smiled at him and said, "Mr Bukow was in court when you and the solicitor got that gentleman released on bail. He was very impressed with both you and Mr Standish, that is why he wanted to hire you. Oh, by the way, Mr Bukow speaks perfect English, when he has to!"

Phillip said, "Somehow, I thought that might be so; you had no need to translate anything I said to him!" and turning to Mr Bukow, "I will do my best for you."

"Thank you Mr Everett," he said in slightly accented English and they left the office.

Chapter 10

On Thursday morning, John Standish rang with a cheery "And how is my favourite private detective this sunny morning?"

"And good morning to my favourite solicitor!"

"I've been told that a policewoman will be visiting Betsy Herne after school tomorrow and will be there if you wish to interview her; her mother has graciously given permission for you to step inside her dwelling at four o'clock for the express purpose of talking to her beloved daughter so you'd better have a wash and brush-up to come up to our Doris's standards!"

"Sarcasm will get you nowhere," said Phillip, but the next day he parked outside the address given and looked around the street of small terrace houses. I suppose she must be renting, or perhaps she was housed by the local council; the exterior could have done with a coat of paint and there was an overflowing rubbish bin at the side of the doorstep. However that was nothing to do with him so he sat and waited for the policewoman to drive up, greeted her and gave her his name.

"I'm PC Jen Whitlock, and I'm here to attend your interview with Betsy Herne; shall we knock on the door?"

After leaving them on the doorstep for several minutes, Doris opened the door reluctantly and said, "She's in here," and indicated a door to the left. Betsy was sat on one side of a dining table, looking scared so Phillip introduced PC Jen Whitlock and said, "I'm Phillip Everett," and they sat down at the table. Doris also sat down, next to Betsy, and said, "Wot do we do now?"

"I would just like to hear from Betsy – is it alright if I call you Betsy or would you rather be called Miss Herne?" he said, with a smile.

Betsy giggled nervously and replied, "Betsy's okay with me."

"Perhaps Betsy will tell me how she came to meet Mr Dunn and what happened subsequently. Actually, there's no need for you to be here Mrs Herne, this policewoman will be present all the time we are talking and I will in no way try to coerce your daughter; all I want to hear is the truth!" Doris showed no sign of moving so Phillip concentrated all his attention on Betsy. She was very hesitant at first and kept glancing first to her mother and then at the policewoman but she gathered confidence as Phillip encouraged her to go on with her story.

It was virtually a copy of what Mr Dunn had told Phillip. Betsy was very unhappy with her life, she had played truant, some oaf in the park had called her "fatty" and it all became too much for her to cope with. She had sat down on the park bench and started to cry. She hadn't even seen Mr Dunn at first until he spoke to her and asked her what was the matter and could he help. This was the first time anyone had shown any interest in her and as for offering to help, that was just too good to be true. He was a very nice old gentleman, perhaps like a grandfather that other kids seemed to have, and for her he had performed miracles. He listened to all she had to say, he asked her what she wanted to do and then he helped her but she had to promise to stop playing truant, cutting herself, pinching money to buy all those chips and doughnuts and she had to keep herself neat and tidy, try to work hard at school, go to the gym and all that.

"The trouble started when, after a bit, I lost some weight from going to the gym and swimming and things and people at school started to take more notice of me. They stopped bullying me and one or two girls said I looked much nicer with my hair being styled and everything; some of the boys started chatting me up a bit and that was great. Before, they used to laugh at me and call me fatty and other things; I even started liking school a bit more, once one of the teachers praised me for the improvement in my work."

Doris interrupted her in a loud voice with, "That's just what I mean, Walter Dunn has corrupted her and she's started thinking about boys and men."

Phillip said patiently, "Mrs Herne, it's completely natural and normal for any fourteen-year-old girl to start noticing the opposite sex, I'm sure you were the same at her age!"

"I was a good girl at her age," said Doris, self-righteously.

"What exactly does that mean?" asked Phillip.

"I didn't fool around with boys," she said.

Betsy said indignantly, "Neither do I, Mum!"

"Please carry on," said Phillip.

"Well, one day, one of Mum's boyfriends said in front of Mum, something like 'you're shaping up quite nicely' and gave me a grin. After he had gone out to get some cigs, Mum lost her cool; she started shouting, calling me names like whore, slag and slut and things and saying I was trying to pinch her man from her!"

At this point, Doris began to shout, "You ungrateful brat, after all I've done for you, now you're telling lies about me; I wish I'd never had you, you've ruined my life, having to bring you up, scrimping and saving when I could have had a real good job in an office or somewhere like that and a bit of fun out of life, instead of…"

Phillip was writing down all these remarks and when Doris noticed this, she tried to snatch his notebook but he was too quick for her. He grabbed her hand and told her it was obvious that if she was too excitable to sit still and keep quiet during the interview, either she should go into another room or they would have to take Betsy to the police station and interview her there, without her mother being present.

Doris sat there, trying to be calm, shaken by the rebuke and Betsy was looking very upset at her mother's outburst. Phillip turned to Betsy and said, "Please don't be upset Betsy, you were doing so well; if you could carry on telling me your story, we can finish quickly and be on our way. What happened next?"

"We had this big row, like a big, you know, falling out, and so I said if she carried on like that towards me, I would tell Mr Dunn and ask if I could stay in his house for a bit, till she calmed down. That's when she got these ideas about Mr Dunn and said she would cause trouble for him because with him buying me all these nice things, he must be getting something back from me and she dragged me down to the police station and convinced them that something was going on and she wanted Mr Dunn arrested for having an illegal relationship with underaged girls, but honestly, there wasn't anything like that going on. I'm not stupid, even if I am only fourteen, and he wasn't like that, honestly he wasn't." She looked shyly up at Phillip and said, "I just imagined he might be like a nice uncle or grandad who buys you birthday and Christmas presents and things and I knew he was a bit sad cos his wife died last year and his son lives abroad somewhere…" She trailed off.

"You have done very well Betsy," said Phillip, "you have explained everything very clearly; would you be able to say this in court?"

"It's the truth and I would say it."

"I don't have much more to ask you, Betsy, it won't take long; can you remember all your meetings with Mr Walter Dunn?"

"Yes, course I can," Betsy said, scornfully. "Now this is very important, so think carefully before you answer, did you ever go to Mr Walter Dunn's house?"

"No, I don't even know where it is!"

"Did you ever meet Mr Walter Dunn in any place which people would call 'private', say just you and him in a room where there was no other person present?"

"No, I only saw him when he took me to the hairdressers or that shop which sold school uniforms, oh, and after he got me a pass to go to the gym as many times as I wanted, he stood in the reception for a bit and talked to the old man behind the desk, the one who answers the phone and lets you go into the changing rooms, that one!"

"Finally, did Mr Walter Dunn ever suggest that he would like to spend time alone with you or invite you to visit his house or to go away anywhere with him?"

Betsy laughed. "Are you kidding? What would a nice refined gentleman like that talk to a thicky like me about? He'd be bored out of his mind and come to think of it, so would I. He's a very nice gentleman but he doesn't know nothing about pop stars or records or anything like that!!"

Phillip finished his notes and thanked Betsy for her clear and accurate answers to his questions. He shook hands with her formally, nodded in the direction of Doris and said to the policewoman, "Thanks for being here, we can leave now."

He started to say goodbye to the policewoman when she smiled at him and said, "I was hoping you would offer to take me out for a drink."

"I'd be glad to but we're both driving."

"Perhaps some other time," she said reluctantly.

"Give me a call and we can arrange something," said Phillip, fervently hoping she would not because he didn't fancy her type. Besides, today was Friday and he had this standing arrangement with Gordon; now he came to think of something, Sarah had not been in touch but he mentally shrugged and put it out of his mind. After a swift visit to a supermarket to buy a few essentials, he put an evening snack together before he took the bus and tube journey to meet his friend outside the wine bar. They greeted each other in their usual insulting way. "How is my Highland friend?"

"Not so bad, what about my Sassenach private dick?"

"From what I can see, your dick looks okay, even if it is on the small size!"

"Listen mate, whatever the size, none of my ladies have ever complained!"

"That is because you always select such timid women who dare not say boo to a goose!"

"Enough of your compliments," said Gordon, "or you will make me bigheaded, let's go and eat."

"I've had something to eat but I'll join you anyway."

Gordon took them to a place nearby where, he said, the food was out of this world. "You mean it's what they give to astronauts?"

"Ha, ha, not funny, this is good Scottish food, Aberdeen Angus steaks the size of a dinner plate."

"Down here, we call those saucers, you know what saucers are Gordon, those little round plates you put cups on!"

"Enough with the daft jokes, you London git," said Gordon. "Now, you've really hurt me, I am not even a Londoner, I was born under a wanderin' star in Buckinghamshire."

"Never mind, don't cry into your beer, I'm paying so you can order what you like."

"There speaks the rich banker to a poor worker in what was the private sector. We'd all have had a lot more money if it wasn't for you bankers lending lots of money to people who couldn't pay it back."

"That's rich, if you don't mind the pun, you were a banker yourself until less than a year ago!"

"Ah, that's where you're wrong, I wasn't – strictly speaking – a banker, I was a—"

"That's just splitting hairs. Let's order, I'm starving!"

"So how's business, private eye business, that is," said Gordon jokingly.

"I managed to find the lost dog!" said Phillip, laughing.

"Oh yea, did it turn up on your doorstep, barking to be let in?" asked Gordon, between mouthfuls of steak.

"No, actually I went to a dog fighting meet and managed to find it in the back of someone's car, by pure chance really," and he told him the whole story.

"You have to be joking, you idiot; from what I've heard that could have been nasty, very nasty!"

"It wouldn't have been much fun for the dog either, if he'd been second on the programme. After what I saw happened to the first dog, it made me so sick I would have done anything to prevent it happening to Bruce."

"So what now?" said Gordon. "Out of work again, are you?"

"No, you big mouthed Scottish twit, I have another case about an inappropriate relationship with a minor."

"You mean an affair between a teacher and a student?"

"How perceptive you are, Gordon! No, I'm certain the ex-teacher in this case is innocent; there is a court case pending so I can't discuss it with you and I've got someone who wants me to find his daughter. She went missing nine months ago—"

Gordon interrupted him, "Nine months ago, do you mean he's just noticed she's not there?"

"Fathers tend not to be very observant, do they? No, so far he's relied on the police but they've told him they have found nothing to indicate foul play and I think privately, they are of the opinion she's gone off with a boyfriend who Daddy doesn't like and they don't want to be found. They are scaling down the enquiry, so unless anything unusual turns up, that's it."

Gordon sat back, replete with his meal and said to Phillip, "You are very unkind to our constabulary, you can't blame them if she just left with her fancy man."

"If that's the case, I would hate to be him if he's found because Daddy's very rich and would no doubt deprive him of his genitals, one millimetre at a time, with a blunt knife," Phillip said.

"Let's find our way to our usual haunt and see if the girls have arrived."

Gordon headed straight for them, beaming at Isobel and giving her a hearty kiss on each cheek.

"Very continental," said Jasmine. "Don't I get one?"

"I'll leave that to Phillip," said Gordon wickedly, "he's more the expert than me!"

Phillip kissed Jasmine chastely on the cheek, and whispered in her ear, "Catch me later and I'll make up for that insipid one."

"Now let's see what we're all drinking, let's get the evening started." They were soon laughing at a very poor but rude joke that Gordon cracked. They ended up at Gordon's flat, this time with Isobel sharing his bed and Jasmine spending all night with Phillip.

Phillip left his friends and arrived home about 1.30 but there were no messages from Sarah and as the afternoon started to drag on, still no sign of Sarah. I guess that's the end, thought Phillip, ruefully, but in a way, I'm glad it's happened sooner rather than later. I've still got Jasmine and she's a lovely girl. Except in his mind he knew this wasn't really true – Sarah had got closer to him than any other woman he had met – but he was not ready for another serious relationship and shied away from any involvement. To prevent him feeling sorry for himself he had the idea that he should do what his mother did every so often, she 'bottomed' the house or in other words, she spring-cleaned. Phillip had lived by himself long enough to know that houses don't just clean themselves and, at the moment, he couldn't afford a cleaner, so he rolled up his sleeves, knowing the physical effort involved would put Sarah out of his mind. He put a load of laundry in a large plastic bag and left it where his laundry service could pick it up outside and just as he was getting a can of lager out of the fridge, he heard a vehicle draw up. For a moment, he almost thought – but it wasn't her.

He sat in an armchair, surveying the results of his labour, when he remembered their Chinese feast, neatly stacked away in the freezer. He took out the dishes to heat in the microwave for his evening meal and when he finished, put the dishes in the dishwasher and, still feeling restless, decided to go down to the pub for a few beers. After a shower, he dressed casually and strolled to his nearest pub. He found a quiet corner and sipped his lager, watching the various people coming and going through the pub, thinking it was a good exercise on observation and amused himself by guessing what people's relationships to each other were or what they did for a living. There appeared to be, more or less, the usual Saturday night crowd enjoying themselves when three young people came in, one young man and two girls, expensively dressed as if going to a party. It crossed his mind as to what these three could be doing in this humble watering hole. When he worked in the City, he himself wore expensive, hand tailored suits and shirts and the young man's suit was of the most expensive cut and style and the girls' evening dresses had certainly not come from Primark or Matalan!

They sat at a table near to Phillip and the young man went to the bar to get some drinks. They were sitting with their backs to him so he was able to study them carefully, without appearing to stare. Aged about eighteen or nineteen, very high-heeled shoes and as their short skirts showed, sheer stockings. They were both slim with good legs but he had to reserve his opinion as to what they had on top as they were sitting with their backs to him. Perhaps they were models, he thought, and the young man was their agent. He was losing interest and turned to look elsewhere when their drinks arrived and they changed their seating positions, turning to face him. He was, he admitted, wrong about them having too little on top. Both were pretty with dark brown hair and although they were wearing short jackets, their cleavages were pretty impressive. Phillip went to the bar to get himself another drink and as he returned to his seat, both girls smiled at him. Costs nothing to smile, he thought, so he returned the compliment. They appeared to be discussing something in quiet voices when one of the girls got up and walked over to him.

"It's a shame to see you sitting on your own, are you waiting for someone perhaps?"

"No," said Phillip, "just having a quiet drink."

She turned and said, "Come on you guys, let's cheer this lonely fellow up!" and sat down next to him. "I'm Penny and no jokes about always turning up, this is Linda and that's Harry, and you are?"

"Phillip."

"What are you doing here?" asked Linda politely.

"It's my local, I can walk here and I don't have to bother about driving back," he said.

"Very useful," agreed Harry, solemnly. "What do you do for a living?"

"I'm that rare breed, a private investigator."

"Wow, I've never met a private detective before."

"Well you have now."

"Do you advertise or something and then people ring you up and ask you to track their husbands or wives, or do you find lost dogs and things like that?" Harry found this very amusing and Phillip was beginning to wish he had never smiled at the girls when Penny said to him, "If you're not waiting for anybody, why not come with us to this party we're on our way to? It's an all-nighter, loads of food and drink, dancing, if you want to, and my partner hasn't turned up so I'll be on my own with these two here. Aw, go on, you're sure to like it?"

Phillip shrugged his shoulders and said, "It sounds great but I'm only wearing casual clothes and you three are all dressed in evening clothes, I don't think I'd fit in."

Penny shook her head vehemently. "There'll be loads of people dressed casually, you won't be a bit out of place and besides," she twinkled at him, "you'll be the handsomest guy there, I'll be lucky to hang on to you!"

"If you want me to come," said Phillip, "then let's go." Penny took his hand and they all walked out of the pub into the car park.

"This is my car," said Harry, indicating a pale blue, sleek Jaguar, with the latest registration number on the back. "Everybody hop in,

Linda with me in the front, Penny in the back with Phillip, and no hanky-panky, or I'll be forced to throw you out." Harry was laughing.

It was dark by now and Harry apparently liked to drive fast. Penny whispered in Phillip's ear that Harry's father was very rich and bought him a new car every year when another registration number came out, and then she started to kiss him. He had heard of French kissing, of course, but never quite as passionate as this. She took her tongue out of his mouth to whisper, "I've come 'commando' tonight, are you going to do anything about it?" Phillip felt under her dress and found she was not wearing any underwear at all, not even a thong, her stockings were held up with special grip tops and he could tell she was ready and waiting for him.

Harry shouted gaily, "What are you two up to in the back there? If you don't stop it now, I'll park the car and get in and join you."

Phillip was using his hand to try and satisfy her, but she was not satisfied with that and before he could try anything she was astride him, they were having full sex. Just after she climaxed, leaving him frustrated, she sat back and pulled down her dress. "Don't worry, I will please you more later," she whispered and squeezed his hand.

Harry pulled his car up with a screech of brakes, in front of a large house, alongside various other cars which would have made a car thief salivate with joy. There were many hundreds of thousands of pounds' worth of every type of expensive car on the market but on patrol were two large uniformed guards with dogs. "Come on, you three, let's get in where the action is. Mr and Mrs Ashley are holidaying on their yacht in the Bahamas," Harry explained, "and Master Isaak Matthias Ashley Junior is in residence. It's him who's giving the party tonight," he said, "so we'd better introduce you to him, you don't get in there without an invitation!"

They went into a large room, probably a ballroom in previous days, containing maybe fifty young, and not so young, people. Settees and armchairs were arranged in groups with coffee tables scattered round and against the far wall were tables piled high with food of every kind. Servants in spotless white uniforms were waiting to serve the guests with food and drink. Penny took Phillip's hand and said, "Come with me, I'll introduce you to our host." They crossed the room to where a young man of medium height was standing; he was of slight build, very slim and wearing a perfectly tailored suit, waistcoat and white shirt but so pale, he looked as if he had never seen the sunlight in his life. "Isaak, this is my friend Phillip Everett," and she was about to say, "and he's a private detective," when Phillip interrupted smoothly, "and he is a banker, pleased to meet you, Isaak," who shook Phillip's hand formally and said, "Bankers I like. Make yourself at home, there's food and drink over there, help yourself to whatever you want; you can do anything you want here, anything goes except hurting someone. Any person found using physical violence to abuse another person will be thrown out of the house immediately."

Phillip didn't quite know how to reply to that statement except he knew some remark was expected of him so he said, "That won't happen with me!"

"Well then, you are very welcome," and Isaak moved away to talk to another couple.

"Why did you stop me telling Isaak you were a private detective?" asked Penny, when Isaak had moved out of earshot.

"Because this does not appear to be the kind of party which would like to have a detective in its midst. That couple over there, the man has his hand up that girl's dress, she doesn't appear to be wearing anything else apart from the dress and she looks about fourteen; there seems to be a couple in that dark corner over there who are having full sexual intercourse and the television screens appear to be showing soft porn films of some sort."

"What do you expect?" said Penny, amazed. "Haven't you ever been to an adults' party before?" and flounced off. Phillip was not sure what he should do but he got himself a drink and sat down in a comfortable armchair, wondering about the best way to extricate himself from this situation, when a pretty blonde girl said to no-one in particular, "I haven't had *you* before, have I?" Phillip sat there in amazement as she expertly unzipped his trousers and proceeded to perform oral sex on him. Unwillingly, he rose to the occasion and when she had finished, he felt relieved, in more ways than one. The blonde pulled her flimsy skirt up and said to him triumphantly, "Now you do it to me!"

Even in the dim light, he could see she was drunk and very excited, and he wondered if one of the anonymous doors which opened out of this area led to rooms containing supplies of cocaine or other drugs and conceded that this was probably true. What a situation he was in! It wouldn't say much for his reputation as a reliable private investigator if this were to be known in many circles. He had to extricate himself as soon as possible; he smacked the girl lightly on her shapely behind and said, "I don't do things like that!"

"What, you gay or something?" she said indignantly.

"By gay, you mean 'happy go lucky'?" he queried, sarcastically. "Let's just say I don't fancy handling used goods and it's about time you went back to finishing school!"

She looked at him with amazement, not sure what she should make of his remarks and then said, "Bollocks to you" and marched off. Phillip looked round at the scene before him, feeling not the slightest sexual frisson for any of the semi naked women, displaying various parts of their anatomies, the men laughing and drinking and moving from one female to another or fondling a man in a suggestive way and in the cold light of reason, he knew he had to get out before he could be involved in any other incident. Once they realised he was not joining in any of the 'entertainments', they would become suspicious of him so he decided to edge his way to the entrance hall and phone for a taxi.

He was never so thankful to see a taxi, as it appeared twenty minutes later, approaching up the drive. He had the door open before the car had stopped and gave the driver his address, sinking back, thanking his lucky stars that he hadn't got involved in anything. At first, when he had entered the large room with Penny, all his male instincts had been aroused at the sight of willing girls apparently eager to be fondled and used in any way for sex and then the alarm bells had started to go off inside his head. His common sense told him that the word 'condom' would be laughed at and how many of these men had been tested recently for HIV or AIDS or, in fact, any sexually transmitted disease? One man could infect only one woman, but she could have several sexual encounters at a party like that and could infect many other men and the circle went round endlessly, most of them not even aware they were infected, due to slight symptoms which they ignored. It occurred to him then that he didn't know how many sexual partners either Jasmine or Sarah had had; maybe he should get himself checked out. He heaved a sigh of relief when the taxi drew up outside his home, jumped out quickly, paid the fare and gave a generous tip to the driver, closing his front door behind him. Thinking back on the evening's events, he told himself off mentally with, You really aren't very bright, are you Phillip, for heaven's sake think with your mind, not with your penis, next time a pretty girl you don't know asks you to go to a party!!

He stayed in all day Sunday, preparing and finalising his report on his interview with Betsy Herne, emphasising Doris's behaviour and remarks while he tried to talk to Betsy. Monday morning he faxed the finished report to John Standish's office and about eleven o'clock the phone rang; it was Walter Dunn, sounding very upset. "I hope you don't mind my ringing you, but you did say if you could help me with anything…" His voice trailed off.

"Of course I did, and I meant it, what seems to be the trouble Mr Dunn?"

"I'm having a lot of harassment and I'm wondering what to do about it. Do you think you could come over and give me a bit of advice?"

"I'll be with you in half an hour," Phillip reassured him but remembering his experiences on Saturday night, he rang his doctor to make an appointment for an AIDS test, but even as he started to press the numbers, he realised that this would go down on his medical records. No, he didn't think he wanted such a personal item as that to be on his doctor's records; what he should do was check on the Internet and find a private clinic to carry out the test, whose confidentiality was guaranteed and he would be the only one to receive the results.

It won't take me long to make an appointment, he thought, so he studied the information about AIDS and HIV and found the number of a clinic who promised they would act in complete confidence. There was no address given, only the phone number but he rang, was answered by a woman with a cultured accent who explained that they tested for a number of conditions and there was no need for him to give his name or address, provided he collected the report himself and paid the £250 fee in cash. They did not take cheques, credit or debit cards, however, and once the amount was credited to their bank account, all the relevant paperwork was shredded.

"How long should I wait before I attend your clinic for the test?" he asked.

"At least four or five days since the last occasion you had unprotected sexual intercourse." He made an appointment for Friday and she gave him the address which he wrote down carefully; a Harley Street address – very posh, he thought, and made a note in his diary of the time.

He pulled up outside Walter's bungalow and noticed that the garden wall had been painted over. He rang the doorbell but there was no reply. He rang again and a voice asked, "Who is it?"

"It's me, Phillip Everett." He heard bolts being pulled back and the lock undone and Walter opened the door, only allowing enough room for Phillip to squeeze in sideways. Poor guy must be frightened to death! he thought.

"I'm very sorry," said Walter apologetically, "I keep the door locked and bolted all the time, it's even worse now than it was on remand. At least the people in there might be guilty of one offence or another, but they don't continually throw it in your face. Here, they are all saints and they behave as if you are the only evil person in the neighbourhood. I went to the supermarket and a middle-aged woman said to me, "You are Walter Dunn the child molester aren't you? You are a dirty, filthy beast," and she spat in my face and walked away. I get people looking at me and saying "pervert, rot in hell". Someone sprayed my wall with the words 'pervert' and 'scum' and I had to paint over it with red paint. So now I spend all my time inside my house, with doors and windows locked. It's worse than being in prison!!"

Phillip said, "How about you make me a cup of tea and then we can sit down and thrash this out between us?" Having given Walter something to keep him occupied, Phillip figured out the best way to help him. They sat down together and Phillip started by saying, "Have you ever had a big dog running towards you barking, showing its teeth and looking as if it was going to tear you to pieces? Well, if you face up to it and stand still, looking it in the eye, and are obviously not going to run away or cringe before it, that dog realises that his plan to frighten you into running away off his territory, is not going to work and so he loses confidence and crawls away with his tail between his legs. In a way, people are the same; if someone accuses you of being a child molester and you cringe with fear, standing there trembling, it's almost as if you are admitting guilt and they go away self-righteously, thinking they have done society a favour and will attack you again and again because they think they are right. The next time this happens, and of course, it will, turn round to them and say 'who do you think you are to slander me in public? I am not a child molester and you should come to my trial and it will be proved to you. I am not the first innocent person who has been accused of some crime I would not ever dream of committing but my name will be cleared in court very soon. In the meantime, you can keep your mouth shut or I shall sue you for repeating falsehoods. Really work yourself up into a frenzy and pretend it's one of your past pupils who you are telling off."

"Phillip, that all sounds very easy when you say it like that, but I just don't have that kind of confidence."

"Walter, you have to get off your knees and fight for justice. The only thing the meek will inherit of the earth is the six feet they will be buried in! The other thing is… why would you want to stay inside your house all the time, worrying in case some vigilante comes and paints rude words on your walls? You are not a poor man, you have a nice car and plenty of money to pay for petrol; jump in your car and drive to places like Brighton or Eastbourne or any one of a dozen places, go sightseeing, walk along the sea front or in the countryside, join the National Trust or English Heritage and visit some of England's stately homes. No-one will recognise you there and even if they do, you are perfectly entitled to be there; look them in the eye and wait till their eyes drop. You could do your shopping when you're out, then you won't have to go to the local one. How do you get on with your neighbours? You said that one lady comes and cleans for you. I'll go and call on them on your behalf and come back and tell you what the situation is." Phillip walked over to the next door bungalow and knocked on the door, which was opened by an older lady. Phillip put on his most charming manner and said, "I'm sorry to disturb you, my name is Phillip Everett and I am acting on behalf of Mr Dunn, your next-door neighbour."

"Oh yes," she said.

"Could I just come in for a moment, please?"

"Of course you can," and she led him into their sitting room where an old gentleman was sitting watching cricket on the television.

"Bertie, this is Mr Everett and he wants to talk to us about Walter, next door," and she turned the set off, much to her husband's annoyance.

"What's the score?" said Phillip.

"Hundred and ten for two," he said, somewhat mollified.

"Sit down, sit down, would you like a cup of tea or coffee? I know you younger people like coffee don't you?" she beamed at him.

"That's very kind of you but Walter's already made me some, so thanks, but no thanks. Can I ask you how long you've known Walter?" asked Phillip.

"Oh it must be years and years, ever since we moved in here, now let me see, was it 1978 or it might have been 1979. No, no, I tell a lie, it must have been 1981 because that was the year our Vera had her first one. Vera's our daughter and—"

She would have carried on reminiscing for the rest of the day but Phillip interrupted her smoothly with, "Then you must know by now that he is not the sort of man to commit an offence against a fourteen-year-old girl!"

"Of course not," she said indignantly, "we never believed that for a moment, did we Albert?"

Albert chipped in with, "Walter's been working with teenagers and young children all his working life, he retired without a blemish to his character, so why would he start messing about now?"

"It's all nonsense," said Phillip, "an innocent man caught up in a feud between an evil mother and a poor neglected daughter and after a bit of a hiccup, we've got him remanded on bail; when his case is heard in court, he will be completely exonerated and his name cleared. There's just one thing I'm a bit puzzled about; he seems to think you're avoiding him!"

Albert struggled to his feet and rather red in the face said, "Well, we're not! We were just waiting for him to say something to us, because we didn't want him to feel embarrassed!"

"Tell you what," said Phillip, "I would be really grateful if you could give him a bit of support, he is very lonely and feels miserable!"

"Well, if we'd known that, we'd have been round there like a shot;

poor Walter, he's still getting over his wife dying like that and these yobs painting stuff on the walls, they want to bring back national service, that'd teach 'em something." He was obviously going to launch himself into one of his favourite subjects when Phillip thanked them and murmured that he wondered how the cricket was getting on, and went to the door to let himself out. "You're a very kind young man, Mr Everett," she said, as she walked him to the door. Phillip took her hand and kissed it gallantly, before walking over to the bungalow at the other side of Walter's.

He knocked on the door and after a few moments, a woman answered the door, perhaps aged in her late thirties. "Yes?" she said, slightly aggressively.

"My name is Phillip Everett," he said, "I am a private detective."

"Oh, so you're not a salesman or anything like that?"

Phillip smiled winningly. "You can rest assured I am not selling anything, nor am I a Jehovah's Witness! Might I ask if your husband is in just now?"

"No, he's at work, come inside for a moment."

"I don't think it's appropriate for me to do that but I wanted to ask how long you have known Mr Dunn, your next door neighbour?"

"Known Walter for years, at least fifteen years it must be, why?"

"I am investigating Mr Dunn's case, have you heard about it?"

"Poor old devil, yes, we heard he'd been put inside for trying to have sex with an underage girl but we never believed it for a moment! Walter, chasing a fourteen-year-old, no way! He was still recovering from his wife's death, if you ask me. It was that girl's mother wasn't it? I shouldn't wonder if she wasn't going to try and get some money from him. You know, agree to keep quiet if he gave her a few thousand and him not knowing if he was coming or going." She was preparing to launch into a diatribe against the whole of society and its ills and Phillip only just managed to interrupt with the reason why he had knocked on her door.

"As I said, I am investigating the circumstances of Walter's case and we've now managed to get him out on bail. However, since he has been at home, one or two people have been extremely unpleasant in their ignorance, insulting him, writing graffiti on his wall and one woman even spat in his face. A kind word from his neighbours would help him to weather this unpleasant period before he goes to court for the trial when I, and everyone connected to the case, will find his innocence proved beyond all reasonable doubt. I was wondering if I could ask you to give him a bit of support, because basically he is such a nice man and his son has unfortunately been called back to America to deal with a business crisis!"

She looked at Phillip and said, "I don't suppose you'd like to come in for a drink or something?"

He recognised the warning signs even as he gave the tiny lie, "I'm so sorry, but after I've told Walter of the support he will be getting from his immediate neighbours, I have an appointment in town, with a client. So sorry!"

"Pity, I'd have liked to have a chat with you – about your work of course, good-looking guy like you must get a lot of invitations eh?"

Phillip smiled at her, "Thank you so much for your help, I know I can depend on you," and beat a hasty retreat back to Walter's bungalow. "I won't come in but I've had a word with both your neighbours and they will give you their support. Don't be afraid to talk to them and don't forget to go out to plenty of other places, use your car and time will soon pass to the trial and then it will be all over!"

"Thank you so much Mr Everett, I don't know what I would have done without you!!"

For the next two days, Phillip set out his plan to commence the investigation into the disappearance of Vasily Bukow's daughter. There was so little real information available to work with. She went to a party and spent a lot of time with a good-looking young man, no-one saw them leave, whether separately or together and that was about the sum total of the information provided. When he looked through his post, he found a thick envelope containing various slips of paper with information typed or written on them and he began to meticulously sort the pages into different piles, each pile to be studied later. There was a note from Barry Spencer which said he hoped that he had enclosed as much useful information as they had in their possession and best of luck. If he needed anything else, just ring on this number. Phillip checked with his bank and found that he had been credited with £30,000 and concluded that it was time to "get the show on the road".

He made himself a cup of coffee and began make a start. The police report showed that they had gone through the usual missing person routine, interviewed all the party guests, but no-one knew who the young man was. There was a photofit picture of him, a compilation of various persons' views but although it seemed to be a detailed description, just how accurate was it? It must have been his first and only time on this party-going circuit, no other female, young or old, had spoken to him and no-one knew his name. What had he been doing at that exclusive party, without being invited? Was it simply a case of one of the girls bringing along her boyfriend, her brother; had parents brought an unexpected visitor and wouldn't own up to it or was he just a gate-crasher after a free meal and drinks, but why choose this party on that night? Was he specifically sent to target Bukow's daughter? It began to look as if everything pointed to that. Was he sent as bait; young, charming, had he lured her outside, perhaps for a 'breath of fresh air' or a clandestine kiss? Then when the two of them were out of sight of the other guests, perhaps she was overcome with chloroform and then abducted. There were an awful lot of maybes; the man disappears completely, never to be seen again and again the question, why was she abducted? There has been no ransom demand and if it was not money the kidnappers wanted, was it some kind of revenge on the father? Was he involved in Russian power politics, even though he denied this; perhaps this was intended as some kind of warning and it went wrong, perhaps the girl died and could no longer be used as a hostage? He filled pages of his notebook until his eyelids started to droop and he realised he had done as much as he could for one day.

He slept badly, dreaming unpleasant dreams where he was standing naked with faceless beings dancing around him, attacking his genitalia, and he woke up in a cold sweat with the coming appointment for his AIDS test overhanging him. He realised if he had become infected with the disease, he would have to change his lifestyle completely. No more casual flings like Jasmine or Sarah, he would have to curtail his easy sex life because there was no way he would pass it on to some unsuspecting woman. His tired brain tried to sleep once more. He dreamed there were young females dancing around him singing "dirty, dirty, dropping off, dropping off". Also other females, but this time the faces in the dream were familiar, Samantha, Jasmine, Sarah, and when he tried to embrace them, one by one, they pushed him away and turned their backs, walking into the distance. He woke again at around five o'clock and decided he might just as well do an hour's workout, half an hour running on his treadmill and then various body exercises, until he was sweating profusely and in need of a cold shower. After a light breakfast, he was ready to face any doctor in Harley Street and he arrived for his ten o'clock appointment in good time, trying to eliminate his fears.

The receptionist was a beautifully dressed older woman who was obviously very experienced at putting nervous clients at their ease. "If you could just give me one or two details about your general health, any allergies and so forth – we shall of course destroy the forms immediately after you have collected the results of your test, or perhaps you might like to keep them yourself?" She asked him if it had been sexual intercourse with full penetration, or was it only peripheral. She told him it was very rare to catch any sexually transmitted disease in that way, but it could happen and he obviously wanted to be absolutely sure. "Please go into Room 4 and the technician will do everything necessary for you." Sounds like a high class brothel, thought Phillip, irreverently, but the young lady was very efficient and half an hour later he was back at the reception desk. A discreet raising of one eyebrow by the receptionist and he handed over his money which was all in £50 notes. This was carefully counted and a receipt written out. "The results will be ready for you at three o'clock this afternoon and I shall be here to give you the report," she said. What can I do to fill my time in between now and then, he thought. I know, I'll become a tourist and go on a sightseeing trip because that way, I'll keep my mind occupied and not worry about the test results.

Like many people who live in or near London, he had never visited large numbers of the well-known tourist attractions so he tried to make up for it in a few hours! He went around parts of the British Museum, there was too much to take in; then took a look at St Paul's Cathedral, had a sandwich and finally caught an open-topped bus with a smart attractive girl giving a commentary on the various buildings they passed. That kept his mind fully occupied until with fast-beating heart, he approached the Harley Street clinic and went in to await his fate. There was the same quiet atmosphere, the same elegant receptionist, and on her desk reposed a plain, white, A4 envelope. "Here you are sir, I hope this is what you wanted?" and she slid the envelope over to him. He turned his back to her and with a shaking hand pulled out the sheet of paper, trying to focus on the typed details which gradually became clearer – *Male person, the results of all tests undertaken have proved negative. This person is clear of any infection or harmful viruses. Blood sample shows normal, healthy specimen, no treatment is required.*

Phillip turned around to face the receptionist who was calmly sitting behind her desk, his smile showing his happiness. "It's good, it's good, thank you very much," and he walked out into the street, ready to celebrate. He returned to his office, planning the celebrations he was going to have that night but felt restless, unable to settle down to work so he got in the car, in high good humour and drove aimlessly south until he came to Sevenoaks and treated himself to a large ice cream, something he hadn't done for years, and drove back.

He met Gordon with the usual greeting, "How is my favourite Highlander?"

"You're in a good mood tonight!"

"I've just got a new case and they've put £30,000 into my account already!"

"What on earth are you going to investigate – whether Hitler is still alive?"

"If he was, he'd be over a hundred and ten years old by now, so we can safely say he's dead! No this money is to investigate the disappearance of someone's daughter and more than that I can't tell you!"

"What about the police?"

"They have done all the usual detective work but turned up no evidence of her whereabouts. That's where I come in – now it's up to me!"

"You big-headed English twit, how are you going to find her when the police, with all their resources could not?"

"Because I'm better than them, so there, see!! Come on, I'll take you out for a meal, before we meet the girls."

"That will be a first," said Gordon. "No expense spared?"

"Now you must remember, dear Gordon, that you are the rich banker and I am the poor, hard-working… er… working man that is, so it will have to be chicken and chips at the nearest takeaway!"

"Empty promises," jeered Gordon. "I knew there had to be a catch in it somewhere, you should have been a politician, not some down at heel private dick!"

They finished up in a small Italian bistro, enjoyed a huge meal of pasta, garlic bread, a bottle of red wine, ending with the guilty pleasures of tiramisu in delicate crystal glasses. After a couple of espressos, they were ready to meet the girls but when they arrived at their usual haunt, there was no sign of them. "Perhaps they're not coming?" said Phillip.

"They are," said Gordon, definitely. "I spoke to Isobel on my mobile and she said they were just about to leave work."

"What time was that?"

"About ten minutes before you turned up," said Gordon. Phillip kept his thoughts to himself but he wondered if this might be the end of their casual relationship; perhaps the girls had found other, more eligible quarry who might perhaps be interested in permanent relationships, rather than the casual sex they had been enjoying; instead he told Gordon to try Isobel's phone again but there was only a recorded message saying the she was unable to answer at the moment, please try later.

Gordon was getting worried. His relationship with Isobel was progressing in what he thought was the right direction. Once he had persuaded her into bed, he found she was a willing partner, though not as experienced as he thought Jasmine might be with Phillip. He had been toying with the idea of asking her to move in with him, but was not sure how this would affect his friendship with Phillip; it all needed a serious amount of thought, a big step to take, etc, etc. There was still no sign of Isobel or Jasmine, nor was there any message; Phillip thought hey ho, this is where it ends but I'm not going to sit here, biting my fingernails, so he went to get some more drinks. He looked along the bar and spotted two young women; his mind went into the usual male overdrive, check them, young, attractive, well-dressed, well-shaped with curves in all the right places. He moved along the bar until he was standing next to one of them. "You don't mind if I stand next to you, do you?" he said politely.

They both looked at him in amazement and the one furthest away from him said in a clear voice, "You may think you're irresistible, but forget it, we don't sleep around!"

"Wow, that was quick," said Phillip, "but sleep was the last thing on my mind, I get enough of that at home."

She continued as if he had not spoken, "I'm telling you this so you don't waste your time, thinking you are going to get one of us into bed tonight."

"Actually, I was hoping to get both of you, you know, a threesome, but one of you will be quite acceptable!" he said, enjoying the look of complete fury which came over her face as she took in what he had just said.

"If that's your chat-up line," said the girl standing next to him, "it's the worst one I've ever heard."

"No!! Don't say that," said Phillip. "How about something else, I have several chat-up lines, one for every occasion."

"I have to tell you it's not working: try harder, OK!"

"My name is Phillip Everett and I'm with that hunky fellow over there and he's called 'Gordon'. We are both very interesting young men, Gordon is a banker and I am a private investigator."

"Are you trying to tell me you are a private detective, go on, pull the other leg, it's got bells on!!"

"I can assure you." He was laughing so much at the amazed expressions on the girls' faces. "Really, honestly, I am, we are, he's a banker and I'm a—"

"If you ask me, you're a complete idiot," but they were both laughing with him.

"It might make it easier for us to communicate if you tell me your names?"

They looked at each other. "Shall we?" said one; "Why not?" said the other.

"I'm Chris, short for Christina."

"And my name is Joan, like Joan of Arc," chimed in the other girl.

"That's a bad choice," he said lightly, "you know what happened to her!"

"Well. it isn't going to happen to me, but you haven't answered my question, are you really a private detective?"

"Yes, I have to confess, that is my profession."

Chris said scornfully, "I thought they died out after the war, or was it during the war?"

"No, there are still some of our elite service aiding the public in their difficulties and here I am, living proof of that dying breed," said Phillip, theatrically, hand on heart. "So what have you got against men?" he asked her.

"You mean those low creatures whose minds can only concentrate on having sex and with as many females as possible?" said Chris.

"There are a few immature specimens like that," said Phillip, "but you two must have been very unlucky to meet them all at once. Most men are like me and my friend Gordon over there, nice, polite, well behaved, who never do anything that we are not encouraged to do."

"And then when you've had enough sex and get bored, you leave," said Joan.

"Statistics *prove* that more men get ditched by women than the other way about!"

"And if you believe that, you'll believe anything!"

"Now surely, you two lovely ladies would have no difficulty holding on to your men?" said Phillip, winningly.

"Watch him Joan," said Chris, "he's switching his chat-up line to flattery!"

At that point, he felt a hand on his shoulder and Gordon's voice saying the girls had just arrived. They were waving at him from the table he and Gordon had been sharing, so he turned back to the server and asked for two glasses of red wine to be added to his order.

"Those two are your girlfriends, are they, and you were just chatting us up until they came?"

"I was just keeping you two ladies entertained while I was waiting to be served."

"Oh yeah, and I suppose if we'd agreed to a threesome you'd have come out with 'No I don't do that sort of thing'."

"Well, I suppose we'll never find that out now, will we?" Phillip said to Joan.

"That's another one to add to our collection, Chris. We get to find them everywhere, no matter where we go!" she said.

"At least I can offer you a drink," said Phillip, "to try to make up for me being a man! What will you have?"

"Vodka martini," said Chris,

"Bacardi and coke," said Joan and Phillip picked up his drinks to take to the table.

Gordon was asking Isobel and Jasmine what had happened to them, and Isobel told them the sad story, all too often repeated. A man had jumped under their train and they had been held up while the police were called, evidence and photographs were taken and the body removed. The most annoying thing was that she had forgotten to recharge the battery of her mobile phone and they had sat on the train, completely unable to reach Gordon until they had arrived at their station, by which time it was quicker to get to the wine bar than make more delays by queuing to get to a phone. They finished their drinks and the girls suggested going back to the flat; it had been a sad and frustrating evening. On the way out, Joan and Chris raised their glasses in salute to Phillip and he gave them a cheerful wave. Back at Gordon's flat they had a final drink and retired to bed, Isobel and Gordon to his comfortable room and Jasmine and Phillip to the twin-bedded smaller bedroom. Phillip was pleased that the sad events of the evening had not dampened Jasmine's appetite for love and her body was just as receptive and eager for his passion as he was to make her feel satisfied. He wondered if Isobel had been as eager as her friend!

Chapter 11

He returned home on Saturday morning, checking his phone to see if there were any messages from Sarah, but there were none. I guess this confirms it, he thought, it's the end of the brief relationship we had. He settled back into the usual routine he followed when he was on his own, and Monday morning he rang Walter Dunn shortly after nine o'clock. "Walter, Phillip Everett here, just checking to make sure you are okay, how are things going?"

"I took your advice Mr Everett and started going out in my car; both neighbours have been to see me and we are all on good terms again and I am getting around much more. I feel so much better, now I have something to interest me, no-one has said anything rude to me and I have even got the odd smile from people, if I have said good morning or something like that!"

"That is really good to know Walter; have you had any contact with either Doris or Betsy?"

"Certainly not, Mr Everett, I don't want to go back to prison again."

"That's very good to hear," Phillip said. "I feel sure we are going to clear you at the trial. Until the court case, act normally and try not to worry too much." They said goodbye to each other and Phillip put the phone down.

Now, he reasoned, let's make a start on Mr Bukow's case. He opened the box file which he kept locked in his safe, and set out in order the varying pieces of information he had been given. The most important task was to find the young man who had last been seen with her – what was her name again? – he turned over one of the folders and saw it contained a photograph of her. Written on the back were the words 'Katia Bukow, seventeen years of age'. She was a pretty girl, dark hair, blue eyes, oval face, and judging by the photo which was a view of her from the waistline up, quite curvaceous, but not fat. He wondered how tall she was.

He decided to start by locating the unknown man and began checking the Internet for anything concerning Russian society in the London area. There were at least three Russian nightclubs, or perhaps judging from the advertising pictures, more restaurant, disco/dance hall, a large bar with plenty of tables and chairs where you could meet friends might be nearer the mark. Everything appeared to be as completely Russian as it was possible to get in South London, Russian price lists in the bars, Russian menus in the restaurants, Russian pictures of scenes from the mother country, everything for the homesick Russian, be he immigrant or a member of the Russian mafia! Each one obviously catered only for the Russian clientele, opened at ten pm until three in the morning, and other nationalities were probably not welcome. This was going to mean some long hours of night work, so he would spend the daylight hours checking the routes he should follow and taking it easy.

He arrived at the first club just after ten o'clock and after walking past the entrance a couple of times, noting a large man with a bulge in his pocket which looked suspiciously like a firearm, he attempted to enter the doorway, only to be firmly repulsed. "Do you speak English?" queried Phillip.

"No English, what do you want?"

"I wish to speak to someone here."

"Who, they Russian?"

"Yes," said Phillip.

"What they called?"

Phillip was getting annoyed so he took out his official-looking card and said in his most imperious manner, "I wish to speak to the manager of this club."

The Hulk on the door looked puzzled and a little uneasy but spoke into his mobile in rapid Russian, and finally said to Phillip, "You wait here, he come."

He only had to wait a few minutes before a sleek, middle-aged man appeared, dressed in an impeccable suit, complete with expensive gold cuff links and a gold ring on his left hand, who asked in perfect, well-modulated English, "May I ask who you are and what is your name?" he said, very politely.

"My name is Phillip Everett" – he showed him his card – "and I am a private detective. I am making some enquiries about a missing person. Who exactly are you?"

The answer came back smoothly, "I am Ivan Chernenko and I manage this club."

"Well Ivan, I need to come in and have a look around." Ivan hesitated. "Of course," said Phillip conversationally, "I could come back with a dozen police officers and start checking all your various licences, whether your guests have genuine passports and if any if the young ladies working here are all over the age of sixteen. Perhaps your 'guests' would not be quite so happy to visit your premises again in the near future, if that happened?"

"I am giving you permission to enter the club but please be discreet, people come here for a quiet meal or a few drinks and I would not like to upset them, you understand?"

"Both you and your clientele have nothing to worry about, you can rest assured I will not harass anyone." The Hulk stood aside and allowed Phillip to enter, followed by his boss and once inside, Phillip asked Ivan if he had ever seen the young man in the photofit picture.

Ivan studied the picture carefully before asking, "Is this a good likeness?"

"Yes, it has been compiled by several persons who saw him close enough to make an accurate description."

"No, I'm sorry, I have not seen this man in the club."

"What about your doorman, he must have to make a close inspection of people who visit here, particularly the ones he has not seen previously?"

"I will show him the picture."

"Would you mind asking him in English if he has seen this man, I want to see his reaction," Phillip said.

Ivan shrugged and went to the door; he asked carefully in English, "Our private detective here wants to know if you have ever seen this man," and he waved the picture in front of him. Phillip watched the Hulk who looked carefully but showed no reaction to the picture and shook his head, "No, I never seen him," so he was either a very good actor or was telling the truth.

"Do you still want to go inside?" said Ivan, hoping the answer would be no.

"Yes," said Phillip. "I promise I'll be very discreet and just act like any one of your guests."

"Very well," Ivan said, and ushered him back through the door. It proved to be very quiet in the bar, lounge and restaurant and although he showed the photofit to the barman, and a couple of men at the bar, nobody recognised the man. "Do you sell beer?" asked Phillip.

"Yes," said the barman, "but only Russian beer!"

"Okay," Phillip said. "I'll have a glass of it."

"Large or small?"

"Large." The barman filled a glass with beer and Phillip handed over a £10 note. "How much is there in this glass?" he asked.

"You ask for a large glass, large glass has one litre of beer in it!"

He thought to himself, that's over two pints and it's strong, very strong, if I'd asked him for a very large drink, do you think he would have served it to me in a bucket? Suddenly, he found that very funny. He found a seat in an area where he could watch, without appearing to do so, all the people who visited the club that night, but by twelve o'clock, he concluded that he was not going to find out very much, finished his beer and left to drive home.

He woke at noon, made himself a large pot of coffee and started to go through his notes. Where else would Russian people go – always assuming that the suspect young man was Russian – shopping? – unlikely, Russian Orthodox church – he might go there but if he didn't, other worshippers might know him. He found out the times of the services at the Russian Orthodox church, the main one being on Sunday at ten o'clock, so he made a number of copies of the photofit and using the Russian language software on his computer, made a note on top of the photo saying, 'I am a detective, searching for this man who has abducted a seventeen-year-old Russian girl. If you have seen him, please ring this number.' Next Sunday he would go along and stand outside the church and when people come out after the service, he would ask them to take a copy; that might possibly have some results.

In the evening, he went to the same night club again and the Hulk at the entrance said "You here again," somewhat ungraciously. "Go in, my boss wants to see you." He was waiting just inside the door and he said quietly, "Mr Everett, if I might have a word? Are you here to sit and watch people like you did last night? If I could suggest something, might it be possible for you to leave your phone number and a copy of your photograph and I will show it to everyone who comes, and that will eliminate the need for you to sit there, eyeing every person who comes into the place! People have been complaining and you will be affecting business if you carry on doing so. I promise to ring you if there are any results."

"That's very reasonable," said Phillip. "Quite a good idea in fact, but seeing as I'm here now, I'll stay for this evening but I won't come here again, will that do?"

"Mr Everett, do you not trust me? If we were protecting this man the doorman would warn him as he approached the entrance and you would not see him anyway!"

"Point taken," said Phillip. "Here's a copy of the photo," and he wrote his mobile number on the back.

Resigned to this small victory, the manager said, "As you seem quite determined to stay, I shall get Tania to sit with you; that way you will not stand out so noticeably and please, do not stare at any of my customers!"

"Alright, if that helps you, wheel her in," he said and went to the bar for a large glass of Russian beer. He chose the same table and planned to make his beer last for the rest of the evening and then looked around to see who 'Tania' might be. A young woman came through the entrance and walked towards him; Phillip thought, oh no, I couldn't be that lucky! She was fairly tall, maybe five feet nine, fair hair slightly curling, shoulder length, quite slim but, as the Americans would say, 'stacked in the right places'! She was dressed like a teenager, with a short skirt and skin-tight top, fashionable platform shoes with ankle straps which showed off her legs to the best advantage, and a large shoulder bag. There he was, thinking he would have to spend another boring evening, sipping beer and trying not to look as if he was inspecting every customer when she walked towards Phillip, saying in faintly accented English, "Mr Everett?"

"You speak beautiful English!"

"But I have only spoken two words."

Phillip said firmly, "Yes, but they were spoken beautifully."

"Thank you Mr Everett, my name is Tania and I have come to keep you company, that is, if you are Mr Everett?"

He stood up, floundering in a morass of half-sentences. "Indeed, that is me, I am it, please call me Phillip."

"Thank you, that is a very nice name, perhaps it is from one of the Mediterranean countries, French or Italian?" she asked, seating herself opposite him at the table.

"Oh no, nothing like that, I'm just a plain old Londoner."

Tania frowned slightly. "But you are not old!"

"No, not really, it's an expression we use in England; English is a funny language, it must be quite difficult to learn, when you're not born here."

Tania laughed and said, "It is even harder to speak it, there are so many things you have to know about pronunciation that… but I must not go on. You interrupted me and I have to tell you that there will be no hanky-panky!"

Phillip nearly fell off his seat, trying not to laugh at her serious face, wondering what his reply should be to that! She continued, "The big guy on the door, he is my cousin and you would not want me to tell you what he does to men who are twice your size, if they try anything with me."

"Your English is very good – hanky-panky – well I'm not normally afraid of men but I never try to force myself on any young woman. The 'hanky-panky' only happens when both partners are willing participants!"

"That is very nice to hear," said Tania.

He said, "I have told the manager that I shall not be coming here again so you will not have to put up with me after tonight." Tania said nothing. "How old are you, Tania?" Phillip asked.

"I am nineteen."

"Barely out of nappies!"

"Why, how old are you?"

"Twenty-nine," he said.

"That is not a big difference. In Russia it is quite normal for a man to be older than the woman he marries."

"In England, there are no set rules about people's ages. Either sex can be older and in fact, most people do not marry, they just live together," he said.

"Is that good?" asked Tania.

"As long as they don't have any children, it's not so bad, but if they decide to start a family, then they should get married before they are born and try and stick together to form a stable relationship for their kids; that's the least they can do, seeing as the kids didn't ask to be brought into this world."

"I think I agree with you," said Tania.

"I have been very rude," said Phillip, "not asking you what you would like to drink?"

"Thank you, I would like a glass of white wine."

"Any particular kind?"

She laughed. "Just ask the barman, he will give you the kind of wine I like."

"I suppose he's another of your relatives!"

The barman produced a large glass of white wine and Phillip paid and carried it back to the table. Putting the glass in front of her, he said, "The barman assures me that this is your favourite wine!"

"There is not much choice in here, Russian people are not known for much wine drinking."

"Their favourite tipple is vodka, isn't it?" said Phillip.

"Yes, I think it's something to do with the climate. Me, I do not like to drink too much alcohol!"

"Alcohol can do a lot of damage to the human body, physically and mentally, if drunk to excess over a period of time." Listen to me, thought Phillip, I sound like some TV pundit, talking like this to a young, good-looking, girl. I must be nuts. "Tell me something about yourself Tania," he said, leaning towards her, sipping his beer.

"What would you like to know?" she countered.

"Where were you born?"

"I was born in Moscow hospital, my parents were some kind of party officials so we were a bit better off than a lot of people. We lived in a better part of Moscow, nicer apartment, a bit bigger than others, I went to better schools. Then after the change of the party system to the so-called democratic government, my parents started to invest their money in power and oil. As oil, gas, electricity were privatised, they became owners of lots of shares in those companies. Then the crime in Moscow got really bad so all our family came to United Kingdom, mostly London but also Manchester and Edinburgh so there are many brothers, uncles, aunties, cousins etc, we are a large family. Everybody is working but my parents decided to be in London and started this club for homesick Russians. We try to keep everything like it was before they came here." She gave a delighted chuckle. "Everybody spends a lot of money, remembering where they came from but they wouldn't go back for anything. Russians are very sentimental." She smiled at him.

"Do you have any brothers or sisters?"

"Yes, one of each but I am the only one living with my parents. They are both older than me – should that be 'older than I' to be correct English? My brother Alexander is twenty-seven, married with two children and he works in City of London, my sister Helenka is twenty-five and works in same office as Alexander, I think they look after financial interests of Russian business people. What about you Phillip?"

It was the first time she had called him by his Christian name and Phillip felt absurdly pleased. Although her English was good, she still spoke with an Eastern European accent which he found charming; he found everything about her to be delightful but, hold on a moment, he told himself, she was completely out of his class, not to mention a ten year age gap. He told her briefly about his work in the City, how he met Samantha at university and they had been together for eight years. When he told Tania how she had walked out on him, she found it difficult to believe.

"You are tall, nice looking, clever man, why would she do that?" Phillip tried to explain that he no longer had a glamorous, well paid job, no longer had a large apartment, a flashy car or could go to the most expensive restaurants with rich friends, all that was lost in a very short time with only the possibility of ever recovering financially, sometime in the future. She just could not accept the change in her lifestyle. Tania put her hand on his and said softly, "Did your heart break?"

"It's always difficult when a relationship breaks down but I'm beginning to think it might have been for the best, I've just got to get on with building up my new life and career."

"What is it you do now?"

"At the moment, I am sitting opposite a beautiful young Russian lady who is holding my hand in the most comforting way!" said Phillip, flirtatiously.

Tania blushed and pulled her hand away. "I'm very sorry."

"Please don't apologise, you have a lovely touch but as much as I am enjoying your sympathy, I have to go now." He got up from the table and said, "Thank you very much for making what was going to be a very dull evening into a very pleasant one."

"Do you really have to go now?"

He picked up her hand and gallantly kissed her fingertips. "I am afraid so, please give your family my regards." And with that, Phillip turned and walked out of the club.

Chapter 12

The next morning found him hard at work at his desk. He rang John Standish and said cheerfully, "Good morning to you, John."

There was a groan from the other end of the telephone and John said in a long-suffering voice, "You're not going to harass me, I hope, I'm having a bad day!"

"It's only just after ten o'clock John, how can you be having a bad day?"

"Well, I am! What is it you want?"

"I was only going to ask you if you'd heard any more about Walter Dunn's trial date?"

"Nothing so far but I did speak to Walter a couple of days ago and he seemed to be quite happy, not at all worried about the date so I don't think there is any particular hurry."

"I sent you my notes of the interview I had with Betsy and the behaviour of her mother, but I am wondering if there is anything more I should be doing, in the meantime?"

"Once the date is set, we can arrange a meeting and discuss our strategy but at this point I cannot think what else could be done that would not have to be repeated later," said John.

"Okay, John, we'll leave it at that, goodbye, talk to you later," and Phillip put the receiver down.

Phillip pulled out his large map of the London area and marked out his second port of call, the next Russian club, which he would visit tonight, and spent what was left of the rest of the morning, trying to obtain information on the Net. He made a large sandwich for lunch and answered the phone when it rang, thinking it might be John. It turned out to be Gordon. "How are you, my old and treasured friend!" in Gordon's best attempt at a Scottish accent.

"I've no money," said Phillip.

"Did I say anything about money, did I mention finance, did I, did I? Anyway, you never have any money! I am forwarding you an email about a lecture which I have to attend, about – wait for it – 'Modern Society and Its Moral Standards'. Actually there are three two-hour lectures but I'm hoping after showing my face at the first one, I won't be missed at the other two but what I was thinking," he said persuasively, "is that the first date is next Friday so I thought if you were to attend the first lecture with me, it's going to be a bit of a laugh, then we can go on our usual Friday night out! How about it, my old pal, do poor old Gordon a favour!!"

"I'll think about it after I've seen the email. Let you know as soon as!"

Phillip downloaded the email and read the contents. Leaving aside the superfluous details and concentrating on the main subject matter, he thought it might be quite a good idea to attend as in his present job, it was important to know as much as possible about people and current trends in their behaviour. He emailed Gordon to say he would meet him outside the lecture hall at the appointed time for the first lecture and then they could go for their usual Friday drinks.

That evening, he arrived at night club number two at half past ten. The atmosphere was completely different, the surroundings were more de luxe and when he showed his card to the doorman (a medium-sized man, not a Hulk!) he was told he was welcome to go in, they liked British people! Phillip asked him to look at the photofit which he studied carefully, only to shake his head and say he had never seen him. Phillip said thanks and went inside. The place appeared to be smaller, there was no restaurant but part of the bar was set out as a counter for serving food and presumably the kitchen was at the back of this area. In the centre of the room, there was a square of parquet tiles, space for dancing, and in the far corner, a trio of players were starting to play Russian music on a minute triangular platform, perhaps fifty centimetres high. The rest of the floor was taken up with tables and chairs, of which a small number were already occupied.

Phillip made his way over to the bar and said to the man behind it, "Do you speak English?"

"Niet," but he pointed to a woman standing next to him. She said, "I speak a little English."

Phillip showed her the photo and his private detective licence card and said, "As you can see, I am Phillip Everett, I'm a detective and I'm looking for this man. He is wanted for abducting a seventeen-year-old girl and perhaps for her death."

The woman looked a little puzzled. "What is abducting?" she asked.

"Do you understand 'kidnap'?" The woman nodded. "Have you or your friend ever seen this man?"

The woman showed the barman the photo and they took a close look, speaking in Russian, then she said, "He and me no see this man."

"Thank you," said Phillip. He ordered a large beer and found a table, not too near the enthusiastic musicians, and considered his position. More people were slowly filtering in, most of them seemed to know at least one other person there so he thought he would wait until the place filled up a bit more then go around discreetly, showing the photofit and asking if anybody had seen him, but first, he asked the woman behind the bar to write in Russian, "Have you seen this man?" on the front of the photo. He thanked her and gave her a tip for helping him. Not that it helped in any way because none of the people he spoke to had seen the man, and he returned home after a fruitless evening.

Friday afternoon came and Phillip met Gordon outside the lecture hall, which was full; Gordon said cynically, "Either they're like me and have been forced to come or there are going to be free refreshments!"

At this point a man walked onto the stage to a round of applause. "There will be three lectures on 'Society and Its Current Moral Values' – or possibly, lack of them," he joked, "and this afternoon I will be talking about the changes and influences which brought about the state that society has reached at this present day. To do this, we need to go back to the end of World War II. The generation that grew up in the early Fifties had to live through the reconstruction of the country after the damage done during the war. They had to work very hard for very low wages but they were convinced they were doing it for their children so that they could inherit a better world to live in.

"In the sixties, society's attitude to sex and drugs was more relaxed. Parents felt that after the restrictions they had to put up with, allowing children more freedom of behaviour should be tolerated, but the human being, given the choice, tends to take the easy way out. It's more difficult to abstain from sex before marriage, drink less alcohol and control your emotions when everybody around you follows the same protocols, but it's far easier to drink more alcohol, have sex whenever you want to, behave without constraint, i.e. commit crimes, if all around you, people laugh at law enforcement and parents perhaps turn away from condemning their children's morals as they know they might be to blame. The seventies produced another generation of parents – single parent families, who started to appear in much larger numbers throughout the country. The boundaries of moral behaviour were pushed even further back and parallel with this, came economic changes which had a profound effect on everyday lives. In the sixties and seventies, all children below the age of sixteen were in full time education; when they reached sixteen they would either continue in higher education or, in the case of boys, take up an apprenticeship, while girls might obtain work possibly in factories, offices or various other jobs, perhaps learning shorthand typing or bookkeeping at evening classes. Unemployment at that time was very low. The majority of teenagers lived at home.

"From the seventies onwards big changes started to take place. Automation started to be used and with the introduction of modern machinery, many companies were able to increase mechanical efficiency, which led to them shedding workers. The worst affected were the young people, both girls and boys, but girls were in a worse position than boys because the girls who worked in factories had fewer avenues of re-employment available to them. Many were unemployed and with no purpose in life, nowhere to go, sex became a substitute for going out and having fun. This seemed to be more prevalent within the lower paid classes and with the number of single mothers increasing rapidly, where the child's father was unable or unwilling to support them, it became government policy to pay them benefit money and allocate a council flat for their use, in the vain hope that at some time in the future the mothers would commence paid employment. This appears to have become the norm; a vicious circle in which with no chance of obtaining employment, if you became pregnant, you could obtain money and a flat and a certain amount of independence from parents, would-be employers or boyfriends. If it could not be proved that they were 'co-habiting' with a partner, two people on benefit payments could live together and use their money in any way they wished.

"Unfortunately, this had an unforeseen 'knock on effect'; as the number of young mothers grew, in some cases they had numerous children with different fathers, which led to instability in home life and as these children grew to sexual maturity, the boys tended to impregnate local girls, not all of them of course and many of the girls followed in their mother's footsteps, in turn becoming pregnant at a very early age and repeating the whole cycle once more – living on benefits and provided with council accommodation. Some years back, the fourth generation of a single mother's family was interviewed for a TV programme because the young boy was caught stealing. The single mother of the boy was asked by the reporter live, on TV, how she felt about her son stealing. Her reply was, 'He's a good boy really, he only steals cigarettes for me.'

"'No,' she said, when asked, she did not feel any shame.

"The early eighties suffered an economic recession, with soaring unemployment and crime rates, house burglary in particular had a massive increase. Newspapers had photographs of the most burgled street in the country, tables of most likely areas to be burgled appeared in the media of where the most house breaking incidents had taken place, it was advisable to ask someone to 'babysit' your house if you wanted to go out for an evening at the theatre or cinema or even round the corner for a visit to friends or a quiet drink. There were areas in the North East where burglars were so brazen they would knock on a house door, in broad daylight, and if there was no answer, they would open the door by some means (kicking was quite popular), enter the premises and take small portable articles such as money, jewellery etc. The main public reaction was a careless 'well, it's all insured isn't it? The insurance company pays up so there's no real harm done'. Stolen property was quickly sold in pubs and clubs and nobody seemed to be aware of any wrongdoing, no matter how cheap an item was, and would sometimes boast that they had picked up an item 'dirt cheap'. The Home Office let the police know that only habitual burglars were to be arrested so the first time a burglar was caught, he would get a lecture, the second time a warning, the third time a caution, and only on the fourth occurrence would he be arrested and charged. With moral standards disappearing and weak law enforcement, there was little to control the way people behaved. Next time, I will talk about various institutions which were in place to show us how we should behave, for instance, the Church. Thank you all for listening."

There was a round of lukewarm applause.

"Come on," said Gordon, "let's go and eat. What did you think of his lecture?"

"Quite interesting," Phillip said. "I was possibly too young to remember most of what he referred to but it's all useful information and will no doubt come in helpful at some time. Where are we going to eat, it's your shout!"

"That steak bar, the one we went to a while ago. I like my bit of fillet."

"You shouldn't be eating so much red meat," said Phillip virtuously, "won't do your arteries any good!"

"What," said Gordon, "are you trying to put poor Scottish farmers out of business, you vegetarian English peasant!"

"I'm not a vegetarian," protested Phillip. "Lead on MacDuff, where you go, I shall follow."

In the end, he enjoyed his steak as much as Gordon, he just liked to get Gordon to rise to the familiar bait. Afterwards, they met Isobel and Jasmine at the wine bar and after a few drinks, it was back to Gordon's comfortable flat. By now, they had settled down to a usual routine, a last drink, perhaps a few kisses with their girls and then bed, Gordon and Isobel to his room, Jasmine and Phillip to the second bedroom. However, Gordon showed them a bottle of Scotch whisky which had been a present from a friend. He displayed it as if it were the Holy Grail and said reverently, "Forty years old, single malt and I am now going to open it and we can drink to our continued good health."

Jasmine looked a little puzzled, not knowing anything about the myths and stories about whisky, and said, "If it's forty years old, won't it have gone off by now, what is its sell-by date?"

The two men howled with laughter at Jasmine's hurt face when she said, "What's so funny?"

"My dear Jasmine," said Gordon, "the older it is the better it gets!"

"Well I'm not drinking any of it," said Jasmine.

"Nor me," said Isobel, wrinkling her nose. "I don't like strong alcohol very much."

"So it's just you and me," said Phillip and they proceeded to become very mellow after the second tumblerful.

"I'm surprised you can still stand up after guzzling that much prime Scottish whisky," said Gordon.

"Listen, you highland jessie, anything a hairy Scotsman can do, an English gentleman can do twice as good," replied Phillip emphatically.

"Oh yeah, then prove it!!" Gordon said and started to strip down to his underwear. "Let's see how good you are at the Highland game of wrestling."

"Okay," said Phillip, "if it's a lesson in wrestling you want, this Englishman's going to show you how it's done," and he thumped his chest and tried to look menacing.

"This must be what men do when they become drunk," said Jasmine to Isobel, "they start acting like little boys."

The two men wrestled each other to the floor and rolled about, first Gordon on top of Phillip, then Phillip getting the upper hand and pinning Gordon beneath him. He crowed, "I've got you now, do you surrender?"

Phillip felt two soft hands on his shoulders; it was Isobel holding him back saying, "Get off him, you big oaf!" He let go immediately and Gordon tried to reassure Isobel that they were good friends and it was just a friendly game, "acting the fool", their mothers would have said, when they were young. Isobel had to be calmed down, she had felt real anger at what she thought had been an attack by his best friend. Women, thought Phillip, they'll never understand what this man to man relationship is all about. Isobel was not to be comforted by their reassurances and told them she didn't like it and hoped they would not act in this juvenile way again! "Shush, shush," said Gordon, and cradled Isobel in his arms, winking at Phillip and saying, "I think I'm ready for bed now, I'm a bit tired. What about you two?"

The following morning, everything was back to normal, everyone happy and choosing a place to go for breakfast. The two men let the girls go ahead and Phillip told Gordon that he thought Isobel was in love with him, so he should consider his next move accordingly, it would be a shame to hurt her. Gordon sighed and said, "I'm in love with her and there's no way I would do anything to hurt her. I'm a very lucky bloke to have a lovely woman like that who feels the same way as I do and we've talked about getting married. Both girls are Roman Catholics and both of them come from deeply religious families. As it happens, I was baptised RC, my parents happened to think it was the right thing to do, although I can't say I've ever been to church much. Why do you think I support Celtic? Anyway, you'll be getting your invitation eventually and of course, I shall want you to be my best man, but in the meantime, what about you? It's about time some female pinned you down and made an honest man of you! I suggested spending a little time living together, before the wedding, but Isobel wouldn't hear of it so it's down the aisle for me. Oh, and there's something else I have to tell you, Jasmine is engaged to be married to one of her countrymen. You knew they came over here to work at the bank from their home in Portugal, didn't you?"

Gordon could tell from the look on Phillip's face that this was a complete bombshell and wondered if they had ever talked about anything during their sexual romping – evidently not – and now he said, "You haven't fallen in love with her have you?"

"No, no I haven't but I have to say I'm very surprised, there was never the slightest hint that she might be, well, seeing someone else. Here I am, making love from the very first night we met, to a sexy, attractive woman – she actually sneaked out of her bedroom and came on to me on the sofa that first time they stayed here, and even last night, there was no lessening of the passion between us, I can't quite take it in."

Gordon outlined the story Isobel had told him. The engagement had taken place before both girls had come to England and was a long standing agreement between the two families. Jasmine was to further her career in banking and Mario was working at the family business to build up his finances and provide a home for Jasmine and the family they hoped to have. Gordon hesitated. "You're not going to cause a scene are you?"

"Of course not, why would I do that? I'm just amazed that she could jump into bed with me – and believe me, she is one sexy lady – when she has a fiancé waiting for her to come back and get married. I could easily have fallen for her but now I feel guilty and I've got to call off this relationship. I feel a bit sorry for this Mario, do you think he knows anything of this?"

"Don't be such a righteous ass," said Gordon, "you can't undo what's been done, after all, don't tell me you wouldn't have laid a finger on her if you had known she was spoken for? Just let things run their course, she is her own person and if she wants to have a little fling before she settles down to marriage and children, well that's her decision isn't it. Women can do that sort of thing nowadays, you know, emancipation, giving them the vote, the pill, condoms etc, just give in gracefully and accept the situation!!" They ate breakfast without noticing that Phillip was rather quiet, and he left at the usual time and travelled home trying to decide what was the best action he could take.

On Sunday morning he loaded the sign attached to a sturdy plank of wood and headed for the Russian Orthodox church, parking outside the main entrance. He waited until the imposing doors were opened and getting out of the car, he stood with the sign prominently displayed where all who exited the church could not help but see it. It caused surprise and many comments, which Phillip guessed to be on the subject of "have you seen this picture, the man has kidnapped a young girl" etc, but none of the worshippers said anything to him directly and Phillip felt very frustrated and disappointed. Still, that was what being a private investigator was all about, he thought, endless time-consuming searching for information and then, with any luck, a good result. He would have to consider whether it would be productive to come here another Sunday, in case anyone had not been attending the service.

Monday came and Phillip decided he would visit his third and last Russian night club and then, if nothing came from that, he would have so speak to some of the police officers involved in the case and pick their brains as to what were their conclusions. Did they think she was dead – if so someone went to a lot of trouble kidnapping her only to end up killing her. They could just have hired a hitman who would have had plenty of opportunities to shoot her. If she went willingly, where had she been all this time and how had she managed to live; her credit cards had not been used. She was a rich little girl, she would be used to all the luxuries in life, could she have been withdrawing money in some other way? But the police would have been aware of that. Phillip rang Barry Spencer, Bukow's PR, and asked him if he knew how his employer's daughter had managed her finances. The reply was, "A monthly allowance was paid into her account, she had a cheque book and a credit card with a limit of £2,000."

"Did she have any of these with her when she disappeared?"

"No, her evening bag was discovered behind a cushion in the main room where the party was being held and the credit card was still in it; the cheque book was found later in a drawer in her bedroom when it was searched after they realised that she was missing. Anything else I can help you with?"

"Yes, actually there is – when you were in contact with the police working on the case, did you ever go with them to a pub they tended to frequent, say after work was finished?"

"It was a place called the Black Horse not very far from the local police station, do you know it?"

"Yes, thanks I'll be able to find it if I need to," Phillip said.

"May I ask how you are getting on?" asked Barry.

"Sure, at this point I am eliminating people and places among the Russian community where the young man in the photofit might have been known, as he was the last person to be seen with Katia. So far, no-one has acknowledged seeing him or knowing him but I'm beginning to get an inkling of how much concentrated work will be needed to sort this thing out, but you know what Sherlock Holmes said, 'Eliminate all which is impossible and whatever is left, no matter how improbable, is the solution to your problem,' or something like that anyway, so I guess I am eliminating all the impossibilities!"

"Good man, I think if anyone can get to the bottom of this, it will be a fresh mind and impartial attitude like yours that will do the trick. Keep in touch and let me know how you get on. Mr Bukow is placing a lot of hope on you!" Phillip put the phone down and planned his evening's entertainment.

Ten o'clock saw him parking his car and walking slowly along the street to his third Russian venue where, standing in front of the discreet entrance stood an extremely large, sour-faced man. Phillip said "Good evening" politely and showed his private detective's licence and said smoothly, "My name is Phillip Everett," and made as if to pass the man and enter the club. The man looked over Phillip's head and announced, "Members only!"

"Nevertheless, I am investigating the abduction and possible murder of a young girl and I need to enter the premises in order to carry out some enquiries." There was no response forthcoming. "Very well, I wish to speak to the manager of this club, would you ask him to come here and speak to me?" The doorman had a short conversation in Russian on his phone, and Phillip waited for several minutes before a young man, immaculately dressed in tailored suit, pale blue shirt and matching tie, came out of the door with a very superior attitude. Phillip took an instant dislike to him, not a thing he normally did. He was slightly shorter than Phillip and simply said, "Yes?"

"As I was telling your man here," Phillip said, keeping his temper with an effort, "my name is Phillip Everett, here is my card."

The manager handed the card back. "You are a private detective and as such, you have no more rights than any other member of the public and I see no reason to allow you to enter a members only club. All this card does is to state your name and occupation. This is a private club and therefore, as you are not a member, there is no reason why I should allow you to enter."

He turned to go back into the club when Phillip said, very quietly, "You are English aren't you?"

"Yes, as it happens, I am English."

"And you are an arrogant bastard," Phillip said.

"If you say anything else like that, I shall tell Olaf to beat you up and throw you out of here."

Phillip said in a deliberate tone, "I think you're the sort of low-life no-one else would employ so you turn to the Russian mafia and kiss their arses to get a job!"

The manager's face went red and he said something in Russian to the doorman. Let's see if all that self-defence training I went through is going to pay off, thought Phillip as the big man moved nearer and lunged at him. Phillip stepped smartly to one side and chopped him on his thick neck with an outstretched hand; the first blow brought him up short and after the second blow he went down like a log of wood and lay there in a heap. Phillip hoped he had not hurt him too much!!

The manager stood with his mouth a little open, shrinking back as if he expected Phillip to do the same to him but all Phillip said was, "May I go in now?"

As if galvanised into action, the manager asked, "What is it you want?"

"Just keep a civil tongue in your head," said Phillip, "and look at this photofit picture, have you ever seen him or has he ever been to this club?"

The manager studied the picture carefully and said, "No, I'm afraid not."

"Show it to the big guy." The doorman had just managed to struggle to his feet and was gently feeling the side of his head, but he took a long look and carefully shook his head. "I'll go inside now," said Phillip, "and show it to your guests, discreetly."

But after exhaustively explaining the reason for the questions he was asking, that he was investigating the disappearance and possible murder of a young Russian girl, he had to admit defeat and bade goodnight to the manager and his burly henchman on the door. As he drove home, he puzzled over why no-one seemed to have seen him and was forced to come to the conclusion that the young man had come from, or been brought into this country illegally from another, and after he had fulfilled his purpose, he had been taken back to wherever it was he had come from or even more likely, killed. The only way to stop the slightest hint of what happened getting through to Vasily Bukow would have been to eliminate the man entirely and this smacked of the Russian mafia.

But why? What reason could there be to kidnap a young girl? To force her into prostitution – but there were other easier targets who could be forced into that way of life. Ransom – but there was no communication from anyone asking for money and no indication whatsoever of a blackmail plan which appeared to leave only one explanation – revenge. Our Mr Bukow must have made some pretty nasty enemies in his previous career in Russia so that would appear to be the answer, the poor girl was kidnapped as an act of revenge and the fact Bukow did not know if she was alive or dead was an act of torture for the poor man, forever twisting his gut in not knowing.

But Phillip's job was not concerned with his enemies but to find Katia alive or to get proof of her demise. It looked like the handsome young man was imported from another area so that he was unknown in London Russian circles and his job was to persuade her to go outside with him where she could be anaesthetised and then the pair of them driven away in a waiting car. Did that mean that someone else who attended the party was a conspirator as well? Poor Bukow, never to know what had happened to his beloved, only daughter, that was some revenge!

The following evening, Phillip decided to go to the Black Horse pub, frequented by the policemen who had worked on the original case. He bought himself a pint and sat at the bar where he could eavesdrop on conversation without anybody really noticing and hoped he might pick up someone who had actually worked on Katia's case. No such luck, for two hours he sat there drinking desultorily and the bar was starting to empty of the original drinkers who had been there when he entered. He was uncertain what to do next; because of his lack of preparation, he had utterly wasted his time so he had to go home and re-think his strategy. On Friday morning, he rang Barry Spencer again.

"Spencer," a voice said.

"You don't sound very friendly this morning," said Phillip.

"Oh, it's you again," said Barry, forcing a laugh, "if you keep on ringing me, people will start to talk!"

"You could do a lot worse than me you know," Phillip said, pretending to sound annoyed.

Barry replied in a similar tone, "Darling, I didn't know you cared!"

"If you can be serious for a minute," Phillip said, "can you remember any of the policemen's names who worked on the original case?"

"I do recall an Inspector Alan Mountfield and Sergeant Ian Bell, if that's any help to you."

"Those names will be very useful, I think. Thank you. Just one other thing, how does Mr Bukow feel about Katia's disappearance?" asked Phillip.

"I don't get you! How would any father feel about his only daughter disappearing? He's devastated," Barry said.

"So they were very close?" said Phillip.

"Close, you must be joking, she was the apple of his eye! Why are you taking this line of questioning?" Barry asked.

Phillip tried to explain: "If it was my daughter, I would be moving heaven and earth to find her."

"He gave the police every assistance he could and now he's hired you, hasn't he?" said Barry, becoming irritated.

"Look Barry, I'm following the theory that this abduction is a revenge attack by someone who holds an almighty grudge against Bukow. He or they are keeping the girl somewhere to make him suffer the pain of not knowing what has happened to her, not allowing him any peace of mind."

"And that helps you how?" said Barry.

"I think I first have to find the motive for this act, then I can carry on from that basis."

"Okay," said Barry, "I see what you're getting at, you think that sometime in the past, Mr Bukow has 'upset' someone or some organisation, so badly that he, or they, have decided to exact revenge in a particularly nasty way, not targeting him but taking what was dearest to him."

"This would appear to be the only possible reason in this case," said Phillip, "and the ideal thing would be if Mr Bukow produced a list for me, giving the names and possible locations of anybody, anybody at all, who would fit this description and then this might give me a lead, something to work towards."

"I think you're asking a lot," said Barry. "Mr Bukow is a very… shall we say, he plays his cards close to his chest and you are asking him to delve back into times and places which I think he would rather forget, but if you say this could help to find his daughter, I know he won't think twice about giving you the information. I'll get on to it right away and explain your reasons for asking; it may be he has thought this himself, but I'll get in touch with you the moment I have anything to tell you."

"I think that will be of the greatest help," said Phillip. "Do your best and tell him it was me who asked him to wrack his brains for old enemies!" and to himself he said under his breath, "So be it, the die is cast and all I have to do is wait for results."

This being Friday night, Phillip met Gordon as usual and they went to a well-known Chinese restaurant, just off Leicester Square. They chatted and Gordon asked him casually how his cases were progressing and without giving anything away, Phillip told him that one was awaiting the date of trial for the first, and the other one had come to a halt while he was pursuing some further information. Gordon nodded his head wisely and said, "I thought you'd have trouble with your second case; after all, if the police have given up, they must have come to the conclusion that there's little chance of solving it."

"Well, I'm still plugging away at it," said Phillip, "but to change the subject, what's going to happen when Jasmine kicks me into touch?"

"What do you mean by that?"

"You'll have Isobel and I'll be on my own, thickhead," said Phillip. "I can't very well sit on my own in the wine bar with you two billing and cooing like a couple of lovesick pigeons; talk about a spare part – I'll stick out like a sore thumb!"

"You could do," said Gordon. "I see what you mean but we're old mates, aren't we, we'll just have to rearrange things a bit – I'll meet Isobel one night at the weekend and we can meet on the other!"

Phillip could see problems ahead, if and when Gordon and Isobel got married, but he shrugged his shoulders and told him to have a word with Isobel about what she wanted to do and left it at that.

"Anyway, it's okay tonight because both of them are coming," said Gordon, neatly avoiding making any decision.

"Always as well to plan in advance," said Phillip, "rather than waiting for events to occur and take you by surprise."

They met the two girls and after spending a couple of hours laughing and joking, they went to Gordon's flat "for a nightcap", he said jovially, and then putting his arm firmly round Isobel's waist, they went into his bedroom. Jasmine could hardly wait until they had closed their door and before Phillip could say anything, she took his hand and led him into the other bedroom. She had been a passionate lover from the first night when she had slipped into Phillip's bed but that night, she seemed to be insatiable, kissing, caressing, encouraging him with whispered suggestions, telling him where to touch her, reaching an explosive orgasm at the same moment as he did and saying suggestively, "That was marvellous, how long will it take you before you are ready to make love again?" Phillip murmured in her ear what she should do to excite him again, but to no avail! Short of waking her up from her exhausted sleep, he would have to content himself with what he already had!

Saturday morning he woke to find Jasmine studying him, propped up on a couple of pillows; as she slid down beside him, he could have sworn there were tears in her eyes as they made love again as energetically as during the previous night. When they had satisfied themselves Jasmine sat up and said she had something to tell him. "I hope you're not going to say you're pregnant," Phillip said, knowing perfectly well this could not be a problem.

Jasmine looked down and said, "I'm not going to be able to see you again. I'm truly sorry, but I'm returning to Portugal soon to get married. You must think I'm bad to behave like this but from the first time we saw you in the bar, I said to Isobel if men can sow a few wild oats, then so can a women and I wanted to know so much about what you were like in bed. Do you hate me?" She began to cry.

Phillip held her and said he already knew about her prospective marriage and that she would be returning home soon. "But it's a free world and it's up to you what you do. Who am I to say what's right and wrong. Now don't cry, you'll spoil your pretty face!"

Jasmine sniffed and looked up at him, saying, "I'm so sad this has to come to an end, I do love you but in a very physical way. You are a wonderful lover, everything a girl could want but I was brought up in a strict Catholic family and they are very important to me, so it has to be marriage or nothing. I know you can't go through life relying on sex to keep you happy all the time and my marriage has been agreed upon for quite a while now. I shall go back to Portugal and you will be just a memory, but I'll name our first baby after you, so I'll never forget you."

Phillip kept a suitably solemn face and tried to comfort her but wondered what Mario would think if his wife wanted to name their first child after a former lover. Jasmine disappeared into the shower room and Phillip wandered into the kitchen to make himself some coffee. He thought he heard the outer door close and when he came back into the lounge, he realised that Jasmine had gone. He wasn't sure whether to be glad or sorry but hoped she would be happy, when she had settled down to her life of domesticity. Gordon and Isobel appeared minutes later, wearing identical fluffy bathrobes and looking as if they had enjoyed sharing a shower together and Phillip explained that Jasmine had told him about her impending marriage, then dressed and left without saying anything more.

"I think she was upset," he said and then went to get washed and dressed. It felt a little odd, just the three of them going out for brunch and Isobel was intrigued by the word.

"I've heard the word, of course, but what does it actually mean?" she asked. Gordon told her it was an Americanism meaning late breakfast/early lunch, hence "brunch" and Phillip decided it was time he left them on their own, but not before Isobel told him that she and Gordon had discussed when they wanted to meet at weekends and she was quite happy for them to continue their Friday's drinking, as it would be more convenient for Gordon and her to meet on Saturdays and Sundays. Phillip acknowledged her remarks and told Gordon he would see him next Friday, privately thinking that he knew who was going to wear the trousers in that relationship!! "Give my regards to Jasmine when you see her," and he set off to return home.

Chapter 13

Phillip prepared to visit the Black Horse on Monday evening and decided he was not going to just sit there, he would question the barman whether many policemen came in and if so, would he point them out to him. He arrived early, took a seat by the bar, asked his question, paid for his pint of lager and tipped the barman. The barman had told him that policemen usually came in between six and eight o'clock and about quarter to seven, the barman came over and told Phillip that Sergeant Bell had just come in. "I hope you're not going to cause him any trouble," he added.

"Course not," Phillip said reassuringly. "I think he might be able to help me with something," and he got up and greeted Bell as if he was an old friend and offered to buy him a drink.

Bell looked at him blankly and said, "I don't think I know you do I?"

Phillip smiled. "Don't think I'm trying to seduce you, I have no ulterior motive, I assure you, but I understand you worked on the case of the missing Russian girl?"

"Yes," he said reluctantly, carrying his drink over to a small table.

"I'm a private investigator and her father has asked me to try and find her because, apparently, the police enquiries have come to a dead end, due to a complete lack of evidence." He fished in his breast pocket for one of his printed cards and showed it to Sergeant Bell, to give some credibility to his presence.

Phillip started conversation going in a casual way, hoping to get Sergeant Bell's co-operation and asked him how long he had been in the police force.

"Sixteen years," said Bell, sipping his beer.

"That's a whole lot of experience there," Phillip said. "Is it right that you were second in command of the squad when you were investigating Katia Berkow's disappearance?"

"The special group that was set up, yes," said Bell slowly. "Can I ask what you have to do with this?"

"Well, as I said, her father is devastated by her disappearance; she apparently vanished into thin air, so to speak, and he's asked me to make enquiries, hoping against all hope that someone like me can come up with a fresh lead of just a hint of what happened, by striking off in a new direction."

"What are you after?" said Bell. "Are you trying to say the police didn't do their level best to find that girl, that they just gave up, weren't really bothered because her father was rich and she was Russian or something? Because if you do, somebody should punch your living daylights out. She was only seventeen, for God's sake, virtually a schoolgirl and from everything we found out about her, she was a great kid. Some of the men on the squad were fathers like me and the thought of one of their kids vanishing and never knowing where they were or what happened to them, kept 'em working far longer on the case than could really be justified, but you can't go on searching for someone when there is not the tiniest shred of evidence to follow up. We've just put the case on the back burner until sometime when a new fact comes to light. Okay," he said belligerently.

"I never thought that for a moment," said Phillip soothingly. "I'm here, talking to an experienced copper like you, to try and get an idea of what could possibly have happened to her and I thought you would give me the benefit of your expertise. People who worked on the case must have had some inkling as to what happened to her. Did they think the girl was dead and they should be looking for a body right from the start, had the girl fallen in love with some unsuitable bloke who would never be acceptable to her father, did she just want to drop out of sight for some reason? What was the general opinion of the men?"

Sergeant Bell considered what Phillip had said, hesitating for a moment before he replied and then said, "There were two schools of opinion in the Squad, one was although we all thought that the girl was alive, the 'romantics' thought that she fell in love and did not want to be found, and the others felt, myself included, that she had been abducted for prostitution purposes and whisked out of the country that night. She was a lovely girl of seventeen and could be used to pleasure very rich clients."

Phillip looked at Bell and said levelly, "That is my theory as well; my only argument with that is, why pick on her?"

"Why pick on any pretty girl?" said Bell. "Any girl who had been abducted would have her mother asking me the same question, 'why my daughter?' Perhaps because she came from a rich family, it adds more to the pleasure of the clients, the abductors would feel – the utter humiliation for the girl and the more perverted satisfaction for the clients."

"I am thinking along the same lines but this angle of 'rich family girl being humiliated' is new to me, I never thought of that," said Phillip.

"How long have you been a private detective?" said Bell, derisively. Phillip had to own up that it was not even one year and Bell told him he had a lot to learn. "I've been in the Vice Squad for five years and could tell you stories that would make your hair stand on end, details of which never surface in public, not even the Sundays get hold of 'em. Revelations that would make your skin crawl; what human beings do and are capable of doing to each other is beyond belief!!"

"So if we assume she has been snatched for the purposes of prostitution, where is the most likely place she would have been taken? asked Phillip.

"Well, assuming she was taken to the Middle East, the most likely place would be Dubai. Wealthy Arab clients like to have white girls but the only thing wrong with that theory is that they can now get plenty of Russian girls. A lot of Russian 'models' make a fortune, prostituting themselves in rich Arab states, and they are most obliging, nothing is too much trouble, if you know what I mean. No, I think possibly Amsterdam would be my guess; in that place, anything goes, any kind of perversion which could loosely be described as 'sex' takes place there!" said Sergeant Bell.

Phillip agreed that his theory might be correct, in any case, it was worth trying to find if Katia had been taken to Holland so he asked Bell, "If it was you, how would you go about finding her?"

"Do you mean 'if I was a policeman' or 'if I was a private investigator'?"

"A private investigator."

"You cheeky devil," said Bell, "asking me to give away my underhand methods of finding the truth, you've got a nerve! But seriously, buy me another pint and I'll have a think about it, try and come up with something helpful, go on!"

Phillip went across to the bar and bought a couple of pints and some crisps, for good measure, and returned to the table where Bell was sitting. Sergeant Bell said, "I've gone over in my mind what might be the best way for you to approach this. As a private individual, the local police might be a bit unwilling to help you, but I would still start off at Central Police Headquarters, show them Katia's photograph and ask for their help; it will depend on how persuasive you are but there's not much goes on in their city they don't know about and when you explain the circumstances, they might be prepared to give you any information they have. It might be home to all kinds of sexual goings-on but they would never condone any method used to force a girl into prostitution against her will."

"What else would you do?" asked Phillip, consigning all facts to memory.

"I wouldn't expect much help from their police in practical ways," he said, "but if you could manage to talk to the Vice Squad blokes, they could provide you with a lot of useful info about various sex dens to search. Er... when I say 'search' I mean of course, making 'enquiries' in the time-honoured way of trawling through bars, brothels and other dens of iniquity for hours on end!! But let's face it, she's been away for nearly a year and unless she's kept herself in good shape, she won't still be in one of the very private places, strictly reserved for rich clients. I can't see that myself; brought up in total luxury, she would have been like a fish out of water and by now she will have graduated to a brothel on one of the streets. Rich clients are always looking for fresh, young faces and bodies and after a few months of being used, they would have passed her on down the line, so to speak."

"What about this country?" said Phillip.

"Similar system, but much more undercover. A girl could start out as a top-rated call girl, only going with rich clients who could pay top whack, but as she ages, she might move down the ladder ending up on the streets, many a time controlled by a pimp and if she doesn't die from drugs, injuries inflicted by brutal customers and can still work, she might move to railway stations or some other sleazy location. You can just imagine the kind of customers she gets! People who deal with the dregs of society such as the police, social services and hospitals, come into contact with all of society's ills, sometimes on a daily basis," said Bell.

"I'm very grateful to you for all that information," said Phillip. "I now feel I have a better idea as to what I'm up against, 'fore-warned is fore-armed', and I'm going to spend time formulating a plan as to what to do next."

Phillip thanked Bell, who said "Good luck", and then he left the pub to drive home. The following morning, before getting absorbed in future plans for the abduction case, he rang John Standish to find out whether a date had been set for Walter Dunn's trial. After John had told him that the date had not been scheduled, Phillip told him he would only be available on his mobile number as he was going to spend a few days in Amsterdam. "Oh, yes," laughed John, "on a guided sex tour is it?"

"Listen," said Phillip, seriously, "if you'd heard what I listened to last night about the sex trade, it would put you off having sex for the rest of your life!!"

"Well, don't tell me what you heard then, I quite enjoy sex," said John.

"I meant sex as it's purveyed in the sex industry," said Phillip indignantly.

"Okay, okay, you're going to Amsterdam to look at the museums and art galleries and tulip fields and windmills, I believe you," said John, highly amused at Phillip's indignant tone of voice. "In any case, the courts usually give us four weeks' notice about dates set for trials and I don't suppose you're going to be in Amsterdam that long, are you?"

"Course not! I wouldn't be able to afford it for that length of time, even on expenses," he said. "I just wanted someone to know where I was going for a few days, in case anybody makes enquiries. It gives me a warm, safe feeling," he said.

"Point taken," John said. "Good luck, see you when you get back. Don't catch anything nasty while you're over there, will you?"

Phillip did not comment at John's playful remarks and put the phone down. He looked up the Amsterdam Tourist Office phone number and asked them to send him the usual pack of information leaflets, lists of hotels, sightseeing tours, places of interest, etc, and any other useful information about the city they had, including police stations, doctors' surgeries, post offices, embassies and similar other addresses, which they were only too happy to supply.

Now to book a flight, thought Phillip. I'll go from Gatwick because that's easy to get to from here, I'll tell Gordon when I see him on Friday night and travel Sunday morning.

He managed to get a flight for twelve noon which would fit in nicely with his schedule. After a meal, he and Gordon went to the wine bar and settled down for some serious drinking, both feeling a little *distrait* by their lack of female companionship. "Strange, not having the girls here, I'd sort of got used to our happy foursome on Fridays and I shall certainly miss sharing the sofa with Jasmine after we got back to your flat, Gordon. The sex was really good but we can hardly be looking round for some interesting talent, with you a soon to be married bloke," said Phillip, somewhat reluctantly, concentrating on his beer.

"Nothing to stop you eyeing the talent," said Gordon. "Don't let me put you off, I'll just sit back and admire your expertise!"

"Might not be able to meet you next Friday, Gordon, I'm going to Amsterdam on Sunday and I might not be back by Friday."

"After all the rearranging I had to do with Isobel, you're saying you might not be here next Friday? Hardly cricket, is it Phillip, what on earth are you going to Amsterdam for, as if I didn't know!"

"Why is it that a fellow can't mention he is going on a short trip abroad without everyone assuming he's just going to get his end away!" Phillip said. "As it happens, I'm going in relation to the case I'm working on and if I have to visit one or two houses of ill repute during my investigations, I can assure you it is with only the purest motives and in the furtherance of my desperate search on behalf of a distraught parent—"

"Oh, shut up," said Gordon, "you sound just like a Victorian novel. When will you know if you're coming?"

"If I don't ring you before six o'clock, I won't be able to make it. Now let's get on with the reason why we're sitting here, your round I think?" Phillip said.

Gordon was curious and wanted to know the whys and wherefores which made it so important for Phillip to travel to Amsterdam. "Come on, let's hear the full story, why is it imperative that you have to go, thereby mucking up our Friday evenings?"

Phillip became serious and asked if Gordon could keep his mouth shut. "The fewer people who know anything about this trip, the better it will be and I'm telling you this in complete confidence, someone's life may be in danger. Can you keep that mouth of yours shut and I mean that absolutely; it's that serious!"

Gordon waited a moment, taking in what Phillip had said and then, intrigued, he said seriously, "I don't work for a bank for nothing you know, there's things I know that could affect the monetary funds of other nations and cause a world collapse in some commodities but have I ever told you, have I ever told anybody, the information I've been trusted with – no – so I can assure you that whatever you tell me will go no further, understood?"

Phillip started to tell him the story of Katia's disappearance and how he had been hired by her rich, Russian father to try and find her, because the police had had to put the case on hold as there were no possible leads to follow up. He had talked to a policeman who had worked on the case and between them, they agreed that it was very likely she had been taken to Amsterdam to use as a prostitute, to humiliate her and her father in revenge for – he couldn't work out what. So that's why he was going to try and ferret out some information in the red light district, to either prove or disprove whether she was being forced to work there.

Gordon was serious again as he took in what Phillip had told him; "I wish you luck," he said, "and I don't need to tell you how careful you'll have to be. There is usually some mafia involvement in the sex trade and you could disappear without a trace, if they think you are a 'troublemaker'!"

"I'm not going to cause any trouble, if I find the poor girl, I shall just take her back to her father quietly. What the rest of the sex trade are up to is entirely the business of the government over there, I have no problems with that. I'm no threat to organised crime!"

"*If* you find her, and I say *if*, whoever has her will not blissfully wave you goodbye," emphasised Gordon.

"I knew that there might be some risk-taking when I became a private detective and that's why I took a six week course in self-defence," Phillip said.

"You didn't tell me that!"

"Well I don't tell you everything, do I, and anyway, you were in the wilds of Scotland at the time so I was hardly going to phone you to tell you all about my adventures, knocking out six-foot-six-inch tall, beefy instructors in the SAS, now was I?"

"What was it, karate, kung fu, or something like that?"

"It wasn't a competition, you were taught about the vulnerable points on the human body, how to disable a person with a single blow, that kind of thing," said Phillip.

"You mean like hitting him in the bread basket?" said Gordon eagerly.

"The human neck is the best area to disable a person because it lies closest to the brain and by hitting it in a certain area, it sends a direct shock to the brain, in the same way as a boxer punching his opponent on the chin and knocking him out. Definitely not to be tried at home!!"

"Perhaps I'd better take this course," said Gordon, with interest.

"What, do you want to disable Isobel so that you can have your wicked way with her?" scoffed Phillip.

"No, no I mean it, seriously," protested Gordon. "It could come in useful, you never know these days!"

Patiently Phillip explained that these courses were not open to the general public. "They'll only put you on a course if you can prove that the job you are doing requires this kind of training and it costs £1000, half in advance and half when you finish."

"Good grief," said Gordon, "that is what you could call expensive!!"

"It's a six-week course, Monday to Friday, you go home at weekends although you can stay over. The accommodation is very basic but comfortable, a bit like the army, but you do have your own room. The food is plentiful and wholesome, it's self-service, none of this being waited on; you pay at a till at the end of the counter and after you've finished eating, you take your tray to a collection point. It's that simple!!"

"It sounds just like being in the army," Gordon said.

"How would you know, you've never been in the army," laughed Phillip.

"So what do you pay £1000 for?"

"You pay for the training, which is very good, and at the end of six weeks, you are extremely fit and confident, you know how to handle yourself in a difficult situation." Gordon pointed out that in time, he would probably forget a great deal and also lose his fitness. "That's why I do strenuous physical exercise three or four times a week," Phillip stated.

"When have you ever had to use your training?" asked Gordon.

"What about the time when we were on the bus and I disarmed that yob in the hood, took his knife away from him, does that count?" said Phillip.

"Oh, yes, I remember that!!"

"And what about the other night; I was trying to enter a Russian nightclub when I was stopped by a big gorilla-type bouncer; he called the manager of the club, who turned out to be a young Londoner and when I called him an arrogant bastard, he told the man-mountain to beat me up and throw me off their property, into the gutter."

"Wow, what did you do then, run?" said Gordon, his attention riveted on Phillip's face.

"He lunged at me, I stepped to one side and chopped him in two places on his neck, he fell down and lay there, unable to get up for a while, not knocked out or disabled in any way, you understand, but unable to come back at me, temporarily."

"What did the manager do?" asked Gordon.

"He thought he was going to be next and started panicking," Phillip remembered, "but I asked politely if I could go into the club to make a few enquiries, and he backed down and ushered me inside. I'm not violent for the sake of it, only in self-defence if I'm attacked and I made sure the bouncer was okay before I went in. Unfortunately, I didn't get anywhere with my questions so it was rather a waste of my valuable time!"

Gordon sat back in his seat and went, "Phew, it would appear the course was not a waste of time or money, if it helped to get you out of a sticky spot like that! Good on yer my man, you can back me up any time!!"

"It looks as if it could be part of the job and I need to protect myself without being openly aggressive. I'm not a policeman, I only have the same rights you have but if I have to go snooping round, asking people awkward questions they would rather not answer, I just need to be able to protect myself. Fancy a wrestling match at the Albert Hall sometime?"

"No thanks," Gordon shuddered, "I can see you winning and me ending up with a black eye, I'll believe you where thousands wouldn't!! If you wanted a safe, easy life, you should have got another banking job."

"Okay, that's enough talk about work for tonight, how are you getting on with Isobel?"

"I've not seen her since last Sunday," Gordon said, reluctantly.

"I would have thought that by now you would be spending a lot more time with her, plans for the wedding, where you're going to live, how many children you're going to have, that sort of thing," said Phillip, sweetly. "Not losing your nerve are you Gordon, afraid to lose your independence?" In a way, he was reassured when Gordon answered that it was only because they were both working all day and she was still living outside London that they were only able to spend time together at weekends and no, he was not losing his nerve, he was quite looking forward to a life spent married to her and who knows, one or two children might come along in time.

A female voice interrupted their conversation, saying, "Well, if it's not the man we spoke to in here only the other week," and as Phillip turned round to see who it was, he recognised the two girls he had spoken to at the bar… when had it been, a few weeks ago?

"Here we are, Gordon, I must introduce you to the two young ladies 'who do not sleep around'. Meet 'I do not sleep around number 1' and 'I do not sleep around number2'."

"So his name's Gordon is it? In his case I'd be willing to make an exception to my rule!"

"Sorry," said Gordon, cheerfully, "I'm already spoken for but my friend here, he's free."

"Just my luck," she said, sighing comically, "all the good-looking men I meet have been nobbled already."

"You have to be up early in the morning to catch a good-looking man like him," Phillip said solemnly.

"We're not getting anywhere here," and the two of them walked back to the bar.

Gordon looked at Phillip curiously and said, "You're fancy free at the moment, aren't you, why didn't you follow up that obvious invitation?"

"Not my type." Phillip shrugged his shoulders.

"She'd be okay for the night," said Gordon. "I'm not that desperate."

"Aren't you going for anybody tonight?"

"Not tonight," Phillip said.

"Well, you're not sleeping with me!" said Gordon, with a laugh. It was strange not having the two girls with them and now that Gordon did not want to pick up any girls, while of course he did, how was the situation going to work out in the future? I'm a selfish sod, he thought, but now that Gordon seems to be settled in his relationship with Isobel, my days spent with him, eyeing up the talent, flirting, trying to get girls to sleep with us, would appear to be over.

CHAPTER 14

Sunday morning found Phillip, suitcase packed, parking his car at the airport long-stay area and catching the flight to Amsterdam. On arrival at the airport he cleared customs, found the taxi rank and asked the driver to take him to a cheap hotel, near the city centre. "Not many cheap hotels near city centre," said the driver laconically, "what about hotel in red light area, depends on whether you want hotel with or without sex?"

"I just want a hotel where ordinary people stay, like tourists, and er... without sex!" Phillip said.

"Okay, I take you to one hotel and if it's not suitable, I take you to another," said the driver, and Phillip got into the vehicle.

The first hotel, although fairly presentable on the outside, proved to be very unsatisfactory inside and Phillip politely left and got back into the taxi. "No good?" said the driver. "No good," agreed Phillip. The next hotel, down an unprepossessing side street, was a plain narrow building, more like a town house but then Phillip went in; he approved the spotless cleanliness and after mentally changing pounds into euros, he realised the terms were very reasonable and decided to stay there. He went back outside, thanked and paid the taxi driver and carried his bag back into the small reception area. Evening meals had to be booked by three pm in advance so he declined the offer and went upstairs to look at his room. Nothing luxurious, but clean and with a miniscule shower and toilet room, double bed and small television set. He started to unpack.

Having settled in, he studied his map of the central city area and decided to start his search straightaway, using the stack of information leaflets sent to him by the Amsterdam Tourist Bureau. He wondered if he should telephone the police station or whether it might be better to pay them a call and talk to them, face to face; it might be a slightly tricky situation to explain over the phone, perhaps to someone whose understanding of the English language might not take in all the subtle nuances which a British copper would have. He thought, what if he was faced by a Dutch cop, trying to explain something to him when he didn't fully understand the language – he decided the best thing would be to find the police station and explain his situation face to face.

He checked the map, and tucking it into his pocket, set off to walk there, always on the lookout for a small cafe where he could purchase an evening meal, in an effort to familiarise himself with the layout of the surrounding neighbourhood. After a short walk, he found the police station and asked if anybody spoke English and after a short time, a policewoman appeared who said politely, "I speak English, may I help you?" Phillip plunged into his explanation as to why he had come to Amsterdam, telling the policewoman of Katia's unfortunate disappearance and how, after conferring with a London policeman, he thought she might have been brought to Amsterdam. The Dutch girl frowned a little and said, "Normally we are asked by your police force, prior to them sending anyone over for this type of investigation."

"I fully understand your position," Phillip said, "but I am a private investigator, acting on behalf of her father and as such, although the police are aware of my work, I am not here with their backing."

"Do you have any ID?" she asked. Phillip handed her one of his printed cards but she looked at it and shook her head. "This only tells me your name is Phillip Everett, private investigator," and she handed the card back to him. "I am not sure why you have come to our police station."

Falling back on the charm, Phillip said, "Apart from meeting such an attractive lady like you, I have many other reasons. I was hoping that maybe I could get help from your police force, as I'm sure you wouldn't like the idea of a seventeen-year-old girl being brought over here and forced unwillingly into a life of prostitution, now would you?"

She smiled at him, just a little flattered, and said, "I am sorry, but we cannot really help you. You should have gone to your own police first, then if they had made a request for our help and co-operation, we could have made it official."

Phillip's face showed his disappointment and he said ruefully, "But perhaps you could display Katia's photograph on your notice board over there and then if anyone can help, if they should see her, they can give me a ring on my mobile." He put the photo and his card next to it on the desk in front of her and she studied it carefully.

"I think we can do that for you but I'm afraid it's not 'official' you understand?"

"Absolutely," Phillip said. "Thank you."

"You must be careful, Mr Everett, Amsterdam can be a dangerous place for a man to go round asking questions, especially in some areas and at night and we wouldn't want to go fishing a young, good-looking private investigator like you out of a canal, would we?!" Phillip thanked her and left the police station, feeling a little disappointed.

Outside, he walked along until he came to a bar and decided to get a drink and some food, suddenly aware how hungry he was. He ordered a large glass of lager and a roll which, when it was presented to him, he thought could have fed a starving family for a week! There was everything that made a sandwich delicious, crusty roll, Dutch butter, cheese, ham, some kind of pate, assorted pickles and garnished with various salad vegetables. Phillip spread his map on the table while he tackled his gargantuan 'snack', so intent on where to go next that he failed to notice a young woman studying him until she came over and stood next to him. "Can help you?" she asked. "You seem to have been studying that map for a long time." She spoke in Dutch and Phillip looked up at her, his mouth full of sandwich, and said that unfortunately he did not speak Dutch, as he only spoke English. "Ah, English, I speak English, can I help you?"

Phillip took a long look at her and said coolly, "I'm not looking for business."

She smiled, not offended, and said, "This can be a lonely city, especially for strangers and at night."

"Don't worry about me," said Phillip, "I assure you I can look after myself. I'm a detective," he announced.

"That's okay, many of my clients are detectives!"

"Good for you," said Phillip, rather rudely, becoming slightly irritated by her presence, when the thought occurred to him that she might be able to help with information. "Perhaps you might be able to help me, but I don't mean on your back."

She teased him, raising her eyebrows and said, "You want it standing up?"

Phillip had to laugh and said jokingly, "So far I've not tried that. No, I am looking for a missing girl and if you could lead me to her, or even tell me where she is, you could earn a lot of money that way. I believe she is working in the same kind of business as you, so there is always the chance you might have seen her; this is a picture of her."

She studied the picture carefully, wrinkling her forehead with concentration, but she shook her head and said regretfully, "There must be hundreds like her but as far as I can tell, I've never seen her; may I keep the photo, I could show it to some friends of mine but I will have to be very careful, I don't want to wake up one morning in a canal, dead!" Phillip told her that the girl was Russian, only seventeen, and had been taken from her family and possibly smuggled into this city, to be used as a prostitute. "Many girls have been brought here in the same way," she shrugged, "especially from Eastern Europe."

Phillip didn't want to tell her that Katia had been taken from London, nor did he want her to know that her father was a very rich man so he asked her to get in touch with him if she saw or heard anything of any use and wrote his mobile number down on the back of a beer mat. She stuffed the beer mat in her bag and asked curiously, "What is your name?"

"It's Phillip; tell me, if you were in my position, how would you go about finding this young girl?"

"Well, if you buy me a drink and let me have a mouthful of your sandwich, I might just be prepared to give you the benefit of my advice, after all, time is money," she said flippantly.

"Oh, sorry, yes of course, what do you want to drink, would you like something else to eat?" She ordered a large glass of lager and nibbled on his sandwich and then proceeded to tell him what she thought he should do!

"If I were a detective, I could flood the red light district with dozens of copies of her picture and wait for someone to ring you with information. However, if her kidnappers panicked, they would just kill her. You have to make your enquiries very discreetly, so as not to spook them. The way the system works here is that there is a constant need for fresh, young bodies and if you kidnap a young girl, and I mean, some of them are only thirteen or fourteen, you put them in top class houses where only the rich bastards can use them. After a while, when the clients have tired of her, she would be moved to a top class brothel where clients could ask for anything or any person, they wanted. When her usefulness was over, she might be moved to a brothel close to the river or just off the streets and finally, the streets themselves, managed by a pimp who takes a large cut of her money. Most girls finish up like that but if she is very lucky and keeps off the drugs, she might manage to save enough to try and start a new life. How long since she was taken?" she asked.

"Around eleven months," replied Phillip.

"In that case, she would definitely be out of the top class houses by now, so you should start looking in the expensive brothels."

"Are there many of them?" asked Phillip.

"About a dozen; they are all in the red light area but I must warn you, don't go inside any of them, waving that photograph around and asking questions. You will never get any answers but will probably be beaten up, warned off and then thrown out into the street!"

"I can look after myself," Phillip said, stoutly.

"What, against two or three big men; in any case, they could call the police and say you raped one of their girls."

"Is that a joke?" asked Phillip. "Raping a prostitute in a brothel!!"

"No, it's not a joke," she said. "We have laws in Holland to protect women. The sex industry is regulated and prostitutes have rights, not to be assaulted or raped, just like any other woman. Why not, they are human beings aren't they, just doing a job meeting the needs of some sections of society!" she said, indignantly.

"Okay, okay," said Phillip. "By the way, what's your name?"

"You can call me Magda."

"Right, listen Magda, I am not in any way trying to belittle or condemn prostitution," he said, "it's been around in one form or another for thousands of years. It wouldn't have survived that long if there hadn't been a need for it. But you were going to tell me how to go about finding where the girl might be!!"

"You have to pretend that you are a customer," said Magda, "you ask to see all the girls before deciding which one you are going to pay for. You have to make them think you are a big spender, come over here from England for a few days of sexual tourism. Most of these establishments have detailed photographs of the girls, in various provocative poses, dressed in the bare minimum so you should be able to tell if your girl is working there."

"Thank you, you've been very helpful," and he gave her a fifty euro note.

"If I come across your girl, I'll ring your mobile. Don't give me the photograph," she said when Phillip offered her the picture, "it's much too dangerous. If the people who took her are anywhere around and word gets passed to them that I am looking for her, I could be tortured and killed. All the various aspects of the sex industry are controlled by some kind of mafia organisation and if their identity is threatened, it would be, how do you put it in English…? 'Small beer' for them to kill and dispose of a body. I think I will remember her face but if I see her, I will not approach her but ring you." Magda finished her glass of lager and said "Are you sure you don't want my business? I am very good at it."

"Sorry, it's not you Magda, it's just that sex is the last thing on my mind at the moment."

"You are very strange, most men tend to get excited as soon as they enter the red light district. Quite a few of them say it's because they know so many couples are having sex, the air is polluted with sex hormones and as you breathe them in, it makes you excited. Is that not so for you?"

"I can't say it's having much effect on me," Phillip said. "I have to go now. Thank you for all the information you have given me; take care of yourself, no doubt I will see you again," and with a smile, he turned and left the bar. Once outside, he could have kicked himself for not getting Magda to tell him where these high class brothels were, then he could have marked them on his map, but he was not going back into the bar. He knew he was in approximately the right area, perhaps they would not be difficult to locate and he came across one before five minutes had passed. Displayed outside the door were several photographs of attractive girls and a sign saying 'Come inside and spend some time with our lovely young ladies'. He studied the photographs thinking it would be too much of a coincidence to see Katia's face amongst them; there were five girls and they would probably not have any more so there was not much point in going in.

Ten minutes later he came across a second sign saying 'The Most Beautiful Girls in Amsterdam are waiting for you – we guarantee you will have most pleasurable time inside'. No photos, so Phillip knew he had to enter the premises. As he walked inside, a big woman perhaps in her forties, dressed so that much of her figure was provocatively displayed, came up to him and said, "Welcome to our house of pleasure sir," switching quickly from Dutch to English when she saw he did not understand her. Phillip reminded himself to play the rich guy who wanted to pick his own partner, a choosy client in fact. "Good evening, madam."

"What can we do for you sir?"

Pretending slight boredom, Phillip said, "You might be able to persuade me to stay by showing me your girls and what they have to offer!!"

"We have ten lovely girls who would do anything to please a discerning client like yourself," she answered.

"Well then, let me see them, so that I can pick one out."

She took a long look at Phillip and said smoothly, "Many of our young ladies are already with clients in their rooms."

"That's a pity," Phillip said, turning as if to go.

Determined not to lose a well-dressed client who appeared to have plenty of money to spend, Madam said, "But we have an album of photographs, showing our young ladies in various poses, some of which we sell as souvenirs of your visit, should you wish for a copy."

"Right then," Phillip said brusquely, "where's this album?" Madam showed him to an armchair and presented him with a thick, Victorian style photograph album, covers embossed in very fancy silks and made of quilted satin. Phillip found his heart beating faster as he opened the book and studied the pictures carefully, one by one. Madam was perfectly correct when she said they had ten lovely girls, all of them appeared to be fairly athletic, judging by some of the poses they presented, both clothed, semi-clothed and completely nude. But Katia was not among them.

He took a last look at a very well-endowed blonde and sighed regretfully, "No, there is nothing here to inspire me," and gave the book back to Madam.

"What exactly were you looking for?" she asked him.

"What I would like is a young girl, not more than seventeen, looking something like your neighbour's daughter, homely, girl next door look, not experienced like those girls are, a bit new to it, you know what I mean," he leered.

"Ah, now, what you are asking for," said Madam, knowing exactly what he meant, "is available only to special clients."

"Every man likes to think they are special," he said, shrugging his shoulders.

"Every man likes to think they will be rich some day, but that will never happen," she replied.

"Being rich is relative; first, it depends on what you mean by 'rich'. Some men are very rich but they don't spend much of their money. Anyway, thank you for your help," he said hypocritically and turned to go. Madam did not look very pleased to see him go, business was very slow tonight, but there was nothing she could do to stop him. Once out of sight of the doorway, he made a quick note of the two addresses he had already called at so that he would not make the mistake of visiting them again.

He found two more brothels, but neither of them had photographs outside so he followed the same procedure, casually looking through the photographs and then saying to whoever who was in charge that none of them excited him enough to want sex with them, and then talked his way out of the building. It was getting very late and Phillip felt tired, hungry and footsore – it was very tiring visiting brothels, whether you had sex or not! – what he needed was another of those large glasses of lager and something to eat. He found a small bistro and went in, asking the waitress who came over to his table if she spoke English. She nodded, "A little." He ordered his lager and the easiest thing on the menu was steak and chips, which he ate with gusto. As he ate, he became aware of a heavily made up young woman smiling at him and attempting to sit down at his table. He said coldly, "I've finished thank you."

"I like English people," she said. "Would you like to order from *my* menu?" Phillip raised both hands in a fending-off gesture.

"Don't sit down, I don't want any company tonight."

"But I could be very good company for you," she emphasized. He was beginning to lose his temper so he growled at her, "I'm a detective and I'm looking for a woman who robbed my client of a lot of money. Do you want me to arrest and charge you with theft?"

"There's no need to be like that, all I wanted to do was keep you company," and she marched off, saying something to the man behind the bar as she went.

Phillip shook his head in disbelief, can't they take a hint when a man is not interested in sex. He had a couple more glasses of lager and then went back to his hotel.

He did not sleep well, constantly dreaming and then waking suddenly. He was dreaming that he was running away from two large Russian men who caught up with him and when he tried to fight them off, he found he could not move. A large fist was coming towards his face ready to smash into it and he woke sweating, trying to work out where he was. After a long time, he fell asleep again but woke tired and bad tempered. He got out of bed and started an hour of punishing physical exercise, followed by a brisk shower, which improved his temper somewhat, then he dressed and went out to find a place to have breakfast. He soon came across a little self-service cafe and helped himself to scrambled egg, a few mushrooms, some croissants and strawberry jam, and two large mugs of strong coffee. Gordon would like it here, he thought to himself and grinned.

While he ate, he planned what he would do during the day. The sex trade never rests, just a different shift takes over, so that would give him the opportunity to talk to a different section of people who might possibly give him some information. He finalised his plans and when he emerged from the cafe, the sun was shining brilliantly so he decided he would take a canal boat trip and see something of the city sights. He found the embarkation jetty, bought a ticket and boarded one of the many comfortable canal boats and prepared to look forward to a pleasant trip in the sunshine. The next thing he knew, the ticket collector was shaking his shoulder gently, saying something to him in Dutch. Phillip looked bewildered until the collector, realising he did not understand him, said in English, "The trip is at an end, you must have been very tired because you slept all the way!!" He tried not to yawn and got to his feet, a little groggily. Nothing for it, he would have to see some of the tourist attractions, at least he wouldn't nod off while he had to walk round.

By four o'clock, he had trailed round a number of buildings, trying to take in the information vouchsafed to the straggling group of visitors he had tagged along with and slipped away to find something to eat and drink, to say nothing of a well-deserved rest. Fully satisfied and refreshed from his meal, it seemed like a good time to recommence his search in the red light district. He sauntered along, trying to look unobtrusive, when he spotted two women leaning up against a building, apparently just chatting to each other. As he came level with them, one of the women said something to him, in Dutch of course, and he said, "English."

"English," one of them said, "you looking for a good time?"

"No," said Phillip, "but perhaps you can help me?" The two women looked at each other, considering what to say, when he showed them the picture of Katia. They looked carefully, saying nothing, and then shook their heads. He thanked them and then walked on a little further, feeling the hairs on the back of his neck standing up, as if someone was following him. Casually, he stopped to look at some photographs of girls, displayed in a window, and thought he saw a bulky looking man, some yards back, who also turned to look in a window at the same time. Without appearing to notice, he took great care to study the people around him but continued to ask any of the women who approached him if they had seen the girl in the photograph.

He was now deep in the red light district and turned down a side street, before realising how narrow and badly lit it was. A voice behind him said, "Hey, English, what you looking for?" It was the bulky man he had noticed earlier. "This is very bad area to be asking questions, people can disappear and no-one ever seen again!!" He was very close to Phillip now, who was getting very tired and impatient with his lack of success and as the man came nearer, Phillip jabbed him in the throat and as he leaned forward, coughing and spluttering, chopped him on the back of his neck, felling him like a huge log. He went down heavily and started to convulse on the pavement. Phillip stood over him, uncertain of his next move, looking to see if anybody had seen what happened and gradually, the big man relaxed and started to come round.

Phillip put his foot on the man's chest and asked, "Who do you work for? And I tell you now, if I don't like your answer, my foot will smash your face so that even your own mother wouldn't recognise you!!" He lifted his foot a few inches off the man's chest and held it over his face.

"Nobody, I work for nobody," the man managed to cough out.

"Then why are you following me?" said Phillip, tersely.

"I'm only trying to protect my girls,;you ask them questions but you don't go with them, it's not good for business. I'm their pimp and I look after them but asking questions don't make any money and we all have to earn a living!!"

"What possible danger could I be to any one of your girls?" Phillip asked. "I'm looking for one particular girl."

"Show me picture, she might be one of mine, then we can do business, I give you a special rate." Phillip showed Katia's picture to him, still lying on the pavement, but he shook his head, "No, I never see her."

Phillip gave him a swift kick in his ribs. "Take a really good look, is she one of yours?" Reluctantly, the big man studied the photo, with aching neck, aching head, aching ribs and again shook his head. "Then I'm no danger to you or any one of your girls, am I?" and Phillip turned and walked away, back into the well-lit thoroughfare he had previously left.

He thought it was now time to continue his line of investigation by locating the brothels he had not yet visited, so he checked on his map and found he was very near where he had finished the previous night. He walked into a bar and ordered his usual large glass of lager and a plate of steak and chips and, suddenly ravenously hungry, he attacked his food with gusto. He found the next brothel on his list and went through the same procedure as the previous evening, asking to see all the girls before he chose one he wanted, reluctantly turning down all the offers because he apparently wanted one special type of girl. He hoped that the madames of the brothels did not phone each other and warn them about this peculiar Englishman who turned down the offer of sex with every one of their girls and who appeared to be making a tour of every house of ill repute in the city of Amsterdam!! Thoroughly disappointed after another fruitless night's search, in the early hours of the morning he returned to his hotel and slept till breakfast time, waking up with the realisation that he would have to review his strategy, if he wanted to succeed in his search.

What further means could he use to speed up his search. An idea occurred to him; what he needed was someone who spent a lot of time in the red light district, but not a 'sex worker'. He had heard the sex trade in Holland was controlled by a special civic administration department, helping both sexes of people who sell their bodies for sex. They could have free tests for AIDS or other venereal diseases, help with drug problems and protection from any kind of exploitation. The only thing was, how did he find out exactly where this department was? It looked as if he needed the help of one of the 'business girls' but although trawling the streets for some time, he couldn't find one! Giving up his search, temporarily, he went into a bar and a woman's voice addressed him in Dutch. "English," said Phillip, without even looking up, and someone said, "Oh, lovely, I'm English as well, darling – are you looking for something?" she asked.

Phillip looked up and quickly assessed what he saw. Peroxide blonde, bit on the plump side, well past thirty, wearing a tight, see-through blouse and shortish skirt, cheerful smile and engaging manner. "Where are you from?" asked Phillip, curiously.

"I'm from London babes, where are you from?"

He replied cautiously, "I'm from the South also."

"You want a bit of company?"

"If you mean, 'do I want any help', yes I do."

"I'm a very helpful person, what kind of help did you want?"

"Well, I don't want help of the sexual kind," laughed Phillip, "if that's what you mean. But on the other hand, I have lots of worries on my mind at the moment!"

She looked at him questioningly. "Not a homosexual are you sweetie? You don't strike me as being that way inclined, a good, healthy, red blooded male, you are, unless I'm much mistaken!! Anyway, I'm very good at soothing away worries, I'm sure I can help you."

"There is a way you could really help me," he said, "but it would take up some of your time."

She looked a little doubtful and said, "Look, honey, I have to earn my living and helping people is okay, but who's going to help me with rent and everything, if I take time off to help you?"

Phillip said soothingly, "How about I buy you something to eat and we can talk over the situation?"

"I might miss a client."

"I don't think so," he said, "at this time of the day everybody is at work and if they're not at work, that means they're unemployed and can't afford your services anyway!!"

"Okay, you've convinced me."

Phillip said, "Where's a good place to eat round here and by the way, what's your name? Mine's Phillip."

She wrinkled her nose and laughed a little. "Customers call me all sorts of names but you can call me Gloria; come on I know a good place to eat, just around the corner." They went into the restaurant and were shown to a table. Gloria sat down and asked if she could have anything she wanted and Phillip reassured her, thinking to himself, it's all on expenses, and asked her what she wanted to drink.

While waiting for their food they started to chat, each trying to obtain information about the other. "What's this help you want me to give you?" she asked, after they had eaten and were finishing the wine.

Phillip brought the photograph of Katia out of his pocket and showed it to her. "Have you ever seen this girl anywhere?" Gloria studied the picture, knowing this was probably the main reason he had asked for her help. She shook her head slowly, "No, I've never seen her."

"Would you please memorise that face for future reference as it could mean a lot of money for you. I won't give you a copy because I wouldn't want to put you in any danger."

Gloria had caught two words, 'money' and 'danger'. She said slowly, "I'm always interested in money but what about the 'danger', where does that come in?" Phillip was annoyed with himself for even mentioning the possibility so he emphasised the easy task he wanted her to take on.

"Look, I'm going to give you my mobile number and all you have to do is ring me if you see her. You don't even need to speak to her or approach her, just ring me and tell me where she is or where she is going, and you will be given a large sum of money, enough to keep you in lunches and bottles of wine for quite a long time. There is no need to do any more than that or give away your identity to anyone and nobody you know should be told about this, that way you will be quite safe."

"Why should there be any danger?"

"It won't be dangerous if you just remain in the background. There is another thing I'd like you to do for me," said Phillip. "I've been told that in Holland, they have a government-sponsored agency which looks after people who work in the sex industry, is that true?"

"I've never used them," said Gloria, "but I know about them. You have to register with the agency and they provide free tests for HIV and other diseases; they also give you advice on some aspects of the sex trade."

"Why haven't you joined, or registered?"

She looked straight at him and said evenly, "I've been in this game for more years than I care to remember and I just like to be a free agent."

"Can you show me where this agency is, on the map?"

"I've never been there but I do know where it is; here, have you got a pencil, make a mark there!" Phillip felt very pleased as he made a slight pencil mark on his map; at last, he was really getting somewhere! Gloria made a teasing remark, "Are you going to join them?" she said innocently, "they look after homosexual men in our profession as well as women!"

Phillip gave an exaggerated sigh and said in a silly voice, "Yes, I know that darling, but I already have a job!!"

They finished their meal, the waiter presented him with the bill and Gloria said, "I take it you'll be leaving me now, although we could still go back to my place if you wanted?"

Phillip answered her politely, knowing full well her reasons for asking the question; "I'm afraid I have a lot of work to do."

"You haven't told me what sort of business you're in, have you?"

"I find people and at the moment, I'm trying to find that young girl."

"You a policeman or something? You seem like a very nice man and I wish I could help you."

"The best thing you can do to help me is give me a ring, saying you have seen her. I'm sorry, I have to go now but remember, it will mean you can expect to be well rewarded for the information. Goodbye for now," and they left the restaurant to go their separate ways.

CHAPTER 15

Outside the restaurant, Phillip headed towards the building he had marked on his map. The agency was in the red light area because, after all, if you were in the business of dealing with prostitutes, male escorts and various other aspects of the sex trade, this was the place to have your offices! He found the correct office, saw a door marked 'Inquiries', went through and found a small waiting room with a large desk against one wall where a middle aged woman was talking to a young girl. There were several chairs spaced out against the other three walls, all occupied. Phillip patiently waited until a chair became vacant, sat down and waited his turn. When he moved into the chair in front of the desk he asked politely, "Does anyone speak English please?"

"Yes, a little, how can I help you?" He brought the now very familiar picture of Katia out of his pocket and asked if she had seen her. She shook her head and so he asked her if she would write across the bottom of the photo in Dutch, the words 'Have you seen this girl?' She wrote some words at the bottom of the picture and handed it back to him. Phillip showed it to everybody sat in the room, asking if anybody had seen her, but there was a universal shaking of heads of everyone waiting. The lady behind the desk said she was quite busy and if he would come back a little later, they could discuss whatever problem he had more privately.

Phillip agreed and went through the door, to be faced with one marked 'Private'. On an impulse he knocked on the door and heard a voice call out. He went in, apologising profusely for having knocked on the wrong door but the short, balding man he saw behind the desk said, "What is it you are looking for?"

"Perhaps you can help me," said Phillip, realising the man had addressed him in perfect English. "I only need two minutes of your time – I am looking for my stepsister; she was only seventeen when she was abducted. I have managed to trace her to your city and I believe she was taken to be used as a prostitute."

"What makes you think that?"

"I have been on her trail for several months now and to explain how I traced her here would take up too much of your valuable time; please just accept that she is here. I need your permission to put this picture of her in the Inquiries waiting room in a position where everyone entering and leaving that room would see the photograph; someone might have come across her and would be able to help me."

The man studied the photograph and acknowledged what a pretty girl she was and looking up at Phillip, he asked, "And what is your name?"

"It's Phillip Everett and if anyone who sees her could ring my mobile, I'm sure I could arrange some type of a reward for them; you can imagine that her father is beside himself with worry and would be only too happy to make it worth their while."

"Well, Mr Everett, you had better write your telephone number on this photograph and if you leave it with me, I will ensure it is displayed in a prominent position where it is sure to be seen, perhaps in the reception area." Phillip must have looked a little doubtful because he said, "I can assure you that I will make all my staff aware of your search and the photograph will be displayed where anyone coming in or out of the building will see it!"

"Thank you very much, I am in your debt," said Phillip, very grateful for the help he was being given.

That evening, he visited a couple more brothels but with no results and he returned to his hotel feeling fed up. In the morning, he put himself through his usual punishing regime of exercise, followed by a shower and breakfast, while he decided what more he could do that day. Perhaps a visit to the police station would show some results so he called round and asked the police sergeant whether there had been any response to the photograph he had left there the previous Sunday evening. The desk sergeant proved less than helpful, whether through ignorance of the facts or a genuine misunderstanding of the situation, and Phillip thought it was rather like knocking his head against a brick wall. There was no sign of the picture, either on the notice board or on the sergeant's desk, which meant nothing had been achieved at all.

In the end, after a tortuous conversation, both men furious because they did not speak the other person's language well enough to communicate clearly with each other, it was established that the photo had been pinned up on the canteen notice board and with that information, Phillip realised there was nothing more he could do. He left the building and cudgelled his brain, trying to think what more he could do, when his phone rang. It was so unexpected that he very nearly dropped the phone as he pulled it out of his pocket and said, "Hello."

"Mr Everett, do you remember me? It's Magda."

"Yes, of course I do, where are you?"

"Not far away, but I need to speak to you urgently. Can you meet me in Ruben Street at a cafe-bar called Kaplinskeys?"

"Sure, I'll find it, are you okay?"

"Fine, look just meet me there," and she rang off.

Phillip consulted his map and found the place with little difficulty; there was no sign of Magda. He bought himself a drink and sat down at a table with a view of the street and settled down to wait. It was only a few minutes before Magda appeared and Phillip got her a drink; she seemed a little unsure of how to start their conversation. Eventually, she asked him if it was true he had beaten up a pimp. "I didn't realise it was common knowledge!"

She said seriously, "It's very seldom anyone assaults a pimp round here; it's a very dangerous thing to do; there are a lot of them and they look after each other. They will go to almost any lengths to control their girls and anyone who tries to muscle in on their territory could, at best, be severely beaten, or at worst, killed."

"Who said I was trying to muscle in on their business?" he said.

"Don't you see, you beat him and made him look weak in front of the others, as if he was not able to control his girls, and the net result is that a few of them are after you now, to break your legs or something worse and they will be coming soon, about seven or eight of them. Each has their own special way of dealing with 'difficult customers' so you've got to get somewhere safe now."

Magda was looking quite distressed so Phillip said soothingly, "It's okay Magda, I was thinking of going back to London tomorrow, I seem to have done as much as I can here anyway."

"I think you should go today, now," said Magda, urgently.

Phillip sighed. "I don't think I can go back today; are you quite sure this posse is after me?"

Magda wanted to shake him; she shrugged her shoulders. "I've come out of my way to warn you; if anybody ever finds out I did this, well I hope you'll be able to identify me when they drag me out of the canal," she said.

"Really, I do appreciate this and I'm grateful to you for taking the trouble to come out of your way to tell me and I'll be very careful tonight, before I go back tomorrow, I promise!"

Magda had to accept that she had done her best to alert him to the danger he was in and said, "I'll keep a lookout for that girl and if I should come across her, I will ring you right away," finishing her glass of wine. "I'd better be going now and look for some clients; this is not really my area," and when Phillip gave her a fifty euro note, she looked at him, surprised. "What's this for?"

"It's for taking the time to come and warn me and promising to look out for Katia!"

She stuffed the note in her purse and got up to go – "Maybe I'll see you if you come over here again?"

"I'm sure I'll be back, either to collect the girl when she is found, or to carry on searching."

"See you next time then," and without a backward glance, she walked out into the street.

Phillip sat, looking into space, before he gave himself a mental shake and ordered a sandwich from a hovering waiter, before he got down to considering what his move should be tonight, to carry on his search, yet avoid the avenging pimps, who according to Magda, were after his blood. He decided the best thing to do would be to visit some of the seedier brothels he had not yet been able to fit in, what with his busy schedule! How Gordon and he would laugh over this when he told him about visiting nearly every brothel in Amsterdam and never getting laid!! In the meantime he rang Flight Reservations and booked a seat on the eleven o'clock plane to London.

He returned to his hotel, packed his belongings ready for the next morning and sallied forth to the red light district again, to continue his investigations. The novelty of searching the red light district was rapidly losing its appeal; it was one blind alley after another or, to put it another corny way, like looking for a needle in the proverbial haystack!! His feet ached, his libido was at rock bottom and he came to the conclusion that he would rather be relaxing in his own home, watching a footie match on TV, with a glass of lager in his hand, anywhere but here. Back to the hotel, he thought, but was suddenly aware of the hairs on the back of his neck starting to bristle; someone was following him. He was annoyed with himself; in spite of being warned, he had been paying no attention whatsoever to things going on around him and in his momentary confusion, he turned into what proved to be a cul-de-sac. As he turned to get back into the well-lit thoroughfare he had just left, he found himself facing a number of men, blocking his way.

Fear gripped his whole being and he felt like a trapped animal, with predators ready to rip him to shreds, with nowhere for him to run. All sorts of thoughts were flashing through his brain as he suddenly realised the eight men all looked like pimps, the kind of bastards who forced teenage girls, some as young as fourteen, to walk the streets, some to be raped and abused by any pervert who had sufficient money to pay the pimp to have sex with them. Phillip felt his anger mounting beyond control; If I'm going to die here, I'll make sure to take as many of these vile creatures with me as I can, he thought.

His mind flashed back to his self-defence course. He recalled the words of the instructor: "When faced with multiple enemies, always strike first! If you wait for them to make a move, you will be overwhelmed by sheer numbers. Weigh up your opponents and strike at the most dangerous one first." The line of eight men stopped, as though they were waiting for someone to make the first move. As there were eight of them, they felt confident of the outcome – there was no hurry. Phillip made a quick appraisal of each man and picked on the smallest one first – he has to be a knife man and thus the most dangerous, he figured. He was the type to creep around your back and stab you several times while you were facing the others.

The guy on his left was the same pimp whom Phillip had beaten up before and thus he was not going to start anything and might still be suffering from the last encounter. The third man on the knife-man's left was bulky, very big and didn't look very bright or very fast, but if he did hit you, you would stay on the floor a long time. The next man was tall and slim and Phillip guessed he was some kind of martial arts exponent – Judo or Kung Fu. Phillip didn't bother appraising the others; I shall be lucky to get past the first three! he thought.

Phillip moved fast. Taking a few paces forward, he kicked the little knife-man as hard as he could between his legs. There was a terrible scream which must have been heard in the City Centre and the knife-man fell onto the floor. Phillip followed this up immediately by punching the next man, as hard as he could, on his nose. The big guy groaned and as the blood started to drip down his nose, he raised his hands, trying to stem the blood flow. With an open hand Phillip jabbed him in the centre of his chest and as the man bent down to ease the pain, Phillip chopped the big man hard on the side of his neck. The man fell down like a sack of potatoes and lay there, supine. Phillip continued to move swiftly towards the Kung Fu guy, who was already putting up his hands like Bruce Lee. Phillip kicked as hard as he could at the side of the man's left leg and he heard the bone crunch. The man fell on his left side, holding his leg and moaning in pain.

Phillip moved on to the next man who turned and started running. The next man was very big, probably an ex-wrestler, but he was slow and as he threw a punch, Phillip was able to step aside. That put the big man off balance and turned him to the left so Phillip punched him as hard as he could into the right side of the man's back; he knew how painful it is to be hit in that area. He had suffered that pain when he had made an attempt to show off during his self-defence course, with his course instructor. The man groaned, but did not go down. He turned to Phillip, who thought, the bastard wants more, so he kicked him in his testicles, hard. This time, the man did fall down and appeared to be having some kind of convulsion, he looked green in the face. Not very technical, thought Phillip, but it always works! Phillip turned to face the next man but there was no-one there. A quick look at the knife-man who was lying on his right side in a foetal position; the man Phillip had previously beaten had gone as well.

With the exit clear, Phillip walked out of the cul-de-sac and proceeded to move as fast as he could, out of the red light area, paying more attention as he went, with the occasional glance behind him, to make sure he was not being followed. He was very careful in case the runaways had laid an ambush and were ready to attack him. He saw nothing and continued walking fast towards the city centre.

When he had walked for some distance and he knew he was not far from his hotel, Phillip was quite sure that no-one was following him. He heaved a sigh of relief and turned into the next bar, ordered a double brandy and a glass of lager and went, with reaction setting in, to sit down at a table before his trembling knees gave way. He tossed the brandy off in one swallow and was about to drink his lager in a very similar way, when the barman said something to him, with a smile. Phillip said, "Sorry, I only speak English."

"Oh, English, we like English, have a nice day, you look as if it was not so good for you? Wait," and he put another double brandy in a glass and brought it over to Phillip's table saying, "On the house!"

The alcohol content of the first brandy was taking effect but he still felt tense although the adrenalin surge was now wearing off. He tried not to think too closely about the danger he had been in and thanked God for the self-defence course. Without that, they would have been fishing his disfigured corpse out of some backwater the following morning and word would have gone round that this was what would happen to anybody who dared to offer violence to one of the sex trade's pimps.

The following morning he made his flight in plenty of time, landed at Gatwick and picked up his car. Once home, he caught up with messages on his answer phone and sat down at his desk to write out a list of expenses, trying to sort out all the crumpled receipts he had collected and marrying them up with the amounts expended. He hoped Mr Bukow was not an ex-accountant who would check every minute detail, when out of the corner of his eye, he saw a smart, new

BMW convertible draw up outside, a young lady getting out a small suitcase from the boot, and when she turned towards his door, he could have sworn it was Sarah. He must be suffering from delusions, following his traumatic experience abroad but, yes, it actually was Sarah and she rang the doorbell impatiently.

He went to open the door, gazing down at her in amazement as she said, pathetically, "You won't send me away, will you?" She looked so sad and miserable, he stood aside to let her enter, for once in his life, speechless.

"Is it alright if I stay for a bit and apologise for my behaviour?"

Phillip realised what was happening and was so happy to see her. "It was my fault…"

Before he could add another word, Sarah's face lit up and looked full of joy. She dropped her case and reached up to put her arms around his neck, murmuring, "I've missed you so much!" For the next few moments they kissed as though they had been apart for years instead of weeks, and when they drew apart, she said, grinning, "I've brought my overnight case with me, I'll race you up the stairs."

Phillip needed no further persuasion and ran upstairs after her as she rushed into the bathroom, reappearing shortly wearing a short, filmy, see-through nightie as he struggled with his zips and buttons! They fell onto the bed together, breathless with anticipation and proceeded to make love ecstatically until they climaxed and fell back on the pillows, exhausted with their efforts. Snuggling together, they became drowsy and drifted off into a light sleep, Phillip waking first, feeling ravenous, having missed anything to eat since his snack on the plane this morning.

He showered and dressed, Sarah being still fast asleep. He sat down on the bed next to her sleeping form and started to nuzzle kisses behind her ear until she surfaced and yawned. She slipped her arms round his neck and would have pulled him back into bed if he had not said lightly, "Get your delicious little bum off that bed and come downstairs so we can get something to eat. After that, I'll see about accommodating you." He pulled the duvet off her and gave her a light smack across her bum. "Up you get!" and he went downstairs before he could change his mind and leap into bed with her again.

When she appeared, not wearing very much, he told her to put her outer clothes on so they could go shopping, unless she wanted a takeaway. She put her head on one side and said, "I don't think I've ever really had a 'takeaway', are they nice?"

Phillip had to laugh, "Come on milady, I think we'd better save takeaways for another time, then I can show you how delicious they taste and how full of calories they are!" They shopped, wandering all around the big supermarket, then went back and ate a large salad and a plentiful portion of ice cream which Sarah had insisted on buying, saying it was years since she had eaten ice cream out of such a huge carton!

They sat companionably next to each other and Phillip told her a little about the case he was working on, without too many details, not wanting her to worry about the danger he had been in. "Do you think you will ever find her?" questioned Sarah.

"I really hope so," he said, "there's quite a lot at stake. Mr Bukow paid £30,000 into my bank account and if I am not successful, it's obvious he'll want most of it back! Now what have you been doing over the past few weeks?"

"I was heartbroken when you told me our relationship was going nowhere, so I thought I had better find someone else and try to forget you. I did a lot of crying, some serious thinking and I got on with my college work. After lectures, a few of us went out for a drink and it turned out to be okay, better than spending time feeling sorry for myself, and it became a routine. Two men of about my age showed a lot of interest and first one of them invited me out. We went for a meal, and when it was finished, he paid the bill although I offered to pay my share, but conversation kind of dried up and he just sat there until finally he said, 'The other chap I share my flat with has gone on a field trip, you could come back with me and er… have a coffee or something.'

"I said, 'Sorry, I don't really know you, I've only seen you at college a few times.' He went a bit red in the face and said, 'Oh come on, I'm only talking about a bit of sex, nothing too serious, you know you girls are all asking for it!!'

"Well I nearly hit the roof, stormed out, phoned for a taxi and went home. He must have thought that because he paid the bill, I should make it worth his while, disgusting creature. After that, I completely ignored him if I saw him in college.

"I missed you very much and wanted to come over here and change your mind but I gave dating another chance. The other chap I'd met when we went for a drink asked me to go out and he seemed quite nice so we went for a meal and got on okay, talking about our various interests and college work and things and I insisted on paying my half of the bill because I didn't want him to think he was entitled to payment in kind, if you know what I mean!! So he had this old car and said he would see me home if I gave him directions and off we went. He pulled up in the lane, you know, at the end of the drive and when I said he could drive straight up to the house, he grabbed me and sort of pinned me up against the seat, started to kiss me and pushed his hand up under my top and started to squeeze my breast!

"Well, a goodnight kiss would have been not too bad, but he was nearly trying to undress me so I slapped his face really hard and while he pulled back, I managed to open the car door and I ran up the drive, scared he would try to follow me. The rotten sod didn't even apologise when I saw him again, just ignored me, and when I told a girlfriend about what had happened, she was amazed I had made so much fuss! Fuss, she called it, when I might have been raped and murdered in my seat," she said dramatically.

Phillip was unable to say anything, his feelings were such a mixture of emotions. "Say something," pleaded Sarah, "don't just sit there!"

He cleared his throat with difficulty and then said gently, "You are a beautiful young lady and I am a very lucky man for you to have decided to make me your friend, lover, protector and anything else you want me to be and I shall do my best to care for you the best way I know."

Sarah wriggled with embarrassment and said, "Aw, that's the nicest thing you've ever said to me, I'll try to live up to it."

On Friday, Phillip gave Sarah the spare key to his house and told her she was free to come and go as she pleased; she must treat it as her home, whether he was there or not. "What about your parents?" queried Phillip, lightly. "What do you think their attitude will be towards their darling daughter moving in with an old roué like me?"

"Don't worry," she said, po-faced, "I won't let them move in!"

"That's a pity, I rather fancy your Mum and I've always wanted an enormous, hairy, black dog to keep the place untidy," he replied, equally poker-faced. "But seriously, how do they feel about you staying here on weekends and at other times? They must know that we don't sit here playing cards or doing our knitting!"

"When I talked to my parents about you I told them that I'm a sensible, twenty-one-year-old girl who doesn't sleep around, doesn't do drugs and I don't binge drink!! I love this one man and I want to spend time with him; yes, we do sleep together and we do make love, but it's a very healthy, loving relationship."

"So what did they say?" he said, curiously. "They said, 'If you ever need help, or you want to talk about anything that bothers you, come to us.' And that was that! With it being Friday, are you meeting Gordon tonight?" Sarah asked.

"No, I wasn't sure how long I would be in Amsterdam so we arranged that if I didn't ring him before six o'clock tonight, I wouldn't be seeing him."

"And are you going to ring him?"

"That rather depends on you; what can you offer me as an alternative to drinking with my best friend? Anyway, Gordon has met someone called Isobel and they are planning to marry, so in a way, our relationship has changed. He did say we should carry on seeing each other on Friday nights but I could tell that he would rather spend time with her than sit in a wine bar, drinking. So I don't think he'll be worried about me not turning up."

"That's good," said Sarah, snuggling up to him. "I can have you to myself for a while and I think I can promise you a more entertaining time than just drinking yourself silly with Gordon!"

They enjoyed their weekend, hardly ever leaving the bedroom except to raid the fridge for food, or indulging in a long, lazy bath together. Inevitably, Monday morning arrived and Sarah drove off to work and Phillip tried to settle down at his desk and catch up on his two current cases, beginning a detailed report to be sent to Vasily Bukow.

Chapter 16

The phone rang and when he answered it, Gordon asked him, "How are things going, my old son?"

"Not so much of the 'old', I know that Scotsmen age quickly, but English guys like me are fit and still young at fifty!!" said Phillip, indignantly.

"Ho ho, you wish! How was Amsterdam?"

"I managed to call in at every brothel in the red light district, without getting laid once, I beat up a pimp and then saw off six of his mates who came to damage my extremities – the other two ran away!!"

"You've got to be kidding, what a load of rubbish, if you beat up six people, they must have been small boys!"

"If they were boys, they were bloody big ones!"

"Are you serious?" said Gordon, sounding decidedly unbelieving. "What did really happen?"

"Yes, I'm quite serious; it's only by the grace of God and my self-defence course that I didn't end up floating in one of the canals!"

"Tell me, exactly what happened?" Gordon asked.

"I will, next time I see you."

"That's why I'm calling; next Friday there's the second lecture on 'Morality in Society' like the one we attended before. Are you interested? It's at two o'clock, is that a date?" Gordon queried.

"Okay, that's a date but remember, no kissing," joked Phillip. "I'm a very inexperienced type of guy and I don't want to have to slap your face," he said, in a silly, affected voice and they laughed with the ease of old friendship.

Later, John Standish rang, informing him of the date for Walter Dunn's trial and asking him to call at his office on the next two Monday mornings, to plan their strategy. "Fine, see you next Monday, about ten o'clock, traffic permitting!" Phillip acquiesced. Sarah rang in the afternoon and after some sexy backchat, she told him she would be a little late that evening as she would be going home to collect a few more clothes, "seeing as how I'll be spending more time at your place." They said a fond farewell and she rang off. That evening they carried her bags upstairs and Phillip told her to put her belongings wherever she wanted. He left her to arrange things to her satisfaction and when she came downstairs, humming a little tune, he asked her, "Have you eaten?"

"I had a meal with Mummy but that seems ages ago so if you waited for me, let's have something now. Do you have anything in the house, after our lazy weekend"

"I'm fully domesticated," he said, virtuously, "so I restocked this afternoon, can't have you going hungry!"

"Wow, a domesticated lover, good at housekeeping as well as good in bed!!"

The week flew by and they found they enjoyed each other's company, even when not making love and when Friday came, Phillip told Sarah reluctantly of the arrangements he had made with Gordon to attend a lecture and then go out for a meal and a few drinks. "Okay, that's fine," she said. "I'll just go over to Mummy's and stay there for the night, I mustn't monopolise all your time. Besides I have some college work I must complete and you are a distracting influence on me!"

Gordon was eager to hear about Amsterdam and he urged Phillip to tell him all about his experiences. Phillip started by explaining his theory and how he was going to make stringent enquiries into the way in which the sex rackets were run so that he could find Katia, if that was where she had been taken. "Tell me about this fight you had with twenty pimps, or whatever it was," said Gordon, obviously not really believing him.

"This guy came up to me in the famous, or infamous, red light district and more or less told me that it was dangerous to ask all these questions and after a bad night's sleep, not getting very far with my investigation, having to fend off every person who thought I was looking for sex, I got really pissed off and lost my cool. I jabbed him in the throat and as he bent down he was gasping for breath; I chopped him on the neck, which causes a temporary shutdown of the brain. He fell onto the pavement, like a sack of cement, and went into convulsions, like he was having a fit, so I stayed until he came out of it, just to make sure he recovered okay; heavens, I didn't want him to die on me if I'd hit him too hard. Anyway, he came round and I met this prostitute and before you ask it, no I didn't have sex with her, but I became friendly with her. Before you say anything else, we'd better get back or we'll be late for the start of the lecture!"

Gordon's face was a sight to see, avid to continue with Phillip's story but anxious not to miss the beginning of the talk!! They just made it to their seats when the Professor mounted the rostrum and began.

He began by stating what the lecture would cover: society and what the socialist government had hoped to achieve. Their supposition was that every person was equal, and how they aimed to bring that about was by using the lowest common denominator, so that everyone was on a similar level of achievement.

He described how women candidates were shortlisted for parliamentary seats, which resulted in unprecedented numbers of female members of parliament when Government then proceeded with various social engineering projects. New legislation was brought in which gave more rights to minority groups in what was seen as 'positive discrimination' and which appeared to destroy all the institutions society had previously relied upon. The traditional institution of marriage, which had proved the best way in which to establish a stable family and a good background for young people to grow up and mature in, was one of the first casualties. Next came moral values, social behaviour, religious upbringing and the work ethic – a fair day's work for a fair day's pay – these disappeared behind a fence of various benefits which were used, not by everybody, the speaker hastened to add, but by good and bad alike, people who seemed to think that the rest of us worked hard and paid our taxes in order to support them.

Divorce numbers spiralled upwards and when twenty-four-hour drinking came on the scene, a section of society seemed to regard it as a licence to drink until they were nearly unconscious and scenes of teenagers vomiting repeatedly in the streets were regarded in some parts of our major cities as part and parcel of life and nothing much could be done about it. The newspaper-reading population were amazed to read of the increase in liver damage and internal illnesses, mainly caused by excessive drinking. Useless to point out that twenty-four-hour opening of licensed premises merely meant that you could obtain a drink at any time of the day, *not drink all day long!*

"With political correctness being enforced by an increasing number of officials, who all have to be paid," the speaker went on, "it appears that respect for others is at an all-time low. If you try to point out anti-social behaviour, such as dropping litter as an example, you might get a foul-mouthed response or even in extreme cases, it has been known for people to be attacked and beaten. Try to ask a devoted mother not to block the entrance to your property by parking her four-by-four across the pavement while she delivers her child or children to the local school, you are liable to receive an answer containing many swear words, mainly beginning with f and s, which she has no reluctance in airing in front of an audience of children and other mothers. What sort of an example is that to any child?

"The most recent survey carried out among young people shows that they are more tolerant of bad behaviour and accept using bad language as a way of life. They accept that getting pregnant while still at school is 'just one of those things' and it would appear that the majority of the younger generation live together without getting married, and when the first child arrives they then go their separate ways, with poor results for their child's upbringing, being brought up by a single parent.

"These children grow up and the whole cycle starts again; little attention is paid to their children's needs and generation after generation is brought up with the same attitude, namely, *if I like something I want it now, if I don't like something I discard it and look for something else which appeals to me.* Who is going to set a good example to our young people? When trouble comes and the media calls attention to it, calls it a scandal, the government come up with quick, ill-conceived solutions which prove to be totally impracticable such as fining people 'on-the-spot fines', and when events have moved on and publicity has died down, the 'solution' is quietly dropped and no longer enforced.

"When the present government came to power, they promised to be always open and honest with the population. What do we appear to have now? An administration which tries to hide its failures; if they are forced by circumstances to announce bad news, they do so at such a time when other events are taking prime place with the media, hoping to divert attention in another direction. If your house is broken into – the police have on occasions been unable to attend immediately; if you say something considered to be out of place to a known homosexual person, the police appear on your doorstop before you have time to turn around!

"You will then be lectured as if you were homophobic and you are warned never to do it again. If a heterosexual couple were seen to be having sexual intercourse in a public place, they would be arrested and charged with indecent behaviour. In an actual case of a homosexual couple who were seen to be in the same situation, a lady who complained to the police was told 'not to walk in that area'. We are assured that this is still a Christian country but when a shop was recently opened, displaying books relating to homosexuality, an elderly gentleman went into the shop and asked if he could display a copy of the bible alongside these publications and permission was refused. Shortly after he returned home, two policemen arrived and subjected him to a long lecture about being homophobic.

"In times past, this country was famous for allowing freedom of speech, when a person could say 'I don't agree with what you are saying, but I will fight for your right to express your own opinion'; apparently, it seems as if the majority may say nothing about a minority. Prince Harry found out about this when he was forced to apologise for calling his friend a Paki. It was not meant as an insult, simply that the man came from Pakistan and in the usual way English people have, they will abbreviate any word which can be shortened in any way. There are too many examples to quote, as each one of you will know. My wife's full Christian name is 'Victoria' but the name is always abbreviated to 'Vicky' and I don't believe she feels insulted in any way.

"The English person abroad has to put up with a number of nicknames, wherever they happen to be, some flattering, some insulting, but we ignore this for the main part and usually laugh, feeling in some way that their Englishness has been recognised. However, it appears that we have reached a point where nothing may be said to anyone, in case they should feel insulted. That was the situation under the Communist regime in Russia and we, in the West, used to say how dreadful if was because freedom of speech was one of the most basic of human rights, to be what you want, to say what you want – it's why they call it a free society. Are we a free society today? Perhaps you should go away and think about that most carefully.

"Thank you for listening. Your comments and questions should be addressed to my secretarial staff and I shall do my best to reply."

As they made their way leisurely towards the exit, Gordon said, "Where shall we eat?" Phillip thought that now was the right time to tell Gordon about Sarah so he told him how she had come to see him, after he had not heard from her for weeks, and they had kind of mutually agreed that she should move in with him and he had given her a spare key, so that she was free to come and go as she pleased. She was going to spend this evening with her parents but in case she was waiting for him, he would ring her when they got to the wine bar. "Ooer, you've got it bad," said Gordon. "That's the first time since I've known you that you felt you had to ring her 'in case she was waiting'; my, my, how you've changed," he said.

"Okay, you can cut the crap," Phillip said, "it's just that she's gorgeous and a bit young and vulnerable and besides, I've just realised I like spending time with her, not just in bed, although that's great as well!"

In the wine bar, Gordon went to get their drinks and Phillip looked for a table where he could sit and make his call to Sarah, when an all too familiar voice said, "Well, look who's here," and Phillip looked up to see Samantha, his ex-partner, standing in front of him, exquisitely and expensively dressed as usual, arm in arm with his old supervisor.

"Slumming it tonight, are we?" she said, with raised eyebrows. Phillip looked up, taking in the whole picture from her black, high heeled shoes, the nearly off the shoulder dress, plunging deeply at the front, revealing her lack of underwear, to the carefully tousled hairstyle, no doubt straight from her pricey coiffeur. The dress was a little too tight, a little too revealing, and Phillip thought to himself, did I really make love to that body, spend several years of my life thinking we were together for ever, only to have her walk out at the first sign of any difficulty and then making a point of flaunting her latest keeper in my face, or have I imagined it all! "Good evening sir, are you with this woman or do you just happen to be standing next to her?"

The old boy laughed good naturedly and said, "Yes, yes I am with this lady." Some devil got into Phillip and he asked if he was keeping her in the manner to which she had become accustomed.

"Come, come, it's not like you to be a bitter loser," said Samantha, knowing full well what he meant.

"Why should I be bitter? I had you first, when you were still young!" said Phillip crudely.

"Now Phillip, don't be bitchy darling," she said uneasily, wondering what he was going to say next.

"I don't think I'm being bitchy, sweetheart, you are much better at it than I am, even if you were not much good at anything else!"

There was a momentary silence, while Samantha's face flushed under her careful make-up. "We must have caught you on a bad night," said her companion, gently pulling her elbow. "Got to dash now," and Samantha, with a wiggle of her backside, pulled the supervisor after her as if he was some sort of lap dog.

"What a woman, in a class of her own," said Gordon, with a glass of lager in each hand.

"Put your tongue away," said Phillip, "you know you always fancied her!"

"Never mind her, carry on telling me about how you beat up that pimp."

"It was a couple of days later and my friendly prostitute phoned me to say I had to meet her urgently. She told me she heard on the grapevine that this pimp had got some of his friends to come after me, but like an idiot, I carried on searching in the same quarter as before, turned down a side street to look at my map and when I turned to go back into the main street, about eight assorted villains were blocking my way. I turned to get out of a bad situation but the little side street happened to be a cul-de-sac and I was trapped."

"Phew, what did you do next?"

"I felt like praying but I rather thought there wasn't enough time for God to come to my rescue. You had a bloody good laugh when I told you about my self-defence course, but believe me, it saved my life! The theory is that when outnumbered, you strike first, where they are least expecting it, because if you wait for them to come after you, you will be overwhelmed. Always go for the most dangerous-looking one first – they somehow think they are superior to you and will least expect to be attacked first. In this case it was the little man with a knife. You must realise that I was thinking this could be my last act. But the thought that these bastards who force girls as young as thirteen to have sex with the sick perverts and then pocket all the money made me so mad, I was determined to take as many of them with me as I could. So I kicked the knifeman as hard as I could between his legs. His screams must have been heard in city centre. Once you start, don't stop or the impetus of your attack will peter out and you will lose any advantage you have."

Phillip carried on telling Gordon, describing the encounter as it happened. When he finished Gordon said, "Wow, that was some fight, I raise my hat to you."

"It was an adrenalin flow and anger which drove me to extend myself," said Phillip. "Suddenly, the place was nearly deserted and I turned and walked very fast to a bar near my hotel. I had a couple of double brandies, one straight after the other; in fact, the bartender gave me the second one 'on the house', he seemed to think I needed it!"

"If I were you," Gordon urged, "I wouldn't tell that story to anyone else. I believe you, where thousands wouldn't, but most people who don't know you will think it's a load of bullshit, besides which I don't think the Dutch Tourist Board would be very happy if a story like that got around – not good for their image eh?"

"I have no intention of telling anyone about what happened. After that I was very careful and watched my back whenever I went out, but

I still searched all through the brothels, looking at the girls to see if Katia was amongst them."

"You mean they parade in front of you?" said Gordon, his mind boggling at the very thought.

"Nah, the madams mostly show you a book of 'artistic' pictures, telling you to pick one you fancied."

"What, nude pictures?"

"Well nearly, showing off all their assets, as you might say!"

"And what did you do then?"

"I had to pretend that none of them were what I was looking for and say goodnight!" Gordon looked unconvinced, knowing that Phillip was a hundred-percent red-blooded male, and let his mind wander over the possibilities. He opened his mouth, about to make a facetious remark, when Phillip said, "Don't even go there!!"

"Anyway, as I said, if you think I'm going to go around boasting of my prowess in foreign parts, you must be nuts," said Phillip abruptly, "and see to it that you don't go blabbing about it at the office or anywhere else, if you want to remain in one piece, my dearest and oldest friend!"

Phillip rang his home number, only to get the answer phone and he said to Gordon, "After this drink, I'll make my way home. I haven't brought the car so it'll have to be good old public transport; pity, it'll take me ages."

Gordon had a sudden thought. "I'll give Isobel a ring and ask her to bring the car round, then she can take us all to see your new place, I haven't even had a glimpse of it yet!"

In spite of Phillip's protestations, Gordon insisted on phoning Isobel and while they had another drink, she drove round to pick them up. It was a rather complicated drive for Isobel, unused as she was to Gordon's car, and once they were out of the centre of London, she gave a sigh of relief. "I don't think I'll ever get used to driving here, I need a lot more practice before I pass my test!" The two men were shocked into silence and then both started to speak at once. "Only joking," she said. "I just thought I'd say that to get your complete attention. That's an example of the British sense of humour, yes?" The two men burst out laughing and Gordon patted her leg and assured her that she did indeed have all his attention and when he'd picked Phillip up off the floor, he was sure he would agree.

They pulled up outside the house and duly admired the sign which said 'Phillip Everett, Private Investigator' and he ushered them through the front door, not really expecting to find Sarah there. She had said she was going over to see her parents while he went to meet Gordon but she had evidently been asleep on the sofa and woke up suddenly as they came into the lounge. Phillip introduced everybody and was aware of a little frisson of ice in the atmosphere. He realised that Sarah, not expecting anyone, was dressed in a sloppy sweater and old jeans which had both seen better days, whereas Isobel was immaculate in a smart trouser suit and Gordon was wearing his usual Savile Row, made-to-measure business suit.

Sarah was obviously feeling a little out of place and fairly bristled with annoyance. Normally, she too would have been smartly dressed, particularly if she had known she was going to be meeting Phillip's friends, but she said stiffly, "Shall I make some coffee or would you like something stronger?"

Hoping to smooth her ruffled feathers, Phillip gave her a hearty kiss and murmured in her ear, "Do you realise how sexy you look in that loose outfit? Makes me think of what's underneath when I force you to strip later on," and said, "Darling, I'll show Isobel and Gordon *our* pad while you make the coffee, okay?"

Sarah brightened considerably, and said, "Yes, you do that and I'll tidy up a bit!"

When the three of them came downstairs, having dutifully inspected all the facilities upstairs and made admiring comments, they all sat down to drink their coffee. Gordon and Isobel got up to go – they had decided to go for a meal somewhere – and as they were leaving, Gordon gave Sarah a kiss and said what a beautiful young lady she was and Phillip was a lucky dog to have found her, he didn't know how he had managed it and Sarah was somewhat mollified. "Perhaps you could come back for another, longer, visit," she said. "You caught me unawares this time, I don't usually slop around when we have visitors," and turning to Phillip, who was kissing Isobel, "A phone call would have been nice!"

"I called you," said Phillip patiently, "it went on the answer phone," and before she could say anything more he slapped Gordon lightly on the back and said he would ring him during the week, saw them to their car and waved them goodbye.

Sarah was looking mutinous, clearing away the coffee cups and stacking things in the dishwasher. Phillip expected an outburst and that was exactly what he got! "You could have told me you were bringing somebody back; I felt a real idiot, dressed like this!" Phillip came up behind her and put one arm round her waist, but she was determined to put him in the wrong and went on, "I came home from Mummy's early because she had her bridge club grannies round for their monthly gossip fest; I thought you would be back about eight but I must have fallen asleep and there you were, bringing in two complete strangers to me – did you think I wouldn't be in?"

"Calm down," said Phillip. "First of all, I didn't expect you to be here; secondly I had a rather annoying meeting with my ex-partner and her comments always rile me, then Gordon and I had a drink and when he found out it was going to take me hours to get back here, using public transport, he rang Isobel and she brought the car round and gave me a lift home. Now I could hardly get out of the car, tell them 'Thanks, but get lost', now could I?" he appealed. "I had to ask them in and to be fair, I had no idea you had come back here from your parents as you didn't answer the phone, so you could see I had to do the gentlemanly thing, didn't I, and invite them in for coffee or a drink?"

Sarah sniffed, albeit expressively. "You mean *she* wasn't with you in the wine bar?"

So that's what it's all about, thought Phillip. "Of course she wasn't. I told you, Gordon only rang her up when he found out I would have a long journey in front of me (and compared to you, her driving is atrocious), hoping he would never be found out!"

"Of course, she's not English, is she?" said Sarah, prepared to be generous. "Our roads take some getting used to," she said smugly. "Okay, I think I might be prepared to forgive you, if you feed me; I haven't eaten yet."

Phillip heaved a quiet sigh of relief and asked her if she was going to change, but she shook her head. "Let's just get going to the nearest pub that serves food and I'll drive so that you can have even more to drink, provided it doesn't make you too sleepy later on!" They ordered from the surprisingly varied menu and Sarah ate, enjoying the cosy atmosphere, only to look across to Phillip's plate, which he had cleared in very short time. "Do you always eat that fast?" she said. "I hope you're not going to be the same in bed!"

Once home, they went straight upstairs and started undressing, and although Phillip assured Sarah he could help her with taking off her sweatshirt, she reluctantly refused his offer and told him to take his own clothes off and be sure to put them away tidily. "I didn't take you out for an expensive meal to come home and be henpecked," he called to her in the shower.

She appeared a few minutes later wearing just her underwear, walking slowly towards him saying, "What was that you were muttering about? Let's see what you're capable of doing now, I'm going to give you marks out of ten for…"

It was a long time before they finally fell asleep with Sarah murmuring sleepily, "I'm not quite sure how many points you got, you'll have to take the exam again!!"

Chapter 17

After the weekend, life went back to a routine, Sarah went to college and Phillip wrote out his report and expenses and forwarded copies to Mr Bukow and then went to visit Walter Dunn. Walter was delighted to see him and welcomed him in, telling him the news about the date being set for his trial and how well he was getting on with his neighbours who were proving to be valuable friends. Phillip asked if he was still living on his own! Walter looked a little shocked. "I suppose that's what my life will be like from now on, what with my wife's death and everything."

Phillip told him he was far too young to think of spending the rest of his life living alone and somewhere there was a very nice lady waiting for him and he should get out more and try and meet some of the women, aged over fifty, who outnumbered men five to one. "You need a companion to share your life with, if you are adamant about not going to live with your son in America; there are too many lonely people in the world, without you contributing to that number."

"For a start off, I've had this case hanging over my head for so many months, I haven't been able to think further than the next day and another thing, where do I meet all these women and how do I know which ones would be interested in an old widower like me and—"

"Come on now," said Phillip, "where's your Dunkirk spirit? That's not the attitude that rescued thousands of stranded soldiers from the war-torn beaches! Wait until this trial's over and I'll show you how to get into the mainstream of dating again." Walter shuddered slightly and Phillip grinned at him. "Has John Standish been in touch with you?"

"Yes, the trial has been set for a week next Tuesday."

"Has anyone been in touch with you with useful information which might help us?" queried Phillip.

"Afraid not, Mr Everett, were you expecting anyone to come forward?"

"It was just an outside possibility but from next Monday, John and I will be meeting to prepare your defence. If you need anything, let me know won't you, and if I don't see you before then, I will be there at the Law Courts for the trial. Do try not to worry and I'll see you there. Be prepared to buy the champagne to toast your acquittal!" and with that encouraging remark, Phillip left him.

He went to John Standish's office and they were soon discussing what form Walter's defence would take. "Who are you calling as witnesses?" asked Phillip.

"I'm going to call you, Walter, Betsy and the policewoman who was there when you interviewed her, with her mother."

"You mean the one who witnessed the wild behaviour of Doris?"

"We shall try and show what an unreliable and biased person she was, try and cast doubts about what she claims took place between her daughter and Walter, and altogether show her as an unsuitable guardian for a teenage girl, even if she is her own biological daughter. If we can discredit what she says under oath, I am convinced we will win the case, hands down." With that they got on with analysing Phillip's evidence and the way in which he would give it and ended the morning thoroughly satisfied with their meeting.

On returning to his office, Phillip found a message on the answer phone from Barry Spencer, asking him to ring asap. Phillip rang immediately and Barry said that Mr Bukow had been asking how the investigation was progressing. Phillip told him that he had posted off a detailed report to him only two days previously, which he obviously had not received. "Actually," said Barry, "it's not such a good idea to put such confidential papers in the post; if you just ring this number we have any number of messengers who will collect packages from you without you even having to put a stamp on the envelope, and then we can be sure there will be no hold-ups." Phillip murmured his agreement and said next time, that was exactly what he would do.

In the meantime, he filled Barry in with some of the details of his search in Amsterdam, without mentioning anything about the fight in which he had become involved. He explained the steps he had taken and told Barry that there were now many eyes and ears searching and he was hopeful that there would soon be some results. Barry expressed some doubt. "How can you be sure that she is in Amsterdam?"

"After my talk with the policeman who was involved in the case at first, I am as sure as I can be of her present location, although I personally could not trace her. If you look at our information, you know that the Russian mafia are running everything to do with the sex for sale industry; that includes alcohol and drugs, in Amsterdam and other places we know; so I wonder if the 'Head Man' could be an old former friend of Mr Bukow? Maybe they fell out and this is his form of revenge?"

Barry thought about it for a moment. "Are you saying that this man kidnapped the daughter of his friend and forced her into being a prostitute?"

"Just imagine if you are a very rich man," said Phillip, "and some old business colleague kidnapped your only daughter, who was your pride and joy, and forced her to have sex with any Tom, Dick or Harry who would pay her pimp for the privilege, how would you feel? How painful and humiliating it would be, for both daughter and father."

"Can you identify the Russian man involved in this act?" asked Barry. "If not, this is just speculation on your part and Mr Bukow would not say whether you are right or not."

"Could there be a man who might have done such a thing? If Mr Bukow could indicate such a person, it might be a positive lead to follow up." said Phillip.

Barry was being very diplomatic and said smoothly, "There might be many men like that, in Mr Bukow's previous business dealings; which one would you investigate?"

"Think this over and speak to Mr Bukow before I return to Amsterdam again; I am hoping for real information from the 'sex workers' I have been in contact with and one in particular, who is working on the inside, could be in a very good position to locate Katia. If Mr Bukow thinks of anyone who could be villainous enough to kidnap his daughter, get in touch with me urgently. In the meantime, I'll make another copy of my report and if you send somebody over, I will deliver it into their safe hands."

CHAPTER 18

The day arrived; Phillip and John Standish arrived at the Law Courts to find Walter already there, waiting nervously for them. John's assistant, loaded down with important-looking files, went to check if their witnesses were present and asked them to sit and wait until they were called by the Usher into court to give evidence. Betsy was dressed in her school uniform and was ignoring her mother who was talking loudly to her solicitor, a bored-looking gentleman who acknowledged John with, "This isn't going to be too long drawn out is it? I'm due for a game of squash this afternoon. How's your game coming along, you were slowing down a bit, last time we played?" John withstood the inclination to start a conversation with the 'opposition' although they were actually long-time friends, gave him a nod and shepherded Walter into court to take their places. Phillip went to sit next to the policewoman and Betsy, awaiting the time he would be called into court.

He offered to buy the two ladies a coffee and by the time he had found a machine, the correct change, pressed all the right buttons in the correct order, they barely had time to take a sip before he was called to give evidence. John had already made his opening speech in reply to the case for the prosecution, who had given Mrs Hearne's allegations that Mr Dunn had tried to groom her daughter for a sexual relationship by bribing her with the provision of clothing and paying for hair styling and gym membership and school books. The spectators in the public gallery settled down, after some amusement, to hear Doris, who was the only witness, give her story, which on the face of it, could provide a very entertaining morning's performance. On her solicitor's advice she had dressed (after much mutinous disagreement) in an old grey dress which came to just above her ankles, a shapeless cardigan-style jacket, flat shoes and thick, lisle stockings.

Walter sat, rather white faced, as Doris told her story, of how he had accosted her daughter in the park and persuaded her to accept clothes, books, hairdos, gym membership, trainers and equipment and such like, undermining her mother's authority until when she had remonstrated with her daughter, Betsy had said she would go and see Mr Dunn because he was the only one who was good to her. They had met, she didn't know how many times, and for all they knew (who this imaginary 'they' were, she didn't quantify) sexual intercourse had already taken place, perhaps several times!! The Gallery settled down to this very interesting story. Who'd have thought that little old white-faced man in the dock there could do such a thing, but of course, it's always the innocent looking ones who are the worst, aren't they, they all agreed.

Things didn't look too promising and Doris came down from the witness box, incredibly pleased with her Oscar winning performance as the wronged girl's brave mother, standing up for virtue and justice!! John had made no effort at cross-examination, after asking the judge if he might cross-examine Doris at a later time, if it should be necessary. He called his first witness speedily, anxious to get Phillip's evidence before the judge started to think about his lunch.

John started skilfully bringing Walter's circumstances to the judge's attention, emphasising his loneliness and his kind-hearted attempt to help a child who was sobbing, while he was taking a walk through the park. Phillip told of his investigations into Walter and Betsy's background, of the abusive mother and her lack of care for her daughter, at which point Doris stood up red-faced and started to shout at him. Nothing could have played into the hands of the defence quite so beautifully and when the judge sternly told her that with another similar outburst, he would have her removed from the court, the gallery was delighted.

After that, Phillip continued his explanation as to the results of an interview he attempted to have to get Betsy's side of the story, how her mother had constantly interrupted, the home circumstances with attention being focused on Doris's numerous different boyfriends and how she had always belittled her daughter and said how glad she would be if Betsy had never been born. He finished with the scene witnessed by the policewoman, who had been present throughout the interview.

The prosecuting solicitor attempted to cross-examine Phillip but it was all too obvious that his evidence showed the whole story to be true; the policewoman was called and verified everything Phillip had said and the judge decided that Betsy should give evidence after lunch. They all adjourned to the adjacent pub, ate a light meal and went back to court for Betsy to take the witness stand. Every sympathy was with her and the judge assured her that she should not be frightened by her surroundings and Betsy played her part as if she had appeared in court a hundred times. At first she was hesitant when John questioned her but gradually she started to speak out and he skilfully asked the right questions, leading her to talk of her life at home, how she was bullied at school for being fat and not being able to afford all the latest gear.

The judge asked her to itemise 'gear' so that the court record could show exactly what was meant by the word used in this context. Betsy obliged by looking up at him and explaining earnestly, "It means fashionable shoes and the latest mobile phones and make-up and trainers and being able to go to McDonalds and have a burger whenever you want, or going to the mall and buying things."

"Dear me," said the judge, "I had no idea so much was involved in the lives of schoolchildren nowadays," and suddenly recalling that the afternoon was progressing, asked her to continue.

The prosecuting solicitor decided to make a desperate attempt to discredit Betsy's story by requesting that she should undergo an examination in order to prove or disprove whether she had ever had sexual intercourse, in other words whether she was a virgin. There was a shocked silence in the court and then everybody started murmuring to the person sat next to them and the atmosphere sounded like a disturbed and angry wasps' nest. "In my chambers, now!" stated the judge, adding as an afterthought, "The jury will ignore that remark until after I have come to a decision," and he swept through the door to his chambers.

"What do you think you're playing at?" he demanded fiercely, when the three of them were ensconced in his room. "I'm aware that you want to win this case but do you really have to get this girl to submit to a humiliating examination to prove your point?"

"As I see it, a lot rests on whether the old man had his wicked way with her and whether she is protecting him by saying they were never alone at any time, either because she is completely under his influence or because she wants to look like an innocent victim of her mother's salacious story. It's in her own interests, as well as mine, for her to undergo this examination and the quicker the better."

John Standish looked ruefully at the judge. "Although it goes against my better judgement, if I were in his shoes, I think I would be tempted to do the same, regardless of Betsy's feelings. What is your decision, judge?"

"Very reluctantly, I shall agree to it but only after you have explained it very carefully to her and made it clear that she is in no way to blame for any findings." They went back into court, the judge announced a recess and allowed John to explain to Betsy in a quiet room, what was going to happen.

"It's alright," she sniffed, "I know what's involved. Anyway, it's not going to hurt, is it? I am still a virgin and I'd do just about anything to win the case and take the smile off her face."

The jurors and audience reconvened in court and the doctor was called to give evidence. When asked by the prosecuting solicitor as to whether or not Betsy had ever had sexual intercourse, he firmly declared, "No, she is a virgin!"

It was a foregone conclusion after that; when the two solicitors had given their closing speeches, the judge in his summing up would virtually instruct the jury as to their duty and sure enough, twenty minutes later, they returned with their verdict of Not Guilty. The judge awarded costs to Walter, congratulated him and left the court.

"Where's the champagne?" said Phillip. "Let's go and celebrate."

"Can I come too?" said Betsy.

They paused and John said gently, "I think there are going to be some difficulties when you go home tonight."

"I've been talking to the policewoman and she says she'll go back with me and if my mother tries to throw me out, she knows a place where I can stay for a few days. After that, I don't know what will happen to me." She looked at Walter. "I suppose you hate me for causing you all this trouble, don't you? I didn't mean to get you into bother, but she kept on and on until, in the end, I told her about you and said you were the first person who ever did anything for me and her dirty mind thought I must have been sleeping with you, to do all those nice things for me." A small tear appeared, which was swiftly brushed away and she said defiantly, "Well anyway, thanks," and she turned away.

Walter was torn between relief at being declared not guilty and concern for Betsy's unenviable situation. "I am sorry, but I am still barred from seeing you or coming anywhere near you. But I can't see your mother doing anything silly after what the judge said. If the worst comes to pass I am still around."

Chapter 19

The following morning, Sarah left for work and Phillip sat down to work out his final bill for Walter Dunn's case. When the post was delivered, he stretched his long limbs and went into the hall to see what new array of bills had arrived, and was intrigued by an expensive cream envelope, addressed in bold, black ink, and immediately slit the top open to read the contents.

It came as a complete surprise! It was, of all things, an invitation to a birthday party. He read the accompanying letter in which Tania's father had written that he had made such an impression on them both, she had asked if he would come to her twentieth birthday celebration the following Friday. A party was to be held at the club and would start about two pm. A reply would be appreciated. Phillip was surprised that they would have remembered him and was of a mind to reply politely, refusing the kind invitation as he had unfortunately made other commitments for that day etc, etc. This had to be thought about and considered carefully. What would Sarah think about attending an extremely pretty girl's party, a girl whom Phillip had known in the past? He would have to explain it all to her.

Sarah let herself in with her much-prized own key, shouting through to the kitchen, "Where's that gorgeous man of mine?" and flinging her arms around him, kissing him generously on the mouth. He returned the kiss with interest and debated whether he should introduce the subject of the invitation now, or later. Sarah chattered about what he was preparing for them to eat and should they go out for a drink or should they stay in and watch a film on television or –

"You're very quiet," she said suspiciously, "what's wrong?"

"Nothing's wrong," he said, rather defensively. "I've received an invitation to a party, that's all and—"

"Oh, goodie," said Sarah. "I love parties, where is it?"

Phillip explained that he had visited a Russian nightclub while he was searching for the unknown young man who was connected with Katia's disappearance. The manager had objected to him watching customers while he was on his own, it would look a bit suspicious, so he had provided a young lady to sit with him, as if he was a genuine 'bona fide' visitor and it turned out that she was Tania, the manager's daughter. Sarah's eyebrows could not be raised any higher. She said abruptly, "Is she pretty?"

"I really didn't notice," he said, nonchalantly.

"Call yourself a private 'dick' and you didn't notice what she looked like, come off it, of course you noticed. I bet she's a stunner, isn't she?" Sarah said.

"Look," said Phillip firmly, "I can't afford to upset my Russian friends; if I do, it might lead to unnecessary complications. After all, they have paid £30,000 into my bank account. If you come with me, you'll see that Tania, although a very nice girl, is not a patch on you and you can partake of Russian hospitality and, er, broaden your outlook."

Sarah looked mutinous and then said grudgingly, "I suppose I'd better come with you, to fend off this Russian chick who has obviously got a crush on you. Perhaps her daddy might have you lined up as a marriage possibility, and I must put a stop to ideas like that!!"

Phillip reassured her that nobody would see him as a marriage prospect, not with his job and a non-existent career pattern and Sarah changed the subject by saying, "I've nothing to wear, I'll have to go shopping for a new outfit, when did you say this party was?"

"How about wearing your birthday suit, just for me, tonight?" he said. "After we've eaten, of course!"

Sarah pretended to be outraged and said the dreaded words, "Only if you come shopping with me tomorrow!"

Phillip gave in with good grace, hoping to wriggle out of the chore, but Sarah would have none of it, although in the end, he quite enjoyed seeing her dart in and out of changing rooms, half dressed, in various outfits before she made her final decision.

Phillip told her they had to be there by two pm and was sitting drumming his fingers on the arm of his chair at 1.30, waiting for her to come downstairs in order for them to get into the taxi he had booked. The wait was worth it and as she came down the stairs, posing dramatically two or three steps from the bottom, she said, "Do I meet with sir's approval?" Her dress was black, demurely knee-length but as his gaze travelled upwards, taking in the top half, with the neckline plunging to show the upper parts of her breasts with a teasing glimpse of a lacy bra, he thought, do we really have to go to this party? He could have ravished her where she stood!

The neckline was accentuated with a small design of a butterfly in iridescent sequins, making sure that all eyes would be concentrating on where that plunging neckline was going. Phillip recollected where he was and said grudgingly, "Come along you half-dressed hussy, you'd be late for your own funeral; for heaven's sake put your coat on or the driver won't be able to keep his eyes on the road!" Sarah laughed triumphantly and put her evening wrap round her shoulders – "Thought that might attract your attention, let's see what the opposition can come up with!"

They arrived at the club and Phillip showed the invitation to the big bouncer on the door, who obviously remembered him. He opened the door for them to go in and they were met by Tania's father who greeted them cordially by saying, "I see you have brought your good lady with you, welcome to you both," and he shook hands with Phillip and kissed Sarah's hand elegantly. "I am Ivan Chernienko, Tania's father," he said to Sarah. "Your good man did not say he had such a beautiful lady to accompany him."

"I'm Sarah Pennington," she said formally. "I am Phillip's fiancée."

"Ah, so you are not yet married?" Ivan said.

"No, not yet, we are making plans but we have not yet set a date."

"Please go through into the club," said Ivan.

The big room had been rearranged, the tables had been placed against the walls so that people could sit and face the central area, some of them, near the bar, set with tablecloths and cutlery and glasses for eating and drinking. There was evidently going to be dancing later, as the central area had had the floor covering removed to disclose parquet tiles, which had been polished to a soft golden colour. "Have you met any of these people before?" asked Sarah. "Yes, one or two of them." A young couple approached them and Phillip recognised Tania, although not the young man with her. Tania introduced herself to Sarah and told them the young man was her boyfriend, Gregory. He was built like an athlete, over six feet tall and well-muscled and very good-looking.

Tania was wearing an attractive dress, with nothing like Sarah's extravagant display of bosom but some very expensive jewellery, a gold necklace, earrings, bracelet and a gold ring with a large diamond in it. Sarah thought real competition, not that she would have said anything of course, but she had a drawer full of expensive jewellery, in much better taste, but she had never thought of bringing it with her when she moved in with Phillip; perhaps it might be a good idea to collect it some time when she went home for a visit!

Tania said to Gregory, "Will you look after Sarah for a moment?" and took Phillip's hand to lead him over to the bar. Taken by surprise, he followed her meekly, and after asking what he would like to drink, she ordered a glass of lager for him. "Are you still looking for that young man?"

"I could find no trace of him so I am concentrating on the search for Katia. Did you know her, before she disappeared?"

"We were at college at the same time but I did not see her very often because, being younger, she was in another class and of course, I left two years before her."

"What was she like?" asked Phillip, curiously.

"As far as I remember, she was a nice, quiet girl, not putting any airs on, even though her father was the richest man we knew. Are there any developments in her case, have you found out where she has gone, or was taken to?"

Phillip was careful in the way he replied and he said lightly, "Oh no, nothing very much; I went to Amsterdam on a wild goose chase really and beat up a few pimps but apart from that, I'm really not much further forward."

Tania appeared to be deep in thought and remarked, "From what our doorman tells me, those men are very nasty, they force girls as young as fourteen to have sex with a few favoured rich men who pay a lot of money for it; they are despicable!"

"I had no regrets about beating up a few pimps, they make a lot of money out of the business but the girls are paid next to nothing and usually end up on drugs or with AIDS or some other sexually transmitted disease, then they're tossed into the gutter to fend for themselves."

Tania chuckled. "I can see you are a fighting man!"

"Only when I am being threatened."

She changed the subject abruptly and asked, "Are you in love with your girl?"

"Yes, very much so, why do you ask?"

"Because I think you are the sort of man I would like as *my* fiancée!" Warning bells rang in Phillip's conscience; this would have to be handled very diplomatically, he couldn't handle two women at once!

Clearing his throat, Phillip said, "You have a very nice-looking young man in Gregory."

She shrugged her shoulders. "He looks like a man but really, he is just a boy at heart, very young," she said, with the wisdom of her twenty years.

"Of course, it's a well-known fact that men mature at a slower rate to girls," Phillip observed.

"At this rate," she said tartly, "I shall be an old woman before he reaches maturity!"

Diplomatically, Phillip said, "You could be exaggerating a trifle there, don't you think?"

Tania smiled and said, "It looks as if everyone has arrived, we'd better go and take our places at the main table… you are sitting next to me."

Phillip looked around the large room for Sarah and finally saw her being escorted by Gregory to another table. Then the feast began. He knew there was sure to be huge amounts of food consumed and made his mind up to eat sparingly, missing out every alternate course and keeping his glass of vodka full all the time. Tania was watching him and asked if the food was not to his liking? He assured her he was enjoying every mouthful but he didn't want to feel too full, he wouldn't be able to move for the dancing. "But in films, all detectives are fat," she said.

"Yes, maybe, and they all wear Fedora hats and have long, trench coats and two-tone shoes but I don't do that and in any case, they probably don't make Fedora hats and two-tone shoes any more. What would I look like, walking round London in that get-up? People wouldn't be able to move for laughing!"

A professional photographer was moving from table to table, and he took several photographs of Phillip and Tania. "Are those for private sale?" he asked. "I think he is from the Russian newspaper which is published here and also in Russia."

"Is it not dangerous? Most people in this room escaped from Russia to live here in England and the comrades left behind may take exception to seeing their happy faces, celebrating an attractive girl's birthday, published in a Russian-speaking newspaper!"

"Russia is a very long way away," said Tania airily. "I don't think anyone here is worried about something like that."

Any food which had not been served was placed on a table next to the bar, for people to help themselves and then the speeches started. Ivan rose to his feet and made a ten minute speech in Russian which seemed to impress and amuse his audience. Phillip caught sight of Sarah, sitting next to Gregory, looking extremely bored, which was hardly surprising. Ivan sat down and there were various other speeches, all in Russian, with numerous toasts in vodka. Some people emptied their glasses each time and it was beginning to have the usual effect. Phillip always raised his glass to each toast but only sipped a tiny amount each time; Tania, he saw, was drinking mineral water.

Eventually the speeches came to an end and Tania pulled him onto the dance floor. The music was Russian dance tunes, played over the sound system from a record or a CD and the dancing was erratic, to say the least. After a very few minutes, Tania whispered in his ear, "Let's go somewhere quieter," and taking him by the hand again, she threaded her way through the dancers and out into the deserted hall. "Don't worry," she said, smiling, "I am not going to, how do the Americans put it, 'jump your bones' or something like that but I have a question to ask you. Do you intend to marry your girlfriend?"

"Eventually, yes," said Phillip firmly. They were standing very close together, too close for Phillip's comfort really, when the photographer came out of the main club room and seeing them together, took two pictures of them. He raised his hand as though to say thanks and went back into the club.

What Tania was planning to say or do was interrupted by Sarah coming through the door, putting her arm through Phillip's and saying possessively, "I think it's time to go home isn't it, darling?" and Phillip acquiesced, asking Tania to say goodbye to her parents and thanking her for the invitation to her birthday party which they had thoroughly enjoyed. "We wish you and Gregory all the best for the future, you make a lovely couple." The look of wrath on Tania's face did not support his wishes and she said carelessly to Sarah, "You'd better take him away before I jump him," and she smiled, petulantly.

On the way home, Sarah muttered to Phillip, "You'd better be good to me tonight, after putting me in the position of being bored to tears for over three hours while you lorded it over the high table, in the place of honour. Goodness knows what would have happened to you if I hadn't spotted Tania manoeuvring you out of the room to somewhere more private!"

"I thought you would like having a handsome young man to keep you company!"

"Handsome he may have been, company he was not! He could find nothing more to talk about other than the latest situation in Russia and failing that, the football results!! I nearly yawned in his face."

"That was very naughty of you," he said. "I can see I'm going to have to spank your bottom and teach you better manners!"

"Pooh, just you try," said Sarah, already forgetting about her boring evening.

Chapter 20

Monday morning had Phillip examining any way in which he could kick-start his investigation into Katia's disappearance when the phone rang and a woman's voice asked, "Is that Phillip Everett?"

"Yes, Phillip Everett here, how may I help you?"

"I hope you remember me but anyway, just listen to what I have to say. You need to come and see me. Meet me at the place you first met me, understand, at about three o'clock tomorrow. Goodbye." Abruptly the receiver went down and Phillip was left with the impression of a faint accent, possibly Dutch? He hoped it could only be the woman he had given the money to before he left Amsterdam and it was something to do with Katia, but why all the mystery? Perhaps she thought her telephone line was tapped, she might even be in hiding, worried that her questions had aroused suspicion in the wrong quarter and that she might be in danger.

He was galvanised into action, booking a ticket for Amsterdam, packing a small bag with essentials, and then he rang Sarah. This was the first time he had rung her at work and she sounded worried when he explained that "something had turned up" and he was going to Amsterdam, almost immediately. "I don't know how long I'll have to be there, but obviously I'll keep in touch with you; you can ring my mobile but only during daytime and early evening, not at night please.

I should be back before you've had time to miss me!"

"Do be careful, won't you," said Sarah. "Miss you already." Phillip put the phone down, checked his bag and passport and drove to Gatwick.

He arrived in Amsterdam, took a taxi to the hotel in which he had previously stayed and checked in. He decided to go for a walk to familiarise himself with the area and also to find the small restaurant where he had met, what was her name, Magda, that was it! After retracing his route, he found the place and went in for a beer, covertly studying anyone who entered, and decided to order a meal, even though it was quite early. If he ate now he would be able to spend the rest of the evening trawling the red light district, to see if he could learn anything further.

An hour later, Phillip emerged from the bar, mentally making a note of his bearings so that he would have no difficulty finding it again, and made his first call to the police station to check if they had put the photo of Katia on their canteen notice board. "No information," they said and he knew it was a complete waste of his time. I'll have to be more selective as to whom I show it to in future, he thought, and so he headed off for the red light area, carrying two pictures of Katia in his pocket. Two women approached him and he glanced round to see if their pimp was anywhere around. He wasn't going to get himself in an awkward situation again where he had to defend himself from numbers of irate 'heavies' and he was very cautious as they spoke to him in Dutch. "English," said Phillip carefully. "Oh, ya, Engleesh, you want trade?"

Phillip realised it would be useless trying to ask them any questions as they did not seem to speak much English, so he took out the picture with the Dutch words written on the back, *Have you seen this girl?* They both looked at it and shook their heads. "Danke," he said. He walked on a short distance and two more women came up to him and started to speak. I wonder why they come in pairs, he thought, it must be for safety reasons. Once again he said "English," and the first woman, probably not more than twenty-five said, "Johnny, you want English girl?"

Philip explained that he was asking them if they spoke English and the second woman laughed and said, "You won't want to speak while you are going jig-jig with one of us."

"I'm not looking for 'jig-jig' at the moment," he said, "I'm looking for this girl," and he showed them the picture with the Dutch writing on the back but they shook their heads. He tried to make them understand that she was a young girl who had been kidnapped and brought here to work in the sex trade against her will but the women shrugged and said, "Many young girls, maybe fourteen, fifteen years old work here." Everybody he asked had the same negative response and he was beginning to get tired of repeating his question when he saw the big pimp whom he had kicked in the genitals standing some distance away.

Neither made any movement towards the other and then Phillip smiled and gently shrugged his shoulders. The big man raised his hand in acknowledgement of a truce and Phillip turned and walked away, rapidly increasing his pace after he had turned a corner. Getting involved in a fight was the last thing he wanted and when he had walked a fair distance, he turned into a bar and ordered a drink. The barman recognised him and said, "You want brandy?"

"No, no, just a nice large glass of your superb beer, thank you, but I would like to buy you a drink. What will you have?"

"Thanks, that's very nice of you but I don't drink when on duty," the barman said, sliding a glass over the bar counter. "Do you like our city?"

"I'm getting to like it," said Phillip diplomatically and took his beer over to a table and sat down to rest his weary feet.

Phillip started to go over in his head what he had achieved tonight. The answer was nothing and he could only hope that Magda had something more positive to add to the sum of his knowledge, otherwise he thought, I'll still be strolling round the red light district when I'm in my dotage!! Back to the hotel where he could give Sarah a ring. Suddenly it seemed very important that he should speak to her and he waited impatiently before she answered, sounding slightly out of breath.

"You're being very mysterious," said Sarah. "Tell me why it was so urgent that you rushed over to Amsterdam in such a hurry?"

"I received a message from one of my 'eyes and ears' over here, saying she had some information she could only pass to me directly by word of mouth. She sounded very nervous and I think she may be afraid for her life. This is quite a small community and if any gossip had circulated that one of their own was giving information to a private detective, for no matter what reason, she could well be threatened."

"Did she ring on her mobile?" asked Sarah.

"I'm not sure; perhaps she was afraid she could be overheard but anyway, I'm meeting her tomorrow and then I'll get to the bottom of this. I'm thinking of you now, getting ready to go to bed, in your thick, flannel pyjamas, with your cup of cocoa, your romantic book and a couple of chocolate biscuits. My mouth is watering already!!"

"Phillip Everett, since when have you ever seen me in pyjamas, let alone with a cup of cocoa; you always seemed to be more interested in getting my clothes off, rather than imagining me in flannel pyjamas!" she said indignantly. "Look, you will be careful, won't you, I mean you could be stirring a hornet's nest. Just take really good care 'cause I want you back here all in one piece, right?"

"I'm going to be extra specially vigilant because I want to get back to you asap. Sweet dreams," and he put his phone away, reluctantly, leaving Sarah not knowing whether to laugh or cry.

Chapter 21

At two o'clock, Phillip took a careful reconnaissance of the area around the bar where he was to meet Magda and could see nothing out of the ordinary. Not many people around, one or two women with shopping baskets, a couple of children hurrying back to school, an old tramp searching the rubbish bins. He sauntered slowly on the opposite side of the road until he wondered if he should go into the bar and get a drink – anybody watching would find it suspicious, loitering along aimlessly. He was on the point of crossing the street when he saw Magda approaching him. She came up to him and smiled, whispering to him urgently, "Pretend you are a punter and we are haggling about the price!"

Phillip raised his voice slightly, "That's a bit too much for me, what do I get for that?"

Magda put her hand on his arm and said, "Oh, come on, that's not so much, I've got a place just round the corner from here and I can do a lot for that amount; you'll like it, I can tell you." She slid her hand down his arm and slipped a small piece of paper into his hand.

Phillip pretended to be considering Magda's offer while he glanced at the paper. *I tracked down the girl, she is with her pimp at this address.* As if she was making casual conversation, trying to persuade him to take up her offer, she asked when he had arrived and when he said "yesterday," she asked him what he had been doing. Without thinking, Phillip told her, "I wandered round the red light district, showing Katia's picture, but nobody I asked could tell me anything."

Magda was furious and her face went red. She hissed at him, "You idiot, you've ruined everything; the girl could be dead by now; she will certainly have been moved from that address I worked my butt off to get for you. What's more, you've now put my life at risk; once they know I came to meet you, they'll want to silence me or make sure I never work again. I'll have to leave Amsterdam for good but where can I go?" She turned and quickly walked away. Philip felt dreadful for letting Magda down and putting her in danger. Nothing can be done now, he thought; I must go and rescue Katia.

Where was there a taxi when you wanted one? He started to walk as fast as possible in the direction she had given him. He stood outside number 45, a two storey apartment block, of which there were so many in this city, and studied the neatly polished brass knocker on the door. He found a large stone in the ornamental window box, knocked loudly on the door and stood back, well out of the way. A very large man with ginger hair opened the door and Phillip moved fast, grabbing him by the arm and yanking him outside into the street. Ginger, caught off balance, started to fall forward and put out his hands to save himself from falling flat on his face and Phillip hit him on the side of the neck as he fell. He went down without a sound except for the air expelled from his lungs, making a slight *whoosh*.

Phillip stepped over him and knew he had a few minutes in which to search the apartment for Katia, before the man recovered his senses. There was nobody in the downstairs rooms. He ran quickly up the stairs; there was no time for hesitation. Two rooms were empty, the remaining one was locked. No time for discretion, he gathered his strength and braced himself to kick the door in. As the door gave way, splintering the frame, he saw a young girl, huddling in a corner, and recognised her immediately from the photograph he carried in his pocket.

"Katia... Katia, isn't it? I've come to take you home to your father; come with me now, there isn't any time to waste." The girl was quite plainly petrified with fear and if anything, tried to squeeze herself further into her corner. Phillip quelled any pity he felt for her; he must get her to come with him now or Ginger would recover and he was not sure he could win a fight with him, and he might also be armed. Without hesitation, he grabbed the shrinking girl, talking all the time, hoping to soothe her; he swung her over his shoulder in the approved fireman's lift position and set off to get down the stairs without tripping. Ginger was groaning on the pavement outside and Phillip took care to give him a well-aimed kick in the region of his crotch! There was a muted scream and he fell back, doubled up in agony.

Phillip was still carrying Katia over his shoulder and now she was starting to struggle. She was hardly dressed for outdoors and had no shoes on but he set her on her feet and slipped off his jacket and wrapped it around her, all the time saying, "I've come to take you back to your father, Katia, don't be afraid, but we have to get away from here as quickly as possible. I don't know how many men they're going to send after us, once Ginger comes to and tells them. Okay, can you walk?" Watching the painful way she was stepping he put her over his shoulder and carried on walking as fast as he could. An old couple were walking toward them and Phillip indicated that the girl had too much to drink. They just smiled and walked past. Phillip saw a taxi and he shouted "Taxi!! Hey taxi!!" The taxi stopped, and still carrying Katia, he rushed toward it; opening the door with his free hand he almost threw Katia into it. Getting in himself he told the driver to go to his hotel.

At last they were outside the red light district and reached the hotel without any incident. He told the receptionist that he was checking out immediately, as soon as he had collected his belongings from the room. "What about the young lady?"

"She is coming with me to the airport." They hurried up the stairs and he urged her to rest for a few moments while he made some phone calls and gathered his belongings together. The first call was to book two air tickets, the second call was to Katia's father, to tell him that he was bringing her back to England.

But Katia's father was not in London; he had gone on a business trip to America and his office, perhaps understandably, was very wary of giving Phillip any details about how to get in touch with him. "Then you must tell him that it's most important I speak to him; it's about a task he asked me to undertake a few weeks ago and I have very positive results for him. Please tell him Phillip Everett called and ask someone to contact me immediately!!" Phillip used every ounce of authority in his voice and could only hope that someone would comply with his request. There was going to be trouble when they reached Gatwick because Katia had no passport! If anyone could sort out difficulties, he was betting Vasily Berkow would be the one.

They had to take a taxi to the airport, against Phillip's better judgement, but with any luck, they would be out of the country before news of their travel plans could be filtered back to the mafia. At the shops in the airport, he purchased a tracksuit for Katia and a sweater. She chose a pair of trainers so that she looked more like a normal traveller and he bought some refreshments from the cafeteria, always on the watch to see if anyone was taking any special notice of them. He heaved a sigh of relief when they boarded the plane, only a little worried that no-one from Vasily's office had contacted him.

He said to Katia quietly, "Because you haven't got a passport, there are going to be difficulties at the airport and we have to agree on what we are gong to tell the authorities. How about we were taking a last look around Amsterdam before we caught the taxi to the airport and your bag was stolen by a pickpocket. There was no time to go to the British Embassy…" He had a thought: "Do you have a British passport, or are you still Russian?"

She frowned., "Do you know, I've never seen my passport; since I arrived in Britain, I've never really been anywhere apart from on

Daddy's yacht and I didn't need one then," she said innocently.

Oh to be so rich, it didn't matter whether you had a passport or not!! "Never mind, I've rung your father's office and alerted them to the urgency of this matter and with any luck, we might be able to explain everything satisfactorily to the officials."

A shadow passed over her face and she looked down at her seatbelt. "I'm not sure my father will want me back, when he hears how I have been living during the past months," she said quietly.

Phillip took her hand and gently squeezed it. "Your father has been searching for you since you disappeared and he is going to be so happy to see you, he won't give a damn whatever you have been forced to do by those thugs; he will just be so pleased to have you with him!"

They landed and Phillip prepared himself for the explanations to the passport control officers and knew when they were requested to "step this way", it was not going to be easy. He gave them the explanation they had agreed on, filled in forms, aware that they were probably being filmed and assessed, and gave Gordon's name for reference as to his good character. It looked very good on paper – Gordon's name, posh address, and place of work the Bank of England; Phillip hoped Katia's Russian name would not arouse any suspicion, but her address was pretty impressive and after a period of silence when they were served with cups of stewed tea, they were finally told they were "free" to go on condition that they called at a local police station to show Katia's replacement passport.

For a nerve-wracking ten minutes, he had to leave Katia alone while he collected his car and the relief on her face when he picked her up was a sight to behold. Her teeth were chattering with nerves and she was nearly in tears when her fiery Russian temperament came to her aid. "I thought you had deserted me," she raged. "Where have you been? What took you so long? I have been thinking every man who came past was going to grab me and take me…" She was sobbing, but Phillip noticed it was with fury and he let her go on, venting her spleen on him, until she ran out of words.

"Feel better for that?" said Phillip, cheerfully.

She glowered at him and apologised stiffly for her bad manners and thanked him for everything he was doing.

Nothing was said and they were entering the outskirts of London. Katia gave him the directions and they drew up outside the Berkow family mansion. They must have been expected because the electric gates swung open without any halt, and he was able to drive straight through.

He helped Katia out of the car and rang the doorbell for her; she was suddenly very shaky and clung to his arm as if she would be unable to let go. The door opened and, suddenly galvanised into action, Katia rushed into the hallway, calling something out in Russian, and straight into the arms of her father. "I'll talk to you later," said Phillip, in the face of the sobbing Russians, suddenly enormously embarrassed by this show of feelings and in a typically English manner, he said ineffectively, "I'll leave you alone now, er… goodbye!" and he got back into his car with the thought that he could not wait to see Sarah.

Sarah was at home, watching a television programme, but as soon as he walked in, she jumped up and rushed to hug him. "I was waiting for you to ring with some news," she said accusingly.

"Sorry, things moved so quickly; we've been held up at the airport because Katia didn't have a passport and we've been interrogated by various officials, filled in loads of forms and I've just left her at home in her father's arms and rushed back here to be with you."

"Thank heavens you're safe, I had visions of you being beaten up, shot, thrown in a canal, drowned."

Phillip's lips closed her mouth with a longing kiss and he murmured, "My mind's a bit confused, let's sit down and I'll tell you the whole thing, get it sorted out in my mind.

"It started when I befriended Magda because she worked in the red light district. She became my eyes and ears and told me how it really was with most of the sex workers there. She gave me a tip as to where they were keeping Katia but when she heard I had already been round asking questions and showing Katia's picture again, she was so frightened that she may be targeted, and knowing how ruthless these guys could be, she was very annoyed with me. She was not safe now to stay in Amsterdam. I felt dreadful for letting her down, but there was nothing that could be done now. She had already slipped the address into my hand of where to find Katia. That was my priority now."

He told her the rest of the story. "You were very lucky to both escape in one piece," said Sarah. Her face showed her amazement. "My hero," she said, with gentle irony. "Is there no end to your talents! I'm just teasing you, you know I think you're pretty special! If you haven't eaten, perhaps you'll feel calmer with some food inside you and maybe a drink or two, then we can go to bed and you can show me how much you missed me!"

Chapter 22

Barry Spencer rang to give him Berkow's congratulations. "He is absolutely over the moon and can't praise you enough; I think you can safely say that your future career is made because his recommendation of you will pave the way to cases you will be able to pick and choose. You've done a great job, where everyone else had failed!"

"How is the girl?" asked Phillip.

"After the first joy of getting home, she's beginning to show signs of trauma," Barry said quietly. "She must have lived through such a terrible time; what's your impression of her?"

"When I found her, she was being kept in a small house with a pimp or minder to guard her, on the outskirts of the red light district. She was so terrified of him that at first she refused to come with me, although you can hardly blame her for that, seeing as I was a complete stranger! I had to nearly knock her out, grabbed her in a fireman's lift and carried her downstairs, giving the pimp a kick for good measure as we went out. I spoke to her in English, telling her that I had come to take her home and after that she was very brave and told me off when I asked her where was her British stiff upper lip – she said 'I am Russian.'"

Barry asked if he had any idea of what her conditions had been like, since it was important that her family knew how to treat her. Phillip said, "She needs plenty of loving care and reassurance that they still love her, no matter what her life has been like over the past months, and she will probably need psychiatric help," suggested Phillip. "And as for what her living conditions had been like – I only know what my contact told me. There is a constant new market for very young girls, some as young as fourteen, and the mafia get their supplies from anyone who wants to provide them. They are groomed, made up and given sexy outfits to wear and put in top class houses for very rich men to use in any way they want. There is only one proviso, there must be no signs of physical violence, no bruises or marks.

"The girls stay there for maybe a year, by which time the clients have grown used to them and they have lost their freshness. Then they are moved on to an ordinary brothel where any man, or woman for that matter, can pay to use them for sex. As they get older, or have not learned to be very good at pleasuring the client, they are passed on to a pimp which means they are working at street level and they sell their bodies for what they can get. The pimp takes most of the money but provides her with enough to live on and a certain amount of protection. Do you want to hear what the lowest level is?" asked Phillip.

"You might as well tell me," Barry said, with resignation in his voice.

"When the pimp realises that a girl is not making enough money for him, he kicks her out onto the street and sooner or later, any pervert can have her. Eventually she might become a drug addict and die of an overdose, she might die from AIDS or another sexually transmitted disease or possibly be killed by injuries sustained in an encounter with a customer."

"That's a terrible story," said Barry. "Of course I knew something about the women in the sex trade out there but I never realised it was such a terrible business. I always thought that prostitution was strictly controlled in Holland."

"So it is, but the authorities don't pay the girls, they still have to earn a living like in any other country. If you don't have the money, you don't eat, you have no roof over your head, nothing, that's it. You can understand their desperation to attract a client, can't you?"

"Okay, I get the picture," Barry said, "but Katia is only eighteen, how come she was already working for a pimp?"

Phillip said, "I expect it was because she was no good at pleasing men, men who paid a lot of money to have sex with her and expected to be pandered to in any way they asked, by a willing, compliant slave. Katia was brought up in a hothouse environment, spoiled rotten by her father and the only person she had to please was herself. She just did not know how, or want to learn how, to please a customer and short of raping her into submission and flinging her out onto the streets, this they were unwilling to do. She was still a valuable merchandise.

"As it is, my life is in as much danger from mafia retaliation as their lives are for kidnapping and using his daughter to try and humiliate him; unless he makes it his business to terrify his enemies in very short order, I shall be looking over my shoulder for several years to come!!"

"Having heard what you said, I would agree with you," Barry said. "Mr Bukow is so very pleased with you, he said he is sending you a bonus cheque for £10,000 and if there is anything left of the original float he paid into the bank for you, please keep that. He also says he does not require any reports or receipts from you, he is just so thankful his daughter was not killed. There's one thing Phillip, your job sounds very exciting; next time you have to go anywhere like that, on a similar assignment, can I come with you?"

"Don't even think about it, there's no way I'm going to take on anything like this case again and I can assure you that you will not be needed, although thanks for the offer and your confidence in me; any time Mr Bukow wants to entrust a nice, easy lost dog or divorce case to me, I'm your man!!"

They concluded their conversation on a note of hilarity and Phillip started to work on a report for his own file. The post came shooting through the letter box and he noticed a stiff, expensive envelope which immediately intrigued him. When opened, it proved to be an invitation to take part in an Advanced Self Defence Course at Stonewell Manor Physical Training Unit. He rang the number on the letter heading, gave his name and reference number and was told there was just one vacancy on a course starting in two days; he would need to pay the full amount of £1,500 immediately and full instructions would be sent to him in that day's post.

Chapter 23

Sarah came in from work and belatedly Phillip wondered how he was going to tell her he would be away for three weeks on a self-defence course when he had only just returned from Amsterdam. Sarah was full of chatter all through their meal and after, when they sat down in the lounge, Phillip plunged in straight away, before Sarah could wonder what was making him a little uptight. Unfortunately, it was not his most diplomatic approach as he said, "I'm going on a self-defence training course in a couple of days. It's an advanced course to include the latest techniques and gadgets used to defend yourself…" He trailed off, looking at the expression on her face.

Sarah looked at him with an expression of rage on her face and opened her mouth but he carried on desperately, "It's a residential course so I'll go on Monday but I'll come back each Friday evening and get back about seven o'clock, depending on the traffic, and it only lasts three weeks so I won't be away too long."

"You've completed your case," she said mutinously. "I thought we could have some quality time with each other, relaxing and perhaps even going on a little holiday somewhere, just you, me and a king size bed; I don't see much chance of that if you're always going to be disappearing somewhere by yourself." The rest of the evening was spent in watching television, with very little conversation. There were no cuddles in bed that night and Sarah was distinctly sulky the following morning.

Phillip spent the weekend preparing for the course, after trying to explain to Sarah the importance of being very fit and prepared for any danger, not that he expected to be in danger, he hastily assured her, but it was as well to be prepared. He suggested that she might like to spend some time with her parents while he was away and gently hinted that this kind of situation might crop up again and their relationship would have to adjust to many different possibilities. She gave a huge sigh and admitted she had been a little jealous, thinking about his time spent in the red light district, wondering if he had been sampling anything offered by the girls, but he showed her that night that she was the only girl he was interested in and she was somewhat mollified!!

Phillip set off very early on Monday morning, leaving Sarah still in bed, and arrived at the manor at eight o'clock. As the word implied, it was an old manor house with three more modern buildings alongside. He guessed that the largest one was probably a gym, and living quarters would be in the older building. The lady behind the reception desk in the hall smiled at him with a questioning look on her face. "Phillip Everett," he said cheerfully, "reporting for duty!"

"Nice to see you Mr Everett," and she ticked his name off her list. "You are in Room 31 in the Annexe and this is your key. You go out of the door and the Annexe is the single story building on your left. Breakfast is at 7.00 to 8.00, lunch 12.30 to 13.30 and the evening meal is at 18.00 hours. There may be some work in the evenings but you will be informed of that by the instructor. No evening meal will be provided for Course members on Fridays as it is expected they will be going home when the Course finishes for the day. On Mondays we start at 10.00 am, to give everybody time to get here, so it looks as if you have time to make yourself a cup of tea in your room before you start. It's all written down on this sheet of instructions but if you have any queries, please let me know but I just have to point out there is no bar here, alcohol is not allowed on the premises and the nearest bar is two miles away!"

Phillip murmured his acknowledgement, picked up his sheet of instructions and room key and turned to walk out of the door. He found Room 31, unpacked, changed into his track suit and trainers, as per instructions, and made himself a cup of instant coffee from the tray and kettle provided and slowly re-read all the instructions again. At 9.55 he located the gym and went inside to meet the others on the course. A very fit looking man stepped forward and announced, "Good morning gentlemen, I am your course instructor, Jonas Park, and this is my assistant, Graham. We only use first names on the course and we commence at 09.00 hours promptly, with the exception of Mondays, when we start at 10.00. We try to finish at 17.00 hours but some evenings we work after the evening meal.

"I hope you all read what this course entails from your joining instructions and I have to emphasise that we expect strict discipline during the time you are here. Without discipline, these courses would be of little benefit to you and we want you to get the maximum for the money you have paid out. This is an advanced course, as you all know, but it is somewhat different from the initial six-week course you went through originally. That was based on physical fitness and the art of self-defence. This is a shorter course but it goes beyond what you learned earlier; it includes not only physical fitness but an awareness of the forces around you and how to deal with possible aggression against you or others. We conduct extra periods of discussion after the evening meal on Tuesdays, Wednesdays and Thursdays but these are completely voluntary and there is no physical effort entailed, only discussions and lectures, but we have to know by lunchtime each day if you are not coming. As you will find out, there is not much to do in the evenings, so you might just as well come to the lectures.

"You have a free night tonight, to write home and complain about us, and on Fridays, you are free to leave when we have finished work for the day, around 17.00 hours. For the first two days, we are going to see how fit you are." There was a chorus of groans. "Please form a line." Graham walked along the line of men, looking as if he was going to greet them by holding out his hand and then aiming a swift blow to their bodies, to test how rapid their reaction to the blow was. He did not hit with the full force he could have used but nevertheless, any man who did not react quickly enough received a stinging blow on the chest or stomach. Partly due to surprise, most of them took a hit and were bruised.

Graham was probably in his mid-twenties but was obviously at the peak of physical fitness and Phillip knew he was enjoying himself, showing everybody how slow their reactions were. As he approached Phillip, he knew that by anticipating where the blow was going to fall, he could outwit Graham and the way to do it was to watch his eyes. Just before an opponent makes a move, his eye will reflect where the blow is going to fall and Phillip spotted the eye movement in a split second, caught his hand and arm, spun him round, twisting the arm round his back and counted to three, then let him go. Graham turned to face Phillip and said, "Well, I'm glad someone remembered what he was taught on the first course!" but his face did not reflect what he was saying. He was clearly embarrassed and felt he had been shown up by a student in the first few minutes of the course.

"As there are thirty-one members on the course, I will partner you for all the exercises where a partner is needed," said Graham. "You've nothing against that, have you?" Phillip shook his head and Graham continued beating up the rest of the students, to varied groans and expressions of pain on their faces as they failed to be as quick as Phillip, then Jonas took over and announced, "Now gentlemen, after your short initiation period, we can proceed to work on getting you into peak condition and physical fitness, follow me!"

They spent the rest of the day running, rope-climbing, doing push-ups, wrestling and then, more running, while Jonas quietly assessed each man's particular strengths and weaknesses. As was to be expected, at the end of the day, all the students were exhausted while Jonas and Graham were as fresh as daisies. After a long soak in the somewhat cramped bath, Phillip crossed the driveway to the manor for their evening meal. It was clear to him that not a great deal of money had been lavished on the interior of the building. It was clean and tidy but decoration was minimal and everything was quite basic, no expensive fitted carpets or antique furniture, but at the moment the only thing on his mind, apart from picturing Sarah arriving home from work or college and standing under a hot shower, was food! He was ravenous after the workout during the day and would have eaten anything put before him. As it was, there were substantial amounts of goulash, rice and fresh vegetables, cooked to perfection, followed by a choice of fruit salad accompanied by ice cream or fruit tart and custard. Copious amounts of iced water, tea, coffee or fruit juice were on hand and the service was quick and efficient.

Phillip casually chatted to one or two of the other students sitting at the same table and then excused himself on the grounds that he needed an early night to be ready for the torture of next day's agonising muscle stretching, and returned to his Spartan accommodation. The small single room contained a bed, a small bedside chest of drawers, a wardrobe for clothes, a flat screen TV attached by brackets to the wall, and an armchair. A door opened on to a small bathroom, with a shower attachment over one end of the bath, a washbasin with a mirrored cupboard over it, and a toilet. Everything was spotlessly clean – no self-respecting insect would dare to land on the ceiling or walls – but everything was completely colourless and anonymous. Still, for only four nights a week, it was not much of a hardship! He rang Sarah and told her about their first day's experiences then he asked her what she was doing. "I'm thinking about Friday, when you get home," she said saucily. And with that he went to his lonely bed and slept like a log.

Next morning at breakfast, there was a great deal of joking conversation about the food, the rooms, overall conditions etc, when a voice said, "I've not seen such luxury since my days in Stalag Luft 17!" Another voice said, "You must be thinking about your house, what would you know about Stalag Luft 17 anyway?" A blond young man chipped in with, "It's not bad, I quite like it here, the regime suits me; I'm due in court straight after this course and if I'm banged up in prison, this is good preparation for it!" Everyone seemed in a good humour, not really moaning, and trooped out to start their second day of tuition.

At the end of day two, everyone felt the same – exhausted. Phillip thought, if this is supposed to make us fit, it's not really working in my case! After the evening meal, before they started their first evening lecture, he rang home but there was no reply so he joined the others in watching an hour long film about the origins of martial arts such as karate, kung fu and other similar self-defence regimes. Apparently it all went back to ancient religious cults which preached that instead of killing or enslaving warlike tribes, using methods of self-defence would defeat the aggression of opposites by showing them that they can be disabled, without being physically injured. Battered and bruised they might be but wounded or dead, they were not! Over the centuries the ideas developed into various disciplines which were used to protect the individual and gradually came to be used as a sporting exercise or in competition.

The film carried on to show various ways of overcoming your opponent but went on to say that your superior knowledge must never be used to do real harm to that person, whatever the circumstances. To inflict serious, permanent harm on another person would result in prosecution and possibly a prison sentence. The film ended and Jonas asked if there were any questions or comments. Nobody seemed to have a word to say so Jonas said, "You must be tired, you've worked well today, I'll let you get off to bed!" Phillip made his way to his room and rang Sarah again. There was no reply so he assumed she must be staying with her parents.

The lecture the following evening was another film, showing different situations which might provoke one person to attack another and how to prevent the attacker from inflicting any harm. Phillip was inclined to think it a waste of time because he had never learned anything by just watching a film; it would be much better to see it demonstrated in an exercise, and he remarked on this, during the discussion afterwards. Graham, who was taking the evening session, looked at Phillip, saying, "Everyone has a different opinion. Tomorrow we start on the self-defence exercises and as I will be your partner, this film was just a reminder of various methods we can use. That's all for tonight." Phillip had the distinct impression that Graham did not like him and it became more obvious as the men practised the different techniques. He used a lot more force than was strictly necessary.

Phillip found himself with much more bruising and sore muscles as he tried to learn the new manoeuvres with Graham but he was noticing that the blond young man, who had talked so much at breakfast, kept trying to engage him in conversation, which was rather puzzling. Phillip concentrated on damage limitation but when Graham, acting as Defender, threw Phillip so that he landed awkwardly on his back, he said, "I think I've got the idea, Graham, but just to make sure I've got it right, let's just try it again." They faced each other, Phillip feinted to the left and Graham caught his arm; he moved so quickly using Graham's impetus to throw him by twisting his arm and Graham flew through the air, landing heavily several feet away with a distinct thud.

His face was contracted with pain as he lay there winded and Phillip strolled over to him saying, "I think I've got that right, haven't I?"

Jonas came over to the two men, asking, "What do you two think you're doing?"

Phillip showed Jonas some of his bruises and said, "Perhaps you had better ask Graham, he's been a bit overenthusiastic with his demonstrations all this week."

Jonas breathed heavily, recognising the aggression between the two men. "Okay, that's it! This is a self-defence course, not some kind of personal vendetta!"

The blond man appeared and said quickly, "I can be his partner."

Jonas nodded and helped Graham to his feet, speaking to him quietly – "See me in my office, before the evening meal. Now let's get on with what we're paid to do!"

When they sat down to eat, Phillip asked his new partner, "What made you volunteer?"

"Because I like you!"

'That's all I need,' thought Phillip. "I think you've made a mistake," he said coldly, "I'm strictly heterosexual!"

The other man burst out laughing and said, "So am I, very strictly!!"

With a sigh of relief he said, "What's your name? I'm Phillip."

"Alexander, but my friends usually call me Sander."

"Why Sander and not Alex?"

"We already have an Alex in the family who is older than I am so they started to call me Sander to distinguish between us."

"Why did you come on this course?" asked Phillip curiously.

"People make the same mistake you did; they think I'm gay and I keep on being approached by guys making propositions so I'm on this course so that I'm physically able to discourage gay men from – well, making suggestions."

"You should learn a few put-downs, comments that will dissuade a lot of them," said Phillip. They discussed various remarks which might put off some aggressors and laughed at some of the more improbable replies.

Friday evening came and Phillip drove as quickly as possible, arriving home, despite the heavy traffic, just after six o'clock. He opened the door; all seemed very quiet and he wondered if Sarah was still staying with her mother, when she jumped out at him. For a moment he almost obeyed his self-preservation mechanisms which had been honed to perfection during the previous week and only just managed to react to Sarah's embrace as he smelled her perfume and returned her enthusiastic kiss.

"I've missed you so much but I was going to act all distant, as if I was annoyed with you, but when your car drove up, I was like a love-sick puppy and I could hardly wait to get my hands on you!"

"I did call you," said Phillip, defensively, "twice on Tuesday, but when there was no reply, I thought you'd decided to stay at your parents' for the three nights, so I didn't leave any message. Anyway, now I'm back," and he hugged her tightly.

"And here's me thinking that you must have some young female gymnast, showing you all the right moves!"

He laughed and said, "There are no females at all on this course, either taking it or instructing on it – wait a moment, I tell a lie, there is one middle-aged, plump lady who is the receptionist and she's worth a cuddle except I think she would not appreciate that!"

"Do you want to eat now?" asked Sarah.

"No, let's wait until I've had a shower and then I can make up for the days I've been away before we think about eating," and they went upstairs. He came out of the shower and found her sitting on the bed, wrapped in a large towel, her hair still slightly damp from the bathwater. "This is 'for your eyes only'," she said huskily, and let the towel drop to the floor. Phillip swallowed, looking at that desirable body, and moved quickly, pulling her onto the bed and starting to kiss her voraciously, covering every inch of soft skin, feeling her growing excitement. After they had reached their climax, he could feel her relax beneath him and he whispered in her ear, "Don't fall asleep, I lack nourishment and if I'm to do you justice, I have to eat, so get your pretty butt off this bed and put something on to make you look respectable, instead of the seductive houri you are, then we can go to the pub and consume large amounts of food and drink." He slapped her bottom and rolled out of bed to search for some casual clothes.

"Just one thing before we go," said Sarah, looking somewhat mutinous. "What is a 'houri'?"

"Come on woman," he said, impatiently, "I'm ravenous."

"Not until you tell me what a 'houri' is," she said furiously.

"Well if you really must know," he laughed at her face, "it's an Arabian dancing girl; haven't you heard of them, the ones who do the dance of the seven veils and then throw themselves at their master's feet, all ready to obey their commands, whatever!"

"Oh, that's alright then, I thought it might be an insult or something."

"It's obvious your education has been sadly neglected," he said, as they walked to the pub. "I shall have to inform you of some of the more worldly items of general knowledge which appear to have been missed by your tutors!!"

Chapter 24

They found a table and he went to the bar to order their meal and drinks. A crowd of people, seven or eight of them, came straight up to the bar, and with a sinking feeling, Phillip recognised one young woman, the cause of his going for the HIV test, and she recognised him. "Hello, my gorgeous friend," she said, in a loud voice.

Phillip would have ignored her but said coldly, "I think you must have mistaken me for someone else," and turned away.

"Oh no," she said, sarcastically. "Who can forget such a moment of bliss!" Phillip tried to ignore her but she persisted. "Come on darling, I would love to repeat the experience. We're all going to a party, why don't you come with us, all sorts of wonderful people will be there tonight."

"That being the case, you should be able to enjoy yourself."

She put her hand on Phillip's shoulder and as he made to shrug it off, he saw Sarah, standing to one side, with a thunderous expression on her face. How long has she been there, thought Phillip, wondering how he was going to extricate himself from the situation before Sarah exploded with temper. In her best upper class accent, she drawled, "You had better take your hand off my fiancé's shoulder, sweetheart, you might contaminate him. After all, we don't know where your hand has been do we? Or even if it's been washed this year."

"Where did you come from?"

"If I hadn't seen you crawl in, I might have asked you just the same question," said Sarah, putting her arm through Phillip's arm, very ostentatiously and possessively, lifting her chin and glaring at the other girl.

Phillip held his breath for what seemed a very long time, when the other girl said to the group she was with, "Oh come on, we'll never get served here, this place is starting to depress me, let's go somewhere with a bit of life!!" and with that, the group wandered out of the bar. Phillip collected their drinks and they returned to their table in silence.

Sarah asked with an aggrieved expression on her face, "Can we never go anywhere without you running into one of your old flames?"

Phillip cleared his throat with difficulty and said quietly, "She is not, and never was, one of my 'old flames' as you put it."

"So how come she knows you?"

Phillip started to explain: "It was a very similar encounter like tonight. A group of them came in and I was sitting at a table, on my own. It was the time you left me and that girl started a conversation, asked me if I wanted to go to a party with them and at that time I was feeling pretty miserable, thinking you would not come back, so I decided to go. We went in one of their cars to a mansion owned by one of their rich friends. It was a young man whose parents were in the Bahamas and he was taking the opportunity to throw a party, with exotic food, drink and drugs.

"I was introduced, told to help myself to anything I wanted and then left to my own devices. I soon found out what sort of party it was; couples were having sex, working through all the positions in the Kama Sutra, girls were moving from one partner to another, and one came and sat on my knee with her legs wide open. Now I'm pretty broad-minded about sex, whatever turns you on so to speak, but strictly in private, and this was an orgy. She was high on drugs and said 'I've not had you yet, have I?' She also smelt revolting, sweating and scrabbling at my clothes as if she was desperate to have intercourse, a complete turn-off as far as I was concerned. I nearly threw up but I managed to push her onto the floor and went into the lobby to phone for a taxi. I was never more relieved when it arrived and I got home safely in one piece, an experience I don't want to repeat, I can tell you."

"I thought men would like that sort of thing," Sarah said.

Phillip thought carefully before he answered., "Some men might welcome that kind of situation, they might go looking for it, if only in their heads, but basically we've evolved over the centuries and we like sex a lot, but with a bit of affection and respect for our partners."

Sarah shrugged her shoulders and said, "I've very little experience in that field but from what I've heard and read, a lot of your so-called 'men' have not changed all that much, no matter what you say."

Their food arrived, they ate quickly and Sarah pulled her coat around her shoulders. "Come on, let's get you home before you meet any more of your old flames in this pub. I think we'd better find a new 'local' to patronise – there aren't any more of your old stamping grounds around here are there?"

"You've no need to worry," said Phillip, virtuously. "The way I feel about you I have no intention of talking to any of my 'old flames', as you put it."

"Funny, but they always seem to seek you out," she said. "It just makes me wonder a bit, just what sort of life you led before I met you." Phillip carefully avoided making any remark in reply to that!!

The rest of the weekend passed in blissful solitude and Monday came, time to return to his course. They concentrated on improving their physical fitness, very like the previous week, and during a break, Sander told Phillip that he had been approached by a man, thinking he was gay, and when rebuffed, the man tried to hit him. Phillip asked, "How did you cope with that?"

"I've got his arm in my room!!" said Sander, laughing. "No, only kidding, I put my hard work into practice and grabbed his arm, twisted it behind his back and he soon got the message. When I let him go, his arm was just hanging limp – I guess it's going to be a while before he propositions another blond young man with unmentionable suggestions."

Admiringly, Phillip said, "That's really good, You've learned to stand up for yourself, if nothing else. As my partner, I must have taught you something worthwhile!!" and ducked before Sander could hit him.

After two days of exhausting physical work, Jonas told them they were ready to move on to the next stage. Graham was fully recovered and back in action. Jonas told them all that he was going to try to raise them onto a higher mental plateau and Phillip was intrigued; he was not sure what 'plateau' he was on, but his body was complaining of the aches and pains inflicted during the exercises and he hoped the old saying about if it hurts, it must be working, was true. Five o'clock on Friday could not come soon enough and he was on his way home.

Sarah was waiting for him as soon as his key turned in the front door lock and she hugged him before he could even say hello. She was wearing her bathrobe and he smelled her soft skin and hair, damp with the perfumed bath water she loved to soak in. "I need a shower," he said, trying to stop kissing her.

"Don't take all night," she said, jokingly, "or I won't keep the bed warm for you!" He needed no further urging and took the stairs two at a time. When they had finished making love, they fell asleep and Philip was the first to wake. He realised he felt ravenously hungry and went to look in the fridge; he pulled out eggs, cheese, bread, milk etc, and proceeded to make huge omelettes. There was no need to call her, the smell of cooking was enough to have her running downstairs and they enjoyed their simple meal together.

Giving Sarah a glass of wine and opening a can of his favourite lager, they went to sit on the settee to relax and talk. "I noticed last weekend, you had some nasty bruises on your body; do they hurt?" she asked.

"It's unarmed combat and although I ache a little, I'm learning something new all the time. The bruises will soon fade, but thank you for caring."

"I thought the whole idea of this course was 'self-defence'; it can't be teaching you all that much about it if you are being bruised and are all aches and pains." To change the subject Philip asked her if she had visited her parents during the week. "No, I haven't been round. I have to get used to living here on my own when you are away; besides, I rather like it here now, it reminds me of you in so many ways."

"There's only another week to go and then I'll be here all the time," he whispered in her ear, "and in the meantime, I might as well show you some of the right moves to make you want to make my time here worthwhile!!"

Chapter 25

On Monday, he returned to the manor, and the team spent the whole of the day going over what they had already learned. The course took on a more psychological agenda, to include yoga and meditation. Jonas announced that the course was not just to make them 'fighting machines', but the aim was to introduce thirty-one tough men back into society. It was not so that they could beat up anyone they wanted but so that they could be responsible adults and use their skills only when all else failed. "This part of the course will teach you to stay calm, even under extreme provocation," said Jonas, "so during this final week, Graham and I will confront each of you and try to provoke you; this will be done individually, away from the rest so there will only be you and the instructor."

"This could be a bit dangerous," said one of the team's members quietly to his neighbour.

Jonas's keen ears picked up the remark. "Of course, there is the possibility that one of you might try to hurt me or Graham," which was followed by loud laughter. "Yeah, that's what I meant! It's Tim, isn't it?" queried Jonas.

"Yes, that's me!"

"Okay, Tim, you've just volunteered to be the first one. Don't worry about hurting Graham or me, after all, we're experts in self-defence and we're well insured!! Wednesday morning you and I will be first to try it out and in the meantime, more meditation and spiritual awareness. Carry on."

Wednesday morning arrived, with Graham taking the first lesson while Tim and Jonas were noticeably absent. Half an hour later they both walked back into the gym and took their places without saying a word. Graham indicated to Sander that he was next and they disappeared, only to return some time later obviously both unhurt. This went on till the break for lunch and Phillip asked Sander, curiously, "How did it go?"

"He started by insulting me, asking what it felt like to be a poof, how did my father feel having a homosexual son, what was it like to stick my dick up another man's bum, all that sort of thing."

"How did you react?" asked Phillip.

"I just listened. These are the sort of things I hear often and after a while, Graham said, 'Well done, you've got very good self-control; I'm sorry I had to put you through it but these are very useful exercises,' and he shook my hand and that was it."

Tension was building up among the people still waiting for their turn to be provoked and Phillip did his best to stay calm. He was hoping it would not be Graham, since they had already had a confrontation. Friday morning came and Graham walked up to him, indicating with a jerk of his head that he was to follow him, being the last person of the whole group to be interviewed. They went into a room, completely empty except for the padded floor, and faced each other. "I've never met anyone like you, big headed git, who thinks he is something special; Sander 'outed' you, you're nothing but a shirt lifter. Are you enjoying your sex with Sander? I suppose you are the one that forces it on him while he suffers? What about your father, is he proud of you?" Phillip was determined not to rise to the other man's taunts and to last out to the end of the session. "Perhaps you don't even know who your father really is? Does your mother know who it was fathered you?" Remarks like this went on a short while longer, then Graham said, "You have done very well, I admire your restraint, one day it will stand you in good stead," and surprisingly, considering their earlier hostility, both shook hands willingly.

The course came to an end and they were asked to fill in a questionnaire about their experiences as honestly as possible, in order to help the arrangers organise future courses and soon Phillip was speeding on his way home. Just as he drew up, his mobile rang and a voice said, "Is that Phillip Everett, the Phillip Everett I know and love and whom I have not seen for a very long time?"

"Gordon, don't say 'love', someone might hear you and think your intentions were less than honourable," Phillip said, delighted to hear from his friend.

"Rubbish," said Gordon, "I want to have a chat with you."

"Is that a short chat or a long chat?"

Gordon replied, "I want to have a long chat with you, how are you fixed for tonight?"

Phillip looked questioningly at Sarah. "It's Gordon and he wants to meet me tonight."

"Not tonight," she said, "I haven't seen you for five days!"

Gordon said, "Why don't both of you come to the flat and stay over, the girls could get to know each other and we could talk; how about if we pick you up tomorrow, around six?"

Sarah nodded so Phillip replied, "That sounds great, see you then. Regards to Isobel, bye."

"I'm not going to share you with anyone tonight," said Sarah, hugging him fiercely, "and I've already prepared a meal so there's no need to go out anywhere. Do you want to eat now?"

"Whatever you want," he said.

"In that case, food can wait till later!" she said.

The following day, Gordon and Isobel picked them up at the appointed time; Gordon stowed their overnight bags in the boot and Isobel drove off towards the city centre. "Have you forgotten how to drive?" said Phillip.

"Nah, Isobel is still at the stage where she likes to drive and in any case, she is going to drop us off at the wine bar for our chat, while she and Sarah get to know each other. Okay with you two?" he questioned.

Sarah said with a slight edge to her voice, "Fine with me but remember to behave yourselves. I don't want you chatting up any stray young ladies while you're having your discussion or whatever."

"As though we would," the two men chorused, simultaneously. They were dropped off at their favourite wine bar, Sarah hopped into the front passenger seat and Isobel drove off to start their 'getting to know you' session.

As soon as they were inside, ordered their drinks and looked around for a vacant table, Gordon said, "She's really hooked on you. How do you manage it, to get all these luscious females lusting after you wherever you go while I, I'm lucky if I get to chat up one girl in a hundred!"

"Don't talk rubbish, you've had your moments and I don't recall any shortage of female crumpet in your life. You've ended up with a gorgeous woman, whereas I got kicked into touch very quickly – my girl went off home to marry someone else – so I don't think you've been short of anything during your adult years," scoffed Phillip. "Anyway, I'm hooked on her as well, you could say we are hooked on each other; she is something else, lovely figure, loving nature, can't wait to get me into bed when I get home, what more could I want?"

"So it's serious," Gordon said. "She is ten years younger than you, isn't she?"

"Nine... nine years," said Phillip.

"Do you think that might make a difference at some future date?"

Phillip acknowledged that it worried him now and again; he had pointed this out to her and said she would be better off with someone nearer to her own age. Then he had not heard from her for several weeks and he thought it was all over, until she pulled up outside the house in her new little sports car, parked the car and rang the doorbell. "She had a small suitcase with her and such a miserable face, I could have laughed if I hadn't known it was a very serious matter for her. She just said, 'You're not going to send me away, are you?' and that was it. She moved in and I promised myself never to hurt her again and apart from one or two slight upsets, as far as I'm concerned, we're together."

Taking their drinks to the table, Phillip asked Gordon what it was he wanted to chat about. Gordon launched into his reasons for wanting to talk. "I've got a beautiful woman who loves me and wants to marry me. I love her but now she wants to set a date for our wedding…"

"And?" Phillip asked.

"I've got this feeling," said Gordon, "what if it doesn't work out?"

"I see," said Phillip, "you've started having doubts. It's a big commitment."

"Even more so in our case; we're both Catholics and want to remain Catholics so divorce would be out of the question."

"But why would you think about that when you haven't even got married yet!!" said Phillip.

"I'm like you," Gordon said. "I'm quite a bit older than Isobel and in time, she might fall for some younger man. I think we should live together first, like you and Sarah. Then she would experience what it's really like, living all the time with someone, namely me!!"

"So why don't you just go ahead and do it?"

Gordon sighed. "Her parents will not hear of it and if we went ahead, Isobel would be very unhappy not to be welcomed into her parents' house again, which is what they're threatening; her parents are very devout Catholics and living together without marriage is a mortal sin and they take that sort of thing very seriously."

"Now let me get this straight," said Phillip, "spending weekends with you and sleeping together is alright but living with you and sleeping together all the time, is a mortal sin!! Where's the logic in that?"

"There is no logic, that doesn't come in to it," said Gordon. "Isobel does not see any problem, she just says 'let's get married and everything will be fine'."

Phillip sat for a moment, drinking his lager. "I think it's a question of whether or not you love her enough," he said eventually.

"Of course I love her," Gordon insisted.

"Then marry her and be done with all your hesitation and doubts, that appears to me to be the only solution!"

"Perhaps I should do what you did, you know, send her away," Gordon said.

"Don't even think about that," Phillip said, sharply.

"Isobel is a lovely girl and she is very much in love with you; if you tried anything like that, she would be deeply hurt and I, your oldest friend, would be very annoyed with you. Now marry her and let's not talk about this anymore."

In the silence that followed, Gordon said wistfully, "I shall miss our nights out, drinking, chatting up the birds, free to do as we wanted."

"It's alcohol talking," said Phillip. "The 'birds' we used to talk to were the ones that couldn't find any other men to chat to!"

"You do make it sound romantic," said Gordon, grumpily. "You know it was nothing like that; all we were interested in was getting a leg over and on to the next female who was willing. You can't live the rest of your adult life like that, you have to grow up sometime!" Gordon's attention was caught by two women sitting at a table by the window. "Hey, those two over there have been watching us for ages." He raised his glass to them and they smiled. "You can sit here all night if you want," said Gordon, "but I'm going over to talk to them."

Before Phillip could say anything, Gordon had pushed his way across the room to start his familiar chat-up line and no matter how annoyed Phillip felt, there was not much he could do. In the past, it had always been Phillip who was first to start a conversation with any available girls; after all that was why they came here on a Friday evenings; there were always plenty of attractive females and it had become a game to persuade them to come back to Gordon or Phillip's flat where it was taken for granted that they would have sexual intercourse. Gordon had been quite shy in that respect at first; he blamed his boys only education at a Catholic school. "Never met a girl until I was eighteen," he used to joke. Let him get it out of his system, thought Phillip.

He jumped as he felt the hand on his shoulder, automatically tensing his muscles, until he turned and saw a young woman standing next to him. "Your friend over there is waving to you, I think he wants you to go over." Phillip sauntered across the room to where Gordon was grinning and beckoning to him and as he opened his mouth to introduce Daphne and Rose, Phillip said coldly, "I wouldn't bother with him if I were you. He has a sick wife in bed and two very young children waiting for him at home!!"

Gordon almost shouted in his fury, "What are you trying to do?"

"Bring you to your senses," returned Phillip venomously. The two women stood up, picked up their drinks and walked away to the bar.

"Listen to me, I am now walking out of here and I expect you to come with me. If you don't come, I shall call a taxi and go to your flat where I shall tell Isobel that you and I had a disagreement and you stayed behind to cool down and have another drink. I shall take Sarah and go home. Now, are you coming with me or not?"

"No need to carry on like that," muttered Gordon, somewhat shamefacedly, "of course I'm coming with you." They flagged down a taxi and a short while later, they were at Gordon's flat.

Phillip sensed tension between Isobel and Sarah, but Gordon with false cheer said, "I'm having a large whisky, anyone else fancy anything?"

Sarah hissed to Phillip, "Come into the other room, you have some explaining to do!"

Phillip raised an eyebrow and Isobel said penitently, "Sorry, I happened to mention Jasmine to Sarah and…"

He walked over to her and kissed her cheek gently. "Don't worry, it's okay," and took Sarah's hand, leading her into the second bedroom. Closing the door gently, he waited for the onslaught.

A furious Sarah spat out, "I didn't know you were making love to Jasmine at the same time you were making love to me!!"

Phillip tried a light-hearted approach and said, "If I was making love to you both, you must have known about it because you would have been there!!"

"Oh yes, very amusing," Sarah said.

"Look, Jasmine happened a long time before you came along and it finished ages before our relationship had even started, before I even knew you."

Sarah looked puzzled. "But the way Isobel told it, it sounded as if you were meeting one of us on Friday and the other one on Saturday."

"Isobel doesn't know anything about the way we met and when our relationship started. It's true that Gordon and I met her and Jasmine at the same time but Jasmine went back home to Portugal to marry her childhood sweetheart, long before you and I got together."

Sarah looked puzzled. "Why did she do that?"

"Apparently they were sort of promised to each other; it was almost an arranged marriage, in a way; both families wanted it to take place."

"Were you very upset?"

"No, not really, she just said she was sorry but she had always known she was going to go home and marry this chap and in any case, the relationship wasn't going anywhere, so I wasn't surprised."

"I hope this never happens to us," Sarah said.

"Wild horses wouldn't drag me away from you my darling," Phillip said and held her close to him, feeling the tension gradually receding from her body.

She glanced up at him and said, "Now you'll have to prove that. Are we alright to make love in here?"

"I think Gordon and Isobel have their own concerns tonight – they won't be bothered by anything we do!! I'm going to devour you now, take your clothes off," he ordered.

"Please sir, I am an innocent young girl," she said, fluttering her eyelashes like a Victorian damsel.

"Not for much longer you're not," he said emphatically and their lovemaking began.

Chapter 26

The following morning, Gordon managed to intercept Phillip before Isobel and Sarah appeared and he apologised for his behaviour the previous evening. "I don't know what came over me."

"You did behave like an ignorant git," Phillip said.

"If you are trying to make me feel guilty, I already feel bad. Isobel said how nice you were to her, almost loving. You've never been that pleasant with her in the past. She said I had better watch you because you could charm food away from a rattlesnake!!"

Phillip shouted with laughter. "Thank her for that compliment will you."

"Were you trying to make me or Sarah feel jealous?" asked Gordon.

"I can assure you that I had no ulterior motive. In view of what happened in the wine bar, I did have a great deal of sympathy for Isobel; are you surprised that I was nice to her? Look Gordon, if you seriously have doubts about marriage, give it some thought and if you feel the same in a month or so, call things off. But whatever you do, don't hurt Isobel, do it like a gentleman."

"Actually, I was going to propose to her and buy a ring this weekend, but I'll do as you suggest and wait a while but whatever I do, I will try not to hurt her or at least as little as possible; I am really fond of her you know?"

"Oh, there was a second reason I wanted to meet you; I might have a client for you, are you interested?"

"I'm always interested in new clients, Gordon; fill me in on the background, what do you know?"

"Okay," said Gordon, "this lady is forty, comes from a well-to-do family, she's not short of cash. She works in the City, made a packet for herself and married a young City banker who's turned out to be a real sleazeball. He is trying to divorce her, citing her 'unreasonable behaviour', and of course, he wants half her fortune."

"I'm not quite sure where I fit in," said Phillip. "What she wants is a good solicitor, someone like John Standish for example."

"No, Phillip, she knows all about lawyers; what she wants is for someone to dig into his background, find out if there's anything questionable which could be used to refute his suggestions about her unreasonable behaviour; what do you say?"

"Get her to ring me and I'll certainly try to help her if I can."

"Good, good, I'll let her know on Monday and she'll get in touch with you. By the way, we're still friends aren't we?" said Gordon.

"Of course we are. We'll always be friends," Phillip said, suddenly embarrassed as they solemnly shook hands.

"Anyway, as soon as Sarah appears, we'd better be on our way; perhaps Isobel might be going to mass?" queried Phillip.

As if prompted, Sarah appeared fully dressed, carrying their overnight bags, and went to Gordon to kiss him politely, murmuring that "we must all do this again sometime" and what a beautiful flat it was and without saying goodbye to Isobel, they left to go to the station. When they arrived home, they both heaved a sigh of relief, looked at each other and laughed.

"Some weekend that was," said Sarah.

Chapter 27

On Monday afternoon when the phone rang, an assured female voice told him that Gordon had recommended him as being a discreet private detective and she wanted him to undertake some work for her. She gave her name as Elizabeth Donnan and said she wished to call on him later that day, just "to put him in the picture" as it were, would that be convenient? Phillip assured her that it would be and when a very smart Jaguar car drew up in front of his office, he knew he was about to meet Mrs Donnan. He opened the door, shook hands and ushered her into his office, asking whether he could provide her with any refreshments. She refused politely and commenced her story while he made a quick assessment of her.

Slim, about forty, expensively dressed in a smart trouser suit, a necklace which looked to be made of genuine pearls with a diamond clasp, a little unusual for today's business woman and with obvious poise and command of her situation.

"I'll just give you my general details, Mr Everett, to explain why I wish you to work for me. Since I left university, I have been building my career and finances in the City of London and perhaps I concentrated too much on the business side of my life and not enough on my private life. As a consequence I married later in life after falling in love with a much younger man. You know that old saying, 'Marry in haste, repent at leisure', well I certainly had to learn that lesson with a vengeance. My husband turned out to be a liar, a philanderer, a cheat and a spendthrift. Although he worked in the City, he never seemed to have any money and expected me to bankroll him whenever he asked, which I usually did as he always had a good story as to why he needed it and I was besotted with him.

"Three months ago he said he had lost his job and when I made enquiries, I found out he was borrowing money, using my name as collateral. When I refused to give him any more funds, he said he wanted a divorce and that he was entitled to half of everything I own. Most of that was built up before I ever met him and while I am prepared to make a settlement, if only to get me out of this failed relationship, I am not prepared to hand over the results of my hard work to gratify his greed."

"Excuse me a moment, Mrs Donnan," Phillip interrupted politely, "did you have a pre-nuptial agreement between you?"

"That is where the 'marry in haste' bit comes in. I was, to coin a phrase, swept off my feet and being rather naive in matters like that, by the time I came to take advice, it was too late. Will you agree to work for me?"

Phillip was thinking rapidly and looking at her he said, "Excuse me, but at this point I'm not sure what you wish me to do. I think what you need is advice from a solicitor as to your particular situation."

"Yes, I have mentioned it to the family solicitor but I'm of the opinion that a check into my husband's background, before he met me, might strengthen my case and I might not have to bankrupt myself to pay him what he claims is his by right. I thought from what Gordon told me you would be willing to do a little investigation work for me yet you simply advise me to consult a solicitor."

"Mrs Donnan, let me explain—" Phillip started when she interrupted him saying, "Please call me Liza."

"Very well, Liza, I can't honestly say I see any work for me here. I charge £30 per hour I have to spend working on a case, plus expenses, and this can work out very expensive, with possibly no benefit to you in the end."

Liza sat back in her chair and said, "You must be an honest man Mr Everett, and there aren't many of those left in this cutthroat world." She laughed and said, "You are also good-looking, charming and a very nice person to have around."

"That makes no difference to your case," he said.

"I would have thought this would be ideal for a private detective, establishing the past history of a shady character and exposing his greed and determination to make money from an unsuspecting woman; lawyers don't move their butts off their office chairs, that's why I want someone to dig up any dirt, if there is some!!"

Out of the corner of his eye, Phillip could see Sarah's sports car drawing up in front of the house. He could not see the point of continuing the interview further as he knew Liza was starting to flirt with him. He took a card giving John Standish's name and office address and said, "I can thoroughly recommend him, we've worked together on a case before and he can represent you in court."

She frowned, holding the card in her fingers. "If I consult him, will he employ you for any investigative work needed?"

"If he thought there was any need for that, he would probably call and discuss what was necessary, yes," Phillip said.

Sarah waved to him and Liza asked, "Is that your wife?"

"No, she's my partner."

"And you both live here?"

Phillip thought she was being a bit nosy so he said, "That's right, we both live here."

She studied the card and then looked up at him. "Thank you Mr Everett, I will hope to see you soon," and he escorted her to the door where he gazed at her car, almost wistfully.

"That's a great car you have there!"

She scoffed. "Typical male attitude, more interested in the car than the female driver. Your partner is a lucky woman," she said, then climbed into her car and drove away.

"Who was that?" said Sarah, as she came out of the kitchen.

"That was a potential new client, the one Gordon mentioned."

"What did she want?"

"She's going through a difficult divorce and she wants someone to investigate her husband's background. I told her to get a good lawyer; I can't see much work for me there so I gave her John Standish's card and she went off with that, quite happy to consult him. If he thinks there's anything for me to do, he'll get in touch, I daresay."

"All the divorces I've ever heard about are messy," said Sarah. "Do you really want to get mixed up in that kind of business?"

"That's the kind of business I'm in, somewhere between a social worker and a policeman," he joked.

Sarah frowned. "But you don't have to do this sort of job."

"But I love doing it, it's different, sometimes it's exciting, it's physically and mentally challenging, and it gets the old adrenaline going. Of course, it could be slightly dangerous but more people get killed crossing the road!!"

Sarah was not convinced. "It would break my heart if anything happened to you." Phillip hugged her and said nothing was going to happen to him and what were they going to eat this evening.

"Let's go out for a meal, my treat," Sarah said, "but not to the local pub!"

"Sounds great to me," said Phillip. "I can show off my beautiful, sexy partner who's keeping me in the way to which I have become accustomed!"

"Wait till you see my dress!" she said.

He protested, "There's no need to dress up too much," but she was already on her way upstairs. The result was worth the wait and when Phillip turned to look at her, his reaction was written all over his face. The dress was dark blue, very close fitting, the narrow straps and décolleté neckline showing off her slender waist and lovely breasts. As she came towards him he could see that all she wore underneath the material was a soft lacy bra and the faint outline of her panties. She was carrying a small clutch bag, decorated with emeralds, to match her gold and emerald necklace and the strap of her wristwatch. She pirouetted in front of him – "Like it?"

All Phillip could say was, "I've rung for a taxi, it'll be here shortly," and wish that they weren't going out for dinner.

Sarah pouted. "Is that all you can say!"

Phillip knew that much more was expected from him so he took Sarah's hand, kissed it grandly and said, "You know you look absolutely gorgeous and I can't wait to take you out and make every other man jealous, wishing he was in my shoes," and he ushered her into the waiting taxi.

The head waiter recognised Sarah as Lady Pennington's daughter and they were shown to an excellent table.

They ordered and while waiting, Phillip asked Sarah to tell him something about her life before he met her. "I went to a private boarding school, all girls, and the headmistress was very keen we should grow up into well behaved girls so if we ever stepped out of line, our parents would be summoned to the school and we would have to confess our faults and give them an explanation. It was mortifying but we never did anything too terrible so I suppose we all became well behaved young ladies in the end."

"So you didn't have much fun there," said Phillip.

"On the contrary," laughed Sarah, "our biggest sin was committed after 'lights out' when we would sit on our beds and tell the most amazing lies about our experiences with boys when we were home for holidays and any other misdemeanours we could invent, but the worst behaviour of all was to go up behind another girl and pull down her pyjama bottoms!!"

"No, what a terrible thing to do," he said, straight-faced. "And is this what you did?"

"It may sound very silly to you," she said, "but it was considered inexcusable. In some cases, unsuitable behaviour was punishable with expulsion!! Obviously our parents were mortified that their children could be such little devils so we were obliged to be good. What about you?"

"As I'm a Catholic, I always attended a church school, primary and grammar, but then I went on to university where there were both sexes, obviously, and all religions and all nationalities."

"Which university did you go to?" she asked.

"London University," he replied.

"So you had freedom to express yourself and grow up there, did you?"

"If by that you mean sharing digs with all sorts of people, some of which were rather unsavoury, yes I did."

"Which were unsavoury, the people or the digs?" she queried.

"Both," he said, remembering back to his student days; "you should have seen the piles of dirty, unwashed dishes and cutlery, empty beer cans piled up, unwashed T-shirts in dark corners."

"Why would it be like that?" she said, having always had someone to tidy up for her and hand her freshly laundered clothes whenever they were needed!

"First of all you get three or four people sharing a flat. You have two bedrooms with two guys sleeping in each, one bathroom, one toilet, one small kitchen and a communal sitting room. Young men are largely untaught in the skills of housekeeping so they can never agree on a rota as to who washes the dishes, cleans the rooms or tidies and throws away the rubbish. They tend to wallow a bit, flaunting their freedom from authority and thus it goes on until finally, someone does something about the squalor and that someone was usually me!"

"You men, honestly, you are not much better than grubby little boys; how did you manage to survive without catching cholera or the Black Death?"

"I saw one of my fellow students lifting all the settee and chair cushions until he found a piece of abandoned pizza, which must have been there for days, and he ate it for breakfast; it's amazing how a human being can survive anything when they are young and short of money!!"

Their food arrived and the waiter hovered over them, pouring wine and generally making himself useful. Phillip joked with him, feeling very happy to be relaxing in the company of the woman he loved, who was obviously attracting quite a lot of attention from four young men at a nearby table, who were a little noisy and downing large amounts of alcohol; they appeared to be celebrating some kind of win, whether a football team, a boxing match or perhaps a horse winning an important race and they made no secret of the fact that they thought she was sitting with the wrong dinner companion.

Sarah and Phillip finished the first course of their meal and the waiter presented them with an ornate dessert menu, asking them if they would like to order anything further and whether they would like coffee and liqueurs. They studied the list, made their choice and sat back to wait for a few minutes when one of the noisy young men walked over to their table, smiled at Sarah, completely ignoring Phillip, and said, "You're very beautiful, do you think your dad would mind if I asked you for a date?"

Sarah put on her haughtiest expression and looked down her nose at him – "Does your mother allow you to be out on your own at this time of night?"

Somewhat taken aback by this remark, he pressed on with, "Er… me and my three companions over there" – he indicated with a jerk of his head – "have been admiring you all night and we was trying to remember the last time any of us saw someone as gorgeous as you. None of us could remember," he finished, in the face of Sarah's fury.

Phillip spoke softly. "One day, when the four of you have grown up, if you're very, very lucky, you may actually meet as lovely a woman as my wife, but in the meantime, I would suggest that you stick to adolescent schoolgirls."

Insulted, the young man said, "What's this elderly man got to offer you that us four fit guys can't provide you with?" indignantly.

Sarah glared at him and enunciated slowly and icily, "You might be more convincing if you wiped your mother's breast milk from your face!" He turned and went back to his friends, muttering something under his breath.

When they had finished their meal, Sarah paid the bill, with a generous tip for the waiter, who had phoned for a taxi for them, and they went home, rather silent. Phillip paid the taxi driver and they went upstairs to get ready for bed. "For once," Sarah said lightly, "I didn't have to fight my rivals for your attention!"

"No, it was my turn," he said.

Chapter 28

The following morning, John Standish rang to ask how he was and Phillip replied that he was "fine, and how are you?"

"Oh, I'm good, thank you very much; I've had a call from an Elizabeth Donnan, she's coming to see me this afternoon. She gave me to understand that she has already spoken to you."

"Yes," said Phillip, "she came to see me about her divorce but I couldn't see much work for me there so I recommended you because she wants a good lawyer. From what she told me, I gathered she is a rich woman, married late in life and made the mistake of marrying a toy-boy banker who's now lost his job and is looking to lay his hands on half of her fortune!"

"I take it she doesn't think that he is entitled to this?" John asked.

"Apparently not; have you ever met a rich person who would be happy to part with half of their money?"

"No never," laughed John. "So what do you think I should do?"

"Why not see her, take her case and do your usual good job; better you do that than some other lazy so-and-so taking her for a ride."

"Okay Phillip, thanks for that remark, I think I get the picture. If need be, we can still work together, yes?" he said.

"Just give me a call any time you need me," Phillip said.

On Wednesday, John called again to tell him that he had spoken to Elizabeth Donnan and she had told him the tragic story of her life, how she had a hard job getting into banking in the City; she had to work her socks off to compete with men. How she always earned less than her male rivals even though in some cases she was better, in some cases much better, than her male colleagues. She concentrated so much on her career and finally earned and saved some money, she put off getting married and finally, when she did marry later in her life, he turned out to be nothing but a lazy bum. He frittered all his money away when he was making plenty, but now that he was out of work, he was divorcing her and wanted half her money.

"What bank did her husband work for?" asked Phillip.

"United Emirates," John said.

"United Emirates, how did he manage to lose his job with a bank like that, an oil-rich state, must have billions of pounds in the vaults." Phillip said.

"It wasn't the bank, it was the customers, and the number of transactions that take place daily that matter," John said. "Also the fact that he was not good at his job could have had something to do with it!"

"Well you know my charges and conditions; I have already told her but I won't start working on any case until money is deposited in my bank account," said Phillip.

"So what sort of a deposit would you want from her?" asked John.

"This could be a messy investigation and time-consuming," said Phillip. "I think £2000 is a reasonable sum, to start with."

"Seems a fairly reasonable amount," said John. "How do you normally receive your money?"

"There is the wire transfer, also a cheque, or she could pay by credit card."

"To do a money transfer I would need your bank details," said John.

Phillip gave him the details of his bank account; "Don't flash my bank account details around the office, I don't want other people drawing my money out."

"Of course not," said John. "If she does not use wire transfer, I'll shred the account details you've just given me."

"Good man," said Phillip. "Tell me, what sort of information am I looking for?"

"I would have assumed you would have asked her that, when you spoke to her."

"To be honest John, I didn't think I would be involved in the case, so I didn't ask too many questions."

"Look, I'll get a lot more details and I'll send them to you, along with some photographs of both of them."

"Her naked on the rug," said Phillip.

"Yes, I think she would look well like that," said John.

"When I saw her, she was wearing a trouser suit so I didn't see too much of her," said Phillip.

"Ah well you missed something there," said John. "She came to see me in a skirt and jumper. The skirt was knee length, and the jumper had a plunging neckline. When she sat down her skirt rose above her knees and when she leaned forward, you could see plenty, and believe you me, that was enough to get any red-blooded male panting."

"I'll take your word for it John, I'll be waiting for the money and your official letter," said Phillip.

Chapter 29

Events moved quickly and two days after speaking to John, the money was in Phillip's bank account, and a thick envelope had arrived for him containing five photographs of Mr and Mrs Elizabeth Donnan, three of them together and two of them individually. Phillip noticed that the individual photo of Liza was when she was much younger and wearing a bikini, and very nice she looked too. The photo of her husband must have been taken recently, probably at work. It was of him standing near an office desk and dressed in a suit and tie, and was just what Phillip wanted. Six inches by four inches, nice and clear, Phillip could see exactly what Ronald Gardner looked like. It also had his current address on the back of the photograph, but no telephone number. There's no excuse now, why he couldn't make a start on the new case. He wondered if there might be any information about Ron, on the internet. Phillip continued planning, working out his strategy on how to deal with the case.

Friday came; Gordon did not ring so Phillip and Sarah decided to spend a quiet weekend at home, just enjoying each other's company. On Monday morning, Phillip had a call from John Standish.

"Have you received all the information I sent you?" he asked.

"Yes, John, and I have made a start. So far I have found out that Ronald is twenty-six years of age. He was twenty-four when he married Elizabeth, so they have been married two years. This is his first marriage, he comes from a middle-class family, his parents still run a plumbing business, so no financial worries there. He went to grammar school and Loughborough University. He graduated in economics and English history, but he was not in any way outstanding as a student, just Mr Average, if you can call any university student average. He has no criminal record, but has always been short of money, which is consistent with what Elizabeth told me. After university, he had three menial jobs. One in a supermarket as a trainee manager – he left, the job was too demanding, but he was not fired; he left by mutual consent. The second job was solicitor's clerk trainee. Not suitable – so there again, he left by mutual consent. Finally the third job was in a police office as a statistician. Reason for leaving – he was bored. Finally he applied for a job at the Bank of Arab Emirates. He was selected from twelve other candidates and has worked there until made redundant three months ago," said Phillip.

"You found that out already?" said John.

"Yes but this is just peripheral information, none of this is any good to us. A lot of the information we want will have to come from Elizabeth herself," said Phillip. "You should interview her as soon as you can."

"Me?" said John. "Why me? You are the one that gathers information, I'm the one who acts on it."

"You are going to represent her in court," said Phillip.

"Yes but only by asking you questions," said John.

"Okay," said Phillip, "but you ring her first, and ask her to bring any paperwork she has, which refers in any way to her husband."

"Such as what?" asked John.

"I'll start again," said Phillip. "The only thing that we can do for her is to make sure she keeps her money. She will have to pay her husband a minimum amount in settlement because he is her lawful husband and when divorce goes ahead, a division of everything that they both own will take place. It would be nice if they reached a mutual agreement, but this is obviously not going to happen, so it will be up to the judge to decide. The law says that division should be fifty-fifty, half each, but we can argue that it only applies where each partner has put in an equal share into that partnership. In other words, his or her efforts contribute the same portion in building up the final sum of what there is to divide. We will have to convince the judge that the husband's contribution has been virtually nil, and in fact, if anything, it was negative, because he spent a lot of her money, while putting in nothing toward the final sum."

"That's very relevant Phillip," said John.

"What else were you going to use to help her case?" asked Phillip.

"I haven't thought about it yet, but I'm happy with your ideas. However, I really think you should ring her. You know exactly what paperwork you want her to bring to the interview, whereas if I ring her, I'll probably get her to bring the wrong information, or miss out on the exact paperwork you want," said John.

"OK, but I will want the lion's share of what she pays us," said Phillip, jokingly. "I have not had a penny from her as yet," said John.

"Could you let me have Mrs Donnan's telephone number?"

"I'll send you an email," said John.

"Thanks," said Phillip and put the phone down. Five minutes later Phillip's computer screen showed 'one new message', giving him the number he had asked for. Phillip rang Elizabeth's number and she answered, "Elizabeth Donnan speaking."

"Phillip Everett here, Mrs Donnan."

"Ah, my favourite private detective," she said.

"Why, how many have you got?" asked Phillip.

"Well, there are several – one is Mr Everett, then there is Phillip Everett and finally, there is Phillip, I like Phillip best," said Elizabeth.

"Whichever of those you prefer to use, in order to work on your case, I need to talk to you," said Phillip, "so I think I had better start again. Are you going to divorce your husband?"

"He is divorcing me," she said.

"Is there any chance of you two reconciling?"

"None at all, I don't want him near me; besides, he is living with his new girlfriend."

"He has filed for a divorce?" asked Phillip.

"Yes, I have received the papers, some days back," she said.

"Did you give the papers to a solicitor?"

"I was going to give them to you but you turned me down."

"Okay, but I am not a solicitor, and you will have to file a counter-claim – only a qualified solicitor can do that. That is a separate issue but In the end, it will finish up in court unless, of course, you two can come to an agreement, and settle out of court. I have to assume that this will not happen. Our aim is to finish up giving little of your money, or possessions, to your husband. My aim is to minimise any amount of money that the court will allocate to him. To do just that, I need to see you and I want you to bring with you all the relevant bills, statements, in fact any paperwork you have received since your wedding."

"Exactly what kind of 'paperwork' do you mean?" she asked.

"Start with the marriage certificate and then all the bills, mortgage agreement, electricity, gas, council rates, water bills, any repair bills and any other bills which have been paid by you. I need your bank statements, for the two years you have been married."

"Is all this necessary?" she asked.

"We need to prove that your husband's contribution to the household expenses has been minimal. Also if you have paid any of his bills, or given him any of your money we will need to prove that as well," said Phillip.

"I didn't realise it would be so complicated."

"Well courts don't just take your word for it, you know, you actually have to substantiate what you are saying and prove it's true. How long will it take you to assemble all those details for me?"

"I'll ring you back Mr Everett."

On the following morning, Phillip received a call from her. "The information you wanted, I think I've gathered all you asked me for, may I come and see you this morning?"

"Yes of course, about what time can you get to my office?" asked Phillip.

"I can be there in half an hour."

"That will be fine," said Phillip. "See you soon."

Less than half an hour later she was parking her car outside Phillip's front door. Phillip opened the door for her saying, "Please come in." He couldn't help but notice that she was dressed to impress. She wore a skirt which only just reached her knees, sheer black stockings and high heeled shoes which made her legs look sexy. She wore a white blouse with long sleeves, a frilly collar and cuffs. It was cut low with a plunging neckline, showing off her well-shaped, full breasts. You could make out her black lacy bra, showing through the white blouse. As Phillip walked behind her into his office, he could see she had a well-shaped full bum; he knew this was going to turn out to be a very difficult interview. He indicated the chair facing his desk and asked her to sit down. "Please call me Liz or Liza, even though you may want me to call you Mr Everett but please call me Liza."

"Liza, please sit down," said Phillip. She sat down and Phillip went around his desk, and sat in his chair. When she was sitting down, her skirt rose nearly half way up her thighs. "Did you bring all the paperwork for me?" queried Phillip. She had a document case with her which she passed over the desk to Phillip. He extracted the documents and returned the folder to her.

He quickly went through the papers. "Is your partner at home?" she asked.

"No, she is at work," said Phillip.

"So we're alone," she said. As Phillip looked up at her, she slowly crossed her legs and then uncrossed them. The thought crossed his mind quickly, was she wearing any underwear? He remembered that in the film *Basic Instinct* it was what the actress Sharon Stone had done, but this mature woman in front of him looked even sexier.

"If it makes you feel easier, you can come back some other time and I will have a female assistant here."

"You misunderstand me, Phillip, I feel perfectly at ease. I was just thinking this is a house, so it has bedrooms upstairs." Phillip couldn't say anything, inside he was in turmoil. This sexy woman with the full figure, just as Phillip always liked them, was virtually propositioning him. He could just imagine her, lying on the bed and slowly taking her skirt and blouse off. Then he would take her bra off. Did she wear any panties? He was aroused now. "This is all the paperwork that I need, thank you," said Phillip.

"Is that all you want of me?" she said coyly.

"Yes, thank you."

"Are we not going to talk about the case?"

"No, not today, I need to go through all the papers first."

"Are you sure, Phillip?" She slowly uncrossed her legs again and re-crossed them even more slowly. No, she was not wearing any panties, damn woman, she was driving him mad. You don't want to lose everything, Phillip, he told himself, just for a good lay, even she is very sexy and asking for it.

"Can I escort you to the door?" Phillip said.

"Oh well, if you don't want to show me your bedroom, then I had better go." As she got up, she leaned well forward and showed him more of her breasts and started walking out. He followed her, keeping a good distance between them. Finally she made it to her car. "Goodbye Phillip, I could do a lot for you." He did not answer and watched her drive away.

Phillip was so pleased when Sarah got home. As soon as she entered the house, Phillip took her in his arms, and started kissing her, with all the passion the other woman had made him feel. As Sarah responded, he lifted her into his arms and carried her upstairs. Laying her gently on the bed, he slowly undressed her. "Just let me take a quick shower," she said, and disappeared into the shower room. Phillip undressed, and went into the bathroom and came out only wearing his shorts. Two minutes later Sarah was out, wearing only a towel and when she lay on the bed, Phillip now unleashed all the lust that he had felt all afternoon. He tried to make love slowly, watching the reaction on Sarah's face and body, and an hour later, they fell back onto the bed exhausted. "What caused this torrent of passion?" said Sarah. "Although you've made me feel marvellous, what have I done to deserve that?"

"I just wanted to show you what you mean to me, and how much I love you," said Phillip. Sarah kissed him and snuggled up closer to him before they both fell asleep.

Hunger awoke Sarah. "Hey, lover boy, it's getting on for ten o'clock," she said. "Come on, I need nourishment."

"Just say what you would like to eat, and we'll go for it. What would you like?"

"There's nothing much in the house," said Sarah.

"Even the pub will not be serving any food at this time, so that leaves us with takeaway – pizza, Chinese, or fish and chips."

"You missed out Indian food," said Sarah.

"Indian it is then. The least fattening is Tandoori chicken and boiled rice," said Phillip. "Let's try that."

Half an hour later, it was delivered to the door. Phillip said, "Eat it slowly, and not too much, or you will be too full to get to sleep."

"Yes master. First you wear me out, and then, you want me to go hungry. I will open some wine, it will help us to get to sleep." Eventually when they both got into bed, there was one thing that worried Phillip. All the time he was making love to Sarah, he had a picture of Liza crossing and uncrossing her legs!!

Phillip worked hard for the next two days. Going through all the documentation Liza Donnan had left with him, he did many calculations: how much money had been spent over the two years of Liza and Ronald Gardner's marriage; out of the money spent on everything but personal items, how much had Ronald contributed? Phillip was amazed to find that bills, actually paid by him, came to about two percent of the total. His claim on the estate, considering the time and amount of his contribution, would not amount to much. Phillip rang John Standish. "John, I did see Mrs Donnan, and asked her for all the relevant papers. I've been through all the documents now, and I estimate that his financial contribution to the overall spending, over the period that they lived as husband and wife, amounts to two percent of the total sum spent. That is everything but personal expenses. Keeping in mind it was only for a short period, there are no children and he was earning a salary of around £50,000, I can't see that he has any sort of claim on the estate," said Phillip.

"If only it was that simple," said John, "but his current position also comes into consideration."

"I think we should meet Ronald Gardner, with his solicitor, and put this to them," said Phillip. "Let's hear what they have to say."

"Do you want to arrange that?" said John.

"Come on John, solicitor to solicitor," said Phillip, "and try to read up a bit more on the divorce law, John, don't leave me do all the work!"

"Cheeky devil, I'll do that after I receive a summary of the work you have done," said John.

"On its way," said Phillip.

A few days later John rang him, "Howdy," he said.

"Have you been on holiday in the Wild West of America, or were you watching too many cowboy films?" said Phillip.

"It's a good old-fashioned greeting, as befits old friends," said John.

"Friends we are, but old I am not," said Phillip.

"Ah, being sensitive about your age is a sign of ageing," said John.

"Okay, what is it that you have got for me?" said Phillip.

"I have spoken to Ronald Gardner's lawyers and they are ready to meet us and discuss 'financial matters', as they put it," said John. "Shall we meet at your house?"

"No way Jose," said Phillip. "We meet them at your office, John, and I want a female presence there – like your secretary. Do you realise what torture it was, having Elizabeth Donnan taunting me, with that *Basic Instinct* crossing and uncrossing of her legs? Do you know what it's like having a voluptuous woman, with a nicely shaped, well-endowed figure, talking to you about bedrooms and what they could do for you?"

"Okay, I've heard enough," laughed John. "She won't do that here because there will be something like seven or eight people there."

"Just let me know when, and I will be there," said Phillip.

"I've received your paperwork, but if you have come across any more information which might be of use, bring that with you," said John.

"I'll talk to you later, sorry I don't know how to say it in cowboy language," said Phillip.

"Get lost," said John, and hung up.

Chapter 30

Later that day, Phillip received a phone call from Sarah's father, Lord Pennington. "Mr Phillip Everett?"

"Yes, speaking."

"Lord Pennington here."

"Good afternoon sir, can I do something for you?" said Phillip.

"I wonder if you can come and see me tonight Mr Everett?"

"Any particular time, sir?"

"About seven," said Sarah's father.

"Is it anything special and should I bring something with me?" asked Phillip.

"It's nothing formal, just that you have lived with my daughter for some time now and I would like to know where all this is going," said Lord Pennington.

"That's fine sir, I'll be there at seven."

Phillip rang Sarah at work and told her about the call from her father. "Don't be afraid of him," said Sarah.

"I am not afraid of anyone, but I don't have any answers as to where our relationship is going," said Phillip.

"I am not sure myself what the question means," she said.

"I think it means are we going to live in sin, or are we going to get married and what about the children, if we have any?" said Phillip.

"I think I see what you mean but I also think I'm too young to consider having a child," said Sarah.

"I totally agree with that," said Phillip.

"So that is one question eliminated," said Sarah. "What do you think about getting married?"

"I think this subject is in a similar vein to the other one. As you know," he said, "I have had one long-term relationship, almost the same as being married, but that did not prevent her from leaving me. So this is what I think at this point," said Phillip, "our relationship is strong and we are getting on very well together. Getting married now would not strengthen our relationship or add anything to it. We have not been living together all that long, but I do believe strongly that if a couple decide to have children, then they should get married first," said Phillip.

"So far, I have agreed with everything you have said. You have got your answers for my father, just tell him as it is," said Sarah. "Do you want me to come with you?"

"I think you should take this opportunity to visit your parents," said Phillip.

"Yes, you're right, best if we go together," said Sarah. "See you soon."

At 6.30 pm they left for Sara's parents and were shown into Lord Pennington's study. The two men shook hands, Sarah kissed her father and he said, "It's very nice to finally meet you Mr Everett. Hallo Sarah love, we don't see very much of you these days, do we? You are allowed to drop in now and then, you don't need an invitation, you know."

"Oh, Daddy, you know how time flies when you are busy," said Sarah.

"Well, yes, you'd better go and see your mother; this is man's talk." Sarah went to find her mother and Lord Pennington said, "Tell me a bit about yourself, Phillip."

Phillip told Lord Pennington about his early life, his parents, education at school and university, keeping it very brief and factual. He mentioned that he had been in a long term relationship, which he regarded as permanent as marriage, but when he lost his post in the City, she had walked out and left him. He had then decided to become a private detective and move to his present address and how this had led to his meeting Sarah and them falling in love. They had then decided to live together.

"That's what I wanted to talk to you about," said Lord Pennington. "Her mother and I wondered where this was going to lead, by that I mean the current situation between you."

"Well sir, Sarah and I have talked and we are both of the same mind on this. After a discussion, we both agree that getting married would not strengthen our already strong relationship. In fact, after marriage, partners are more likely to start taking one another a little for granted."

Lord Pennington interrupted. "Not necessarily, my wife and I have not done that. Oh, I know that over the years, relationships do change, it's inevitable, but love for each other grows deeper. You understand, I'm talking about love and respect, not passion and sex. The latter will cool as a couple get older, that's a natural process and it is only right that it should happen. Couples who build their relationship on sex alone, will not stay together for long; as the novelty wears off, they will inevitably drift apart."

"I understand where you stand on this sir; I can assure you that it has worried me for some time. Sarah is only twenty and I am twenty nine; that is quite an age gap and it can lead to problems. Luckily Sarah is not the usual kind of twenty-year-old girl, who wants to spend her time going to parties, night clubs and socialising. When we first met I discouraged her from thinking of me as anything more than an acquaintance, an older friend. Nothing sexual took place and after I found her dog and dropped him off at your house, I was quite prepared for it to end there but we continued to see each other. When I realised I was falling in love with her, I panicked and told her our friendship was at an end, that she should start seeking company with people of her own age. I said that our relationship was going nowhere and she was better off not wasting her time with me. I am sorry to say, I was rather cruel and selfish but I was worried that sooner or later she would leave me and look for a younger partner. I have already lived through one painful break-up when Samantha left me and I didn't want to live through something like that again. But I was fortunate enough to have Sarah come back and I have tried to put these thoughts of her leaving out of my mind. Sarah is in love with me and I love her very much."

"That's all very well but there is also the fact of respectability," said Lord Pennington. "Both my wife and I are not very happy to have my daughter living, and perhaps having children, outside of wedlock, a rather old-fashioned word but there it is."

"Sir, we have discussed this and we both agree that when we do decide to have children, we will get married first. At this point, we both think Sarah is too young to have children but both of us would like some in the future because we both like children."

Lord Pennington sighed. "Well that's some consolation I suppose. This job of yours, private detective, it seems a bit of an odd choice?"

Phillip laughed. "Not really, sir, it's the kind of job that sits between the police force and social workers."

"Is it dangerous?" asked Lord Pennington.

"No more dangerous than a policeman's job," said Phillip.

"But once you are married and have children, you should not risk your life unnecessarily, you wouldn't want to leave your wife a widow and your children without a father," said Lord Pennington.

"I will have to reconsider my circumstances at that time, sir."

"I could always find you a job in my organisation," said Lord Pennington.

"I am sure you could sir, and thank you for your offer, but you wouldn't think very much of me if I started sponging on you already," said Phillip.

"It's not sponging, I would expect you to work as hard as any of my other employees," said Lord Pennington.

"Thank you, sir, perhaps one day I will come and ask you for a job but for the time being, I prefer to make my own way," said Phillip.

"Are you good at your job?"

With quiet pride, Phillip said, "So far I have been successful in keeping an innocent man out of prison, I have recovered your dog Bruce, found a Russian oligarch's daughter and brought her back from Amsterdam. The police had let her case lapse because they had come to a dead end but I managed to find some fresh information so overall, I am earning a steady income and I am now currently working on a fresh case." Lord Pennington was curious to know what this present case might be about so Phillip told him he was gathering information in order to stop a ne'er-do-well adventurer trying to gain half his wife's assets in a divorce case, as no pre-nuptial agreement had been signed and she was quite a wealthy woman in her own right. Lord Pennington was suitably impressed and although he would have preferred it, as a father, if Sarah and Phillip had had a proper wedding before they had started to live together, he realised it was a little late for that.

"My wife and I will have to get used to the idea and if Sarah is happy, that must be our first concern. I don't think you are the kind of man who would harm her in any way and if she were made to suffer for whatever reason, you would find that I would make a nasty enemy!"

"I can assure you, sir, that will never happen," Phillip said. "Well, I expect Sarah and her mother will have had a good old chat over the coffee and cakes and she'll be thinking it's time to rescue you from my clutches. Very nice to have met you and I hope we'll see a bit more of you, now that we've been introduced, so to speak!"

On the way home, Sarah asked about his interrogation with her father. "How did it go?"

"Very formal, he asked me about my life so far, are we going to get married, what are my prospects, would I go and work for him, etc, etc, in fact, the questions I will be asking my potential son-in-law, sometime in the future. Was I any good at my job, how was it going, wasn't it rather a funny career for me when I'd worked in banking, was it dangerous, that kind of thing. I think it cleared the air between us but both he and your mother would have been much happier if we had stuck to tradition and married first before we shacked up together, as it were."

"They're a bit old-fashioned in that respect" Sarah said, "but I don't think they mind all that much, just so long as I'm happy and I told my mother all about you and I'm sure she understands."

The next morning, John rang to say that a meeting had been arranged with Ronald Gardner and his solicitors for ten am the following Tuesday at his office. "What do you mean by 'his solicitors'?" queried Phillip. "How many has he got?"

John laughed. "I'm not sure but we shall find out next Tuesday, won't we? Don't forget to bring anything which might be useful to us."

"Is Mrs Donnan going to be there?" Phillip asked.

"Yes, of course she will be present, why, are you afraid she will pounce on you?"

"Of course not," said Phillip crossly, "but I hope she will be quietly dressed for the occasion, we don't want Gardner's solicitors to get the wrong impression about her!!"

"I did tell her that it's a business meeting so with luck she might take the hint," John said.

Phillip arrived at John's office ten minutes early and found him and his secretary arranging the chairs in his office, ready for the opposition to make an appearance. Shortly afterwards, three men arrived and were shown in. Roland Gardner introduced himself and the other two men, one of whom was a thin man of medium height, whose name was Angus McKay and he spoke with a pronounced Scottish accent, the other man was called Richard Holmes. He was above average height, perhaps in his late twenties, good-looking, well-muscled like a sportsman and was McKay's assistant solicitor. Both were impeccably dressed in dark business suits, gleaming white shirts and suitably expensive-looking ties. On the other hand, Ronald Gardner was a tall man, built rather like a rugby player, who was beginning to go to seed, still good-looking but starting to lose his hair. Phillip could see why Elizabeth would fall for someone like that, a sex machine. He was casually dressed, trying to look as if he was a high school sportsman thought Phillip. John introduced his secretary, Mavis, himself and Phillip and offering them tea or coffee, which was refused, the meeting began.

"Who's going to start this discussion?" said John, blandly.

"Our case is quite simple," said Ronald Gardner. "As Elizabeth's husband, on the occasion of our divorce, I am entitled to half of everything we own. I have moved out of the marital home, taking nothing but my clothes and a few personal possessions; I think I am now entitled to an equal share of everything we owned." He emphasised *we* firmly.

"Mr Gardner, when you married Mrs Donnan, can you tell me what you brought into the marriage, quite apart from anything she owned?" asked Phillip.

"What exactly do you mean, 'what did I bring in'?" blustered Ronald.

Gently, quietly, Phillip said, "I will try to make it simple for you: after the marriage, where did you live?"

"We lived in Elizabeth's house."

"And when you moved into Elizabeth's house, did you need a large removal van to move your possessions from your previous address?"

"No, actually, I used my car."

"So the things you moved into Elizabeth's house were just your personal possessions?" asked Phillip.

"Yes, why?" said Ronald.

"Bear with me a moment; you also said you had taken your clothes and personal possessions with you when you moved out of the marital home?"

"That's correct."

"Therefore Roland, all you brought with you into the marriage and marital home, you have already removed and taken back?"

"Yes, yes."

"Where are you going with all this?" interrupted Angus.

"Very well, now I'll place the facts of our case before you," Phillip said. "Mr Ronald Gardner has been married to Elizabeth Donnan for two years. After the wedding, he moved into her house, bringing nothing except personal possessions, i.e. his clothes, his razor, toothbrush and not much else. In the time he lived there, his contribution to their living expenses has been nil. He has not paid a single bill of any kind, be it for food, rates and taxes, heating and lighting, mortgage or household expenses of any kind, in spite of the fact that he was earning £50,000 per annum from the bank where he was employed. Not only that, he was also borrowing money from Mrs Donnan, during the time they were man and wife, and none of that has ever been repaid."

Ronald smirked and said, "But the lady got her payment in kind."

"What precisely do you mean by that?" asked Phillip.

"The lady was always very satisfied when it came to her other needs," he said.

"If you are referring to your services in the bedroom, I think you will find that according to your wife, you were inadequate as a lover and I quote, 'like goods which appeared appetising on the cover but the product inside turns out to be somewhat disappointing' – her words, not mine, I can assure you."

Ronald leapt to his feet and lunged at Phillip "You bastard, you're making all that up, I'll knock seven bells out of you for saying that."

Phillip rose to his feet, putting his hand up. He raised his finger as though to say "careful now" and that really riled his opponent. Ronald swung his right arm and aimed at Phillip's jaw, endeavouring to punch his face, but Phillip swiftly moved his head to one side and caught Ronald's wrist. He gave the arm a swift jerk and everybody could hear the crack of the shoulder joint and Ronald's loud yelp before his arm fell limply to his side and he fell back into his chair, sweating and swearing profusely.

There was a moment of shocked silence and then Angus said furiously, "We shall sue you for that unprovoked attack on my client."

Surprised, Phillip looked at him and said, "Don't be stupid, he aimed at my head and with his size and weight, he would have at least knocked me out, if not caused a more severe injury. I was using quite justifiable self defence against my attacker and if anything, I should sue him!! I would be happy to refute your assertion that I attacked him, if it came to court. Now let's conclude this meeting. Another fact which I have not yet mentioned is the number of affairs Mr Gardner has conducted with various other females, during the time he and Mrs Donnan were married."

"I'm sure in this day and age that a little flirtation with another person could hardly be classed as an affair and I feel Mrs Donnan has been unusually sensitive as to her accusations about my client," said Mr McKay.

Phillip said sarcastically, "You must have heard the words 'infidelity' and 'adultery', which are justifiable reasons for divorce, but when everything is taken into consideration, your claim for half of Mrs Elizabeth Donnan's assets will be laughed out of court. We are going to advise our client not to pay your client one penny in settlement of their divorce," Phillip finished.

"In that case, we shall see you in court," said Angus McKay, smugly. "By the way, why is your client not here with you today?"

"There was no need for her to attend any exploratory meeting as we are acting completely on her behalf and she was not prepared to come here to be insulted by her estranged husband. Naturally, she will attend when matters are concluded satisfactorily."

"In that case," said Mckay, "we shall meet again sometime in court."

As the three men walked out of John's office, Phillip said to Ronald, "Your arm will recover in two to three days' time, just rest it in a sling."

The other man glared at him, supporting his right wrist with his left hand, obviously in a great deal of pain.

John looked at Phillip admiringly. "That was just a two-man show you produced there, I certainly wasn't needed to present the case, but I don't know how well it will go down in court. Perhaps you don't need me anymore!"

"With a bit of luck, it may never reach court," said Phillip thoughtfully, "they may think it over and come back with an offer we can't refuse."

"I don't think so," John said. "The two lawyers will want paying for their time, Gardner has no money to pay them, they might have taken on his case on a 'no win, no fee' basis, but someone has to pay and as far as they're concerned, it's not going to be them! You see my point, Phillip. I wonder what happened to Elizabeth?" queried John.

"Probably couldn't find her knickers," said Phillip, crudely.

John laughed. "That's not a very nice thing to say about our client, I'll give her a ring." He picked up the phone. Evidently Elizabeth answered and there was a short conversation. Putting down the phone, John said, "It's as I thought, she just didn't want to face her soon to be ex-husband and his lawyers but she will obviously attend any court meetings or appearances which are scheduled."

"She'll have to attend those," Phillip said.

"I've not finished – she said she would like to arrange a meeting in your office so that you could brief her on the latest position!"

"Not on your life," growled Phillip. "You are her solicitor, John, you brief her."

"You're a coward Phillip, all she needs is a good 'seeing-to', to quote a popular saying!"

"If you're so clever, why don't you make the supreme sacrifice for the enhancement of your career?" asked Phillip.

"I am a respectable married man, I can't go around sleeping with my clients, think of my good name," John said.

Chapter 31

After a very odd sort of week, Phillip looked forward to a quiet, relaxing weekend, hoping to show Sarah how much he loved and cared for her, when on Friday morning John rang.

"Something tells me that you are the bearer of bad news," Phillip said.

"Afraid so," said John. "Remember Betsy Herne; she has tried to commit suicide by overdosing on aspirin tablets but luckily she was found in time by her mother, Doris; she was rushed to hospital and they pumped out her stomach and she will be fully recovered in a few days. The doctor at A & E said in another two hours she would have been dead."

"We had better go and see her," interrupted Phillip.

"Wait, there's more bad news to come. When our friend Mr Dunn got to hear about it, he drove to the Herne's house and attacked Doris Herne; he was arrested on assault charges and is held in custody at the police station; he is to appear before the magistrates in the morning."

"We'll have to go and rescue him," Phillip said.

"I've already arranged to represent him, and in the meantime, if you meet me at my office, we can go and see Betsy," John replied.

Phillip arrived at John's office, only to find they could not visit her until two o'clock at the earliest so they had a quick lunch at the nearest self-service cafe. Upon arrival at the hospital, they were told that Betsy was now recovering in a general ward, but attached to a saline drip.

She was, however, fully awake and when she saw them coming towards her, she gave them a weak smile. They found a couple of chairs and sat down and asked her how she felt. "Okay, I guess."

"Can you tell us what happened to you, since the court case?" asked John quietly.

Betsy's eyes filled with tears but she answered his question by saying, "Without Mr Dunn's help, everything went back to what it was like before. There was no money for anything, no gym, no swimming, no hairdresser. Back to wearing second-hand clothes because I started to put on weight and my nice ones didn't fit any more; it all just went back to what life was like before I met Mr Dunn. No-one seemed to care about me anymore and I just got more and more depressed until I'd had enough of it all. There was no point in going on. My mother was even more horrible to me; I was blamed for everything – she kept on saying that if I'd never been born, her life would have been completely different, she'd have been married to a rich man and lived a high class life and things like that."

Overcome by tears, Betsy came to a halt and Phillip took hold of her hand. "Your mother is a stupid, selfish, delusional woman; no rich man would come within a mile of her, never mind dating her. You are a lovely, good-natured young woman and I would be proud to have you as my daughter," said Phillip, fervently.

Betsy looked sadly at him. "There's nothing for me to live for, it's either living with my mother or being taken into care and I don't think I could face that."

Phillip squeezed her hand gently. "Just you concentrate on getting better and we'll try to sort something out. We'll be seeing you again very shortly, so keep your chin up."

They walked out of the ward with Betsy looking a little more cheerful. John said, "I appreciate you trying to cheer her up but there's nothing much we can do for her, you know."

"I've got an idea that just might work," Phillip said.

"What are you thinking of now?" questioned John.

"I know of an older couple who have the money and means to give Betsy a nice home," Phillip replied.

"But would they take her?"

"They just might, if I work on them a bit."

"What a devious man you are, Phillip Everett, but I think your heart is in the right place!" John said.

"Well, we'll have to wait and see; now perhaps we had better go and see Walter Dunn, to prepare for the hearing tomorrow in the Magistrates Court."

John introduced himself as the solicitor acting on behalf of Walter Dunn at the sergeant's desk and said he wanted to speak to his client in an interview room. The policeman made the arrangements and when they had shaken hands with a visibly worried Mr Dunn, they all sat down and John asked him to tell his story as simply as possible. He told them he had had no contact with Betsy or her mother since the court case earlier in the year, but he had been watching the local news on television one lunchtime, when he heard that a fourteen-year-old schoolgirl named Betsy had taken an overdose of pills and been taken to the nearest hospital, where her condition was unknown.

"I jumped in my car and drove to Betsy's house to find out if it was her and when I knocked on the door, Doris opened it. As soon as she saw me, she started shouting, calling me a pervert, saying that I had driven her daughter to suicide and if it had not been for her finding her in time, she would be dead by now."

"When she said that, I completely lost my head and I shouted at her, called her a filthy, cruel bitch, and smacked her hard on the face. She burst into tears and I left, although I never saw Betsy, and before I knew it, I was at home. Then the police arrived and arrested me and here I am," he said, with a bewildered air.

"Don't worry, Walter," Phillip said. "John and I will represent you in court tomorrow and get bail for you."

Walter looked a little doubtful, and said, "It's Saturday tomorrow; are you sure the case will be heard in the morning?"

John nodded reassuringly. "We were told to attend court at ten am tomorrow so that's when we shall be here to request bail for you. Try not to worry and we'll see you then."

They left the police station and Phillip asked John what he thought the charges against Walter would be and the possible consequences. John said he was not sure whether he would be charged with GBH – "In which case the magistrate will pass it on to a higher court and Walter should get bail but if the charge is common assault, he might just be fined, hopefully not too much and perhaps bound over to keep the peace."

"Okay John, I'll see you tomorrow; I'd better go and phone Sarah, to tell her of my plans."

Back in his office, Phillip rang Sarah, who was flattered that he wanted to talk to her even before she got home that evening. Phillip told her he was going to show her how much he cared for her as soon as she walked in the front door, but in the meantime, what would she think if he asked her mother and father to sponsor a fourteen-year-old school girl.

"I'm not sure what you mean," she said.

Phillip phrased his reply carefully. "This girl, whose name is Betsy, is recovering in hospital after she attempted to commit suicide. Previously, there was an older man who used to sponsor her, take an interest in her welfare, but because he is a widower and lives alone, the girl's mother went to the police and claimed he was a paedophile who was grooming her daughter for sexual purposes, despite the fact that there was no ulterior motive in his actions in any way. She claimed that they were already having sex which was complete rubbish and this was proved in court and he was cleared of all charges. He was forbidden to have any contact with the girl or her mother and without his support, the mother went back to treating her daughter as badly as before and

Betsy became very depressed, ending up by taking a massive dose of aspirin tablets. John Standish, the solicitor, and I have been to see Betsy and she is in a bad way; she cannot see a way out except the choice of staying with her monster of a mother or going into social services care. Can you imagine a pretty fourteen-year-old girl, who by the way is still a virgin, in the care of the local authorities?

"I thought your parents might like to take an interest in the girl's welfare, a little like godparents. It would only require a little of their time and some financial help," Phillip explained. "She is in hospital now and is very depressed. If we could give her some hope that things can change, it will make all the difference to her life."

"What about her mother?" queried Sarah.

"Well when Walter Dunn, the man who sponsored her before, paid attention to improving her appearance, her schoolwork, her general situation, she blossomed and became a different girl. She became more confident, her school attendance and work improved and she took pride in her appearance, just because someone cared a little about her. On the other hand, her mother constantly complains that it's her fault they are so poor, if she had not been born she would have found a rich guy, got married and had a wonderful life. She tells Betsy that she's worthless, nothing but an obstacle in her mother's life and you can imagine how that makes Betsy feel, to be constantly told she is useless, which has led to these feelings of depression and suicide."

Sarah was amazed at Phillip's story; she could not imagine a mother treating her daughter in such a manner, although she knew there must be much about human behaviour she had little knowledge of. "Okay, what do you want me to do?" she asked.

"If you could talk to your father about him and your mother becoming like godparents to Betsy, taking an interest in her, showing a bit of care and understanding with perhaps some small financial aid, it would then be easier for me to sell the idea to them. That is what Walter Dunn was doing; he was a lonely widower who felt sorry for a young girl and because of the help he gave her, he was accused by her dreadful mother of being a paedophile and dragged through an unsavoury court case," Phillip said.

Sarah replied by saying she would talk to her father immediately; she thought he would be in his office just now and she would see Phillip tonight.

Putting down the phone, Phillip hoped his idea would work and when Sarah arrived home that evening, he asked her while they were eating, whether her conversation with her father had borne any result.

"I can't say what the result was, if any; he just heard me out and said he would speak to Mum so I think we have to wait until they have discussed the subject."

"That's totally understandable and something I expected would happen. I've just remembered I have to be in court by ten am tomorrow so we won't have to be in bed too late."

Sarah was puzzled. "I didn't know that courts were in session on Saturdays," she said.

"It only happens in Magistrates' Courts; it's a question of 'charge me or release me' and we want to get Walter out on bail so that he spends as little time as possible in a cell," Phillip said.

"All the same, this is an intrusion on our time together so you'd better make up for it tonight!"

"I'm straining at the leash," he said, "just say the word…"

Sarah stood up and said, "Word," and ran up the stairs.

Chapter 32

The court hearing began and Walter was charged with breaking the court's restraining order by trying to enter Betsy's place of abode and going within the two-hundred-yard prohibited zone. In answer, John politely pointed out that Betsy was in hospital at the time and the case was held up while the magistrate debated on the exact words of the charge and that point was dismissed, leaving only the charge of common assault. John waited until it was his turn to speak in defence of his client and said in mitigation, that his client was only attempting to ascertain what had happened to Betsy, as he was very worried about her. He had heard on local television news that a schoolgirl called Betsy was in hospital after having ingested an unknown quantity of aspirins; he wanted to find out if it was the same girl and how it had happened. Not knowing what hospital she had been taken to, his only recourse was to call at Betsy's home address, to make his enquiry.

Doris opened the door and started verbally abusing him, calling him a pervert, a child molester and a dirty old man. In his anxiety, Mr Dunn lost his temper and lashed out at Mrs Herne who was by this time shouting hysterically, and unfortunately he caught her a blow on the side of her face, although fortunately, she did not suffer any serious injury. The magistrates deliberated for a short time then announced that they found Walter Dunn guilty of common assault, with provocation, and fined him £100 with £50 court costs and after paying the fine, he was free to go. Outside the court building, Doris Herne walked away without a word to anyone.

Walter thanked John and Phillip for representing him and said he had to rush off home. "Who's going to pay you?" asked Phillip.

"The court, seeing as I was appointed by them as defence solicitor for the case. Who's going to pay you, are you going to send Walter an account?"

"I was well paid by his son initially, so I'll leave it there I think."

"Coming for a drink or a bite of lunch?" queried John.

"You must be joking, Sarah was not best pleased when I had to come to court this morning. She said it impinged on our time together!! So if I don't get back quickly, I'll get a telling off," said Phillip.

"Ah, what it is to be in love!!"

Sarah was busy when he let himself into the house, attempting to make the washing machine work while she tried her hand at some rudimentary dusting and vacuuming. "Thank heavens you've got here; how does this stupid machine work?" she fumed. "I've tried everything but it won't start!!"

Phillip took a quick look and said smugly, "How about switching it on at the plug, think that will do the trick?"

"Here I am being domesticated, cooking, cleaning, washing, ironing, when all you can do is stand there and make stupid remarks!" she glared at him.

"I used to do all that myself, prior to actually getting any cases," he protested. "I think you're doing a great job, particularly when you're used to being waited on hand and foot at home!" and ducked when she threw a dish mop at him. "Anyway, I'll help you later, doesn't do to get out of touch with the chores; how about finding out how your mother and father feel about my proposition?"

"Do you want me to ring them first?" she asked.

"Yes, please."

She spoke on the phone for about ten minutes and when she put the receiver down she said, "They would like to see us both, I think you have some persuading to do!"

Phillip frowned slightly. "I don't want Betsy to go home to her mother from hospital without some hope that things will change for her. If they're in, perhaps we could go to see them now?"

Sarah thankfully abandoned her housework and half an hour later they were sat in Lord and Lady Pennington's sitting room. Lord Pennington asked Phillip where they came into the picture and whether it was legal to interfere between mother and daughter. "We would probably need the court's permission to approach Betsy and we feel sure the mother would object. What do you think Phillip?"

"Not if you were classified as 'sponsors' or 'friends'," he said.

"Well, here is our position, as I see it," said Lord Pennington. "My wife and I have discussed your request and we like the idea of helping a young schoolgirl; financially, there would be no difficulty for us to help her out with the expenses you mentioned, we might almost see her as an adopted daughter but we are not willing to do anything which would be seen as against the law. It would be better if we could win the mother over on to our side so what we would like to do now is meet and talk to Betsy and see what she thinks, is that possible?"

Phillip was pleased and said, "We could take you to the hospital and introduce you both to Betsy, how about tomorrow?"

Lord Pennington looked at his wife and she nodded in agreement. "Okay, tomorrow it is."

On the following day, they approached Betsy's bed, Lady Pennington with a posy of pretty flowers, some magazines to suit a teenager's taste and a gift box with some toiletries in it and Phillip said to her, "Hallo Betsy, I've brought some visitors to meet you, this is Lord and Lady Pennington and their daughter Sarah. I've been telling them about you and they thought they'd like to meet you, to get to know you a little better; how are you feeling today?" Phillip arranged two chairs at her bedside for Lord and Lady Pennington to sit down and then said he and Sarah would be back later to see how things were going.

"Where shall we go for an hour or so?" he asked Sarah.

"The nearest pub, I should think," said Sarah. "You'd better tell me a bit more about Betsy." Phillip filled in the background of Walter Dunn's case and how he had come to meet Betsy and her mother, the generosity of Walter's son in not asking for the return of any money he had deposited in his account, and his attempt to manage his accounting system, in case the Inland Revenue ever came to check them. At the end of an hour chatting, they returned to the hospital and said their goodbyes to Betsy, who was looking decidedly tearful. She thanked them for coming and for Lady Pennington's inspired gifts, which had "cheered her up no end", and watched them leave the ward.

"What do you think?" said Phillip eagerly, as they drove Sarah's parents' home.

Lady Pennington said thoughtfully, "She seems a nice girl who is very unhappy with her life. From what she said, the thing that worries her most is the fact that on her discharge from hospital, she has to go back to live with her mother."

"This is the point that worries me also," said Phillip, "but the alternative is to have her taken into care by the local authority, which might be just as bad. A young girl, approaching fifteen, is a prime target for sexual abuse and there is always some predator waiting for an opportunity to pounce."

"As I see it," announced Lord Pennington, "in a way the law is the biggest stumbling block in resolving this situation, that and Betsy's mother. We cannot legally adopt her, if that was our aim, until she is taken into care and even then it would take a very long time until papers could be processed. We cannot become her unofficial 'aunty and uncle' unless her mother agrees and we are therefore limited in what we can do for her. I can't see any way round it."

Phillip explained that the way Walter had arranged matters, he had paid for her membership to a health club for her to get into good physical shape, for visits to a hairdresser, for school uniform and casual clothes and gradually her confidence had improved and she had started to enjoy a normal teenage life. "Unfortunately, she started answering back when her mother complained about her as she noticed the clothes and how pretty her daughter was becoming," Phillip explained. "Matters came to a head when one of Doris's latest boyfriends commented on how nice Betsy looked and all hell broke loose. Doris was wildly jealous and badgered her to tell her where the clothes had come from and then, when Betsy blurted out Walter's name, had the idea of taking him to court; perhaps she thought he might pay her off to drop the case, I don't know, but the poor man was literally thrown into jail, with a solicitor who didn't enquire too closely into the circumstances, and left there to put up with poor treatment from people who presumed he was guilty because of what Doris said. It took John Standish and me a long time to clear his name but when he was tried, the jury declared him innocent of all charges brought against him. However there was still the ban on having any contact with Betsy. As a result, she sank into depression, thinking she had been abandoned by the only person who had ever taken an interest and helped her; her mother was as nasty as before, no help at all, so in despair, she took a large dose of aspirin in a suicide attempt. I will ask the police authorities if I may visit Doris and sound her out about you two participating in the care of her daughter and I might be able to persuade her to see sense."

Phillip was as good as his word and contacted the police, asking if he was permitted to interview Betsy Herne's mother. After some questions as to his interest in the matter, the desk sergeant put him through to Inspector Clarke and he repeated the story of Betsy's situation and his attempts to help the troubled teenager. "Can you outline what you want me to do?" asked Inspector Clarke.

"Because of Mrs Herne's attitude to her daughter, I have been advised that when speaking to her, a policewoman should be present and I would like you to authorise this, if you would be so good," he said.

Inspector Clarke sighed and said, "I could let you have a policewoman today for a couple of hours but no longer, we have other work to do you know."

"That would be great," said Phillip, "I'll drive to Mrs Herne's and wait for her to show up."

"Her name is WPC Sylvia Bennett and I want her returned to her post all in one piece, is that understood?"

Phillip stressed how grateful he was for the inspector's co-operation and set off after first ringing Doris, stating who he was and explaining that he had been assigned to help her, a little white lie but he thought it was justified in the circumstances. She was a little suspicious, telling Phillip it was she who had saved her daughter's life by finding her with a bottle of pills in her hand and calling an ambulance and he praised her for her quick thinking; he also asked if he and WPC Bennett could explain his plan to her. "Why do you want to go bringing the police into this 'plan' you want to tell me about?"

Phillip thought quickly and answered, "That's so you have a witness to what I say and you can be quite sure I'm 'kosher'!!"

Another quick call, this time to Sylvia Bennett, telling her he would pick her up and would explain the situation on the way to Doris Herne's house. "Much quicker if we only take one car." Having picked her up he drove to Doris's house, helping her out when they arrived. "I'm not going to flash my knickers at you," she said, "if that's what you're hoping for."

"The thought never crossed my mind!"

"You're a nice kind of guy, do you say that to all the girls to get them into bed with you?"

"Well, the old method of clubbing them over the head is no longer allowed," he said, as he knocked on Doris's door. It opened, displaying

Doris in all her glory, cigarette in hand and wearing a tight pair of crimplene trousers and a top which was straining at the seams. Once inside Phillip summoned up all his not inconsiderable charm and smiled at her, saying, "Let's look at it this way Doris, may I call you Doris?"

"If you like."

"I'll come straight to the point. In a few days, Betsy will be coming home from hospital and she will still be in a fragile state, relatively speaking, and you, even as her mother, might not be able to prevent her becoming depressed again. She might even attempt suicide again and who knows, you might not be there to save her or she could take something more dangerous, more damaging to her system."

Phillip paused for a moment to let this sink in and Doris said plaintively, "I have to live in these circumstances all the time, I don't get depressed and want to do away with myself!"

"Ah, that's because you are more mature and try to make the best of your life. Betsy is only a young girl and can't be expected to take your wise attitude to life," Phillip said, piling on the flattery. "So I have a proposition to put to you, which will benefit both you and Betsy – let me explain. I don't think you would like to lose your daughter altogether, either in a suicide attempt or being taken into care by the local authorities, but I have been approached by a well-to-do couple who have heard of you and Betsy's plight and they want to help."

"They're nothing to do with that Walter Dunn are they? I don't want him interfering and coming back into her life, I won't allow it," she said.

"No, no, they have no connection with Mr Dunn but," he emphasised, "they are quite well off, have brought up a family of their own and would be prepared to take an interest in her, help with expenses which we know teenagers incur."

"Do you mean they want to take Betsy away?" said Doris, seeing all the advantages if Betsy was taken away from her; who knows, there might be something to her advantage in this arrangement.

Phillip pressed these advantages home by carrying on with, "Betsy would stay at home, a normal teenage schoolgirl and because an arrangement could be made so that some of her expenses were paid, you would gain because more money would be available to you by not having to spend it on your daughter." Doris said nothing, trying to work out the possible advantages in such an arrangement. Then he said casually, "Of course, there would have to be some sort of legal document, stating your agreement to Lord and Lady Pennington's being joint carers, but your signature is more a formality than anything else."

Doris gasped, "Did you say they were a Lord and Lady?"

"I can assure you that they are; they live a little out of London, in a mansion, very impressive. When all the formalities have been completed, I expect they'll ask you to visit them!" That should clinch the deal, thought Phillip.

"In that case," said Doris, "I can see that it would be in the best interests of my daughter to agree to this arrangement and I'll sign on the dotted line. When will the paper be ready for me?"

"As it happens," said Phillip, "knowing you had the welfare of your daughter uppermost in your mind, I took the chance and brought along three copies of the document with me, one for you to retain, one for Lord and Lady Pennington to have and one copy which I will keep in my office, for my records. I can assure you, Doris, you are doing the best possible thing for both you and your daughter."

Sylvia, who had kept quiet as a mouse, witnessed the three signed copies of the document, one which Doris kept, and the other two stored safely in Phillip's briefcase. Phillip gave a huge sigh of relief that everything had gone just as planned, ushered Sylvia out of the door and shook hands with Doris, reminding himself of the need to see Lord Pennington as soon as possible so that he and Lady Pennington could collect Betsy from hospital and take her home, to ease her back into her surroundings.

"We don't have to go back to the police station immediately," said Sylvia, when she had settled herself comfortably in Phillip's car. He looked at her, surprised. Up till now, he had hardly noticed her, except to think she was rather a tall girl and a little skinny, a pretty face but not the sort of figure he normally admired.

"I'm afraid that I have other urgent business to deal with so I'll have to take you straight back. I want to thank you for your co-operation back there, I think it made all the difference to my dealings with Doris."

"Pity," she said, "we could have had some fun!"

Phillip dropped her off at the police station, returned to his office and filed one document, putting the other in an envelope addressed to Lord and Lady Pennington. Then he rang Sarah. When she answered he said in his smoochiest voice, "Is that the Sarah Pennington whom I love and adore?"

"It all depends on how many Sarah Penningtons you know; anyway, my mummy told me not to talk to strange men."

"Your mummy is perfectly correct; even I try not to talk to strange men," he said.

"It depends on how strange they are," she said. "Sometimes they're capable of igniting the wild side of me, but you didn't ring me for that did you?"

"I've managed to get Doris Herne to agree to let your Mum and Dad be joint carers of Betsy, by obtaining a document all signed and sealed and perfectly legal because it's been witnessed by a policewoman. I've got a copy here for your parents and I'd like to give it to them tonight so that we can make arrangements for taking Betsy home from hospital and explain future arrangements to her."

Sarah rang to tell her parents they were coming over during the evening and Phillip gave them the document to study. After they had both read the paper, Lord Pennington said to his wife with great satisfaction, "My dear, we can now be considered joint guardians of Betsy."

Phillip now asked them if someone from their household could take her home when she was discharged from hospital. "The reason I'm asking you this is that, in her present state of mind, she shouldn't just be ferried home by taxi or ambulance because if she gets the impression that everything is going to be just the same as before, she could get miserable and depressed again."

At this point, Lady Pennington interrupted, "I shall pick her up in my car from hospital and take her out somewhere for a light meal with perhaps a little shopping trip before dropping her off at her mother's place. That way," she chuckled, "I shall be able to meet her mother and impress the gorgon with my suitability as a joint carer!!"

"I'm very grateful to you," said Phillip. "If we're to become joint carers, we might as well start on the right foot.

"I'll ask the hospital reception to inform you when she is to be discharged and this should give you a little time to make arrangements. I can't tell you how grateful I am for what you are doing—"

"You leave all that to us now," said Lord Pennington, jovially, "we'll see that she regains her health and give her a future to look forward to!"

On the way home, Sarah said, "You seem to have mastered my parents; I shall have to watch you."

"Why? You know your Mum and Dad will love doing things for Betsy; it will be like having a daughter of school age and financially, things will not be a problem for them."

"Oh, I'm sure they'll get to love it and it will be good for Betsy, but I meant the way in which you manipulate people."

"Thank you darling, I take it that was a compliment?" he asked.

"Not really, it means that you are devious and manipulative. It's all very well for Betsy but it's going to put a whole new load of responsibilities on my parents and our family."

"I don't see quite how. If we all felt like that, no-one would ever do anything for another person, thinking 'there's nothing in this for me' so

I'm not going to put myself out to help; what about caring for others less fortunate than ourselves?"

"If you're going to lecture me now…" she trailed off.

"I don't understand you tonight," he said. "Are you jealous that Betsy is going to take your place?"

"Don't be so patronising," said Sarah. "And another thing I don't like about you is whenever we go out together, you always finish up with some female making sheep's eyes at you and hanging on your every word. I always finish up looking like some spare part, someone you brought along to make up the numbers. You tell me I'm beautiful, sexy, but no-one takes the slightest bit of notice of me when you're around – I can't see that ever changing. At this rate, even my own parents will probably stop paying any attention to me!!"

As they arrived home and got out of the car, Phillip struggled to reply to Sarah's outburst. "I can see where this is heading, but none of it's true," he protested. "You are a very pretty, attractive young lady with a sense of humour and very good company for anyone. Those things you are saying about me are exaggerated and out of all proportion," he stated, indignantly.

"Oh yes, as always you are right and I am in the wrong," said Sarah. "It doesn't matter what I think so I won't say any more," and with that, she ran up the stairs.

Chapter 33

Phillip judged it best to leave her on her own for a while and went into the kitchen to get some beer out of the fridge. He filled a large glass with two cans of lager and went to sit down and have a quiet drink. Looks like the honeymoon is over, he thought ruefully. It looked as if things had been building up in Sarah's mind for some time and now it had all come to a head. He remembered when Samantha left him, she said he had taken her for granted and he should have learned by now that women are sensitive and don't like being ignored or not having affection shown; he had paid a lot of attention to his career, concentrated on being the provider and making progress with his career but had not taken all that much interest in her personally. Looks like I've fallen into the same trap with Sarah! he thought; I've been busy fixing other people's problems and forgot the one person closest to me. What's the best thing to do now, he puzzled. Do I go against my natural character, which is as the provider, at which I'm pretty good, or do I crush my natural instinct and start being more like a personnel manager, taking care of how other people feel and trying to serve their emotional needs at the expense of my own? If I did take that course, which I've always found difficult to do, how long would I be able to keep it up? Would that be a good thing to do or would that result in changing me as a person? At the end of the day, you have to be yourself; you cannot keep on pretending to be what you are not. It's a case of 'love me, love my dog' even if the dog comes with fleas. He looked down at his glass and realised he had drunk both cans of lager while he was philosophising. Ah well, time you were in bed Phillip, he told himself, and climbed the stairs.

Sarah was in bed with her back to him. Phillip undressed, got into bed and put his arm around her. Very gently, he started to kiss the back of her neck but there was no reaction and he fell asleep. In the morning, Sarah was already up and dressed by the time he had shaved and showered and was standing in the kitchen when he came downstairs.

She cleared her throat and announced, "I'm moving back into my parents' house. I've packed all my things and I'm just waiting for the handyman to come and collect them; I'll take my car over there with some clothes I want." She looked at Phillip, waiting for some comment and looking very sad.

He said quietly, "If that's what you have decided, then there's not much else I can say is there?"

Sarah turned away from him and went into the lounge. He made himself some breakfast and wondered when the workman would be coming to move her possessions and what time she would drive away, putting an end to another phase of his life.

He sat at his desk, staring into space. It was always the same; if someone said to him, I no longer wish to see you or be with you, he never tried to change their minds, he couldn't see any point in trying to persuade the other person to change their minds. He figured that even if that person changed their mind, it could only be temporarily and it was only postponing the inevitable. Sooner or later they would leave anyway, so why bother?

He rang John to ask if anything had been heard from Ronald Gardner's solicitors but he said nothing had been heard from them. Either they were trying to come up with something to negate Phillip's excellent presentation of the facts or they had given up. "I can't imagine them giving up so quickly," Phillip said.

"Why not? They probably found out that Mr Gardner has no money of his own and since they don't feel they could win the case, they didn't want to waste any more of their precious time – lawyers seldom work for nothing you know!"

"Let's hope you are right."

There was not much else Phillip could do and he didn't want to be cooped up in his office all day when Sarah was going to walk out any time now. "I have to go out," he said in a strained voice. "Just lock up when you go and pop the keys through the letter box flap."

She just said quietly, "Okay," and he left.

Unable to think of anywhere to go, he headed for the south coast and ended up in Brighton. He walked aimlessly along the sea front, eating a hamburger for lunch and an enormous ice cream cone mid-afternoon, anything to waste time so he didn't have to go back to the empty house. He was staring out over the sea, leaning on the railings, when two young women approached him and one of them asked him what time it was. Phillip noticed that both of them were wearing wristwatches so he commiserated with them, saying it was a pity that both their watches had stopped at the same time! The blonde one said cheekily, "I really meant to ask what was the time in Tokyo."

He said, looking at them closely, "Now, you have come to the right person. I can tell you it's night time in Tokyo." It was quite a cool day but both were wearing skimpy summer dresses. Of the two, the blonde girl had a shapely figure, her hair fastened up in a ponytail, and she was rather pretty. The other one was a redhead, a little plump, but well-shaped in all the right places.

"If you're both interested in Tokyo," he said, "you've come to the right person, you're talking to an expert about that city; what would you like to know?"

"Actually, it was more you we were interested in," said the redhead.

"That's a very nice compliment, what can I do for you?"

"We both wondered what's a nice man like you doing, looking out to sea with a rather sad face?"

"I was just feeling rather sorry for myself thinking that on a nice day like this I didn't have any female companionship," said Phillip.

The blonde girl giggled and said, "Listen to him, we shall have to watch him Pen, he's got all the answers!"

"I know what you mean Jackie," replied the other one.

"Tell you what, why don't I take you both for some refreshments, then you can watch me more closely," said Phillip, tongue in cheek.

"See what I mean, Pen, he already wants us to watch him closely. Very forward he is," said Jackie.

"Now that I know you are Penelope and you are Jackie, my name is Phillip."

"That's a lovely name," said Jackie.

"Why thank you," he said, "we seem to be getting on very well, what's next?"

For a moment there was silence, then Jackie said, "Are you taking us for something to drink, or what?"

"Yes, but as I don't live in Brighton, I don't know any good places to drink, so why don't you two ladies lead on."

They walked a short distance and then went into a bar with the girls saying, "As there's two of us, we'll get the drinks, what are you having?"

Phillip asked for coffee and Pen looked at him in amazement. "Is that a joke?" she said. He laughed and said that as he had a long drive back, he couldn't risk drinking any alcohol, so she told him to sit down and they would get the drinks. Phillip studied them and decided that while Penelope was better looking, she was rather thin for his taste, whereas Jackie had a full figure but was rather plain. If one could put them both together, you could make a very nice young woman from the pair! He supposed it didn't really matter as he would have to go home soon anyway.

They came to the table, carrying some exotic looking cocktails and told him that his coffee would be ready in a moment. "Where are you from?" asked Jackie.

"I live in London, Croydon to be exact," he said.

She laughed,. "Goodness me, the way you said it, I thought you must live in Scotland or somewhere. London, that's only sixty miles away, only takes you about an hour to get back wouldn't it?"

"Anyway, it doesn't matter where he lives, he's not going anywhere now!" said Pen.

"What does that mean?" he queried.

Pen answered him with, "Because you can stay the night with us in our flat."

"You share a flat?" he asked. "Are you just good friends or—"

"Do you mean are we gay? No, not exactly, you could say we're bisexual, the best of both worlds." Phillip kept silent, not knowing what to say.

"Come on Phillip, most men would give an arm and a leg to meet two women like us. We know men like to watch two women making out. Don't you?"

"In my time I've been to an orgy where people did everything to each other, men with women, women with women, anything and everything went on. A couple of women came and tried to do things to me but I can't say I was taken by it. I guess orgies are not my thing. Afterwards I was so worried I went for an AIDS test and spent some anxious weeks before I found I was clear."

"Are you worrying you might catch AIDS from us?" said Jackie.

"All I know is that while I don't want to suggest or to imply anything to offend you, I would rather err on the side of caution."

"That's insulting," said Jackie, "do you think we're just a couple of slags?"

"No," he said, "but Brighton is the gay capital of the south of England."

"From where we're sitting, London is supposed to be the gay capital and as you live in London," said Jackie, "you could have AIDS!!"

"I'm sorry," he said, "I'm just having a very bad day and I should have told you that I have to get back tonight and left it at that; I'm going to do just that now."

He started to stand up but Penelope put her hand on his arm and said, "Please don't go just yet, you haven't drunk your coffee." She took a sip of her drink and started to talk to him. "We don't sleep around, we don't normally chat up strange men and we don't have any STDs, but I liked you as soon as I saw you, you're good-looking but there's more to it than that. You're the type of man that's very attractive to women."

"Well, thanks for that," he said, wondering if her opinion would still be the same if he told her that a woman had just left him, but he stopped himself in time. Jackie urged him to stay the night, saying he would enjoy their company.

"It won't be an orgy," she smiled, "it's just the two of us. We can do things to please you and you can watch us making love if you like."

The coffee still hadn't arrived and Phillip said, "Look, enjoy the rest of the day and good luck to you both, but I really have to go now."

"What about your coffee?" pouted Penelope.

"Don't worry about that."

"Well, don't forget, the invitation is open any time, here's my card," she said and Phillip put it in his pocket, and waving goodbye, he left the bar.

When he arrived home, he checked through the whole house and everything that belonged to Sarah was gone. That's that, he thought, locked the door and went to the pub to get a meal with a glass of lager to wash it down with. While he waited, he looked round for a table, taking note that the room was quite full, unusual for a week night. After he had wolfed down his food – high emotion always made him feel hungry – with a second pint of strong lager, he desperately tried to stop thinking of Sarah. Images of her running up the stairs in front of him, and naked in the shower, would not leave him and he could visualise her now, opening the shower room door and coming into the bedroom wearing only a lacy bra and panties, with that fresh, fragrant smell of her soft young body. Suddenly, lust overwhelmed him and he was determined to have a woman tonight, to relieve his frustration. He started to look around the room and saw a young couple, sitting a short distance away. The woman was quite pretty and very curvy, just how he liked his women to be, so he started his seduction technique. First a glance, then a longer look; when he caught her eye, she responded with a lingering glance and he gave her a gentle smile. She smiled back, flirting with him at a distance until the young man noticed, said something to her and she lowered her eyes, as though in guilt. The man got up and walked over to where Phillip was sitting and said truculently, in a loud voice, "What the hell do you think you're doing?"

"I'm sitting down," Phillip said, peacefully.

"You've been trying to get off with my fiancée, I should knock your block off!!" the man said. Phillip remembered his last self-defence course, when he had learned especially how to respond in a situation such as this. He also remembered the instructor stressing that they were not teaching you these skills so that you can go and beat up others – you use these skills only when you are attacked. That was why it was called a 'self defence course'. Always remember 'pride comes before a fall' and you must behave with humility. Philip knew he was in the wrong and said, "Sorry, mate, I didn't realise I was doing that." By now, the whole room had gone quiet and everyone was watching and listening. The apology only served to encourage the man, who now shouted, "Sorry does not do it for me, come outside and I'll get some satisfaction by giving you a black eye."

"Well I'm afraid 'sorry' will just have to do. Please apologise to your young lady," and with that Phillip started to stand up and made as if to go.

"Come on," the other man shouted, "I don't want to hit you while you're sitting down, are you a coward?"

Phillip sighed inwardly; so much for humility and in a quiet voice full of menace, he said, "You had better go back to your young lady, unless you want to be humiliated in front of her and all these people."

The other man was caught by surprise and outfaced by Phillip's height and menacing attitude, the courage left him. For a moment he stood there and then with a red face, mumbled that the apology would do and walked away. He walked back to his 'fiancée' and two minutes later they had left the pub. There was a ripple of applause. Phillip was not quite sure what it was for, but the barman walked over to him, put another drink on his table and thanked him for defusing what could have turned out to be a very difficult situation. Phillip finished his lager and then walked home to clear his head; before he fell asleep, he was mentally kicking himself for not staying the night with Pen and Jackie in Brighton.

Chapter 34

Phillip found the next two weeks very difficult to live through. During the days and evenings, he felt lonely; at night he slept badly, by now unused to sleeping alone. He tried to keep himself busy with all the house maintenance chores he could find and his only case, Elizabeth Donnan's divorce, seemed to have come to a standstill. He finally weakened and rang the two girls in Brighton. A woman's voice answered and he asked if he could speak to either Penelope or Jackie and the voice answered, "It's me, Jackie speaking, is that Phillip, I thought I recognised your voice!"

"How are you two gorgeous girls getting on?"

"All the better for hearing from you!"

"Seems like I don't have a lot of work on at the moment and I thought I might spend a day or two in Brighton and look you up."

"That sounds great, please come," Jackie said.

"How will I find you?" he asked. "The best thing to do is meet us at that pub we went into for a drink, do you think you can find it again?"

"Should be able to do that quite easily."

"When are you coming down?" Jackie asked.

"I was thinking of this afternoon, should be there about five o'clock," he said.

"Great, we'll both meet you there, I'm beginning to feel excited already!"

"Well keep your engine running," he laughed, "see you both at five."

Phillip found both the girls waiting for him when he arrived in Brighton and gave each of them a friendly kiss on the cheek. "Took me some time to find a safe place to park my car, but I found one eventually. Are you two ladies well, you certainly look in great shape."

They smiled their thanks at the compliment and suggested that they all have a drink. "We can go to the flat later and have something to eat," said Jackie, naughtily. "You'll be able to move your car and leave it outside our building; a mate has gone on holiday for a week and you can have his reserved space. I'll show you where it is later."

They chatted and laughed while they had a couple of drinks then Penelope told him that they had rushed out after his phone call and bought food and wine so there would be no need to go out again once they got to their flat. They showed Phillip the reserved parking space outside their building where he could leave the car without worrying and went upstairs to their first floor flat. It turned out to be a pleasant, spacious two bedroom apartment, with an entrance hall, lounge, kitchen-cum-dining area, a bathroom and toilet and even had a distant sea view. "Do you two ladies work?" he asked.

"Of course we do," said Jackie, "we are both designers and we run our own business. We have ten people working for us."

"How is your business coping with the present financial circumstances?" he asked.

"It's doing fine," said Jackie, proudly. "I manage the company and Pen here is my senior model and partner."

"You make yourself comfortable while we get things ready," and the girls disappeared in the direction of the kitchen. Phillip looked around, taking a peek in the bedrooms, one of which had two single beds and one with a double bed. You could tell the flat was occupied by ladies; although it was neat and tidy there were many pictures on the walls, little ornaments and all sorts of bric-a-brac placed on shelves.

In his own house, there were just the most essential items, things he needed to use every day. He began to feel a little impatient after waiting about twenty minutes but when he turned away from the sea view, it was worth the wait. Both girls had changed into skimpy bras and panties, red for Penelope and black for Jackie.

"Come and get undressed," Jackie said.

"Is it compulsory?" he asked.

"Yes, it is," she emphasised.

He was reluctant to undress in front of them but eventually, he stood there, just wearing his shorts. "Aren't you feeling comfortable, wearing just your shorts?" asked Penelope.

"I don't usually walk around the house wearing just my underwear," he said.

"It's no different to sitting on the beach wearing swimming trunks," said Jackie, a little amused by his attitude.

"I know you're right there," he said, "it's just that I've been brought up conventionally, where you only undress to go to bed!"

"And you are a man of traditions?"

Phillip laughed. "You're exactly right there. I suppose I must be a bit old-fashioned."

Jackie said seriously, "You have a marvellous physique and should be proud to display it; do you work out at the gym?"

"Not at a gym exactly, but I take regular exercise because I want to remain fit; the job I do requires me to be in good physical condition."

"Why's that?" Penelope asked. "What sort of job is it?"

"I'm a private detective, a private investigator, that is, and I need to keep fighting fit because some people don't like other people prying into their affairs and sometimes they object physically, so I have to make sure I can handle it and look after myself, otherwise I become their victim."

There was silence. "Why would you want to do a job like that?" asked Jackie.

He replied, "Why does anyone want to become a policeman? Somebody had to do it and I like my job, it can be very rewarding. Don't tell me you don't like me any more because of what I do for a living?"

"No, no," they protested, "we like you very much; you do what you want to do, why should we object? Let's all go into the bedroom."

They sat down on the edge of the double bed and invited Phillip to watch them as they started to make love in front of him. They kissed and stroked each other, gently at first, then gradually with more passion and eagerness. Phillip saw both girls becoming more and more excited, their bodies glowing, their breathing accelerating, almost ignoring him. The two girls turned to him and slowly began to include him in their lovemaking until after a very few minutes, he was a full participant in the game. He had never made love to two women before but it soon felt completely natural, first one then the other; it went on for nearly two hours until all three were exhausted.

"You're a wonderful lover," said Jackie as she kissed him. "You've worn the pair of us out! Let's rest awhile and then we'll eat." The two naked girls snuggled up to him and all fell asleep.

Phillip stayed with them for one more day and night and when he was leaving, the girls begged him not to leave it very long before he came to see them again. As he was driving back, he was thinking what a pleasant, loving relationship the three of them had established. Free loving, with no commitments. When he got home, there was a message from Gordon, asking him to meet on Friday as usual. He said he had broken it off with Isobel and would tell him more on Friday. How ironic, he thought, both of them back to being single!

Chapter 35

Phillip sat down, after he had settled in, and thought how difficult it was to keep relationships going these days. That must be why there are so many single mothers. A man and woman stay together until she becomes pregnant and then before or after the baby's birth, they find they can't live together anymore and split up. Thank God neither he nor Gordon had added to the number of single parent families. Probably more by luck than good judgement, he thought, but if that's the reason for Gordon splitting up with Isobel, I'll kick that Highland git all the way back to Scotland.

Friday evening came and they met at Gordon's flat. After the usual greetings between old friends, he said, "I have one important question to ask, you've not made Isobel pregnant have you?"

Gordon was indignant. "What sort of heel do you think I am?" he said. "I'd never do a thing like that; no, it was my dithering about setting a wedding date that she finally lost patience with. She said she didn't want to be the oldest woman to walk down the aisle."

"What was it that held you back?" questioned Phillip.

Gordon thought and said, "It's really difficult to put your finger on, but it might be because her family's Portuguese, not that I have anything against the Portuguese," he said hastily, "but if you marry the girl, you also marry the whole family and I couldn't see myself fitting in to that way of life!"

"In that case, I think you've done the right thing," Phillip said. "Better to find that out now before you get married and then regret it forever."

"That's what I was thinking too," Gordon said. "Anyway, what happened with you and Sarah?"

"It's a bit complicated." Phillip tried to explain. "I tried to help someone I knew from one of the cases I dealt with earlier this year, a teenage girl called Betsy."

"I remember, her mother charged some old feller with trying to seduce her and you investigated him and found he only had the highest motive for helping the kid, didn't he?"

"When the law and her mother stopped him from taking an interest in her, she got depressed and tried to commit suicide so I got back on the case and tried to help her; I couldn't just abandon her and perhaps make a better job of it in the future, now could I?

"You know me, a fixer of everybody's ills, so while she was still in hospital, I convinced Sarah's parents that it would be good for them to become her kind-of adoptive parents and as Sarah had now left home to live with me, it would give them an additional interest in their lives."

"Did they see it like that?" asked Gordon.

"You should know me by now, Gordon, I can sell snow to the Eskimos; yes they visited her in hospital and liked her very much, Betsy's mother signed an agreement that they could become 'carers' and take an interest in her, probably because of their title – Lord and Lady Pennington – Doris was very impressed. Everything was going swimmingly when Sarah suddenly realised that all their attention would be focused on Betsy and not her and she didn't like it one bit. She told me I was manipulative and arrogant and she couldn't stand the fact that when we were out anywhere, it was always me who was getting all the attention. Wow, you can imagine my amazement, when we got home she went straight upstairs to bed and in the morning she told me she was moving out."

Gordon was suitably impressed and said, "What did you do?"

"I got out of her way and drove to Brighton. At first, when I got back, I missed her terribly, she was such a beautiful girl and very sexy, but life goes on and as a matter of fact, I had a bit of luck in Brighton!"

"You're not going to tell me you have a woman in Brighton already?" scoffed Gordon.

"I'll tell you about that later, what about you and Isobel?"

Gordon considered his reply. "Isobel was a lovely lady and I miss her very much and I haven't found another woman to take my mind off her, not like you were hinting!"

"Well," said Phillip expansively, "you and me had better do something about that, let's go for a meal and start looking, there's no time like the present!"

After their meal, they went to the wine bar and as it was Friday, it was very busy with nowhere to sit down. "Let's get our drinks and then we can find somewhere to sit." They stood at the bar, sipping their drinks when they saw four people preparing to get up from a table. "Let's go over and stand near them, to kind of hurry them up, otherwise they'll never make up their minds to leave," Phillip said.

"You're incorrigible," said Gordon but sure enough, when they moved over to hover next to the table, the occupants told them it was theirs and headed for the door.

"I don't know how you have the nerve," said Gordon. "I couldn't do it, stand over people with that sort of 'are you going to move or do I make a scene' kind of attitude."

"It goes with the job I do," laughed Phillip; "you have to be a bit pushy, to get results. You'd be amazed how much time you can waste, allowing people to go at their own pace, when you need to hurry them along a bit, to make them concentrate!!"

"That's probably what Sarah meant about you manipulating people," Gordon replied.

"Gordon, I know my own shortcomings and I could have probably fixed up my relationship with Sarah but I'm not going to do that. This dog comes with fleas and I can't spend the whole of my life with anyone where I would always be worrying what to say or what *not* to say, don't do this and you can't do that – it's just not *me*! If I'm going to have a lasting relationship with any one, it will have to be love me, love my fleabitten dog. They will have to take me, warts and all."

Gordon looked at him over the rim of his glass and said pityingly, "I think, my best of friends, you are destined to spend most of your life on your own."

Phillip shrugged his shoulders. "I'm not going to be a slave to anyone; my idea of a relationship is that you like and accept the person for what he or she is, and not what he or she pretends to be. But enough of this philosophising; this is not the time for serious social studies, this is a time for making out and there's not a dame in sight."

"You always take the lead, so I'll follow you to the ends of the earth, if necessary," Gordon said, facetiously.

Philip looked around the bar, studying the various women present and asked Gordon what were his preferences nowadays? "About the same as they always have been," he replied, "depending on whether you mean a one night stand or a more permanent engagement in the battle, if you see what I mean!!" Gordon shook Phillip's arm and said in a whisper, "Your ex-partner Samantha has just walked in, accompanied by a young woman!"

Phillip glanced casually toward the entrance of the bar and sure enough, there was Samantha with a very attractive girl at her side. Samantha looked great, still very attractive with a slender figure, well dressed. Her companion might be classed as 'curvy', maybe even a little on the plump side, but that was just the way Phillip liked them! She had a pretty face and the dress she wore emphasised her cleavage, of which she was showing plenty. Gordon whispered to him, "She's not turned gay has she?"

"I shouldn't think so," Phillip said. "Not unless that girl is very rich and can afford to support Samantha financially in the manner to which she became accustomed!! Tell you what Gordon, this could be your chance to finally get Samantha into bed with you."

"Wouldn't you mind?" he said, amazed.

"Of course not, every second man in London must have slept with her by now, providing they had plenty of money, so it must be your turn by now," he said crudely.

"She still looks fabulous," Gordon said, enviously. "Don't be so unkind to her!"

"Stay here and I'll go get another round of drinks and we'll see what happens; she never could pass without coming out with some nasty comment about me, she's sure to notice when I go to the bar!"

As he thought, while facing the bar ordering their drinks, he heard a familiar voice behind him saying, "Well, here you are again, propping up a bar as usual!"

Phillip turned round to speak to Samantha, standing close to him, and said, "Times are hard nowadays, who is your new friend?"

She performed the introduction. "This is my good friend Helen and this is my ex-partner, Phillip."

"I'm very pleased to meet your good-looking friend, Samantha, can I buy you two anything to drink?"

"You seem to have won Phillip over already; usually whenever I spoke to him previously, all I ever got were sarcastic comments!"

To Samantha's total surprise, Phillip leaned over and kissed her on her cheek. She was completely overcome by surprise but kissed him back lingeringly, on the lips. Phillip spoke directly to Helen, smiling at her, and said, "As you can see, it was a very amicable split up and we are still good friends!"

Samantha was torn as to whether she told the truth, that it had been she who walked out and deserted Phillip when he lost his well-paid job, or whether she made some unkind comment, but decided to bide her time and asked for a vodka and tonic for her and Helen nodded agreement. "Come and sit down with us, we've got a table over there." Phillip indicated vaguely. "You know Gordon, don't you Samantha?" They threaded their way through the crowd with their drinks and sat down. "Look, Gordon," he said brightly, "here's Samantha and her good-looking friend Helen."

Gordon stood up with old-fashioned courtesy and shook hands with both of them, saying smoothly, "It's a pleasure to meet such lovely ladies!"

"As you can see, Gordon is a real charmer," she said to Helen.

Phillip said, "He always fancied you Samantha; even when you came here with other men he was always saying to me how lovely you looked and what a lucky man he was, whoever was with you, to be escorting someone like you!!"

Gordon blushed at this fulsome praise. "Why, I do believe Gordon's blushing, it shows that he's human and still has normal, human feelings," said Samantha, defending him.

Helen was feeling a little embarrassed and changed the subject by saying, "What are you two guys doing here?"

Phillip picked up her hand and planted a smacking kiss on the back, saying, "In my case, I've been waiting for a pretty, voluptuous, sexy girl like you, with a figure to die for, to walk into my life!" Helen looked amazed and he apologised immediately, saying, "I hope you were not offended by what I said, it was meant as a compliment." He kept holding Helen's hand, wanting to make it quite plain to Samantha what his message was – he was unavailable but Gordon was only too willing. Just looking at Helen, he had thoughts of laying her naked on a bed next to him, and already he was aroused.

What's the matter with me tonight, thought Phillip, I'm feeling like a randy teenage schoolboy and I don't even know if Helen would be willing to come with me tonight. I wonder if the waiter has slipped something in my food tonight, he thought ruefully! "How did you two meet?" he asked them.

"Helen is my neighbour," Samantha said.

"Are there any vacancies in your building?" Phillip enquired, jokingly.

Helen replied, "It's a very large block of flats, I expect there may well be some vacancies."

"I think I'll come with my guitar and serenade you outside your window!"

"Samantha and I both have flats on the second floor so how are you going to find the right one?"

"If you start serenading anywhere outside our building, you'll probably get a bucket of cold water thrown over you, by me, if no-one else!" said Samantha, tartly.

"Where has all your romance gone?" sighed Phillip.

"I met you, lived with you for eight years, during which time all the 'romance' was knocked out of me."

"Don't listen to her, Helen," he pleaded. "Er... I am deeply romantic."

"Hah, so deeply romantic it was never expressed." said Samantha.

"Gordon, please say something to make Samantha remember how romantic I am so that she will stop being hurtful to me and I can impress Helen!!"

Helen was laughing and saying, "Of course you are, I believe you, I won't pay any attention to what they say, I like you."

"That's all I wanted to hear," he said. He nudged Gordon surreptitiously, willing him to say something to catch Samantha's attention.

Gordon took the hint and said, "I think you're being very cruel to Samantha," and gave her a beaming smile. "Would you ladies like another drink here, or shall we try somewhere else?"

"And where would that 'somewhere else' be, not your flat by any chance?"

Gordon pretended to look amazed, "Well, it's a bit more spacious than this bar and very comfortable, we could have a few more drinks before we take you home!!"

"Now how did I know that this suggestion was going to be made sooner or later?" said Samantha, ironically.

"You are just a cynic; all we were thinking of was your comfort and convenience," protested Gordon.

"Of course you were, and where could we be more comfortable than in bed!" she said.

Phillip looked at Helen and she smiled – not a definite "yes" but then again, perhaps not a "no" either, but don't rush it, don't rush it, good things are always worth waiting for. "I'll go get the drinks while you chat to the ladies, Gordon. You've hardly said a word tonight." Standing at the bar, he noticed two women he had seen before Samantha and Helen had walked in, and asked the one nearest to him, "May I stand here, next to you?"

She turned to look at him and then said to her companion, "Geraldine, I wonder if we should let him stand next to us while he orders his drinks?" The other woman replied, "I don't think so Gemma, he looks a bit dodgy to me."

"Oh come on," protested Phillip, "take a look at my innocent face, honest as the day is long!"

"Ah, but that's where you're wrong, the day is not long, in fact it will very soon be over!"

"You're not being very kind to me," he said. "I shall tell my mother about you two."

"Isn't he pathetic," said Geraldine with mock concern.

He carried the drinks back to the table, to be met with, "I thought you loved me and there you were, chatting up two other birds," said Helen indignantly.

Phillip kissed her and said, "Not only do I love you, I admire you as well!"

Helen smiled and said, "That's better."

Phillip was encouraged to lean over and whisper in her ear, "I can't wait to take you in my arms and cover the whole of your body with kisses," he murmured.

Samantha said crossly, "Oh, for heaven's sake you two, stop that or else I'll pour ice cold water over the pair of you."

"So what were you talking about to those two women at the bar?" asked Gordon.

"I just politely asked them if was alright if I stood next to them while I got my order and they started a debate about whether they should allow me to stand next to them. Just silly conversation you have with people while you are waiting to be served."

"It didn't look like idle conversation to me," Gordon said.

"Okay, I asked both of them to come to bed with me, satisfied?"

"That's more like it," he said, chuckling.

There was a short silence when Samantha asked, "What was their reply?"

"One of them said 'why don't we just make love here, over the bar stool' and the other one said 'okay but I want to be first because I just can't wait'; are you satisfied with the answer?"

"I don't know where you get these ideas from, it's absolute rubbish," Gordon said, in disbelief.

"You were the one who wouldn't believe me when I gave you the correct version!!"

Helen broke up their discussion with, "Actually, I'd like to see Gordon's flat. I want to be sober enough to defend myself before I have any more to drink!"

"And I want to be sober enough to be standing up!" said Phillip.

Waspishly, Samantha asked, "Do you mean you as a whole, or just certain parts of your body?"

"Both," he said.

"This conversation is deteriorating by the minute and I'm only an innocent young girl to be listening to all this!" said Helen.

"I wish I was still an innocent young girl," Samantha said.

"So do I," said Gordon.

"Why would you want to be an innocent young girl and have an old lecher like me after you?" Phillip asked him.

"Huh, I could handle two of the likes of you, even if I was young and innocent," said Gordon, triumphantly.

"It's a good job you're not my type," Phillip riposted and so the conversation went on, getting sillier and sillier until all four couldn't stop laughing and decided they had had enough.

They arrived at Gordon's flat in high good humour and he showed Helen all his facilities, as he called them, pointing out that one bedroom had two single beds and the other one, a double bed, the couch which opened up into a comfortable bed. Helen refused another drink and, taking Phillip's hand said, "If it's okay with you Gordon, we'll take the room with the double bed," and she pulled him inside, quickly shutting the door. As soon as the door was closed, she put her arms round Phillip's neck and murmured, "Now you can do all those things to me you mentioned back there, in the bar."

Phillip felt as if he was an eighteen-year-old on his first night of love and he tried to unleash his passion slowly, kissing Helen's face and neck as he started to undress her, until she was standing in front of him clad only in her black lace bra and knickers, displaying her voluptuous figure. He was beginning to lose control as he ripped off his own clothing and slipped her bra over her shoulders, fondling and kissing her bare breasts. He picked her up and putting her on the bed, he lost all control and ravished her. Their lovemaking seemed to go on for hours, Helen meeting his passion equally, until they were sated with each other and she put her arms around his neck and whispered, "You were sensational, you made me feel wonderful; I could say you were the best lover I ever had but that wouldn't be much of a compliment because I've had very few."

Phillip kissed her gently, saying, "You are gorgeous, Helen, and making love to you was a privilege. Curl up round me now and we'll have a rest." It felt so good to have her naked body cuddled close to his and they both fell asleep.

In the morning, he woke up to find he was alone so he quickly showered and shaved and went out to find both Helen and Samantha in the kitchen drinking coffee. "Want some?" Helen said.

"Yeah, thanks, is there anything to eat? I'm starving. Where is Mine Host?"

"I left him fast asleep," Samantha said. So they must have slept together, thought Phillip; he was pleased, it would be better if she and Gordon became an item. He knew Gordon had always fancied her, even when she and Phillip had been together and it was time she stopped going from one man to another or sooner or later, she would come to grief.

After half an hour, Gordon appeared, looking like a smug tiger and beaming from ear to ear. He gave Samantha a smacking kiss on her lips and announced, "Are we all ready for me to take you out for breakfast? Whatever you want, you only have to order it, I'm feeling very generous this morning!"

"What about the washing up?" Phillip. "Surely you don't expect these ladies to dirty their hands working, when you invited them here just for a drink!"

Gordon pretended to be hurt by his remark and replied with, "Thanks, I always knew you were my best friend, of course I wouldn't expect them to wash up, I have a dishwasher and a cleaning lady to do that, whereas you of course, being so poor, have to do all the housework yourself!"

"Take no notice of them," said Samantha to Helen, sighing, "they are the best of friends really but play this game of insulting each other whenever they meet, it's a 'man' thing apparently."

"What are you going to do now?" asked Helen.

"I'll go home!"

"Don't you spend the rest of the weekend together?"

"Not normally, no," he said. "So what do you do for the rest of the weekend?"

"I don't know what Gordon does but I do jobs round the house and generally tidy up," said Phillip vaguely.

Helen was surprised. "Do you not have anybody to clean for you and get in a workman when you want something mending?"

Gordon chimed in with, "He likes pottering around the house, he hasn't got a real job 'like what I have'."

"Gordon's quite right actually," Phillip said, "with him being a banker, still working in the Bank of England, he earns an obscene amount of money so he can afford a 'lady what does' and the maintenance charge for these flats is outrageous so he gets all his little jobs completed without him having to worry about anything; whereas I, on the other hand, am self-employed and have to earn every penny. Therefore I have to watch the pennies carefully and I do most of the jobs around the house myself; I'm rather good at it, if I say it myself! What about you two ladies?" asked Phillip.

"Helen is a PR for one of those huge conglomerates, an international firm which nobody's heard of and I went back into finance with a bank which has not been too involved in the recent fiasco of money troubles. They have managed to keep their heads above water and are doing quite well; I'm trading in commodities," said Samantha.

"What about you, Phillip, was Gordon's joke about you not having a proper job correct, or is it a secret?" said Helen, curiously.

Samantha laughed and before he could reply, she said "He's a private detective, in other words a snooper!"

"What made you decide to do that?" asked Helen, puzzled.

"I find the job interesting and quite rewarding; I used to be in banking and although the work was stressful, it was also boring so—"

"Come on," said Gordon, "we're not going to sit here and discuss work all weekend, let's go and get some breakfast!"

"We've eaten something so we don't need anything at the moment but perhaps you could always buy us some lunch later?" Helen said.

"Not for me, I'm afraid," said Phillip. "Time's getting on and I'm heading home."

"Is it okay if I come with you to see your new house?" asked Samantha.

Phillip was caught completely by surprise and for a moment, he could think of nothing to say. Finally he said, "It's just a four bedroom, detached house out in the sticks and I haven't got the car with me, I'm travelling on public transport," hoping to discourage her.

"I travel by public transport every day," she said, quietly.

He shrugged his shoulders and said simply, "Okay."

They were just about to leave when Helen, coming closer to Phillip said, "I hope to see you again soon."

"All being well, I'll see you at the wine bar next Friday," and she gently squeezed his hand. Having said goodbye to Gordon who asked plaintively, "What did I do, you're all going and leaving me on my own!" Phillip and Samantha headed for the station to begin their journey out to Croydon and Helen waved to them and went to do some shopping. Samantha and Phillip said virtually nothing to each other while they travelled but once they were inside the house, Samantha turned to him "Why did you manoeuvre me into going with Gordon, or to put it bluntly, sleeping with him?"

"I did nothing of the sort; you know the layout of the flat, after all we used to live in the same building at one time, and when Helen took my hand and said we were going into the bedroom with two single beds in it, you didn't seriously think I was going to say no, did you? I didn't know, nor did I care, where you and Gordon decided to sleep, whether together or apart; he's a nice gentle guy and he wouldn't have pestered you and would have taken a simple 'no' for an answer."

"You went after Helen straight away, as soon as you met her," accused Samantha.

"We have slept together enough to last a lifetime and I seem to remember you saying you were bored with my lovemaking and it no longer excited you; well nothing's changed, I'm still the same man!" he said.

"I wanted to tell you that some of the time now, I have greatly regretted walking out on you like that. It's partly the fact that I was very young and you were my first real lover. I had very little experience of lovemaking and I somehow felt that I didn't have enough knowledge of men and perhaps I was missing something in our sex life."

"Well you certainly got to know a lot more men since you left," he said.

"Not as many as you obviously think," she said, defiantly.

"There's plenty of time yet for you to get to know a lot more," taunted Phillip. "Who's the lucky guy now?"

"I'm not seeing anyone at the moment and I haven't been in a relationship for some time now," she said indignantly.

"Don't you count Gordon as a man?"

She was silent, then she said, "Sleeping with Gordon was not something I particularly wanted to do, you could almost say I was obliged to do it, the way things worked out. You walked off with Helen and I was left with Gordon who was very flattering and he obviously thought I was willing to go to bed with him, so I couldn't spoil his illusions."

"There is nothing wrong with Gordon, you could have done a lot worse; you've been out with all those other men; don't tell me it was love each time you had sex with one of them," sneered Phillip.

"Okay, maybe I deserved that but at least it was my choice, I didn't find myself in a situation where I couldn't really say no."

"Now listen to me, Samantha, you came and sat down with us and you could see right from the start that I fancied Helen. If you thought you were being pushed towards Gordon, you could have left, or not come to the flat with us."

"I told you, I didn't want to spoil it for you three!"

"Come on, I know you better than that. Consideration for others has never been your strong point."

After a short silence she said, "I guess I must have changed then."

"Good for you; just think of it as your good deed for the week, you made Gordon a very happy man. A very noble gesture to a decent guy, who likes and admires you, far better than making love to some rich git who has plenty of money; you must know that even while we were together, he lusted after you!"

"You are being very nasty to me," she said in a low voice.

"It's difficult for me when I've seen you with a lot of different men who all had money and I know that that was one of the reasons why you left me. When I took redundancy from the bank and you knew I wouldn't get a large salary or even larger bonuses any more, you thought you were losing all the advantages you had from living with me so you just walked out!" he threw at her.

"There were other reasons as well," she said.

"I'm sure there were but what is it you really want? Why did you come here with me? Is it just to have an argument, if so that's the last thing I want!" Turning to look at her, he saw she was crying silently, tears running down her cheeks and he felt gutted. He could always tell when people cried if it was for real or just because they were sorry for themselves, or even faking. He could see Samantha was deeply hurting. "Please don't cry, if I hurt you, I'm sorry," said Phillip.

"I can't stand it when you're mad at me, I know I've made a lot of mistakes and now I have to live with them," she sobbed. He put an arm around her shoulders to give her a comforting kiss on the cheek, when she turned her face up to his and put her arms around his neck and without warning, they were frantically covering each other's faces with kisses.

Somehow they found themselves in a bedroom, tearing off their clothes, and when they were both naked, he lifted her onto the bed and started to make love to her, something that would stay in Samantha's memory for a long time. Unlike with Helen, he had more control over his movements and he built their passion slowly, keeping himself in check as he watched Samantha's reactions to his lovemaking. He concentrated on the areas where he could see the maximum response, revelling in the way their bodies were attuned, and as he realised she was about to reach her climax, he allowed all his control to vanish and they climaxed together. Finally they separated and both fell back onto the bed exhausted until she raised herself on one elbow, saying, "I don't smoke but if I did, this would be the perfect time!"

He smiled at her. "And why would that be?"

"To show appreciation to the master, you've certainly learned plenty since I left!"

Phillip made himself comfortable on a pillow and said, "Actually, after you left, I had no sex for nearly ten months."

"I hope it was not because I upset you too much," she said mockingly.

"There were a lot of different factors; I had to start rebuilding my life, I was without a job, nowhere to live and my long-term relationship had collapsed so I had to start all over again. Decide on a job, buy a place to live and work from and all that took time."

"Did you feel a grudge against me or was it against all women?" she asked.

"Neither, really, I didn't want to get involved in a new relationship, I thought it better to be on my own, away from any distractions. I was a bit of a loner but I didn't deliberately avoid people, I just didn't seek their company and then Gordon came back from an assignment in Scotland. He contacted me, we went for a meal and a few drinks and it all took off from there."

"Thank heavens you didn't become a hermit," smiled Samantha.

"It would be a bit difficult to do that, when I needed to meet people to do my job! What about you, what happened in your life?"

"At first I really thought I had found what I was searching for because I met a lot of different men with money to spend on me. I lived in the best houses, luxury apartments, was driven round in expensive cars and ate in the best restaurants. I could order clothes and just about anything I wanted and charge it to someone's credit card but of course, it didn't take me long to realise that I was deluding myself. I know it sounds a bit hypocritical in this day and age, but I didn't love any of them, it wasn't really the kind of life I was looking for. I was really being used as a high class whore, to show their money, regardless of how they made it. Other people, to them, were just a means of making money, completely expendable. I became so disillusioned with my life when your supervisor came along. I became really fond of him; he was a decent man and although I can't say I fell in love with him, we became very close."

"So how did that affair end?" he asked.

"Rather tragically. He kept on asking me to marry him as we were already living together and although I couldn't see any point in it, he was old-fashioned enough to want to 'make an honest woman of me' as he put it. You'd have to go a helluva way to do that but after a while, to make him happy, I agreed and we made all the arrangements for a church wedding, me in a white dress (can you imagine?), matrons of honour, champagne reception, the whole palaver. I was being fitted for my dress when my mobile rang and he had been taken to hospital with a 'slight' heart attack. The heart specialist examined him and reassured him that with a few days' rest he would soon be back to normal, but in the meantime, he had been given a sedative to make him relax and sleep, so there was no point in going round to see him that day; I should have visited him the following day but they called me the following morning to say I should come quickly, but by the time I got there, it was too late. They were very kind, brought me a cup of tea when I got there and said he had a massive heart attack early in the morning and he must have died very quickly, with no suffering. I asked to see him and he looked so pale but very peaceful and instead of arranging a wedding, I arranged his funeral."

They lay there quietly until Phillip said gently, "That must have been very sad for you, I had no idea you were so close to him."

"It was like losing a lifetime friend, a best friend, if you know what I mean, and afterwards when the solicitor gave me Steven's will to read, the wonderful man had redrawn it prior to our wedding and as he had no close family, apart from one or two bequests, he left everything to me. I couldn't believe it, a big house and everything that came with it, a fortune in various investments and even some money in a Swiss bank account. You are looking at a very rich woman," she said, mockingly.

"I'm very pleased for you, it would have been tragic if you had ended with nothing," he said. "But how is it you're living in a flat?"

"There was no way I wanted to stay in that big house without him," she said. "Besides I wouldn't have wanted to run the place. Steven needed to employ several staff to look after the property and I just couldn't be bothered to do all that. So I sold the whole place with the condition that the new owner employ all the staff for at least a year or pay them twelve months' salary instead. Then I looked around carefully and bought this luxury flat in a modern block in one of the *best* areas," she emphasised. "I never have to worry about money ever again!!"

"Are you happy with the way things have turned out now?" he asked.

"As you know, financial security is very important to me. I know people say that friends are more important than money but a person who's broke, you will find, doesn't have all that many friends. You try living in poverty and see how many friends you have!!"

"You may be right," he said. "I never went out of my way to cultivate a lot of friends. Experts say you only make friends in the early part of your life and very few past the age of twenty-five; after then, you just make acquaintances. People are very different, some always need a crowd around them, perhaps it's because they need reassurance; some might lack self-esteem or have little understanding of what makes them tick, whatever it is they always want to be the centre of attention in any group. Just a handful of people will do for me," he finished.

"Sometimes one is more than enough," she said, stroking his arm. "What shall we do for the rest of the day? Have you any programme in mind, or now that you have had your way with me, do you want me to go?"

"If you like," said Phillip, "you can stay for the rest of the weekend, although I don't think you will find that very exciting."

"I'd like to stay, please, what do we do now?"

"Normally, when I'm alone, I keep myself busy around the house. When I have guests, say a lady friend, which is very rare, after we've made love we rest a little to recoup our energy then have a shower and get ready to go out for the evening. The only drawback is there are no top quality restaurants within a short distance, so it means getting a taxi there and when you've finished your meal and want to get back, you're hanging around waiting for another taxi, which seems to take ages."

"So what do you usually do for a meal if you're not cooking it yourself?"

"If it's just me, I stroll along to our local pub; they do cooked meals, snacks, salads, everything from hamburgers to beef bourguignon, by way of chicken and chips or mixed grills etc, oh, and my favourite toffee sponge pudding with custard to finish with!"

"Let's do that then," she said, "and by the way, how are you fixed for money, Phillip?"

"So far, I'm doing reasonably well with my clients paying on time, so I'm keeping my bank manager very happy with my current and savings accounts!"

"Nevertheless, tonight's on me," she said.

"Okay, I'm not one of those men who would say, 'Oh no, you don't have to do that, I'm the man and I should pay.' You obviously have a lot more money than I have so if you want to pay, that's fine with me!"

"Now that we've settled that, perhaps we should have that little rest you mentioned before. I certainly used up a lot of my energy, making love with you, let me curl up round you like I used to do," and after a lingering kiss, they fell asleep.

He awoke to hear her singing in the bathroom; he remembered from the past that when she was happy, she always sang in the bath. He showered and dressed and waited downstairs for her, impatient to eat and drink and when she appeared she said, "It's a pity I have nothing to change into."

"You look great, you'll be the best looking woman in there tonight. Come on, we're walking you know, I don't drink and drive, I can't risk losing my licence for anything stupid like that!"

"I can still walk," she said indignantly. "I go to the gym three times a week, and Helen and I do lots of walking at weekends."

Once in the pub he said, "Let's find a table."

She gave him her credit card, told him the pin number and said, "Order whatever you want and pay for it with this. I'll have a vodka and orange and I'll look at the menu and decide what to eat. What are you having?"

The barman said it would be easier if he paid for everything at the end of the evening so he put the card in his pocket.

"I think I might have that pasta dish," he said, looking sideways at her. "It's what marathon runners eat before a race, helps to replace energy, so I'm told!"

Samantha laughed. "Are we going to run a marathon then?"

"It always helps to be prepared, you never know when you'll need it, the energy I mean."

"I think you've convinced me, I'll have the same as you! I'll blame you if I feel worn out halfway through the marathon we're going to run," she said cheekily. "I can't be responsible for anything you eat in here."

"Why, does it say that on the menu?"

"No, but I'll bet the chef has that written into his contract!" He went to order their meal and when he came back and sat down, Samantha asked, "Did you go on a course on how to be a good lover?" she said, archly.

"No, but if there is such a course, I'll certainly join it."

"I wonder how many practical lessons there would be on such a course, how many partners you would have to practise with! I expect you'd enjoy that part of it," she said wickedly.

"What made you ask that?" he said.

"You seem to have improved your technique since we were last together," she said.

He grinned at her. "That's because I've had a great deal more practice," he said. "I've really applied myself to my homework."

"Are you blaming me?"

"Samantha, it's no longer relevant, let's not go blaming one or the other, it's all in the past."

"Just one thing Phillip, tell me who is better in bed, Helen or me?"

"I'm not sure that's entirely relevant, let's not spoil our evening delving into things like that."

"I don't want to put it crudely Phillip but you have made love to both of us within the last forty-eight hours, so who was the better lover, me or Helen?"

"If you're asking for marks out of ten, I don't do that sort of thing, I don't make comparisons between lovers. Each lady is an individual…" he was searching desperately for the right words "… and each one is different!"

"You're very gallant," she said, pressing for an answer. "What was she like?"

"Okay, you asked me for an answer so I'll tell you. As soon as I saw Helen, I saw she had the kind of figure that arouses lust in most men and when I saw her standing there just wearing a black lace bra and panties, I felt so randy that I lost my normal cool. Rather than making love to her, I ravished her as if I were an eighteen-year-old boy who was having his first sexual encounter with a willing young woman." Suddenly, he realised that he had raised his voice a little and a young couple who were sitting nearby must have heard what he was saying. Phillip looked at them and apologised if he had said anything which might have offended them and the girl gulped, blushed and mumbled, "No, no, it's okay, we weren't really taking any notice of you!!" He turned back to Samantha and smiled at her. "See what you made me do, make an absolute fool of myself."

She looked across at the girl and replied, equally quietly, "I think she was really enjoying that, she looks sorry you stopped!!"

The food arrived and they ate quickly, both hungry. "Would you like anything for dessert?" queried Phillip.

"Do they have something that will give me lots of energy for later on tonight?" she asked demurely.

"We don't want anything too stodgy, how about we have ice cream with strawberries and chocolate sauce, that should finish off our meal nicely?" They ate their dessert and sat drinking and chatting until Samantha gave a little yawn and said it was time they were going. He paid the bill with her card and they walked back, arm in arm. No sooner were they inside the front door, than Samantha put her arms around his neck and murmured huskily, "I want you to ravish me tonight; after that meal you should have enough energy!"

He looked at her seriously. "Are you sure? I can be a bit rough!"

"Oh, I don't mean I want you to beat me up" she scoffed. "I just want you to be tough and demanding, do you know the kind of thing I mean?" He nodded his head, almost unable to speak. "Give me five minutes then come upstairs undressed." Mutual enjoyment of their sex encounter went on and on until, exhausted, they both fell asleep. He awoke in the morning to hear Samantha singing in the bathroom again!

Chapter 36

After a lazy breakfast, they dressed and went for a leisurely walk. Samantha asked, "What's on the programme for today?"

"Later on, I'm going to take you home in the car."

"Trying to get rid of me already" she pouted.

"No, I just want to make sure you get home safely" he said, "women travelling alone on public transport on a Sunday can be the target of all sort of weirdos, teenage gang members, pickpockets, drunks, you name it, attacks have happened and I can't have that happening to you!"

"So that's the end of our relationship?"

"We've been there, done that, and we don't want to follow that path again, at least I don't," he said. "I've had three long-term relationships with three different women and they've all walked out on me. I've come to the conclusion that there's a flaw in my character which only appears after a time and I'm now resigned to the fact that long term relationships are not for me and I'll have to live with that."

"Does that mean you're giving up on all women?" she asked.

"By no means, I like women. I'm very good at chatting them up and to give you an example, I've got to know two bisexual girls and I have a great time when I'm with them; they keep on asking me to go see them more often."

"Two women at the same time, how does that work?" she said, jealously.

He shrugged and said, "I asked myself that same question but I can assure you, it works fine! The two girls are lovers, but being bisexual, they both like making love to men and so it works perfectly."

"Don't you think that's debauchery, behaving like that?"

He said impatiently, "It's just like making love in the usual way, there's nothing kinky about it, we don't do anything that we didn't do last night and anyway, I only told you about it to emphasise the fact that I make friends with women easily and I've no intention of giving them up." Samantha was silent.

They walked back to the house, not saying anything until they were sitting in the lounge when Samantha said, with some hesitation, "But you're giving me up, you don't want to see me anymore?"

"I didn't say that; I'm more than willing to be your friend, anytime you feel like you could do with my company, whether it's to make love or just have a chat, just ring me and if I'm here alone, just come round. If I should happen to have company, we can always arrange a time to meet when it would suit both of us. But please ring my mobile number, my job can take me all over the place, even abroad, but I always have that with me."

"Can I take you out to lunch, then I could show you my new flat?" He was relieved that she had changed the subject and agreed it was a good idea to eat out. Samantha gave him directions to one of her favourite restaurants and the service was excellent. There seemed to be a waiter for everything, good for employment, thought Phillip, but the customer pays through the nose for it! Phillip would not drink but Samantha ordered some wine and if it affected her in any, well she always could hold her drink without appearing to be inebriated. They enjoyed their steak, beautifully cooked, and finished with a very light dessert.

Her flat was in a modern block with a basement car park. They went up to the eighth floor in the silent lift and she opened her door and stood back for him to enter, waiting for his reaction to the view over the river. He had a short guided tour, the flat was similar to Gordon's, two bedrooms, both with en-suite bathrooms, small but fully fitted kitchen area with a dining table and a large comfortable lounge. "All mod cons," said Phillip, turning to her.

She shrugged carelessly. "Everything was here, it was fully furnished. I think it was the show flat so all I had to do was just move in, which suited me."

She made them coffee and they chatted desultorily until abruptly she said, "Would you like to examine my collection of underwear, bras and panties etc?"

"You should know by now my love, I'm always willing to look at something which interests you!!"

"Make yourself comfortable," she said, "and I'll have a shower," and she disappeared into her bedroom. Minutes later, she emerged again but they only managed to get to the first matching pair in her collection before they had to retire to the bedroom to judge their quality! Two hours later, a rather sad lady watched him leaving her apartment. He entered the lift, went down, picked up his car and drove home, thinking, what a weekend this has been.

The following Thursday, sitting at his desk, Phillip was wondering what further steps he could take regarding the Gardner divorce case when John rang him. "We've got a problem," he announced.

"Why, what have you done now?" said Phillip, jokingly.

"Don't try to be funny," snapped John. "This is serious. Ronald Gardner has been killed; that is, he's been murdered!"

Phillip was completely shocked. "How? Tell me what happened."

"His lady partner found him when she returned from work yesterday evening."

"How was he killed?"

"The police say it was 'blunt force trauma' – in other words he was bludgeoned to death with a heavy object. The bad news is that Elizabeth Donnan has been arrested for his murder and she is currently being held in police custody, to appear before a magistrate tomorrow morning. Can you come to my office now, straight away?" John sounded rattled out of his usual good humour. "We have to interview her and prepare our case for getting her out on bail."

"I'm on my way."

As soon as he reached John's office, they both left for the police station. They showed their identification to the desk sergeant and told him they wanted to interview their client, Mrs Elizabeth Donnan, without delay. "You mean the woman who bashed her husband to death," he said, with interest.

"Sergeant Hopkins, you should know better than to make that assumption; you know perfectly well that under English law, a person is innocent until proven guilty. Now, I want to see my client, immediately."

The chastened police sergeant said, "Come this way sir," and told them Mrs Donnan would be in the interview room shortly.

Phillip studied Elizabeth carefully. She looked nothing like the sex symbol she had appeared to be when she came to his office; instead she was looking very pathetic, her hair was unkempt and her clothes were creased as if she had slept in them. "Can you tell us what happened?" said John gently. "And have you been charged?"

She seemed to concentrate and said carefully, "It was yesterday morning, I decided to call on Ronald to try and finalise the details of our divorce. I wanted to settle things so that I could get on with the rest of my life and this seemed to be the best way. I got there about ten o'clock; he let me in, there was no-one else in the place. He said his partner had gone to work and he did not have a job. When I said that I wanted a quick divorce, he started to get nasty, accusing me of trying to cheat him out of his proper share of our property and money. I tried to tell him I wanted our marriage to end amicably but quickly, and he started calling me names. He was impossible to deal with so I left, just before eleven o'clock, and he was fine, standing there mouthing insults. I have absolutely no idea what happened after that; the next morning I was arrested and allowed one phone call so I rang you, John. What am I going to do?"

John patted her hand to reassure her and said, "Someone must have seen you enter and leave the premises but the police will assume that as you have a motive and you were the last person who had seen Ronald alive, you must automatically be guilty. He said he wanted half of everything you owned, you didn't want to lose half your fortune, so you took matters into your own hands, perhaps lost your temper when he wouldn't be reasonable and picked up some heavy object and hit him with it. Is that what happened, Elizabeth?" She silently shook her head. "The police can build a reasonable case against you for his murder. It's our job to establish your innocence but the first thing we have to do is get you out of prison on bail. You'll be appearing in court tomorrow morning and I shall represent you. Try not to worry too much and Phillip and I will make sure that everything will be done to prove your innocence." Elizabeth looked up at them as they prepared to leave, fearful at being left in a strange place, and her shoulders slumped, she was very near to tears.

The two men left the police station and discussed what had happened while driving back to John's office. "What do you think, Phillip? As I understand it, she went round to see her husband and after she left, somebody who had been watching gained entrance to the flat, whether Ronald admitted him willingly or not, and killed him with a heavy object – why, we don't know. We'd better discuss our strategy when we get back to the office."

Phillip stated the case as he saw it. "The strong points, as I see them, are she is an upstanding citizen, well thought of by her peers, highly educated, no police record for even a parking fine or jay-walking, just a woman who was getting a divorce who went to see her husband, from whom she was separated, to discuss the amicable resolution of the case. He proved to be totally unreasonable so she gave up and left. There is no evidence that she was there during the attack, other than that she had been to see him that same morning. What was the exact time of death?"

John said, "The time of death has not been established exactly; that will be introduced at a later date, but in the meantime we have enough facts to put the police case in some doubt and that's what I will be working on. See you in the morning, try to get here about nine, if you can."

In court the next morning, the prosecuting solicitor told those present that the police had received a phone call from a hysterical woman who said she had returned from work to find the body of her partner lying on the floor in the lounge of her flat with very serious head injuries and she thought he was dead. The police confirmed that they had followed up the call and found the body, as she had described it, and certified that the man had been dead for some time. A witness said they saw Mrs Elizabeth Donnan coming out of the building around the time when it was assumed the victim had been attacked, which subsequently led to his death. The police had questioned Mrs Donnan and she said she had visited the flat around ten o'clock that morning, leaving well before eleven. The man was identified as Mr Ronald Gardner, who was married to Mrs Donnan. She still used her maiden name for business purposes. He had admitted her to the flat because she wanted to discuss with him details of the settlement of their forthcoming divorce, of which she was contesting the terms of his entitlement to a large share of her money and property.

The accused said that Mr Gardner had become difficult and abusive to her so she left, but she maintained that he was still alive when she exited the building. She did not remember the exact time, but she was quite certain she was home by 11.20 am. The police pathologist estimated time of death on or about eleven o'clock that morning. It would appear the motive for killing Mr Gardner was due to the accused wishing to finalise the divorce arrangements between them, but when she confronted her husband and said she was not going to allow him to take half the money and property she owned, they began to argue.

"We think it likely," said the prosecuting solicitor, "that Mrs Donnan lost her temper with Mr Gardner, in view of his reluctance to accede to her request to expedite the divorce proceedings by settling for a much smaller amount, and in her rage, she picked up a heavy object and attacked him, perhaps hoping that he would agree to her suggestion. Realising that she had given him a fatal blow to the head, she rushed out of the building and went home, trusting to the fact that no-one had seen her enter or leave the building and perhaps hoping to give herself an alibi by saying she had not left her home that morning."

As the prosecuting solicitor sat down, John rose to his feet and began Elizabeth's defence statement. "It is true that Mrs Donnan visited her husband, Mr Ronald Gardner, in order to discuss their impending divorce case and the monetary settlement which he was pressing for. He was deliberately wasting time in the hope that she would become weary of waiting and acquiesce to his quite outrageous demands for a settlement and it is also perfectly true that their meeting was not conciliatory; in fact Mr Gardner became extremely rude and offensive to my client and she was so upset, she realised that nothing was going to alter his wish to obtain every pecuniary advantage he could, even after only being married such a short time. She realised that she must leave everything in the hands of her solicitor and a saddened and crushed woman gave up her efforts to get him to agree amicably and went home. She was working at her own residence that day and had no further need to go out; therefore it was a complete surprise when a member of the police force called and told her that her husband was dead and murder was suspected. She co-operated in every way possible and went to the police station to give a statement and then, to her surprise, was arrested and charged with causing his death. It would appear from the evidence at present in our possession that Mrs Donnan left her husband's residence at least half an hour before he was attacked.

"That being the case, it is very obvious that Mrs Donnan could not have attacked her husband and has been wrongfully arrested; until further investigation and statements have been taken and verified, Mrs Donnan should be released forthwith on bail which I hereby request."

The magistrate asked the police representative what his thoughts were on the matter and after considering the matter he told the court that Mrs Donnan was to be released on bail, to appear in court at a later date to answer the charges. John and Phillip escorted a tearful Elizabeth out of court and asked if she wished to be taken home. "Could you stay with me for a short while?" she pleaded with Phillip. "I've hardly got used to the fact that Ronald is dead – whatever he was, he didn't deserve to die like that – and I feel very unsettled."

"Yes, of course," said Phillip, sympathetically. Now that Sarah was no longer with him, he felt he was a totally a free man; he no longer needed to avoid her and after collecting his car, he drove her to her home. This turned out to be a large, detached house in Hampstead – a long way from Croydon, thought Phillip.

They went inside and Liza said, "I'll show you around in a minute. I just want to put the kettle on and have a cup of tea or coffee, I can hardly believe I'm free to do just that!" They sat silently over a cup of instant coffee and then she said brightly, "Okay, I'll give you the guided tour I promised you."

The property was probably eighty to a hundred years old but was in excellent condition and apart from the five bedrooms and two luxurious bathrooms upstairs, downstairs consisted of a pleasant lounge, looking out onto a flower filled garden, a spacious kitchen, separate dining room and a study, the walls being lined with bookshelves.

"How do you manage to keep it looking so beautiful?" Phillip asked, knowing it would take several employees to maintain the house in its lovely condition.

"This was my father's house which I inherited when he died. I'm hoping to sell it but of course, nothing can be done until the divorce is finalised." She smiled wistfully. "My father used to love to sit in the study and read his books, but anyway, I mustn't get morbid must I? Please make yourself comfortable, I simply must have a bath after spending two nights in a police cell without even a change of underwear, ugh, it was horrible." She shuddered. "I won't be very long."

He sat down in a large comfortable armchair, resting his head against the upholstered back; the next thing he knew was hearing a noise which seemed to come from the kitchen. He found Liza, wrapped in a bathrobe, getting out some pans from a well-stocked cupboard. As soon as she saw him, she came over and putting her arms around his neck, she gave him a lingering kiss. "I'm just thinking about making a meal," she said.

"You're not seriously thinking of starting to cook, are you?" he said.

"Why not? I'm an excellent cook and there's plenty of food in the house!"

"I don't eat large meals and I usually go for something very simple so there's no need to bother on my account," he said.

"Are you normally so difficult to please, or it is just with me?" asked Liza, with a smile.

"No honestly, I'm just telling you there's no need to spend a lot of time preparing and cooking anything for me. I'm just as happy to walk over to the nearest pub and have something there, or even a takeaway," he said apologetically.

"I was going to show you what a good cook I am but if you're happy with pub food, let's get a takeaway, but I don't want to go out at the moment. I've just had this wonderful, long bath and I just want to relax and feel glad because I'm at home, safe for the moment."

"Don't worry about it, I can easily pick something up on my way home!" and he walked towards the door.

She came close to him and looked into his eyes, pleadingly. "Please stay with me tonight, I need you, I would feel so depressed on my own."

Phillip found himself considering what he should do for the best and decided he ought to stay with this vulnerable woman. "I'll stay here for tonight," he said, "but perhaps you should get a friend or relative to stay with you for the next few weeks?"

"Would you like to ring your partner, to explain what's keeping you?" she asked.

"Sarah has left me, moved all her things out completely, I'm back on my own again!" He shrugged his shoulders.

Liza almost purred; inside she felt the greatest pleasure but she only said, "That must have been very upsetting for you, I'm sorry." He looked away from her sympathetic face and told her that life goes on. "Well, that being the case, there's no reason for you to rush back is there?"

"I can stay tonight but remember, I work for a living and I'll have to get back to my office tomorrow."

"That's tomorrow and this is now, shall we eat first or later?" and with that, she slipped her bathrobe off her shoulders, allowing it to fall to the floor.

She was wearing clinging lacy stockings, held up by a tight suspender belt, with matching lace panties and a soft, net bra. Her shoes were black also and had very high heels – the effect on Phillip was instantaneous. Through his mind there flitted the picture of making love to this sexy woman with her full breasts and generous backside straining against her panties; it brought out all the male lust in him, and pulling her into the lounge, he pushed her down onto the carpet, muttering, "Food can wait!"

She was insatiable and met every one of his moves with one of her own; it was almost a wrestling match until finally they came to a halt and just lay there, satiated for the time being. Liza kissed him, lingering slowly on his lips and said, "If you were charging for that performance, I would be out of money in no time. A man as well equipped as you would make a very good professional escort!"

"What, like a gigolo, you mean?" he said indignantly.

She poked fun at him, gently: "That's a very old-fashioned word," she said, teasingly. "I mean an escort. Take all the successful, professional women, going out for the evening, with someone to make sure they have an enjoyable time, finishing up with this sort of lovemaking we've just enjoyed. I'd be first in the queue!"

"The very idea of it turns my stomach," he said.

"Why should you feel like that, it's not really all that different from what happened tonight?" she questioned, puzzled.

Phillip tried to organize his thoughts. "It's completely different," he insisted. "Today, we are just two adults who know each other and unfortunate events have brought us together. It so happens that we are both free with no other ties or obligations, you are now single and so am I. We felt like making love so we did. That's entirely different to being paid for it when you would have to do what that person wanted or told you to do. If they were not satisfied with your 'performance' in any way, they could make subtle complaints against you which might get you the sack or some women might insist that you have sex with them doing things you might personally find revolting. I suppose you've seen that film with Richard Gere in it, when his pimp tells him to make out with men, if there are no women who need his services?"

"Sorry," said Liza. "My you are touchy, I was only trying to say what a wonderful lover you are and most women would give their eye-teeth to have you in bed with them!"

"Why thank you my dear," he said. "That's very kind of you, praise from someone with so much knowledge and experience, a renowned expert in the field."

She punched him lightly on the shoulder and said with mock ferocity, "Watch it buster, don't try to be funny with me or I shall devour you!"

"Well, are you going to feed me or do you aim to starve me into submission?" he demanded.

"We can send for a takeaway after we've had a little rest upstairs on something a bit more comfortable than a fitted carpet!" she laughed. "Come on."

Chapter 37

They were so hungry, they opened the carton of foods and started to eat without delay. Liza opened a bottle of excellent wine and they settled down to eat their fill. She disposed of all the debris in the kitchen and then, when they walked into the lounge, she brought out two crystal glasses and poured a generous serving of brandy into each of them. Phillip said, "You certainly know how to live well," as he looked round the comfortable room and at the brandy balloon in his hand, swirling the amber coloured fluid round.

She said quietly, "Our family, and later on me, always had money and we lived well, although you don't always realise this until you see how other people exist. Talking about money, I think I'd better give you another cheque. I'm sure the first amount I gave you must be running out by this time."

He nodded his head, saying, "That would be appreciated, thank you; there's an awful lot of hard graft to do now. The police will be working like beavers to find the evidence to convict you of murder but I have to find out who really killed Ronald, to be sure of establishing your innocence." He accepted the cheque for £10,000 and slipped it into his pocket.

Next morning, Liza asked him to remain with her for another day but he refused, somewhat reluctantly, because he had to get back and start his enquiries on her case. He rang John who asked him, "How did you enjoy your weekend? It's alright for you single blokes, us married men have to look after our families, it limits our scope of activities. I can't be spending my time coping with sex-starved females, trying to take their minds off their predicament, as much as I would like to!"

"Dear, dear, you'll make me cry in a minute," Phillip said. "It was your choice to get married."

"Someone had to assume responsibility for bringing up the next generation of decent, responsible people and you can't be running around half dressed, on the lookout for some female to lay," he laughed.

"You must be mixing me up with someone else John, I really am just a shy, innocent young man."

John swore loudly and said, "The whole of that previous sentence is wrong; you are a horny, middle-aged, irresponsible, chasing-anything-in-a-skirt type of man who uses what charm he has to get them into bed!!"

"Now, now John, let's get down to business shall we? We have to find out who the witness is who says they saw Elizabeth coming out of Ronald's flat and driving away. Why would they bother to look at the exact time, where was this witness standing, and how could they be so positive about identifying her if she had never been there before? This person had to be close by."

"I agree with you," John said, "but how do we get this information? The police must know who it is but the prosecution might not disclose the evidence until much nearer the date of the trial."

Phillip said, "Leave all that to me, I'm not called a private detective for nothing! I'll take a look around the area and see what I can discover. Ring you when I get some results," and with that, he rang off.

He reasoned that the witness had to be a neighbour with a good view of the entrances of all nearby properties, therefore he would make discreet enquiries as soon as possible, while events were still fresh in people's memories, a sort of house to house enquiry. He found Ronald's last address and the street turned out to be a cul-de-sac. He began to systematically knock on people's doors, making notes as to who answered his knock. Those with drawn curtains where tenants had probably gone to work, and the ones who answered. The first door he knocked on, an old lady answered after a considerable wait, and said in a quavering voice, "I'm not going to let you in!"

Phillip put on his most disarming smile and said, "You're quite right, madam, here's my card. As you can see, I'm a private detective and I'm making enquiries…"

She eyed him suspiciously. "You're not a reporter from one of those newspapers are you? I'm not going to say anything to you if you are."

"No I'm not a reporter, I'm a private detective," he said patiently.

"Nosing into that murder are you? The police have been all over, looking for clues, and I'll have you know this is a respectable area. I've lived here for, well I don't know how many years, but it's a long time and that sort of thing doesn't happen here!!"

"I know, it's very bad for you having to have the police questioning you and letting down the nice tone of the area," he said.

She nodded. "Of course, I feel sorry for that nice young lady; fancy coming home from work and finding a dead body on your living room carpet, such a shock. Of course," she whispered to him, "they weren't married you know, he hadn't been here all that long; some people thought she was wasting her time with him and some people said he had a roving eye but he was always nice and polite to me!!"

Phillip managed to choke down his sudden laughter and nodding his head, agreed with her absolutely. "Did he have many visitors? I understand he was temporarily unemployed?"

"I don't know about that, but she was a very nice girl and I don't know how she's going to sell that place, now there's been a murder there!"

"And I don't suppose you saw anybody leaving the place on the morning of the murder?"

"I should think not, I wouldn't be able to sleep in my bed if I had seen a murderer in this street."

Nothing more was to be gained here. He looked around again and saw the 'no parking at any time' notices and rang Elizabeth to ask her where she had parked her car when she visited Ronald. "I parked on the main road, next to the street entrance, because there's absolutely no place to park in there and you have to have a special permission to park in the street."

"Was it on the same side as the road entrance or on the opposite side of the road?"

"The opposite side of the road."

"Could any person, looking out of their window, see you leave the entrance to Ronald's place and get into your car?"

"No, I don't think so, unless they lived in the end house; I'm almost sure there are some windows looking out onto the road there." So it looked as if the witness lived in the end house if they saw Liza get into her car, how could they have seen her enter or leave the scene of the murder?

He walked back along the road and studied the one small window in the wall of the end house. It must be for a toilet because it was on the second floor and the glass was opaque which meant of course, you couldn't see through it. The windows on the ground floor were normal size and could be opened, in which case, someone would have to lean out of the opening to have seen anything in the main road, in which case they wouldn't have been able to see her leaving Ronald's. Why would they go to all that trouble? Something wasn't quite right; he had to ask questions of Ronald's immediate neighbours, hear what their version of the story was. He tried one side but there was no answer so he knocked on the other door and eventually, an old man answered. "Excuse me, I'm sorry to bother you but here's my card, I'm a private detective looking into the death of Mr Gardner."

The man interrupted quickly with, "I thought the police were doing all that!"

"They are, of course, but I'm investigating a different aspect of his death on behalf of his family," said Phillip, mendaciously.

"Oh, you mean like an inheritance or something!"

"That's very perceptive of you," flattered Phillip.

"I might be getting on a bit but my mind's still sharp as a tack," said the old man.

"I wonder if we might go inside?" Phillip asked. "It doesn't seem quite right to discuss a man's life or death on the doorstep, does it?"

"Sorry, you're quite right, come in, come in, that's my wife Agnes over there, this gentleman's a private detective and he's looking into the death of that fellow next door and he wants to talk to us," he said, without a stop.

Agnes said, "We don't really know all that much about him."

"Nice to meet you Agnes, my name is Phillip Everett and I thought that you, as close neighbours, would be able to help me. How did you get on with them?"

"She's a lovely girl, but although I don't like to speak ill of the dead, he was a real idle rat! While that poor girl went out to work, he just stayed at home having lots of different women come to visit him and we've seen any number of them, haven't we Alf?" He nodded. "The place belongs to her and he only moved in with her fairly recently. I don't know what she saw in him, really I don't!"

Alf chipped in with, "Mind you, he was a big handsome bloke, and she's young and needs a man so she must have thought he was right for her!"

Agnes muttered, almost under her breath, "She should be glad he's dead and out of her life now. She's a very pretty girl and could have done a lot better for herself!"

Phillip asked, "Did they appear to have arguments or rows at any time? I know that with the way some of these modern properties are built, you can hear a pin drop in the next room sometimes?"

"He used to shout at her from time to time and I didn't hear her answering back," Agnes said.

"Did you notice anything in particular about the women who came to visit him, was there one you noticed more than the others?"

"Funny you should say that," Alf replied. "Just lately, that young woman from across the street at number 10 seemed to be there a lot, always when the other one was at work, of course!"

"Could you describe her to me?" asked Phillip.

"Tall, nice figure, good-looking sort of girl, you know!"

"Typical man's description," snorted Agnes. "You forgot to mention the tight see-through blouses she wore and the short skirts showing off her bum. I don't know what things are coming to nowadays with girls all but walking about wearing next to nothing, some of them are a disgrace!! I don't approve of that kind of carry-on."

Phillip interrupted before husband and wife could start arguing about their different descriptions of the same person and asked, "Does this girl go out to work?"

"Calls herself some kind of a model but her working hours appear to be very flexible, to say the least. A car sometimes picks her up, fairly early in the morning and we assume she's going to work."

"Come on Agnes, don't be so unkind to her, she works most weekends and lots of other days as well," said Alf.

"Well, she seems to have plenty of money to spend, whatever it is she does!"

"How often, would you say, has she been over to see Ronald?"

"We don't spend all our time nosey-parkering into our neighbours' affairs, peering out of our windows, you know," said Agnes, somewhat sanctimoniously.

"No, no, I wouldn't have thought that for a moment," said Phillip. "I just thought alert, kind neighbours, as I am sure you are, might have noticed occasionally, people passing by?"

Somewhat mollified, Agnes said, "Well there have been times when we heard them laughing and singing, you know, talking loudly but we can't complain, it's always during the day. When the girl is at home during the evenings, we've never heard anything, not even a TV programme."

"Thank you very much, you've been very helpful to me," and with that, Phillip made his exit.

I need to talk to somebody else, thought Phillip, to get a better perspective view of events. He crossed the street and rang a doorbell. The door was answered by another older looking man and he went into his usual explanation but this time, he was invited to enter straightaway. "How can I help you?" asked the man courteously.

"Could you tell me anything about your neighbour at number 10?"

The man smiled. "Young, pretty, nice figure, a model I believe, works odd sort of hours."

"Have you had any difficulties in the area, noisy late night parties, people coming and going at odd hours, lots of shouting or arguments, that sort of thing?" Phillip asked.

"No, nothing like that," said the man. "If she did any partying, it wasn't in her own place!"

"What about men, have there been any men visiting?"

"Not to stay, just to pick her up and drop her off; I have seen her going over to where that man was killed but it was always in the daytime but quite a few people were of the opinion that they were having an affair," said the man.

"What is your opinion?" asked Phillip.

"There was definitely something going on, which is a shame because he already had a partner and she is a lovely, gentle person so he must have been cheating on her. But, unfortunately, in this modern climate, people don't care. Today's youngsters don't appear to have any respect for partners, other people's feeling or emotions, just themselves."

"Could you tell me the name of your neighbour?"

"It's Jane Watson."

"Do you think she is capable of intense jealousy and rage?" asked Phillip.

"Everyone is capable of violence, if sufficiently aroused, Mr Everett; perhaps a more appropriate question would be 'could she control such strong emotions' and the answer is that I don't know her well enough to judge!"

"Thank you very much for your time, I can't tell you how helpful it has been to me," said Phillip and took his leave.

Outside the building he thought that he had been speaking to an intelligent man – he might make a very good witness for the defence. He would keep a note of him. Feeling hungry and not knowing the area, when he saw two women walking towards him, he showed them his private detective identification card and asked if they knew of any suitable places where he could get a sandwich and a coffee. One of the women was a little older than the other, who could possibly be her daughter, there was a certain similarity in the cheekbones. "In fact, if you live in this street, perhaps I could treat you both to lunch, if I could ask you some questions. How about it?"

"Are you from the police; we've had enough of them poking around here to last us forever!"

"No, I assure you, I'm not from the police, I'm working for a solicitor," he replied, somewhat vaguely.

"Oh, well then, if you only want to ask a few questions, there's a nice pub, just round the corner; we wouldn't mind a sit down and a sandwich or something!"

"My car's just over there," he said, and they drove the short distance.

Phillip ordered coffees and sandwiches for them all at the bar and began to ask his questions. Turning to the mother first, she told him a great deal about Ronald and Jane Watson. Listening to her he realised that the two of them were the street's busybodies and they observed the movements of everybody and listened to every conversation they were in a position to hear! Ronald and Jane's affair had been going on for at least three months; it was always Jane who went into Ronald's place and they saw her at least twice a week, crossing the road. She used to stay in the house for approximately two hours and when she came out, she always looked dishevelled, as though she'd dressed hurriedly. However her face and attitude showed she was happy – "Just like a cat who's been at the cream!!" said Mother. "However in the last week or two, things seemed to have cooled off; we were passing Ronald's place and heard an argument and we were sure it was them, I would have recognised that voice anywhere!"

"I don't suppose you could hear what they were actually saying could you?" he asked.

"Well we did stop outside, just for a moment, but it was mostly her talking very loud and it sounded something like 'Now you find me boring, do you' and his voice replying but it was so quiet, we couldn't hear what he said," the daughter answered.

"You are being a tremendous help to me and I don't even know your names," said Phillip apologetically.

"That's easily remedied, I'm Hilda Jackson and my daughter's name is Gertrude. Not married yet, are you Gertie, but it won't be long now!"

"As you know from my card, I'm Phillip Everett, pleased to meet you," and they shook hands.

Hilda carried on: "After that, I can't say as I remember her going over there again, so there's not really any more I can tell you."

"Just one more thing," said Phillip. "Can either of you remember another woman going into Ronald's place three days ago, it would be about ten o'clock in the morning?"

"Sorry, can't help you there love, we work in the mornings, we were on our way home when we bumped into you."

"Thank you very much, this information is a great help to me; can I get you ladies anything more, a drink perhaps?" Phillip asked.

Hilda looked at her daughter and said, "A glass of port would be nice; what about you Gertie, could you fancy something?"

"A tot of brandy would go down very well," said Gertie.

"Brandy it is and did you say port for you Hilda?"

"On second thoughts, make mine a brandy as well!" He ordered the drinks from a waitress who was clearing their table of coffee cups and sandwich plates, and watched in amazement the speed with which the two women drank their brandies. "I have to go now," he said, "but can I give you a lift anywhere?"

"Yes please," they chorused, so he drew up at the end of their street to let them get out of the car and Hilda asked him to come in to either of their homes. "Really sorry, but I have an appointment with someone and I must go now, bye bye!"

He drove away but only about two streets, parked in a lay-by and got out a pad and pencil, drawing a plan of the cul-de-sac and numbering all the properties on it. He entered the names of all the occupants he knew, including Hilda and Gertrude Jackson and he would fill in any other details later. He began to jot down the information that Hilda had given him about Ronald's affair and the arguments they had heard. When he had noted everything he could remember, he made a list of his expenses, coffees, sandwiches, two brandies etc, placed the receipt with his pad and drove home.

There were two messages on his answerphone, one from Gordon reminding him that this Friday was the last of the three lectures on 'Society and Its Ills' and did he remember the first two? Apparently, this one was how to put all that right and was he coming? And the second message was from Liza asking him to please, please come and stay with her this weekend.

He rang Gordon and told him he would meet him in the usual place to attend the lecture and afterwards, they could go to the bar for their night out. Then he rang Liza to say he couldn't come over on Friday evening. "But I'll come on Saturday night and stay until Monday, how's that?"

"That would be lovely," she said. "I'm looking forward to it already!"

"I'm making some headway in finding out who killed Ronald but so far, this is all theory but I have some evidence to support my ideas. I want you to think back to the morning you went to see him, try and concentrate on what you can remember. First of all I want to know exactly where you parked your car."

"It was on the opposite side of the road, at least ten metres before the entrance to the cul-de-sac, I'm quite sure of that because I couldn't see the street from the car," she said.

Phillip made a note of that. "The second important thing is the weapon used in the killing. The police description is that it was a heavy instrument which was smashed over his head, fracturing his skull. My theory is that whoever killed Ronald did it on the spur of the moment; it was not premeditated in any way and he or she used anything they could grab hold of. Now think carefully, when Ronald was living with you, did he have any kind of a statue or ornament amongst his possessions which might be classified as 'heavy' or 'bulky', something which might have given a heavy blow if someone struck out with it?"

Liza wracked her brains, trying to remember Ronald's presence in her house and when picturing the lounge she thought of something. "He had a rugby trophy," she said, excitedly. "He had this statuette of a rugby player with the ball under his arm, on a round base and whenever it had to be moved, for any reason, it felt very heavy, as if it was a genuine bronze figure!"

"That's brilliant," Phillip said. "Now can you remember seeing it on the morning you visited him and if so, exactly where was it positioned?"

"I'm thinking but I was a bag of nerves when I decided to battle it out with him, about the split of our finances, I mean, and I didn't pay any attention to the contents of the room but I know that trophy or whatever it was, meant a great deal to him, something to do with his team winning a cup when he was playing with them and to him that was a major achievement in his life; he didn't achieve much else to be proud of, with the exception of seducing women," said Liza.

"In the end, this got him killed, I'm pretty sure of that!" Phillip said. "Okay, carry on, you got out of the car, what happened next?"

"I knocked on his door but several minutes went by before he answered and he just said, 'It's you is it, you'd better come in.' I started by saying I wanted to settle our divorce amicably and he said, 'If by that you think you're going to talk me out of claiming half your estate, you might as well go home.' I said, 'Let the court settle that,' and he said, rudely, 'I've instructed my solicitors not to agree to anything less than half of everything and I don't care how long it takes.' At that point he came up to me, and I felt very threatened so I could see there was no persuading him to come to his senses, I was just wasting my time, so I left the house, went back to my car and drove home."

"One other thing," said Phillip. "From the time you got out of your car and walked to the house and the time you went back to your car, did you see any other person, man or woman?"

"Not a soul; of course somebody could have been watching me through their lace curtains!"

"That's about all for the moment, I'll see you on Saturday afternoon."

He drew a detailed plan, noting Ronald's, Jane Watson's, Hilda and Gertrude Jackson's properties, and indicated where Liza's car had been parked and entered it in his computer, together with all his notes he had taken of the interviews. He typed his conclusions which were: Ronald Gardner had conducted an affair with a model called Jane Watson, who lived in the property almost opposite to where he was staying. This went on for several weeks, according to Hilda and Gertrude Jackson, and the two met mostly in the afternoons, while Ronald's partner was away at work. It appeared as though he was losing interest in her because Hilda and Gertrude heard an argument between them in which she was shouting words to the effect that "you find me boring, it's not been that long since you couldn't get enough of my body". After this time, Hilda and Gertrude could not remember seeing Jane

Watson crossing the street to visit Ronald and they concluded that the affair had come to an end.

It would be reasonable to assume that Jane was not happy on being told she was no longer attractive to him and when she saw Elizabeth Donnan knocking on his door, at ten o'clock that morning, she thought it must be his new mistress. She might have been seething with rage and as soon as Elizabeth left the house, she might have gone to confront her former lover Ronald about this new woman who had just left the house. Phillip didn't know what Ronald might have said but whatever it was, it could have enraged her and she might have picked up the nearest heavy object and struck him on the head. When she realised that he was dead – I am guessing here, thought Phillip – she wrapped the object up in a towel or something similar, perhaps concealed it in a plastic bag, and carried it to her flat. When the police were carrying out their house to house questioning, she volunteered the information that she had seen a woman leaving Ronald's house about eleven o'clock and that's how she became chief witness for the prosecution's case, when of course, she was probably the actual killer. At this stage, Phillip thought, we urgently need more proof and a copy of the forensic report. We need to know exactly what the case is against Mrs Donnan.

He printed a copy onto paper and placed it in an envelope; then he made a CD and rang John Standish. "Sorry to wake you from your afternoon nap, but I need to see you first thing in the morning."

"Is that my favourite gumshoe speaking? A greeting or salutation would be nice."

"Forgive me, this is your humble servant addressing you, by the name of Phillip Everett, I do apologise for offending you by not addressing you as 'Your Majesty'."

"That's quite enough of that," said John. "I'll see you in the morning."

"May Allah bless you and reward you with one hundred camels and two hundred wives!!"

"Goodbye, Phillip," said John firmly, and rang off.

In the morning John asked what was so urgent. "How do you want it," asked Phillip, "the modern way or the old fashioned way?"

"What's the difference?"

"One method is using modern technology and the other is using papyrus and quill!"

"I hate watching a computer screen, I do too much of that already."

Phillip passed him the envelope and John took out the document, to start reading. Phillip went into the other office to talk to Edna, John's secretary

"Hiya, my sweet," he began.

"Oh, it's you," she said suspiciously, "you'll have to offer me a lot if you want me to run away with you. I'm a happily married woman!!"

"Sadly, all I can offer you is my deeply devoted love."

"Love is no longer a negotiable currency in my book," said Edna. "You'd have to offer me considerably more than that to tempt me!"

"I shall give you a list of my assets – let me think, first I'm nice and cuddly, I don't snore, I don't leave the toilet seat up and I promise never to call you 'honey' or 'what's your name', how's that?"

"You forgot not leaving your dirty laundry all over the bedroom floor, not leaving a dirty mark round the bath when you've finished and not forgetting your house key when you've been on a boozy night out and expect me to get up in the middle of the night to let you in, starting to make love and then falling asleep after two minutes, inviting your mates to come over and watch the football and leaving the place like a pigsty while you all disappear down the pub. Wait a minute, I haven't finished yet, when you forget anniversaries and birthdays, refer to us as 'the wife', and take charge of the TV programme changer!!"

"Phew," said Phillip, "I think you've just summed up the failings of the male population. I'm sorry I came now, no need to open the door, I can just crawl underneath!!"

"It's only right that every grown man should be brought down a few notches, every so often," said Edna. "Anyway, a big, bright young man with your good looks can stand a bit of criticism and you seem to be full of it this morning; have you won the lottery or something?"

"I only wish I had!"

John came into Edna's office and asked Phillip what he was doing, chatting up his secretary? "Sorry John, I must have missed the sign on the door that said 'John's secretary, Exclusive, Keep Out'."

"Very amusing, come back into my office now and we can discuss your report."

"We've a long way to go yet but it forms a very good basis to work from. We need the autopsy report and what forensic evidence the police found when they went over the room Ronald was killed in."

"I feel sure that the statue or trophy holds the key, if that was used to crack his skull. Unless it was premeditated, the killer would not have brought a heavy object with him, it would have to be something grabbed on the spur of the moment, the nearest object he could have got hold of," Phillip said. John asked Phillip to give him an idea of how events had occurred and he replied, "As I see things, logic says Jane Watson was very angry at being dropped by Ronald; she could have been looking out of her window and seen Elizabeth going into his house and leaving an hour or forty minutes later. She went over to 'have it out with him', after first following Elizabeth to make sure she had driven away in her car. Seething with rage, she never intended to attack him but you've met Ronald, diplomacy and politeness are not two of his qualities and perhaps he insulted her until in a frenzy, she picked up the nearest object and hit him.

"It was never her intention to kill him, she might have wanted to spell out all her attractions, compared to Elizabeth, emphasised that she had a better figure, was prettier and younger and perhaps better in bed. If Ronald did not respond and was insulting and did not try to pacify her, told her to go home and stop bothering him and mind her own business, this might have enraged her even more. He could have turned his back on her contemptuously and that was when she struck."

"So what happened to the weapon she used?"

"As I put in my report, she must have wrapped it in some fabric, a towel perhaps, put it in a plastic bag and taken it home with her. She would have been shocked at what she had done but it looks as if she was a cool character, she calmed down quickly and saw that it was an opportunity to implicate his new lover – Liza Donnan. All Jane Watson had to do was get rid of the weapon and sit tight. Eventually she knew the police would be carrying out house to house inquiries and Jane could then say casually that she saw a woman (Elizabeth) going into the house around ten o'clock and some time later, she saw her rushing out and going along the street to the main road, where she had a car parked. From Janet's description of that woman, the police soon traced it to his soon-to-be ex-wife who, when questioned, told them of the circumstances of her visit to Ronald. The police thought this constituted a motive for the murder, given that Ronald was insulting and refused to move from his decision to claim a large amount of her assets."

"What if Elizabeth had denied she went there to see Ronald?"

"You know the police always suspect relatives first in a case like this; they could have ordered an identity parade and Janet Watson would have picked out Elizabeth immediately. Elizabeth would have been accused of murder and lying would have made the circumstances even more suspicious."

John thought for a moment and then said, "What's the best way for me to approach this situation and what are you going to do?"

"If I were you, I would insist that I received the same information which the police have in their possession, the forensic evidence collected at the scene and also the autopsy report so that we know precisely how he died, then you'll be able to form a credible defence. In the meantime, I'm going to gather every bit of information I can root out so that we can rebut the charge of murder and I'll let you know what I come up with. I'll be in touch soon," and with that, they said goodbye and Phillip went home.

On Friday afternoon, he met Gordon and they found themselves good seats to listen to the lecture 'The Moral Standards of Society Today'.

"I wonder if he'll tell us how the current ills of society can be put right?" whispered Gordon.

"Shouldn't think so," hissed Phillip back. "Anyway it's only his opinion we're going to listen to!"

"In which case, why aren't we in the pub, instead of sitting here!" Just then, the professor came onto the stage, carrying a sheaf of papers, and launched straight into his lecture.

"Good afternoon, ladies and gentlemen, welcome to the final talk on society's moral standards, which could be called 'Society as it is Today'. What exactly do we mean by moral standards and do we need them? If you look back to early civilisation, people lived just like the animals around them – survival of the fittest specimen. Many centuries later tribes of stronger people enslaved other tribes, taking over their lands and their women and killing the weakest – the old, sick and any children who could not survive or be useful to them. You could say that is nature's way, the weak perish and the strong survive and reproduce. But human beings have slowly broken away from other creatures and although it took thousands, possibly a million years, we developed into an intelligent, free-thinking, tolerant civilisation with the ability to care for and respect other people's opinions. However, looking around us on the events happening today, perhaps many specimens have not quite made that standard.

"In the Oxford Dictionary, the word 'moral' is described as 'concern with goodness or badness of character or disposition, or with principles of what is right or what is wrong'. So when we refer to a society which has 'lost its moral standards', we mean a society that no longer cares about anything, whether it is right or wrong. Therefore, if we think in those terms, where are we today? In the last two lectures I covered that subject but I will just mention this fact – no one body has done more to create a fractured society today as the present government.

They have attempted to break up all the well-known, long-established institutions and social groups by trying to enforce what they perceive to be an 'equal' society."

At this point a young man stood up and shouted, "You are a hypocrite, stop slagging off the Labour government. I am a strong Labour supporter and of what they are trying to do for this country!"

The lecturer remained very calm. "This young man illustrates a perfect example of the results of what the present government's policy stands for – intolerance, a total inability to listen to other people's point of view and afraid to hear any argument against them!!"

At this point the young man was on his feet again. "People like you should be in jail for trying to spread lies against a very good government, you are a traitor and scum." Many voices now started to shout, "Sit down and shut up." The young man sat down and the crowd in front of him turned around to stare and some started to hiss, some began to shout "shame". He lost his nerve and began to shoulder his way out to the exit, with many still hissing and booing at him. He turned to the audience and gesticulated, giving a rude, two-fingered salute to the audience. A big man stood up in one of the end seats and caught the young man's hand, gripping it very hard. He said menacingly, "If you show that sign again, I will rip your hand off and shove it right up your arse, get it?" The young man pulled his hand free and ran out of the building, while the audience applauded the big man's actions.

While all this was going on, the speaker remained totally calm and when things had settled down, he continued with his lecture. "I am not trying to insult or deride anybody's actions but one has to recognise the truth and point out the causes, otherwise there would be no relevance to these public meetings. As I was saying, the government was so determined to create an equal society, they completely forgot the lessons of the past. We only have to look at the Communist system of equality to note where that failed. Even China has, to a great extent, abandoned their earlier devotion to Communist principles and is slowly changing into a vast commercial entity. We must acknowledge that there are going to be some differences in a just and fair society. That does not mean that everyone should not have equal opportunities, just the opposite, but it has to be acknowledged that human beings are very different – some are very academically clever, some are talented musicians, some are skilled with their hands, be they sculptors or plumbers and electricians and make no mistake about this, we need everybody's skills and must place equal importance on every facet of human ability. We must encourage and recognise every skill, or people could become demoralised if they think society does not think them worthwhile. Not everyone can be a Mozart or a Picasso but let's face it, who do you need most when your boiler breaks down, an artist or a plumber?!!

"There could also be a danger in that when full acknowledgement of people's skills is not given, frustration could lead to bad behaviour or even criminal tendencies and by not giving them due recognition we do both ourselves and them a disservice. It is vital that we, as a society, harness the energy and skills of everybody and use them to provide a just environment for us all. Where are we now? You do not need me to tell you where we stand at this point in time. By picking up any national newspaper, you will have read of the present situation to which our moral standards have been reduced. Greedy, selfish, intolerant, materialistic, apathetic, uncaring – these are just some of the adjectives used to describe our present society. What sort of society attacks its medical staff who are trying to help them in Accident and Emergency Departments? Who lures firefighters with false 999 calls and then pelts them with bricks and other missiles? What kind of mob or gang attacks totally innocent people going to or coming home from work? People have been shot, stabbed or just clubbed to death only because they asked a group of youths to stop making loud noises or throwing stones or quietly requested someone to pick up a piece of litter! Whole families have perished in house fires, sometimes by a mistaken act of revenge, and I could go on and on, quoting newspaper headlines from the past couple of years alone. How does that equate to a more equal and tolerant society which the government say they are creating? It would seem that they falsify statistics, manipulate communications, anything to make things appear more favourable, and this would apparently be their policy, anything except revealing the truth. However there are some facts which cannot be hidden, such as the general direction in which we are heading. Do we need to change our course? I leave that decision up to you, hopefully a cross-section of the general public.

"We have to ask ourselves, how does society restore its moral values? Looking at the past, there are many examples, some with a religious background such as the Biblical story of Sodom and Gomorrah where God intervened, but a poignant story tells us that God sent his son to be sacrificed to atone for our sins. In more recent times, society was changed by more violent means: we had French and Russian revolutions, with cruelty and great bloodshed, leading to the unnecessary loss of millions of lives. We must hope that this never occurs in our country, our revolution must be totally peaceful! We could start by reversing the process from the roots: the most basic need is for us to restore the family structure, with married couples bringing up their children in a stable background, one mother, one father, both sharing the children's upbringing responsibly. This is the very foundation of any society, the building blocks, if you like, on which other institutions are based. We should never rely on politicians or governments to dictate to us how we are to live. We elect politicians and they are there to serve us, we are not subservient to them and laws which are necessary for improvements to our own lives should be passed. That it is where it all has to start. John Kennedy, a former United States President (who may have had his faults) knew how to deliver a rousing speech and to paraphrase, a key sentence in one of these was, 'Do not ask what your country can do for you, ask what can you do for your country.' I will finish now by putting to you the question 'IF NOT YOU, THEN WHO?'"

The audience rose to its feet and applauded. Outside Gordon asked Phillip his opinion of what they had just heard, and he replied, "Very powerful and convincing!"

"What shall we do now? It's too early for an evening meal and going to the bar, if we started drinking now, we'd be legless by eight," Phillip said.

"Oh, I agree with you there, let's be real touristy and visit some of the sights!" said Gordon,

"Where shall we go?"

After a lot of good-natured bickering, they agreed on Buckingham Palace, made their way there by bus and paid the entrance fee. "You pay that and I'll pay for our meal," said Gordon, generously.

Phillip groaned. "If you're going to start doling out your money on that basis, you stingy, Scottish haddock, I'll send you a bill for everything you drink tonight!"

"That doesn't make sense, stop your blathering and let's look round."

"No, we'll toss a coin for who pays for what," Phillip said.

"Not likely, you'll use that double-headed coin when you always win!!" Gordon complained. They carried on walking and heard loud voices behind them. "What language is that?" asked Gordon.

"Sounds like that Scandinavian chap in The Muppets," Phillip said.

A woman's voice said, "Excuse me, are you two Englishmen?" and they both turned round to see a very agreeable sight – two blonde young women!!

Phillip gave them his charming smile and replied with, "Well I am English but he's a wild Scotsman so you will have to be careful of him."

The woman who had questioned him asked in a puzzled voice, "Why should we be careful?"

Phillip took in the fact that she was a tall, slim, blonde girl and replied with a very straight face, "Because he could snap at any moment and start making love to you, especially as you are two such lovely young ladies."

"He would not do that," she said, doubtfully, "would he?"

"Don't encourage or provoke him as he can be very unpredictable," said Phillip, looking serious.

"But he looks so nice and peaceful!" said the blonde.

"That's not what his mother says about him," averred Phillip.

"I think you are joking, aren't you?" she said, suddenly realising from Phillip's attitude and Gordon's furious expression that he was being humorous. "Did I say something wrong?" she asked innocently.

"You're right there, he's a joke," said Gordon, laughing. "How can we help you?"

"Wait a moment," said Phillip. "I object to being called a joke and I demand satisfaction!"

"I am very sorry for calling you joke but I did not quite understand," said the blonde earnestly.

"An apology is not acceptable, you have really hurt my feelings and if you were a man, I would challenge you to a duel!"

"People do not, how you say it, duel in London."

"Oh yes they do," laughed Gordon. "They use swords or pistols!"

The other blonde girl said, "How do they do that, Hanna, you are not allowed to carry weapons in public; it said so in our brochure, no weapons are allowed to be carried anywhere!"

"Smart girl," said Gordon. "What do you say to that Phillip?"

"Ah well, the law says lots of things but it doesn't mean that people take any notice of it," Phillip said.

Hanna said, "Is your name Phillip? That is a very nice name."

"Thank you," he said, "and his name is Gordon."

The other girl said, "That is a nice name as well. My name is Greta, how do you do."

"Greta," mused Gordon, "like Greta Garbo the film star who wanted to be alone."

"Yes, I'm always being told that but I do not want to be alone."

"Does that apply to night time as well?" asked Phillip.

He had been taking a good look at the two girls and decided that of the two, he like Greta more, she was the taller one and had more curves in the right places. She looked directly at him and then said, "Maybe." They started to walk along in step and Gordon asked them where they were from. "We are from Sweden, a little town you would not have heard of," said Hanna.

"Where are you staying in London?"

"It is called Purley Hotel in Gloucester Road, just a tourist-type cheap hotel but we are only staying in London until Wednesday so we do not spend much time in hotel," Hanna replied.

They chatted away and walked round the various state rooms until Phillip happened to glance at his watch. "They'll be closing up here shortly," he said, "and it's time we left and planned our evening!"

Gordon agreed and then Hanna enquired, "Where are you going?"

"Well we usually go for a meal and then on to a little bar we know, and have a few drinks."

Hanna, moving close, put her hand on Phillip's arm and said, "You are not going to leave us all alone, are you? I owe you satisfaction in our duel."

"And how are you going to pay me back?"

She looked at him a little coyly and said, "You will have to wait and see!"

Phillip looked at her, thinking, nice figure, pretty face, looks a bit like a schoolgirl with that lovely young skin, putting it all together, quite a nice package for a man who liked younger girls. "Hanna," he asked, "how old are you?"

She gave a pretty pout and said "Nearly nineteen!"

"Gordon," he announced, "we cannot desert these two young ladies, strangers to our shores; we must protect them from the kind of wicked men they might meet tonight; the least we can do is feed them before we return them to their hotel beds!"

Gordon agreed heartily and told them they could easily walk the short distance to a restaurant nearby, not too grand, where they could all have a good meal. Hanna and Phillip linked arms and Gordon did the same with Greta and off they all went in search of the restaurant, Hanna assuring Phillip she felt very safe with him.

"Safe, with him, you have to be joking," laughed Gordon. "He's the biggest rogue under the sun!"

"Ah yes, but when the sun goes down, I'm a real gentleman," quipped Phillip.

"How can you say that and keep a straight face?" said Gordon.

"Take absolutely no notice of him," said Phillip. "Scotsmen are known for being jealous!"

"Are you two friends?" said Greta, doubtfully. "You do not behave to one another like friends, I think."

Phillip laughed at her and tried to explain: "You could say it's a British thing, we always talk to each other like this but I can assure you, we are the best of friends, have been for years. We just kid each other!"

"What is kid?" asked Hanna, puzzled. "I thought in English it meant 'small child' or 'baby animal'?"

"Don't worry about it," said Gordon. "It means 'joking' or – well let's not go into that, here we are at the restaurant."

They were all hungry and ordered steaks with all the trimmings, and a pudding, the girls sharing a bottle of red wine and the men having two glasses of lager.

After they had finished, Phillip gave the waitress his credit card and gave her a generous tip. "Not many people tip nowadays," she said. "I think it's something to do with the recession. Thank you very much sir."

"Where do we go now?" asked Greta.

"That depends on you two girls. What normally happens," Gordon said, "is we have a meal and then go to our favourite wine bar. He," indicating Phillip, "then seems to attract two young ladies to come and sit with us and after a few more drinks, we head for my apartment."

"What happens then?" said Hanna, knowing full well what the answer would be.

"We have a few more drinks and then go to bed!"

"And what are the sleeping arrangements?" she asked.

"Well that all depends on the two young ladies; just because they came to the flat, it doesn't mean they have to sleep with us; if they say 'no thank you' then they can sleep in one bedroom with separate beds, Gordon sleeps in his room and I sleep on the pull-out sofa in the lounge which opens out into a double bed!"

Phillip explained, "It's very comfortable, I've slept on it several times."

"After the wine, I don't really want to drink much more," said Hanna looking sideways at Greta. "I think we might like to go and see your apartment now." She looked straight at Phillip, saying, "I'd like to enjoy tonight!"

They phoned for a taxi and when they arrived at Gordon's flat, the two girls were very impressed and walked round murmuring to each other in Swedish. "This is a wonderful apartment, do you own it?" and when Gordon nodded, they were even more impressed. "Would it be okay if I had a bath?" asked Hanna. "In our hotel there is only very small shower and it would be lovely to have a bath, not that your shower isn't lovely, Greta thinks that perhaps she could have one because she prefers to shower. Is it okay?"

"That's fine with me," said Gordon. "You'll find everything you want in there, take your time," and the two girls disappeared.

Greta was the first to appear, wearing one of Gordon's fluffy bathrobes. She asked if it was alright to put her clothes in Gordon's bedroom and turned to him, asking, "Are you coming in with me?" He needed no further invitation and followed her into in to the room, closing the door carefully behind him. Phillip waited for Hanna to finish her bath when his mobile rang.

"Hallo Phillip, it's Helen. Samantha and I are just on our way to your wine bar, are you and Gordon going to be there tonight?"

"Sorry, but Gordon and I decided not to go out tonight. What a pity, I would have loved to meet up with you again!"

"Perhaps we could come round to Gordon's flat without calling in at the wine bar?"

Phillip felt a little embarrassed but said, "Actually, we've got company here tonight so that might be a bit difficult for everybody!"

"What about tomorrow night?" asked Helen.

"Sorry, I'm working on a case over the weekend and I have to consult a client on Saturday. Unfortunately, my working hours are not fixed and whether it's a weekend or weekday, my work dictates the hours, it's something I can't always anticipate."

Helen said, "I feel so disappointed…" but Phillip's attention was focused on Hanna, standing in front of him, wearing only a bathrobe; when she saw him looking at her, she let the robe drop slowly to the floor. Phillip's gaze was transfixed; she looked ravishing naked, a lovely nymph-like body, slim waist, flawless smooth skin, her face a little flushed from her warm bath or perhaps from excitement.

He said in a thick voice, "Have to go, speak to you soon!" and pressed the 'off' button.

He picked Hanna up and carried her into the other bedroom, kissing and nuzzling her body on the way there. He put her on a bed and started to rip off his clothes, then he began to kiss her in every delicious place, making her more and more excited, as he explored her lovely young body with his expert mouth and hands. Slowly, slowly, he could feel her approaching a climax and their bodies melted into one, each satisfying the other. It seemed they could never tire of constant lovemaking and after a short rest, they pleasured each other again and again.

Phillip woke the following morning to find Hanna's naked body still wrapped around his and lay there patiently so as not to disturb her, thinking of all the pleasure she had given him during that exhilarating night. Thank heavens she was not a virgin, he thought; he would hate himself if he had been the first one. He felt her stirring and he smiled. "Good morning, how did you sleep?"

"Mainly on my back," she said, seriously, "but that's because you are such a wonderful lover. I didn't know it could be so exciting, lovemaking. You are my first one!"

"What do you mean, your first one? I know a bit about women's bodies and—"

"You mean, you did not see any signs of my being a virgin?" asked Hanna, chuckling. "That is because I have made a break myself!"

Phillip leant on his arm, looking down at her. "I'm not quite sure what you mean," he said.

"As a matter of fact," she said, "some time ago, us girls were talking and other girls who had already done it said the first time it was very painful and there was a lot of blood. The girl does not enjoy it, her partner is frustrated if it is difficult to enter her and it might even put him off having sex with you. So I took care of it myself; it was a bit painful and there was some blood but I did it!" Phillip stared at her, wide eyed with amazement. "What is the matter?" she asked, anxiously. "Should I not have told you? Is it not correct to say things like that?"

In answer, Phillip kissed her forehead, her eyes, the tip of her nose and lips gently. When he touched her lips, her arms encircled his neck and she pulled him down firmly. This lovely young girl and he was her first lover! She rolled over on top of him, moving against him and all other emotions than the need to possess her again flew out of the window, and their lovemaking went on for what seemed like hours. Finally, both fell back on the bed and slept all morning. When Phillip woke, he glanced at his watch and groaned, it was twelve-thirty pm. He dressed, and without showering or shaving, went into the kitchen where Gordon was sitting talking to Greta.

"Sorry chaps, got to go, thank you," he said and went to the door.

"What happened to you?" yelled Gordon.

"Overslept," said Phillip as he went out of the door, after saying a quick goodbye to Hanna and telling her to take good care of herself.

On the way back to Croydon, he became aware of people staring at him. Surreptitiously he checked – his flies were not open, his shirt was not hanging out, there was nothing out of the ordinary so okay, what was it that was drawing so much attention to him. He sniffed, he didn't appear to smell of BO, even though he'd been in too much of a hurry to wash or shower before he left Gordon's place so what was it? Across the aisle, two women were looking at him and then one smiled so he smiled back. A thought struck him; he knew he could pick up both women – why was that? And then he remembered watching a documentary about a man in his late twenties who said that he had slept with over one thousand women and the theory was that he never used any toiletries, such as soap or cosmetics, when bathing or showering, he just used water. Somehow that meant that testosterone remained on his body and females responded to this unspoken signal which made him a desirable object to women. At the time, he thought it was a load of silly nonsense but this man had been speaking to the Oxford University Students' Union and he was asked the question, "Are there any female students desiring you at this moment?"

"There will be some," he stated and the camera panned round to the audience and focused on one rather plump woman, who seemed to be extremely attentive and was not aware that the camera was showing her image! One had to assume that she was one of those who would be happy to sleep with him but at the time, Phillip thought he must be a man who had gone for quantity, not quality, if he had slept with over a thousand women. Phillip thought, it's nothing to be all that proud of, sleeping with such a large number, but thinking about the reaction he seemed to be causing as he travelled back home, it appeared there might be something in the theory.

A wicked thought occurred to him – shall I put it to the test? Not either of the two women who were sitting across the aisle from him, who had smiled at him, but if he got up and walked along the carriage towards the toilet, he could see how many other young women there were and test the theory. He came out of the toilet and noticed an attractive brunette sitting on the first seat and with a quick glance, sat down opposite her. At first nothing happened but after about five minutes, she glanced at him. Phillip looked at her and when she gave a little smile, he smiled back. He had to be careful, he thought, don't push it, just ignore her now for a minute or so and then, before she loses interest, give her another glance, which he did and she responded by smiling and looking at him again.

"Are you going far?" he said casually.

"Two more stops," she said.

"That doesn't give me much time to get to know you, does it?"

She rummaged in her handbag and produced a card; she handed it to him and said, "Give me a call on my mobile, it will be worth your while!"

"That sounds very encouraging, haven't you got a guy waiting for you when you get off the train?"

"Nobody who can't be put off for you!" She jumped to her feet and said, "This is my stop, do ring me," and as she turned, she lost her balance slightly and leaned over him, her face very close to his. Near enough to kiss, but he held back. "Goodbye for now," she said, with a backward glance, then the train came to a stop and she was gone. He looked at the card she had given him and read 'Gabriella Morris, Public Relations Agency'. What did that mean, wondered Phillip. When he arrived home, the first thing he did was to shower, shave and brush his teeth!! "Goodbye testosterone, I'll just have to rely on my fatal charm!!

Chapter 38

He was just about to go to see Liza when he realised how hungry he was. It must be over twenty hours since he had eaten and there had been a lot of physical energy used in the meantime. On his way, he stopped at a takeaway and bought two portions of fried fish, one portion of chips and a carton of mushy peas. Sheer heaven. He sat in the car and ate the lot and feeling replete, he drove to Liza's house. She opened the door, saying, "I was worried about you, you're a bit late!"

"Hey there, we're not married or anything, and I come when I can."

"Sorry," she said, "it's just that I was expecting you about lunchtime. Have you had anything to eat?"

"Yes, thanks, I've just had a takeaway, but I could do with a drink."

"Tea, coffee, or I've got some of that lager you like; it's in the fridge."

"I'll have a lager please, are you having something to eat?"

"Yes. I'll make myself a sandwich," and she went into the kitchen. He sat drinking his lager, thinking about where his relationship with Liza was going. He did not want it to develop into anything permanent and although he very much enjoyed having sex with her, he began to be worried in case she tried to turn it into something more permanent. He made up his mind to put a stop to it, keep it on a strictly business basis, after this weekend, that was.

On Monday morning when he was saying goodbye to Liza, he told her he would not be able to see her for some time because he was very busy and would have to work at weekends to catch up. Oddly enough, he did not know how true this would turn out to be. Liza said nothing and he left the house quickly, not looking back although he knew she was looking sad.

He drove to the police station where Liza had been kept and showed his ID card to the desk sergeant. "I'd like to see the inspector in charge of the Gardner murder investigation, please."

"Yes, sir, that would he Chief Inspector Hamish McCready. Can I tell him what it's about?"

"I have some new evidence for him regarding Mrs Donnan's innocence."

"Very well sir, I'll check to see if he's free." Phillip waited impatiently while the sergeant rang the Chief Inspector and then allowed him through the security door, indicating which was the correct office to enter.

Chief Inspector McCready shook hands, asked him to be seated and studied his identity card curiously. He looked up at Phillip and said, "I've never met one of you before, that is a private detective. What is this evidence that you have which proves Mrs Donnan is innocent of murder?"

Phillip handed him the copy of his report of the investigations he had carried out and the inspector sighed, almost inaudibly. "You've given me quite a bit to read here, I hope it's all relevant to the case?"

Phillip said firmly, "I can assure you it's very relevant."

While the Inspector read, it gave Phillip a chance to study him and draw a few conclusions. He was tall, must be over six feet, rather overweight, probably in his mid-forties, perhaps going to seed with a generous midriff and for some reason, Phillip took an immediate dislike to the man. He put down Phillip's report and said, "Okay, I've read everything but I don't quite see what this has to do with the case!"

Phillip tried to contain his impatience and said, "As I see it, inspector, it means that your witness is probably the murderer!"

"That is a preposterous suggestion," said Hamish arrogantly. "You have not a shred of evidence to support your theory!"

"The same could be said for Elizabeth Donnan," said Phillip. "She has never denied that she went to see her husband. Your witness says she saw her go into the house and later leave but she also says she saw her drive off, which was impossible. There is no way she could have witnessed her drive away unless she followed her down the street. Mrs Donnan had parked her car well out of sight of the end of the cul-de-sac and no-one could see her drive away."

"What difference would that make?" Hamish said, rather irritated by Phillip's line of reasoning.

"Can you think why she would follow a complete stranger down the street, just to check if she had a car or she went to catch a bus – that's ridiculous," said Philip.

Hamish started to bluster, making up his own story as to why anyone would do that. "A young model, staying at home that morning, she could be bored At that time of the morning they probably never get any visitors coming into the street and when she saw a smart, middle-aged woman going inside the house opposite to hers, it must have aroused her curiosity. So when the woman came out a while later, our witness followed her, just to see where she would go, and that is why she saw Elizabeth Donnan drive away," he announced triumphantly.

"Not a very plausible story," said Phillip. "Is that what she told you? And did she say which model car Mrs Donnan was driving? The colour, style, has she described what she saw?"

"Well you know what women are like, they never can describe a car exactly, something we men think of straightaway. Anyway, that's what she stated and I believe her, why should she lie?"

Phillip controlled his temper and replied patiently, "She is lying because she attacked Ronald Gardner and is attempting to get away with murder. On the other hand, Mrs Donnan fully admits that she visited her husband on that day but she left as soon as she realised that he had no intention of coming to an amicable settlement of their financial affairs before their impending divorce. What about the weapon used to kill Ronald Gardner?"

"So far, it has not been found."

"I assume the police have carried out a very thorough search of the locality near the house and Mrs Donnan's premises and car?" asked Phillip.

"Naturally, we have conducted a painstaking search for the weapon but so far, it has not been found."

"Ronald Gardner was a big, strong man, an ex-rugby player, therefore it's plain that the weapon used had to be of a substantial weight to fracture his skull, what do forensics say about this?" asked Phillip.

"Their report says that a blunt instrument was used, delivered with substantial force onto the back of the head, fracturing the skull," said Hamish. "When it's found, they will be able to confirm this."

"What about fingerprints?"

"There were many fingerprints found in the house, apart from the owner and Mr Gardner. We're in the process of tracing and eliminating the owners of those prints but it takes a long time to do this."

"Did you find any prints belonging to Mrs Donnan?"

"No, but she told us that she was wearing gloves, and as she assured us it was the first time she had visited this address, we didn't expect to find any."

Phillip said, "So apart from what Mrs Donnan told you herself, you have nothing to support your theory that she murdered her husband and what would be her motive?"

Hamish replied as if talking to a halfwit, "The obvious one of course, money. He was asking for half of everything she had, which I understand to be a very large amount, and she did not want to part with it!"

"And how would killing him help?" said Phillip. "It just means that if she is convicted, a lot of other people will benefit and she will spend a very long time in jail. She's a sensible, logical businesswoman who's employing a first rate solicitor who will make sure that Ronnie won't get too much of her money. If she had wanted him out of the way, she could have hired a hitman and been nowhere near when the crime took place, with a perfect alibi. She is not physically capable of attacking anyone, she has never been in trouble with the police, not even a parking ticket, and it would not occur to her that the only way out of a little difficulty with a recalcitrant husband would be to eliminate him!!"

Hamish said, "Our witness has never been in trouble with the police either," and Phillip realised he was wasting his time trying to make the inspector accept what he had discovered. He said goodbye and decided against showing his file to the CPS; he went back to his office thinking he would have to investigate Jane Watson more closely if he wanted to come up with any further evidence against her. He rang John to tell him about his meeting with Chief Inspector Hamish McCready but John was doubtful as to whether it was a good idea.

"I thought I might convince him to start looking more closely into Jane Watson's background but he was quite unmoved. As far as he's concerned, they have their killer. The key lies in that sports statue, I feel sure that's what was used to kill him."

"That's as may be," said John, "but how do we find this missing item?"

"How indeed? I would love to search Jane Watson's house but I know there's no chance of ever getting in there, as things stand."

"What did the Chief Inspector say about the weapon used in the attack?" asked John.

"They reckon they're still looking for it," Phillip said.

"Well that's good for us; they have no evidence against Elizabeth except that she told them she had gone to see Ronald and it doesn't mean that another person didn't go to see him after she had left. I think your case against Jane Watson is very reasonable. By all means gather more information about her but we want to clear Elizabeth in a court of law, not just have the case dropped from lack of evidence!"

"Yes, I agree with you but I want to talk to Jane, see if I find out anything about her."

John emphasised, "Make sure you meet her in a public place, not her home or even in the street, or you could get into trouble and be accused of harassing a police witness and it might prejudice our defence. Perhaps you should try to watch her, establish her movements, where she goes when she goes out, that sort of thing. It might take you longer but then it could seem more of a coincidence if you were to meet casually. You're a private detective aren't you? You should be good at this. Be like one of those detectives in films, sly, underhand but clever with it!"

"Leave it with me, John, I'll watch Miss Watson so casually, she'll never even know!"

The following day, Phillip sat in his car at the end of the cul-de-sac, waiting to meet Hilda and Gertrude. It was about this time they usually came home from work and he was hoping they would be along soon. He had guessed correctly and saw them approaching so he jumped out of his car and said, "I hope you ladies are well?"

"About the same as we were last time we saw you," said Hilda, eyeing him speculatively.

"I wonder if you two ladies would be interested in earning some easy money?"

"Depends on what we have to do, but yes, I think we're interested aren't we Gertie?"

Confidentially, Phillip said to them, in a lowered voice, "Can you find out for me where Jane Watson goes on her nights out, clubs, pubs, bars, that sort of thing. Just write down the names and addresses where she goes and also, if you could, where she goes on the days when she's picked up in a car."

"For a start," said Hilda, "she normally works every weekend, being a model."

"Yes, I know that, but you could observe her quite easily from your house, as you live nearly opposite to her."

"We won't be able to follow her when she goes out in a car, will we?" said Hilda reasonably. "We don't have a car ourselves," Gertrude said.

"I tell you what," said Phillip, "you let me know when she starts getting ready to go out and I'll come as quickly as I can. Knowing how you ladies take such a long time to prepare yourselves for an evening out, if you ring my mobile, I should be here in plenty of time before she leaves her house, then I can follow her!"

Hilda looked at Phillip, obviously wondering about his motives and then asked bluntly, "Why? What's your reason for all this, what are you going to do?"

"I just want to find out where she goes, nothing sinister in that, is there? I might offer to buy her a drink and have a chat about the murder in your street, that's all!"

"What's your interest in this murder?" asked Gertrude.

"Natural curiosity, okay? Now, can you do that for me?"

"Yes, of course we can but what's in it for us, what's our reward going to be?" probed Hilda.

"How about £50 for each of you?" Phillip asked.

Hilda considered this and then said, "Rather than paying us money, we'd like you to take us both out for a meal tonight."

Gertrude nodded her agreement so Phillip said, "Done, pick you up tonight about seven o'clock?" The two women glanced at each other and nodded their heads.

He booked a table in a restaurant, nothing too exotic, and picked them up, dressed for the occasion. That was a mistake, he looked very smart and handsome, too handsome. He was not worried about the cost as it was part of the investigation into the case and therefore could be classed as expenses, so they enjoyed their steak and chips with all the trimmings, the two women enjoying an enormous dessert which Phillip laughingly refused. He was trying to keep sober as he had to drive back to Croydon that night, but the two women finished their meal with double brandies, which on top of the amount of lager they had been drinking, meant when he took them home, both became amorous. He ended up nearly having to fight them off when he was pressed to come in for another little drink. He didn't want to offend them in case, when they sobered up, they decided not to do the task he had asked them to undertake. With a sigh of relief he wriggled out of Hilda's possessive arms and firmly said goodnight to both of them and escaped to his car, praying they would not follow him out into the street and start shouting. He made sure they had his mobile number by leaving at least three Post-It notes stuck in various places and arrived home exhausted, overcome with relief at his narrow escape.

Chapter 39

Two days later Barry Spencer rang, sounding very worried.

"We're in deep trouble," he announced.

"I've not done anything," said Phillip, immediately on the defensive.

"Well, in a way you have. You remember Tania, Ivan Chernienko's daughter, the Russian club owner? Tania's been kidnapped!"

"But whatever for?"

"I can't talk over the phone, her father and I must see you."

Twenty minutes later they arrived at Phillip's office. "You probably won't remember a photographer taking a picture of you and Tania at her birthday celebration; well it appeared in a Russian language magazine with a caption which said 'Tania and her husband to be'."

"That's absolute nonsense, I was engaged to Sarah Pennington at the time!"

"We all know what these magazines are like, anything for a story, and it looks as if your face has been noted by the Russian mafia and they have kidnapped her, to make you and her father suffer. Can you take on this investigation immediately and try and rescue her?"

Phillip's decision was instant: "Of course I will, but I'm going to need some money for basic expenses and things!"

"Don't give that a thought, Ivan will wire the money directly to your account; but it's vital you start straight away, before the trail gets cold!"

"Why did they pick on Tania?" asked Phillip.

"When you rescued Katia, Vasily Bukow's girl, you made them very angry and this is their way of getting back at you! They expect you to try and rescue her and once they lure you away from London, you are theirs for the taking," said Barry.

"What are you planning to do?" asked Ivan Chernienko.

"Let me think for a moment. We have to find out exactly where Tania has been taken. Can you use your own resources to help here?" said Phillip.

"In what way?" said Barry.

"You can forget this country, Tania would have been smuggled out of here almost immediately. What's the name of that Russian mafia boss?" asked Phillip.

"Mr Bukow and he used to be friends and partners in the old days but when Peter Stanek got into prostitution and drugs, Mr Bukow managed to get rid of him from the group they were controlling so that when they kidnapped his daughter, it was an act of revenge," Barry said.

"How is Katia?" asked Phillip.

"She is fine now," he said, "but she never goes out without a bodyguard and we think that is why they picked on Tania!"

"I take it that Stanek's empire covers Holland, Belgium and parts of Russia; I think we can assume that he would not use Holland again so the most likely place he would take her would be Russia. He thinks that on his own turf he is invincible, so that's where we'll start. Mr Chernienko, how would you smuggle Tania out of this country and into Russia?" asked Phillip.

In despair, Ivan said, "I have never smuggled anyone out of any country, I cannot help you there."

"Okay Barry," Phillip said, "let's put ourselves into the minds of these gangsters and assume they want her alive. By road, it's risky and would take too long, rail would mean a lot of changes and in any case, how do you smuggle a live, very unwilling person through stations and passport checks without drugging her which would immediately lead officials to be suspicious we hope; by ship – not very likely, so that leaves us by plane."

Barry agreed. "If they could take her on a flight from some small, little used landing strip, perhaps somewhere quite near London, that would be ideal from their point of view; a flight plan could be filed saying they were just hopping over the Channel with a freight cargo and once in the air, they would disappear off everybody's radar screen."

"If only we could trace a flight such as this, we could assume they would connect with a Russian flight somewhere on the continent and I think we can work on the theory that to start with, Tania is in Moscow somewhere."

"Right," Barry said, "don't forget I am coming with you!"

"Oh no you are not, you'd be just another handicap to me."

"I'm going to insist, I think."

"You can insist as much as you like, you're not coming, I don't want to see you die somewhere in Russia."

"What about you then?" Barry said, outraged.

"It's my job and I take risks because I'm being paid for it; it's not some kind of boy's comic adventure or a Hollywood film. Do I have to spell it out for you? When you're killed, you're dead and you don't come back. These people kill for pleasure – if they're in a good mood they kill you quickly, but on a bad day, they will take the greatest pleasure in torturing you, just so they can tell your friends how you suffered. Nowadays, they'll probably film it on their mobile phones and have a good laugh!"

Barry was annoyed. "I'm not some sort of imbecile, I've played rugby, I can handle myself!"

"That's what I'm worried about," said Phillip, laconically. "People think they're not afraid but when someone's pointing a gun at you from only a few feet away, you can turn into a wobbly jelly, which would be no help to me at all!"

"I still want to go," he said, stubbornly. "I understand the risks I'm taking and I can be of great help to you – you don't speak Russian – I do, fluently," he said triumphantly, "and two brains are better than one!"

Phillip considered it for a moment and then looked at him. "Okay, you can come but there are two conditions. One: you sign a disclaimer form saying you are coming to Russia with me voluntarily and entirely of your own accord, and two: you must accept that I'm 'The Boss'; whatever I say, goes. In our situation there will not be any time for consulting the rule book, no time for reaching a consensus of opinion!!"

"I agree, I agree," said Barry, and Phillip typed out the disclaimer form, printed two copies and gave one to him to sign and stored it in his desk.

During this time, Ivan Chernienko said nothing. "When I get the money credited to my account and we've confirmed the flights to Moscow, we can sit down and discuss our strategy and after that, it's to Russia with love," Phillip stated.

When the two men left his office, Phillip rang John.

"Oh, it's you again, is it?"

"Yes, afraid so, I thought I would tell you that I'm going to Russia, Moscow in fact, and it may be some time before I'm back, it's a bit difficult to assess!"

"What the hell are you talking about?" gasped John.

"Remember, some time ago I told you about a girl called Katia who had been kidnapped and taken to Amsterdam?"

"I remember vaguely you saying something like that but I don't think I was involved, was I?"

"No, but the same thing has happened to another Russian family; their daughter has been taken and her father wants me to investigate and get her back, if possible."

"What about our own police force, can't they do anything?" John asked.

"She's out of the country now so it's out of their jurisdiction."

"How do you know she's in Moscow?" said John, sounding amazed.

"Because it's the same people involved who kidnapped Katia!"

"But what about Elizabeth Donnan's case, what am I going to tell her? That you've decided to visit the Bolshoi Ballet in Russia or something?" fumed John.

"Calm down John, there's not much I can do on her case at the moment until the date is set for the hearing," he said patiently.

"Well, if you have to go to the aid of another damsel in distress, I suppose you have to go, but keep in touch, good luck and make sure you return in one piece. I should hate to have to start all over again with another cheeky private eye!"

Later that week, Phillip checked his bank account and found that £50,000 had been credited, but he hadn't yet heard from Barry. He checked online and there were plenty of flights for Moscow, so they would have no problems getting tickets. Late afternoon and to his surprise, he received a call from Hilda who told him Jane Watson was getting ready to go out.

He drove fast but kept an eye on speed cameras – couldn't be having points taken off his licence for speeding – and parked near the end of the cul-de-sac where Liza's husband had been murdered. He waited, strongly tempted to walk to Hilda's house to see if Jane had left already, but half an hour passed and nothing happened. Just as he was cursing himself for not ringing Hilda, he saw a young woman approaching the car. She was very smartly dressed with an attractive figure and he knew it must be Jane as she crossed the road in front of him and went to stand alone at a bus stop. He pulled out and waited for a gap in the traffic before pulling over to her side of the road. He pretended to be looking for something and winding down his window, he called out, "Sorry to bother you but can you tell me where… it's Jane Watson isn't it, you're a model in that… hang on a minute and I'll remember the name of that magazine… I'd have recognised you anywhere. You look even better than you do in those glamorous pictures!"

This broke the ice and she smiled at him, saying, "Which magazine was that? I appear in quite a few of them nowadays!"

"Do you know, I can't for the life of me remember just which one it was, but I remember you. Can I give you a lift anywhere? It seems a shame that anyone as gorgeous as you should be standing at a bus stop!"

She thought for a moment and then said, "I could do with a lift, it's a bit chilly standing at a bus stop with just a short skirt on. What's your name?" she asked as she got into the passenger seat, next to Phillip. "Were you parked over there waiting for your girlfriend?" she said coyly.

"No, just pulled up to make a phone call; law abiding citizen, me, don't make calls while I'm driving. Where can I drop you, anywhere special?"

"Just carry on along this road, there's a night club on this side and a big pub on the other; you can drop me off anywhere around there. I usually go to the pub for a few drinks before I start clubbing, that's where I meet my friends, inside the club."

"That sounds great, perhaps I could buy you a drink?" he asked.

"That sounds nice, what is your name anyway, you seem to know mine?"

"Well, to tell you the truth, it's Malcolm but I never really cared for it so all my friends call me Harry."

"I think Harry's a nice name, but there's nothing wrong with Malcolm either," she said, determined to be fair. He pulled into the pub car park and they went inside.

"What will you have?" he asked.

"Vodka and orange, please, I'll go over there and get us a seat."

As he waited to be served, he looked at her, wondering how it was possible for her to have killed a man, no matter what the provocation; nevertheless, he was convinced she had smashed Ronald's skull with the rugby statuette and somehow he had to find out more about the circumstances.

Sitting down next to her with the drinks, he said, "What kind of modelling do you do?"

"Mainly clothes but any kind of modelling really, sitting on leather settees for furniture adverts, underwear, I even model next to cars, but I don't model nude or any of that porno stuff!"

"Isn't that where the good money is?" he asked.

"I don't know about that, I'm not that interested."

They chatted a little and then he got up to get her another double vodka and orange; he wanted to be quite sure she was relaxed when he started to probe for answers to his questions. She took a sip of her drink and looked at him, "That's a bit strong, what have you been putting in it?" and she giggled. "I'll just finish this and then I'll go over to the club, will you be coming with me?"

"I'll have to think about that," said Phillip, wondering how to play the situation to its best advantage. After two more double vodkas and oranges, keeping to the J2Os himself, he judged the time right to try and obtain the information he wanted.

"I just remembered something," he said. "Isn't your little cul-de-sac where a man was killed not long ago?"

The reaction was immediate and despite four drinks, she stiffened and said, "I don't know anything about that!"

The atmosphere had become tense and Phillip tried to ease the tension by saying casually, "It was only that I was passing the end of the street and it was the same name I saw in the paper." He said confidentially, lowering his voice a little, "I've got a mate in the police and he was telling me all about it, you know the gory details and such; he said this guy had his head smashed in with a heavy object and they're blaming his wife! What kind of woman could she be to bash her husband over the head, I ask you? You might have seen her leaving, it's such a small street, only five or six houses long. I bet everybody knows everybody else, did you know him?"

"As a matter of fact," she said, icily, "I hardly know anyone in the street, I mind my own business and I'm not constantly tweaking my net curtains to see what other people are doing!!"

He continued, almost as though she hadn't spoken: "Anyway, my mate in the police said they'd arrested the wife but since then, new evidence has been discovered. They've got a witness who identified the wife entering the victim's house but the wife's not now their main suspect. Something else has come to light so they're building up a case against another person! There is some talk that the original witness is the suspect now. Anyway, I've got to be going now, sorry I can't stay and chat, got to meet a man about a dog, you know the sort of thing. What's the matter? You've gone a bit pale, is it too much vodka, or is something worrying you? Enjoy your night out, see you another time!"

Leaving the pub, Phillip got into his car, wondering how things were going to work out; he hoped he wouldn't be arrested for intimidating a witness!

Early next morning Barry rang, saying he was coming round immediately. Twenty minutes later, when he came in he was waving a piece of paper. "I have plane tickets, and visas, I have my passport and the flight leaves Heathrow at twelve noon tomorrow," he announced triumphantly.

"What are you so happy about?" asked Phillip.

"I don't know about you but to me, it feels exciting. Mr Bukow has given me leave of absence and wishes us both success in our search for Tania and hopes we will bring her back, just as you did with Katia!"

"You won't feel quite like that when we get to Moscow," said Phillip dryly.

"Don't be such a spoilsport, where's your spirit of adventure!"

"You've been reading too many Captain Marvel comics; unfortunately, real life is not quite like that. However, let's get down to some serious planning. First, what time is the check-in and how are we going to get there?"

"Nine am and Mr Bukow's chauffeur will give us a lift."

"Okay, when we get to Moscow, we can stay in a modest hotel, no need to draw attention to ourselves. We are not going as tourists but we're going to need maximum publicity to find Tania, I want the kidnappers to come to us!"

"How do you work that one out?" asked Barry.

Phillip explained, "We would never be able to find Tania in the way that I located Katia. That was in an EU country and this is Russia; we'll get no help from anybody in authority and the only way is to get maximum publicity from TV and press. We appeal to a hidden audience, saying some evil criminals have kidnapped an innocent Russian girl, to force her into prostitution and we, her rescuers, must find her before it is too late. We know that Russian people are decent, honest, hardworking, and these people who took Tania (here we put in a picture of Tania) are nothing but scum, the dregs of Russian society. We hope that the Russian people can help us to find this girl and return her to her grieving parents. Now, the message to Peter Stanek and his evil gang – we will find you and put you where you belong, in hell. There is a contract out for your life placed on you by our Muslim brothers and as you know, they never give up!!"

"Wow, what are you trying to do," gasped Barry, "start a World War or something?"

"We need strong language to provoke them, get them to show their hand!"

"You mean so they can get a hitman to kill us?"

"I don't think our Mr Peter Stanek would allow anyone else to kill us, I think he will reserve that pleasure for himself!" Phillip asserted.

"That makes me feel a whole lot better," said Barry sarcastically.

"I did warn you that it's going to be dangerous but you wouldn't listen."

"Yeah, I know but I didn't think we'd fly to Moscow with a sign on our backs saying 'Dear Mr Stanek, we think you are scum' and a target on our chests with the inner circle being placed directly over our hearts!!"

"Don't worry," said Phillip, shrugging his shoulders delicately. "They can only kill you once!!"

"I'm going to have nightmares about this," Barry said, "but just for the sake of argument, let's discuss your plan."

"We land in Moscow airport," said Phillip, patiently. "We wangle our way into the VIP lounge – there are always reporters hanging around there, hoping for some story – and this is where you come in, Barry, you being fluent in Russian. You try to gather as many reporters as you can by telling them why we are here, because this gangster Peter Stanek and his crew of criminals have kidnapped this young, innocent girl and they are holding her hostage. We want this criminal to know that his days are numbered; we know all about him and his murderous gang and we shall hunt them down. We have a large number of agents supporting this operation and the hunt for Stanek has already started. That is our message to him! Are you writing this down?" asked Phillip.

"Er… yes, I'd better do that because I could never put it so well – it's more like a suicide note really – if we want to die, that is!"

"Don't exaggerate," said Phillip, calmly.

"What else do we need to do?" Barry asked.

"Flights booked, all the paperwork we need, passports at the ready, overnight cases packed, yes that seems okay. You'd better go home and do some exercises now to get fit!"

"You must be joking, exercises, if I'm not fit now, I never will be. And just what do *you* intend to do?"

"I shall do my packing, have a meal and go to bed early."

"No drinking?"

"Definitely no drinking!"

"And how long do we have to lead this monastic existence?"

Phillip shrugged again. "Look at it like this, you're going on a dangerous mission, you've got to be fit, physically and mentally, so postpone any drinking until we have something to celebrate."

"I'm going home now and write my will," said Barry flippantly, "but I'll be back to pick you up about eight o'clock, see you then."

Later in the day when the phone rang it turned out to be Chief Inspector McCready, who wanted to let him know that Jane Watson had come to the police and confessed to the murder of Ronald Gardner, showing them the murder weapon, which happened to be a statuette of a rugby player holding a ball, still covered in the victim's blood, wrapped in a kitchen dishcloth and plastic bag. He had informed John Standish, he said, rather pompously, that all charges against Mrs Elizabeth Donnan had been dropped, in view of the signed and witnessed statement from Jane Watson, confessing to her crime, lodged with the public prosecution services, and profuse apologies had been proffered to and accepted by Mrs Donnan for mistakenly thinking that she had been to blame and the police would have followed their policy of keeping an open mind in the circumstances, but his intervention had been noted and his investigations had, as it happened, been correct. Phillip held his breath. "Of course," said Hamish, "we can all be wise after the event and it seems that Miss Watson confessed because someone told her that another person was being investigated, that fresh evidence had come to light and she could not bear the stress and tension of waiting to be arrested. I wonder who that person could have been?"

"Well, Chief Inspector, the right person has now been arrested so justice will be done."

"Yes but by whose intervention?"

"God works in mysterious ways, Chief Inspector."

"Yes, that person is very lucky, is he not, the way it worked out for him."

"Have a nice day, Chief Inspector, goodbye."

When the Chief Inspector had finished his conversation and rung off, Phillip immediately rang John to celebrate the news that Elizabeth had been cleared of all involvement in her husband's murder because of a mysterious person who had frightened the life out of Jane Watson and made her confess! "Something else, John, before I go off to Russia and as I might not come back, I want you to do something for me and if you don't do it, I will haunt you to your dying day and you will never get a decent night's sleep ever again!!"

"Knowing you, that's just what you would do," said John, resignedly. "Well go on, what is it I must do?"

"Get bail for Jane Watson. She did the world a favour getting rid of Ronald Gardner, a real swine if ever I knew one. Married one woman for her money, left her and lived with another poor girl working her heart out to provide for both of them while he sat on his arse and entertained himself during the day while she was out, screwing other women, including a local model!!"

"You do mean Jane Watson, *the* Jane Watson who confessed to his murder?"

"She's actually a nice, hard working person and after the way he dumped her, it could have driven anyone into a rage. He derided her, told her she was a poor lover, swore at her and told her he never wanted to see her again and she was so upset, she just snapped."

"Oh come on Phillip, that's hardly a case for killing someone. If it was, a few more million would die every year on this planet of ours!"

"Please John, just make sure Jane Watson gets bail; I don't want to think of her lingering around in some women's jail."

"Am I to take it then that you want me to represent her during the initial hearing which I think is tomorrow. That's a bit short notice don't you think!?"

"Yes John, thrice yes!"

"Okay, I'll do that, now piss off and go to Russia and give me some peace to start preparing her case. Goodbye and good luck, take care!"

Phillip now rang Barry, when he assumed he had reached home, and asked him where Tania's passport was.

"Hello, I thought you were ringing because you were missing

me! I've no idea where Tania's passport is; she obviously didn't take it with her, so I assume her father must have it. I will go and find it immediately, Herr Kapitan. See you tomorrow!"

The following morning, everything went like clockwork and sitting in their places on the plane for Moscow, Barry asked if they should discuss their movements on arrival.

"Best to rest and sleep if you can," said Phillip, so nothing much was said for the rest of their flight.

They landed, recovered their bags and went towards the VIP lounge. "I guess you'd better take over from here," Phillip said, "you being able to read and speak Russian." So Barry asked a man in what looked like airport-style uniform and he was given directions. They went through passport and visa control and entered an impressive looking lounge where many people were milling round, some with cameras.

"What do we do now?" asked Barry.

Phillip took a careful look around and said, "We bloody well draw attention to ourselves, where are those pictures of Tania? Let's walk over to that small dais with the microphones in front of it." Once Phillip stepped up onto the dais, he grabbed the microphone and hissed urgently to Barry, "I'll speak and you translate," and he found the switch to turn the microphone on. Phillip's words, "Could I have your attention please" boomed around the room. "We have a very important announcement to make!" For a moment the room fell silent and the men with cameras and the journalists with notebooks faced the dais, craning their necks to see who had spoken.

"We are here," said Phillip, "because of the actions of a vicious gangster called Peter Stanek and his men, who are known to be members of the Russian mafia who try to run this country." He waited for Barry to translate, and having riveted the attention of the audience, he continued: "They have kidnapped this lovely girl, a totally innocent young lady, who has been brought here to Moscow to be forced into prostitution." At this point, he showed the photograph of Tania and then passed it to the group of reporters. "If anyone here has seen this poor girl with anyone, please let us know. We would like to add that we have not come here just to find Tania, but we are going to find Peter Stanek and bring him to justice, to put an end to his criminal empire and the activities of his inhuman gang. If anyone wants to contact us, we will be at the Hotel Moskowich. Thank you very much for your kind attention."

After Barry had completed his translation, they put the microphone down, thinking there would be reporters shouting questions at them but nothing much happened. "If this had been in London," Phillip said, "we would have been inundated with questions. Are you sure you translated it correctly?"

"A bit might have been lost in translation, some of the words you used don't exactly have Russian counterparts, but I can assure you that they've got your message and so will Mr Stanek."

"That's the whole idea, I think we will be captured and taken to Mr Sleazeball himself and it will get us nearer to the girl. He won't be able to miss an opportunity like this to show off his captive!"

They headed towards the taxi rank. Barry said, rolling his eyes, "I think it's more than likely that we will be dead long before reaching that stage!"

"Well think of it like this," Phillip said, "you don't want to die of old age, a long and lingering death like an unwanted vegetable, do you? Much better to die when you are young, fit and well, with a smile on your face."

"Thanks, you've cheered me up no end!"

"Don't worry, I have a plan," said Phillip, grinning at him.

"Oh, so you can outrun a bullet can you?" asked Barry.

"Nah, I don't think we'll have to do that."

They took the first taxi in the rank and Barry gave him directions to the hotel they had chosen. They were shown to their rooms and after a short time freshening up, Phillip went to Barry's room, only to find himself facing three men with Barry sitting on the bed, his hands tied behind his back and black tape across his mouth.

"Are you Stanek's men?" asked Phillip. All three men were armed with automatic pistols which Phillip had seen before. They were made in China, fast firing and deadly but not very accurate, although from this range, they could hardly miss. Phillip stepped further into the room and repeated his question loudly.

The largest of the three men spoke in heavily accented English: "Yes, we take you to see him."

Phillip spoke again, "You'd better let Barry loose, you can't take him out looking like that!"

The man closest to Phillip raised his hand to strike him across the face but before he could reach it, Phillip's hand shot up and caught his hand at the wrist. The man's face looked amazed at the speed of Phillip's reaction but not for long; Phillip dug his thumb into the soft part of the wrist and said menacingly, "Do not try to pull away or your arm will be totally paralysed for the rest of your miserable life." The man looked petrified and Phillip said calmly, "However, there's no need for violence, we will co-operate with you, we want to see Mr Stanek."

Phillip dropped the man's arm and it fell limply at his side. "It will recover in a few minutes' time. Do you speak English?" The man nodded silently. "Well, if you untie Barry and free him, we will go with you."

Moments later, all five men walked out of the hotel, the Russians with their weapons hidden, and outside a limousine drove up with darkened windows. "Get in and put these over your heads."

"Is that really necessary?" asked Phillip, in his best cut-glass British accent. "After all, we're not likely to live another day are we?"

All the Russian would say was "orders" so they put the black hoods over their heads. After what seemed like a very long drive, the car stopped and they were hustled out and made to walk through an echoing building – they could hear their own footsteps on a concrete floor – through some doors and then they were allowed to stop.

Chapter 40

There was an eerie silence and then a voice said, "You can take hoods off now." As their eyesight became accustomed to the light, a quick glance around showed they were standing in a large office-type room but with very little furniture.

"What happens now?" asked Phillip.

"We wait." All three gunmen were standing near to Phillip and Barry, one with his pistol tucked in his trouser band, one with a gun in a holster and one had his gun trained on Phillip.

Trying to sound casual, Phillip asked in a loud voice, "And where is this apology for a man called Peter Stanek? I know he's a complete chicken who gets others to do his killing and hasn't the guts to face real men!"

As he finished his sentence, a door flew open and a tall, thickset man with blond hair entered the room. "You will be very sorry you have said that, I was going to let my second-in-command interrogate you, but now I shall take great pleasure in doing it myself!"

"Are you Stanek?" Phillip said, putting a wealth of derision into his voice. "You can't be. Mr Bukow's description of you is completely different."

"You mean the Bukow who was my partner, who cheated me and threw me out of the organisation we had formed, like a pariah, without a penny to my name, when I had built that organisation up into a profitable business? Yes, I remember him, but I managed to get his daughter, his precious Katia, to sleep with me first, before all the others. When my associates became bored with her, I threw her out and let her earn her living, walking the streets, which was all she was good for!"

Phillip had heard enough; this was definitely Stanek and that was all he wanted to confirm. In a split second, Phillip was behind the big man and he whipped out his pistol. He shot the gunman who was pointing his weapon at them and took everybody completely by surprise with the speed of his reaction. He shot the man holding them at gunpoint in the throat and blood spurted out as the man's life wheezed away; the next two shots hit him in the chest and he collapsed on the floor as Phillip turned the gun on Stanek and shot him twice; he also fell to the floor. Another of the gunmen was desperately trying to pull his gun out of its holster when bullets hit him first in the groin, then in his head, and he went down like a ninepin. Phillip moved his gun to the small of the remaining gunman's back and said, conversationally, "I'm going to ask you once," he said politely. "I know you speak English so you will understand me perfectly well. Unless you know where Tania, the kidnapped girl, is, you are completely useless to me and I will shoot you here and now, just like your boss and friends, so the question is 'do you want to die?'."

The man gabbled in his eagerness to escape the fate of his friends, his English suffering somewhat in his rapid answer: "Yes, yes, I know where she is being kept!"

"That's very good," said Phillip. "Now you can take us there; and remember, one wrong move and I will shoot you in your spine, maybe not to kill, but to paralyse you for the rest of your miserable life – I take it you can understand the message?"

"Yes, yes," shouted the man, "I take you, please don't shoot." Phillip told Barry to pick up the gun from the floor and leaving theree bodies lying in pools of blood, they followed the gunman. "There will be men coming to this room soon, to check everything is alright," said the Russian.

"You mean they will have heard the gunshots?"

"No, this room is soundproofed but they come to check all the building before locking up; we must go through these rooms and then down some stairs, they lead to cellar and she is down there."

"Is there anybody with her, any guards outside her door?" He prodded the man hard in his back.

"No, I don't know, I don't think so!" He was obviously terrified.

"Make your mind up," he said, fiercely. "Your life depends on this!"

At the bottom of the stairs he shouted, "Tania, are you okay? It's Phillip Everett and a friend, do you remember me?" A weak, muffled voice said something which they could hardly hear. "Go and get her," he said to Barry, "while I keep this person quiet."

Barry kicked down the door, which wasn't too sturdy, and galloped down the stairs, coming back up holding a girl in his arms. He said worriedly, "They must have been starving her, she can't walk, she's so weak!"

Phillip turned to the gunman, raised his pistol, saw the tears in his eyes as he pleaded: "Please, do not shoot me. I have a wife and four children please, please, I can help you get out of here, I know where the car is and how to get to the airport. I will help you, please don't kill me!"

"This would appear to be your lucky day," said Phillip. "I won't shoot you – yet – but if you put a foot wrong, you're dead man, do you understand?"

Whether he understood or not, he nodded his head vigorously and beckoned them to follow him, up the stairs and through several empty rooms and a complex of buildings out into the darkness. "Come," said the gunman, "we go to where big car is parked. I was driving so I still have the key."

There appeared to be nobody about, any workers having apparently gone home, and they found the car to be unlocked. Who would attempt to steal a car from Peter Stanek and risk having their hands chopped off!! The gunman inserted the car key and the engine started smoothly. "I will drive you out of this commercial area and then I will leave you and the car. This is a very good car and will take you wherever you want to go." He must have been considering his options in the present circumstances and said hesitantly, "When they find Piotr Stanek dead, Moscow is not best place to be, and I think I take wife and kids for long holiday, far away so I can't be connected to crime! There is some vodka in bar, I show you." He pressed a button and a drinks cabinet opened at the back.

"Ooh, look at this," said Barry. "Look at all this lovely alcohol and even some fancy chocolates; after all we've been through, this is just what the doctor ordered!"

"No alcohol for you and me, we have to be strictly teetotal," said Phillip. "We've got to keep our wits about us even more now, we've still got a long way to go." He turned to Tania and said gently, "You must have something to drink, try sipping some water or fruit juice, and then later on, when you're feeling a bit stronger, you could have some of those chocolates when you feel able to keep them down."

He turned to the driver, saying, "If you take us to the next petrol station and fill up the tank, also you must buy a road map of Russia. You can drive to where you want to get out and then I'm afraid we'll have to leave you. You can have your freedom but I hope you are not going to be stupid enough to betray us to the authorities?"

"No, I cannot go back to Stanek's mob; they would kill me for sure, they would know that I helped you to escape so I'll go home and pick up my wife and family and run. I know a place we can go to where they'll never find us, hopefully." At the next service station he had the tank filled with petrol and bought the road map; they pulled up a little further down the road for him to get out. "I'll get home quite easily from here; by the way, my name is Mishka, goodbye and good luck." They wished him goodbye and good luck and drove on, hoping he would be true to his word and not inform the authorities.

"What do we do now?" asked Barry.

"I had thought of going via Belarus, but we don't have visas and they are very particular about who enters their country, being about the last Communist state around here, so I think I will drive in the direction of St Petersburg." Phillip halted the car and checked that he was familiar with all the controls, making sure that he would not be confused driving on the right hand side of the road. He also checked the map for directions. "I'll drive for now and you," he told Barry, "you look after Tania and get some rest if you can; I'm heading in the direction of St Petersburg and I hope we can manage to cross to one of the Baltic States." He kept at a steady speed. "I cannot read Russian road signs so when we come to some signs, you tell me what they say!"

"There you are," bragged Barry, "see how much you needed me. I could do with something to eat, by the way; perhaps we could stop somewhere and get a sandwich." He turned to Tania. "I bet you could do with something to eat, couldn't you?"

"She can have one or two expensive chocolates, but for now we must get away as fast as we can," said Phillip. "She is dehydrated so must drink as much liquid as she can."

Tania gave Barry a weak smile and started to cry, releasing some of the tension of her terrifying ordeal. Barry put his arm around her and said, "There, there," like comforting a baby. "Come on, don't cry, you're safe with us now; by the way my name is Barry, how do you do!" Tania tried to smile, but she couldn't quite manage it. Instead she closed her eyes and tried to rest.

"Look out for the road signs, the driver can't read Russian so he doesn't know where he's going!" shouted Phillip. For some reason this struck them all as being uproariously funny.

"Where exactly are we going?" Barry asked, puzzled.

Phillip told them he was going to try for Smolensk, then to Naumovo and on to Alol, after that, hopefully, across the border into Latvia. Once across the border he thought they would be safe; they could have a rest, drive to Riga and then catch a flight back to London. At first Barry called out the names on all the road signs, but after a while, there was silence. A swift glance back from the driver's seat showed that both Barry and Tania were fast asleep but he was now on the correct route so he let them enjoy their rest and put his foot down. He was completely familiar with the controls now and he was enjoying driving the powerful luxury car. The speed crept up – ninety kilometres per hour, one hundred, one hundred and ten; they seemed to be just gliding along the road silently, you could barely hear the engine and of course, nothing could get past them at that speed. Phillip just had to be careful to watch out for cars in front of him. At that time of the evening, the amount of traffic was very light.

They approached Smolensk and after waking Barry for a few minutes to make sure they were on the right road to Naumovo, he drove on, the adrenaline still flowing after such a stress-filled day. He felt wide awake, driving having a calming effect on him, and he started trying to remember if there was anything he must do before approaching the Latvian border. Suddenly it struck him that there were loaded pistols in the car; if those were found by the border crossing officials, they would be arrested and returned to Russia, probably put into the custody of the police, and they would certainly be arrested for complicity in the deaths of Stanek and friends. He must get rid of them but in such a way there would be no fingerprints to identify and incriminate them; he tried to remember which of the guns had Barry's and his prints on them and came to the conclusion that they must be eliminated in such a way they would never be discovered. He wracked his brains and went over the road plan he had made, and remembered that before they would come to Alol, the map showed a lake. That would be a good place to dump the guns and even if they were found, the water would probably have washed off any incriminating evidence. He drove on until he saw what he thought was a sign for Alol, pulled off the road to park and woke Barry. "Wake up, Barry, what does that sign say?"

"It says 'Alol'," said Barry, trying hard to concentrate.

"Around here there's supposed to be a lake and we've got to dump the guns, that is, when we can find it. Get in the front with me and study the map, tell me when you see a sign saying 'To The Lake' or words to that effect," said Phillip urgently.

They drove on slowly, searching in the headlights for signs to follow and eventually, after what seemed like hours, the lake came into view. Phillip drove as near to the shore as possible, praying that the margins of the water were not too soft and the car would not sink into mud. Phillip switched off the headlights, in case they could be seen from the road and in the eerie darkness, when their eyes became accustomed to the low light, he asked Barry how good his long-distance throwing skills were. Barry boasted, "I used to play rugby and I'm no slouch at throwing a ball!"

"Okay, get as close to the edge of the water as you can without falling in and then throw each gun as far as you can," Phillip instructed. Barry flexed his shoulder muscles and took one or two practice shots, aiming as far from the shore as possible, and then he tossed first one and then the other gun into the water and heard the faint plop as each one hit the surface of the lake. They hesitated, listening carefully, and then walked back to the car in silence. Phillip slid behind the driving wheel, slowly drove the limo back on to the road surface, switched on the headlights and drove towards the Latvian border.

He was beginning to feel very tired and nearly veered off the road a couple of times. He had to do something about this sleepiness before he crashed the car so he stopped, climbed out and forced himself to run a short distance and back again, several times, concentrating on breathing deeply to fill his lungs with oxygen, until he felt more alert. It was just starting to become lighter on the eastern horizon and he returned to the car. Barry and Tania were still sleeping the sleep of exhaustion as he checked the amount in the petrol tank – still nearly half full, thank goodness. In Russia they often had to drive long distances so a large fuel tank would be a necessity; God bless large fuel tanks, thought Phillip, we should be able to make Latvia okay, and he drove on. They were approaching a border control area with large signs in two languages, neither of which he could read! He drove slowly and was stopped by a uniformed Russian, yawning in the early morning light. "Barry," he called, as he lowered the window, "wake up and help me out here!"

"I'm awake," Barry said, and he started to talk to the official. It seemed like ages to Phillip, but then the Russian waved them through.

Next was the Latvian side of the crossing, where the official spoke to them in a language neither of them understood. "English?" said Phillip, questioningly, hoping against hope that the border guards spoke that language, only to have them shake their heads – "No English," they said. Barry started speaking in Russian and that they did understand. "Tell them that we are English and have been holidaying in beautiful Russia and now we are on our way to Riga to catch a flight back to London," Phillip said.

"They want to see our passports," said Barry.

Their passports were with their luggage, in the Hotel Moskowich, which did not go down too well with the border guards. Eventually, after a great deal of dialogue between an eloquent Barry and surly border guards, they were allowed to park the car on the other side of the barrier, just off the road, as Barry went into complicated explanations as to how and why their passports had been left behind in Moscow. The guards were not very happy about Barry's explanations and then Phillip said desperately, "Try this one on them and see if we can get them to believe it; say that we were having a lovely time sight-seeing in Moscow, and then Tania, who is my fiancée, collapsed and was rushed to hospital. The good Russian doctors x-rayed her and told us that she had a brain tumour and she would die if she did not get immediate surgery. Their own surgeon was not confident enough but said if you could get her to Riga, there was a brain surgeon who specialised in just this type of brain tumour and he could save her life, so we hired this limousine and drove straight here without even going back to our hotel to get our luggage. We were so worried about her we completely forgot we had left behind our passports until you reminded us but we know what good-hearted people the Latvian people are and knew if we explained everything to you, you would do the right thing."

Tania had woken up and was listening to this with an open mouth, and she gave a moan and collapsed across the back seat. One of the guards peered into the car and after a hurried consultation with his compatriot, and a lot of what sounded like swear-words, waved the car through the barrier with Phillip and Barry shouting their thanks.

"What on earth did you say to them?" questioned Phillip.

"Well I sort of hinted that she probably had meningitis – the highly infectious kind which could be passed on quickly if they so much as asked us to get out of the car – and I think that this incident will not be reported to HQ in case they get into trouble! Whatever it was, it worked!" Hardly able to believe their luck, they were waved straight through the Latvian border control and found the road to Riga. They arrived in Riga and stopped at a small hotel, booked in and asked the receptionist, who showed no surprise at their lack of luggage and Tania's tattered dress, where they would be able to sell their car. They were given the standard tourist map and told there was a garage about a mile away which might be interested in purchasing the vehicle.

"You take Tania to our room and let her get a bath or shower and try and do something with what she's wearing, otherwise we're going to get some funny looks from people, then get some food into the pair of you while I go and get rid of the car."

Phillip was bone weary but he knew he must get rid of the car as it could incriminate them if the Russian police chose to follow up any sightings on their journey here. He found the garage and took a careful look around at the used cars on the lot, some of them second-hand limos, and tried to work out the price of three airline tickets to London in his tired brain. A salesman approached him and Phillip asked, "Do you speak English?"

"A leetle bit," said the salesman and in his most impressive manner. "What can I do for you!"

Phillip showed him the limo and asked bluntly, "How much for this limousine?" The young man took his time, inspecting everything carefully, the paintwork, the interior, poking the tyres, checking the mileage and then quoted a figure in the local currency. Phillip pretended to consider. "That's not bad, how much is it in euros?"

"May I look at your paperwork?" requested the salesman.

"No paperwork."

"Sorry sir, but that is no good."

"Come on, all that means is you will have to re-register it, that's all!"

"No paperwork means that this car is stolen!"

"No, no, you are mistaken, the car was a gift from my fiancée's uncle, very generous of him, but that is the person he is. We completely forgot about documentation before we set off for home!" The salesman considered; the limousine was a top class vehicle, in excellent condition and although in need of a wash, altogether was worth very much more than he had quoted.

"Come inside the office and speak to my manager," he said.

Inside the office, a little fat man was sitting behind a desk and he listened very carefully to what his young salesman had to say. He didn't believe for a moment the car was a gift; it must have cost many thousands of roubles and this Englishman was obviously desperate to get rid of it. He made a decision. "I offer you four thousand euros, take it or leave it, that is all."

Phillip pretended to think it over and then said, "Cash?" The fat man nodded. "Okay," he said with a smile, "I know you're robbing me blind but I accept; could I have the cash now, do I have to sign anything?" There was no signing anything and Phillip waited while the fat man disappeared from the office and came back with a stack of notes and Phillip handed over the keys. "Could you ring a taxi for me?" he inquired politely.

"I will give you a lift back to your hotel," said the young salesman, perhaps wanting to check where he was staying, and Phillip arrived there with a pocketful of euros, and a smug expression on his face, thinking, not bad for an hour's work!

He went to Tania's room to check on her state of health and although she still felt very weak, she wanted to thank him for rescuing her. Phillip was a little embarrassed, which he hid by advising her to keep drinking lots of fluids and eating small amounts of food every couple of hours, and when she wanted him to come in, he told her he still had to try and get their passports back before they could book flights for London. He gave her a gentle kiss on the cheek and, after going to his own room, rang down to reception to ask them to obtain the number of the Hotel Mosokwich in Moscow and if possible, connect him. He sat down near the phone to wait for his call to come through and inevitably he fell fast asleep but when the phone rang persistently, he woke up and found he was connected to the manager of the hotel. "I don't suppose you speak English do you?" he asked.

"Yes, sir, I can speak English."

"Oh, good, my name is Phillip Everett and I was staying in Room 506. By the way, who am I speaking to?"

"This is Dimitry Sokow, sir, I am the manager of the hotel."

"Well as I said, I and a friend, Mr Barry Spencer, had checked into your hotel and were going to stay a few days but unfortunately, there has been a medical emergency and we had to leave Moscow almost immediately, which meant I have been unable to pay my bill. There is also the matter of our luggage and passports which were accidentally left in our rooms. I shall pay the bill immediately, of course, with a substantial tip in euros, for all the trouble you have gone to. However, I need you to do something more for me. Please pack our suitcases for us, including the passports – most important those are – and take them to the airport, addressed to Hotel Olympus, Riga, Latvia, and once the suitcases are on the plane, ring me here at the hotel and tell me how much the bill is. I'll then wire you the cost of what I owe you, plus a substantial bonus!" Phillip made absolutely sure his instructions were understood and the address of the hotel noted, and put the phone down, heaving a huge sigh of relief.

He was close to collapse after his hours without sleep and the stress of the journey. He wearily took off his jacket and loosened his tie, thinking he would just rest on the bed for ten minutes, and was finally woken by what sounded like the buzzing of an impatient wasp, zzzing, zzzing, and bleary eyed, he reached for the phone. "This is Dimitry Sokow here, manager of the Hotel Moskowich," said an anxious voice.

Phillip answered groggily, "Phillip Everett here."

"I have done everything you asked me to do, just as you said, the two suitcases are on a flight to Riga as we speak, including the all-important passports, and everything should arrive at your hotel some time tomorrow morning!" He sounded very pleased with himself.

"If you would just give me your bank details, I can wire the money to you. How much do I owe you?" Sokow itemised the bill – one night's stay, two rooms, packing two suitcases including three passports, taking them to the airport and asking a friendly pilot to make sure they got to Riga and would be delivered the following morning, and quoted an exorbitant amount – five hundred euros. "I'll wire you seven hundred euros and what you do with the extra amount is entirely up to you!!" With that, Phillip put the phone down, turned over and fell asleep like he had been pole-axed!

Chapter 41

When he woke up it was 6.30 in the evening and he was starving. He quickly showered, shaved and was sorry he had to put on yesterday's shirt and suit, but there was a knock on the door and he was alerted to possible danger. He shouted, "Come in!" and saw it was a young chambermaid, asking if she could turn down the bed covers. She couldn't have been more than eighteen and in her black uniform with white collar and cuffs, black stockings and shoes, she really looked rather cute. When he assented he noticed that her skirt was slightly above her knees until she bent down and as he stepped out of her way, he could see the white part of her legs above her stockings and her pink panties. Phillip was transfixed at the sight in front of him, trying to control his instinct to grab her and start making wild love to her. She stood looking at him and said, "Is there anything else I can do for you, sir?" and he shook his head and hurried out of the room.

He knocked on Barry's door and found that he too was ready to have a drink and a meal; he was glad he'd given him some euros earlier on that day and told him to check Tania's size and then go to the nearest shop selling ladies clothing and pick out something for her to wear, plus some ladies' toiletries, so that she could get out of the tattered remnants of a dress she was wearing when they rescued her. They went to Tania's room and Phillip had to hide a smile as he looked at Barry's choice of clothing, but she seemed reasonably happy with her jeans and sweater and they headed straight for the bar and restaurant.

They ate their meal, Tania being very careful not to overeat, and after they had seen her back to her room because she was still not fully recovered from her ordeal, they spent the rest of the evening in the bar, unwinding. "It's funny," said Barry, "but when we were being held prisoner, I kept saying to myself, if we ever get out of here, I'm going to get completely blotto, but now we've got away, I seem to have lost the urge. What about you, Phillip?"

"I think it must be that now the adrenaline has stopped pumping through our veins, everything feels flat and dull and what seemed like the most important thing to do then, now there's no big rush. Never mind, cheer up, a good night's sleep and we'll feel on top of the world!!"

The next morning their suitcases arrived and Phillip went out to find a bank where a cashier spoke English. As he had promised, he wired the money to Dimitry Sokow's account – which he noticed was not the same as the Hotel Moskowich, but who cared, the man had done what he said he'd do and that was all that mattered. He booked three flights to Heathrow and when they were sitting on the plane, Tania with tears in her eyes, they all shook hands solemnly to celebrate the success of their mission. On arrival, a jubilant Phillip rang Mr Bukow, who sent one of his luxurious limousines to pick them up and take them home.

They stopped at Phillip's house first; all three got out and stood there, feeling a little awkward. "We owe you our lives, Phillip," said Barry, "and I'll never forget that or stop admiring the way you move, the speed and that you killed three men, two of them armed. It will always stay in my mind; I thought there was no way we would come out of it."

Phillip shuffled his feet and said bracingly, "Well, we did come out of it so get back to your girlfriend and make love to her and make sure you never go to Russia again!"

Tania kissed Phillip and said, "Thank you for saving my life. I had given up all hope of seeing my father and England again!"

"You get fully recovered and give my regards to your father," and with that there seemed to be nothing else to say so they climbed back into the limo and it drove away.

The next morning, he received a letter from Ivan Chernienko, expressing his gratitude for rescuing Tania, relatively unharmed; he said he would be his friend forever, along with all the members of his family. He hoped to see him at some time at the club but in the meantime he enclosed a cheque for £10,000 as a token of his gratitude!

The next few weeks seemed flat and dull, a bit of a let-down after the excitement of the Russian trip. He met Gordon on Friday as usual but none of the ladies they knew appeared at the bar and they had no luck chatting up anyone else for a couple of Fridays in succession. "I think you're getting old, Everett, you've lost your Casanova touch," jeered Gordon.

"What about you?" said Phillip.

"Hah, we've always been a team, you corral the ladies and chat 'em up and I provide the accommodation for seduction!" said Gordon.

"So I do all the hard work and you just enjoy yourself!" Phillip riposted.

After another few weeks of striking out, Gordon came up with a fresh idea. "Why don't we start going to a gym? A mate of mine at work tells me that there are some very attractive girls strutting their stuff in the gym he goes to so fit, handsome blokes like us should have no difficulty in chatting up a few birds! That's the place to meet them nowadays!"

"You'd have to join a gym for at least six months and the fees for a city centre gym are probably astronomical, plus the fact that you'd need to go at least three times a week before you would improve your middle-age spread!"

"I totally resent that remark," said Gordon, "but as it happens, my bank pays my membership every year and I've only been once; we could go and I can sign you in as a visitor, just to see the lie of the land!"

"Okay," said Phillip doubtfully, "let's go next Friday and see what we can find. I'd better buy some new gym gear, I haven't really got anything suitable."

The following Friday, he dressed in his keep-fit outfit and a look in the mirror told him he looked good! When he met Gordon, he suggested they try the facilities at the gym first and then go for a meal.

"You mean I have to wait all that time for something to eat?" wailed Gordon, "I wish I'd never suggested coming here in the first place."

"You're not supposed to exercise after a meal and five pints of lager," laughed Phillip.

"You don't seriously suppose I was going to prance around showing off my sexy body in front of any women did you?" Gordon grumbled.

"Heaven knows, we shouldn't put any strain on your system by going to a gym to exercise but the best looking women are always there between five and seven o'clock in the evening!!"

"Alright," he sulked, "but if I die from malnutrition, it will be all your fault!"

"You have enough fat on your body to keep you going for three days without any food whatsoever!" Phillip said, derisively. "Die of malnutrition, don't make me laugh!"

They surveyed the various instruments of torture in the gym, debating what to try first. Phillip was very fit but Gordon, whose idea of exercise was walking to the coffee machine at work, was making heavy weather of a treadmill workout. Two young, toned women walked over to them, trying not to laugh at Gordon, and the taller of the two asked casually, "Are you two regulars? Haven't seen you before."

"Gordon here is a member but I'm just a guest for the evening."

"Are you thinking of coming here every Friday evening?"

"If you offer us some encouragement, we'll certainly think about it!"

The slightly shorter of the two girls said to her companion, flirtatiously, "He's a bit cheeky, isn't he?" Phillip was not attracted to either of them so he made no further attempt at conversation. Two men with bulging muscles walked over to the two women and said casually, "You'd be far better off with us!" Phillip ignored them but Gordon said pugnaciously, "Better off, how?"

"They want young men, not two old gits like you!" said one of them.

"What makes you think you two boneheads are better men than us?" said Gordon.

They laughed. "Because we're young and virile, that's why."

Gordon appealed to the girls: "What do you think, ladies?" but there was no answer.

"Do you two old men want to test us? We're ready and waiting."

Phillip was becoming tired of the confrontation and told the pair of them to go and play with their Action Men! "What did you say?" said the taller of the two young men, incensed with rage.

"Listen, you schmuck, piss off and go before you get seriously hurt!" Phillip said.

"What did you say?" and the man threw a punch towards Phillip but he side-stepped and as the other guy bent forward, Phillip used his hand to chop behind his ear and he fell down like a log and lay convulsing on the wooden floor.

Phillip said to the others, "He'll be okay after a minute or two," and slowly the man stopped twitching, opening his eyes and wondering what had happened to him. He started to struggle and Phillip put out his hand to help him stand up. He said quietly, "Just because you're big and have plenty of muscle, it doesn't give you the right to bully and intimidate other people because they happen to be smaller than you." The two young men said nothing and turned to walk away.

The taller girl said, "Wow, we are impressed"

"I did not do it to impress you," said Phillip. "They made fools of themselves and I'm not particularly proud of how I lost my cool. I should have known better as I've been taught restraint and humility and I did not follow the teaching. Come on Gordon, let's get changed and follow our usual Friday night routine."

They enjoyed their pasta at an Italian restaurant, indulging themselves with a dessert of rich ice cream, and later in the bar, with a glass of lager in front of each of them, Gordon reminisced about what had happened to them that evening. "That didn't go down all that well, did it?"

"No I'm afraid it didn't," said Phillip ruefully, "but it happens. I guess that what I was taught about humility on my last course flew out of the window.

"Well," excused Gordon, "if you had shown any more humility we would have been classed as cowards and they would have walked all over us; as it is, you've taught two bullies a lesson! Hey, I don't believe it!"

"Hell, you must be getting old, you sound just like Victor Meldrew, what was it he used to say – 'I don't believe it!'"

"No, not that, you fool, I've just seen Isobel and Sarah appear in the bar, they've just walked in!"

Phillip was sitting with his back to the entrance so he was unaware of anybody coming or going through the door. Slowly he turned his head, feeling as if his heart was in his mouth, and sure enough, Isobel and Sarah were standing in the entrance as if they were looking for someone. Isobel gave them a little wave and Phillip leapt up immediately and walked across to them. His voice was a little strained so he fell back on his usual opening chat line, "Hello you two lovely ladies, can we buy you a drink?"

"Hello to you," Isobel said.

"Would you like to join us or are you waiting for two other hunks?" asked Gordon, beaming at them.

"Hello Phillip," said Sarah, quietly. "We were hoping you two would be here."

Phillip led them across the room to a hurriedly found table. "What's everyone having?" asked Gordon, beaming from ear to ear.

While he went to the bar, Phillip asked Isobel if she could tell him what had happened between them. She shrugged. "My parents wanted me to go back to Portugal and marry a man whom they have known for many years; I went with them on holiday but I found that the man who they had wanted me to marry from childhood, had grown from a pleasant boy to an unpleasant man and I didn't want to live in Portugal either. I guess I have adopted London as my home although I will always go back to see my parents when I can."

Gordon was back from the bar, balancing four glasses with difficulty, but when he heard the last sentence, he said sincerely, "I'm so pleased you came back, Isobel."

Isobel looked up at him and said, "I was hoping you would be glad, now put those glasses on the table before you spill everything!!" She turned to Phillip, asking him what he had been doing during the last few months.

"I've been working quite hard, actually. I've travelled to Moscow, done a bit of private investigation into a murder, you know, just humdrum, day to day stuff." He pretended to sound cool.

Gordon looked at Sarah and told her, "Sarah, Phillip is a brute, he just beat up a guy twice his size before we'd even had our first drink!"

Sarah said quietly, looking at Phillip, "I can't imagine him ever being a brute!" and sipped her drink.

"So what now?" said Gordon. "Shall we paint the town red or—"

"Do you still have your flat?" said Isobel, abruptly.

"I certainly do!"

"Well perhaps you could show us some of your famous Scottish hospitality!"

"You don't have to say it twice my love. I will ring for a taxi," Gordon almost shouted.

They phoned for a taxi and when they got to Gordon's place,

Isobel took his hand and said, "I suppose the bedrooms are still in the same place? You must show me if you've made any changes in there while I've been away…"

"Yes, it's still where it was but if you don't like it, you only have to say and I'll have it moved immediately!"

"Just follow me," said Isobel and closed the door behind them.

As soon as they disappeared, Sarah rushed to Phillip and threw her arms around his neck. "I've missed you so much. I don't know why I left, it was the stupidest thing I ever did." He stopped her mouth with a kiss and lifted her into his arms to go into the other bedroom, kicking the door shut behind him. They nearly tore each other's clothes off, each wanting to feel the other's naked body while they made love.

In the morning, still entwined, Sarah asked if she could spend the rest of the weekend at his house, and he nodded.

On Sunday she moved all her things back, to Phillip's delight, although he couldn't help but wonder how long it would last!